ALSO BY
CHRISTINE KLING

Surface Tension

CROSS CURRENT

Christine Kling

BALLANTINE BOOKS | NEW YORK

CROSS CURRENT

*

A Ballantine Book
Published by The Random House Publishing Group

Copyright © 2004 by Christine Kling

www.ballantinebooks.com

Library of Congress Cataloging-in-Publication Data
is available from the publisher upon request.

ISBN 0-345-44829-4

Manufactured in the United States of America

10 9 8 7 6 5 4 3 2 1

First Edition: October 2004

Book design by Barbara M. Bachman

To the memory

of Red Koch,

captain of *Hero*

"Se bon ki ra."

Good is rare.

—Haitian proverb

ACKNOWLEDGMENTS

I would like to thank the following people:

Mark Tavani, Tracy Brown, Judith Weber,
the Community Policing Division,
Fort Lauderdale Police Department, Bon Mambo
Racine Sans Bout Sa Te La Daginen,
Fred Rea, Ed Magno, Michael Black,
Barbara Lichter, Kathleen Ginestra, Ross Prim,
captain of *Island Girl*, Marcia Spillers,
Caren Neile, Neil Plakcy, Ginny Wells,
Sean Holland, my readers, family, friends, and
most important of all, my son, Tim Kling.

CROSS CURRENT

i

Looking down at the old wooden Bahamian cruiser *Miss Agnes*,
resting on her side on the white sand bottom, it was hard to imagine
that people had died here. Every detail, from the peeling, eggshell-
colored paint to the frayed wire at the base of the radio antenna, was so
sharp, it was as if I were peering through a camera lens in crisp focus.
It didn't look as if it were underwater. The cruiser and the water above
were so still and clear that as I leaned over the bow of my boat, I felt like
I was floating in air.

"I just can't picture a vessel that size carrying over fifty panicked
people." I turned and saw B.J. standing outside the tugboat's wheelhouse door, dripping seawater, his wet suit unzipped to the waist, his
long black hair slicked straight back. He joined me at the rail and
stared down into the crystal water. "You know, Seychelle, it was like
three generations—old people, young, even kids—all jammed in there
like cocktail wienies in the can. Hell of a way to go."

"Cocktail wienies, B.J.?" I turned around and squinted at him,
my elbows propped on the aluminum bulwark behind me. We both
had to shout to be heard over the rumble of the generator on the
barge. "I didn't think a guy like you even knew such things existed."

B.J. was my sometime deckhand and mechanic, a sort of New Age
natural foods surfer; the only one I'd ever known who didn't make all
that seem kind of fake and wacky. He certainly was not your typical
blond surfer dude, since he had at least two college degrees compared
to my zero—and an ancestry that was mostly Samoan but included a
dash of every other ethnic group that had passed through the Pacific in
the last hundred years. Though he'd never been to his islands, you
could see in his smooth brown skin and almond-shaped eyes that he
carried part of his homeland in him. "Natural" was not a fad to B.J., it
was how he lived his life.

"You're right, I'd never *eat* such a thing, but I do like to observe the habits of the people around me. Take those guys, for example." He jerked his thumb in the direction of the men working the crane on the barge to which *Gorda,* my forty-foot tugboat, was moored. We were anchored a couple of thousand yards off the Hillsboro Inlet lighthouse. "Between them, they have three completely different ideas as to where I should put the straps under the hull so that when we lift this wreck to the surface, we won't break the back of the old derelict. Not a one of them is willing to compromise."

I looked at the characters he was referring to, and I suspected that not a one of them was hangover-free or had used a razor within the last three days. They looked like a labor pool collected from the Downtowner Saloon at closing. "I gather we're going to be here awhile?"

B.J. nodded, then moved into the shade, sitting on the deck box at the front of the wheelhouse. He began to scratch Abaco's ears. She was the black Lab I'd inherited along with *Gorda* and the Sullivan Towing and Salvage Company when my father, Red Sullivan, died not quite three years ago.

"I got tired of swimming around while they try to make up their minds," B.J. said, "so I came out here to bug you." He peeled the wet suit off his broad, brown shoulders. "It's too early to be this hot."

I turned away from the view of his chest. Today I had to concentrate on business. After working with B.J. for years, and swearing to myself I would never allow the relationship to change into something different, something romantic, it had changed. The how and why were a long story, but shortly after finding his toothbrush and coconut soap in my bathroom, I'd asked for a hiatus. I wasn't sure yet I was willing to give up my precious solitude.

The business at hand was a much-needed insurance job. Working for the corporate world beat working for the little guy—you gave them the bill and they paid it. They didn't cry and complain and try to wheedle you out of every nickel. *Gorda* and I were here to take the Bahamian cruiser under tow once these guys from Gilman Marine brought her to the surface and got her pumped out. Gilman's tugs were all huge monsters designed for moving ships, so while they had the barge crane to get the *Miss Agnes* off the bottom, they had subbed this towing job out to me. My father had designed *Gorda* and had her built specifically for the small boat and yacht trade back in the early seventies.

I had deck loaded two big thirty-gallons-per-minute gasoline pumps, and as long as she wasn't holed, we should be able to keep *Miss Agnes* pumped out and get her down the coast, into Port Everglades, and up to a boatyard. Old planked wooden boats like her would usually leak through their caulked seams, but my pumps should be able to stay ahead of the flow.

I leaned out over the water again to examine the wreck resting on the bottom. The sand beneath her looked as though it had been raked into neat furrows, the product of the swift current that flowed through the inlet. The illusion of flying was harder to maintain now as I spotted a school of smallmouth grunts darting in and out of the open pilot-house windows and a foot-long barracuda hanging motionless over the wreck. "Are you sure they said fifty people, B.J.?"

"Yeah."

Neither of us said anything for a while. That was one thing about B.J.—he never felt the need to fill the silences with unnecessary talk. When he spoke, finally, his voice was quiet, and I had to lean in closer to hear him. "See the jetty back there, off the north side of the inlet?"

I looked to where he pointed. The Hillsboro Inlet lighthouse stood back from the broad beach tucked in among the scraggly pines and low sea grape trees. The nearly one-hundred-year-old skeletal frame had been painted recently, white on the bottom half, black up top. A small rock jetty jutted out into the Atlantic along the sandy point at the base of lighthouse.

"Seems the Coast Guard patrol boat was sitting back in there," he said, pointing to the small cove formed by the point. "It was a moonless night. The smugglers prefer that, but the bad news for them was it meant they didn't see the patrol boat until they were almost into the inlet. When the Coasties turned their spotlight on, the Haitians panicked—tried to push their way to the far side of the boat. The weather was real quiet that night, and the crew had left all their windows and hatches open. She just rolled over and went *glug*."

"I heard six people drowned," I said. I also had read in the *Miami Herald* that two of them were children, little girls, ages ten and twelve, but I didn't say it out loud. I knew that B.J. knew, just as he knew that I knew most of the details of the events that had taken place here the night before last. It was our habit, though, to talk about these salvage cases, to rehash the details when we were working. All too often when salvaging wrecked boats there were also ruined lives, and B.J. and I usually did what we could to get around that, joking and laughing and avoiding the image of how it had happened. Those images would eventually catch up with me, often in that twilight moment that comes between wakefulness and sleep, when my imagination would sneak in the vision of those girls struggling in the water, surprised at the sudden cold, screaming for their parents, gasping what they thought was air but sucking in the sea in its stead.

"Fifty people is really only an estimate," he said. "These days, Haitians will do or pay anything to get to the States, and the way the smugglers pack the boats, it could have been more."

"I hope they catch the bastards and charge them with murder."

B.J. was staring at the little strip of sand inside the jetty. "Some of them made it to the beach and managed to lose themselves into the city. Probably got into waiting cars. Immigration picked up twenty-seven. They're either in Krome Detention Center or already back in Port-au-Prince."

"The Land of the Free," I said, "but only if you come from the right island."

"*Gorda, Gorda,* this is *Outta the Blue,* over." The transmission from the tug's VHF radio was barely audible above the rumbling of the generator on the barge.

"Damn." I slapped the palm of my hand against the top of the warm aluminum bulwark. "Not again." When I turned around, B.J. was laughing. "Stop it, you," I said. "It's not funny."

"Bet you he did it again."

"No way I'm taking that bet."

I swung around the door into the wheelhouse and grabbed the VHF radio mike hanging above the helm. "*Outta the Blue,* this is *Gorda.* You want to switch to channel six eight?"

"Roger that."

I punched the numbers on the keypad. "Hey, Mike, this is *Gorda.* What's up?"

"Hey, Seychelle, isn't this a scorcher of a day for June? Not a breath of wind out here."

"Yeah, yeah, Mike. I know you didn't call to discuss the weather. What's wrong?"

"Well, I've been out here fishing all night with my buddy Joe D'Angelo. Him and me, we go way back. Used to work together. We had some good times back in the eighties, boy." I made a circling motion with my hand to B.J. when he shot me a questioning look through the wheelhouse window. Mike rambled on.

A former Fort Lauderdale police officer, Mike Beesting had walked in on a disgruntled city maintenance worker who had brought a shotgun to argue an issue with his boss. The end result was that Mike saved several lives but lost his lower right leg to a short-range shotgun blast. Rather than work a desk, he retired from the department and, thanks to a nice settlement from the city, he now lived on his Irwin-54 sailboat at a dock on the Middle River and ran sunset cocktail cruises and chartered day sails.

"Cut to the chase, Mike."

"Well, we had one light on as we were drift fishing last night, but when we started catching fish, I turned on the spreader lights and kinda forgot and left them on. Joe was nervous about us drifting around out there, so he insisted on watching the radar all night, and then we were playing my whole collection of Buffett tunes . . ."

"So you can't start your engine. Your batteries are dead. *Again.*"

"I'll pay you, Seychelle, you know that. We're only about six or eight miles out off Pompano. I think."

"Mike, the last two times this happened I told you to get somebody down to the boat and rewire it so you could keep your engine-starting battery in reserve."

"And I'm gonna do it, Sey. Next week. I promise."

Mike was the kind of boat owner—and I'd known lots like him—who would much rather spend his money on stuff he could see, cool new toys like an electronic chart plotter or an ice maker, than something necessary but near invisible, like a replacement for a cracked chain plate or a starter battery. He had his boat so loaded down with gadgets it was more like a floating condo than a sailboat.

B.J. appeared at my side in the wheelhouse doorway. At six foot, he was only a couple of inches taller than me, and for a moment I flashed on how pleasant it would be to slide my hands around his waist and pull his body to mine. Being tall, big-boned, and having the shoulders of a swimmer, I still often felt like the gawky kid I once was, the one who had already grown to five feet eight by the fifth grade, the one other kids called the Jolly Green Giant. But with B.J., since the first time we'd made love, there had always been this sense that we just fit together so comfortably, as though my body belonged in his arms. Maybe that's what scares me, I thought as I pretended to be interested in the goings-on aboard the barge and walked to the far wheelhouse window.

B.J. said, "I know you. Somebody's in trouble, and you're itching to go out and save him. Even if it is just Mike. Look, it's going to be at least three hours before these guys get this cruiser up, and then they've still got to pump her out. You've got the time."

"I know, and like always, I need the money, but . . . " The fellows on the barge were still clustered in the shade of the crane, arguing. I wanted to do the right thing here. Working with Gilman Marine meant more referral business in the future. I couldn't afford to screw it up.

Mike's voice erupted from the radio. "Sey, Joe says he really has to get back. Says he'll double your regular rate."

I turned and grinned at B.J. as I punched the button on the side of the mike. "Just give me your GPS coordinates, and I'll be on my way."

B.J. untied my bowline and handed me the neatly coiled line. Once I was at the helm in the wheelhouse, he pushed the tug's bow away from the barge. Watching my stern to make sure it didn't bump anything, I put her into gear and slid over the top of the sunken cruiser, where she rested in about fourteen feet of water. I still had a good seven feet of clearance above her cabin. Walking to the end of the barge, B.J. followed our progress as far as he could, and at the corner he stopped and waved. Abaco ran to the stern and danced around, barking at his receding figure, as though to tell me I was making a mistake, forgetting someone. Watching B.J. stand there, his hand raised to shield his eyes, bare-chested and flashing me the whitest of smiles, had my stomach doing its own gymnastics routine.

Once clear of the last channel marker, I put the tug on an east-southeast heading, about 120 degrees, running at 6 knots. I engaged the autopilot, switched on the radar, found a baseball cap in the wheelhouse, and threaded my shoulder-length hair through the gap in the back. For the last few years, after my father had died from one more melanoma, I had been taking sun protection quite a bit more seriously. I hoped it wasn't too little too late. Red had had the typical redhead's complexion, and though I took more after my mom, with easily tanned skin and sun-streaked brown hair, I had enough freckles on my nose and arms to keep me slathering myself with SPF 30 every morning before going to work.

Out on deck, I began to clear away the mooring lines and to prepare a towline for *Outta the Blue.* Periodically I looked up from my work and gave a 360-degree horizon check to see if there was any boat traffic around me. It was a very quiet Wednesday morning—only one freighter visible farther out in the Gulf Stream, and a little drift fishing boat close into shore. Mike had been right about the stillness out here. There was no way a sailboat could sail herself home right now. It felt good to be moving; the breeze from the boat's forward motion made my neck tingle as the sweat began to dry. I pulled my damp T-shirt away from my skin. The way the smooth, silvery water reflected the high clouds, it looked like *Gorda* was motoring through liquid mercury. Tiny particles of dust rested dry on the surface of the sea. Abaco found a spot in the shade of the wheelhouse and stretched out to sleep, her belly flat on the still-cool aluminum deck.

I wondered if the day would ever come when I would be able to put it all behind me, go back to being B.J.'s buddy, forget about the nights we had spent together. In the first years we had known each other, from the time I met him when I used to work as a lifeguard on Fort Lauderdale Beach, to the days he'd starting working for me on *Gorda,* I had watched him go through a string of beautiful girlfriends, none of whom lasted more than six months. Even though they'd always parted on good terms and remained friends with him, I swore to myself I would never allow my attraction to him to put me in the camp of B.J.'s ex-girlfriends. And here I was, after only four months.

This time, though, I had been the one to put on the brakes. I was the one who said *time out.* If I were honest with myself, I'd have to admit that it wasn't only that we were practically living together. What really scared me was the way B.J. had started looking at and talking about families. B.J., the Serial Dater, talking about kids? Even though the end of my twenties loomed only a few months away, and most women my age were thinking about finding a man, settling down, buying a nice little ¾ out in the western suburbs close to a day-care, I just couldn't picture myself there. The very thought of kids scared the hell out of me. I like sleeping alone, leaving the bathroom door open, getting up at 5:30 and going down for a sunrise run on the beach, or driving over to Lester's Diner for a piece of pie à la mode at 4:00 in the morning when I can't get back to sleep. And not being responsible for anyone but me.

About half a mile to the south, a big sportfisherman was heading my way. The thing was throwing up a huge wake, burning about a bazillion gallons an hour, and with no one on the fly bridge, they probably couldn't even see me from the inside steering station. I slowed down and altered course so he would pass in front of my tug.

Astern, the beach was no longer visible, only the tops of the buildings. I guessed I was seven miles offshore and almost far enough south. According to the GPS, I was only a couple of miles away from *Outta the Blue.* I took the binoculars out of their bulkhead mount case and scanned the hazy horizon for the sailboat's mast. Other than a flock of circling gulls, I didn't see a thing. Now that the sun was climbing higher overhead, it would be more difficult to spot the sailboat, and the day's heat was making the horizon dissolve into undulating heat waves.

The sportfisherman's wake hit us, and though the tug was nearly as big as their boat, the wake made *Gorda* rock and buck. Before cranking the engine back up to cruising RPM, I went out to the foredeck with the binoculars to try one last time to spot Mike's sailboat. Starting left, I scanned the horizon, slowly panning across the water.

Wait a minute. I'd seen something flit past in the viewfinder. Under those birds. I swung the binoculars back to try to focus on it, but I wasn't entirely sure I'd seen anything at all. Had I imagined it? Where was it? I scanned back, found the seabirds circling tightly over a small area—white birds flying low, then swooping down at something on the surface. Perhaps it was just a school of fish feeding, and the gulls were picking off the skittish baitfish that leaped clear of the water only to discover another predator above.

No. There. I saw something in the water. Some kind of floating debris, perhaps something washed off the deck of a cargo ship in a long-passed storm out at sea, maybe a black trash bag, maybe something more. Here in the Gulf Stream we often saw logs, jerry jugs, even plastic-wrapped bales of marijuana that had been carried up from the Caribbean, the Gulf, or as far away as the coast of South America. Once, out in the Northwest Providence channel between the Bahamian Islands of Great Abaco and the Berry Islands, I had seen a ship's container, like the kind they load onto the backs of tractor trailers. It was barely awash, just waiting for some unsuspecting boat to come crashing into it at eight knots.

I tried to refocus the binoculars. I could make out something that looked like a black spot, and the water around it appeared ruffled. Perhaps it was nothing more than a black garbage bag tossed from the deck of some jerk's boat—there were certainly enough jerks out on ships and boats who didn't give a damn about trashing up the ocean. Of course, sometimes there were other things floating out here wrapped in trash bags. The locals called them square groupers. If it *was* a bale, I'd drive on by—wouldn't want to touch it or get involved in any way. My dad had instilled in me from a very young age that drugs were a no-no because the authorities could impound your boat. But if it was a small boat just awash, it could be worth something. That black thing could be a mooring ball.

"*Gorda, Gorda,* this is *Outta the Blue,* over."

Mike and his buddy were getting impatient. I really needed to boost the RPMs and get moving. I was wasting time here. The Gilman crew back at Hillsboro Inlet would sure be mad if they got that boat up and I wasn't there to take her under tow.

I set the glasses down on the deck box and wiped my hands on my shorts. Damn, it was hot. Stepping around the big aluminum towing bitt on the bow, I steadied my right hip against the bulwark and gave it one last try, attempting to hold the glasses still just long enough to make out what those birds were so damned interested in.

Then it moved. The black spot lifted up out of the water and appeared to float there for several seconds. I blinked, not at all sure what I was seeing. Then the shape of it changed, it was turning and, through the binoculars, I began to make out features. My sweaty fingers adjusted the focus with the knob above my nose, and I sucked in air so hard the binoculars bounced. I was looking straight into the dark face of a child.

i i

I lowered the binoculars and spoke aloud—"What the . . . "—and squinted at the object, trying to verify what I had seen, as though perhaps the glasses had been playing tricks on me. I sighted the speck on the horizon easily now with bare eyes, thanks to the circling birds. Several seconds ticked by as my mind flipped through possibilities: a sinking, a fall overboard, a rental dinghy blown out to sea. Another look through the glasses and now it was difficult to see the child in the round, dark object. The head was down, face almost in the water, no longer moving.

I dashed back into the wheelhouse and took a bearing. After pushing the throttle up to max RPM and adjusting the helm to aim just to the right of her, I reached for the mike, then paused, my arm hanging in midair.

I knew the rules: You sight a vessel or a person in distress at sea, you call the Coast Guard. But the rules about what would happen next were really lousy. I knew for sure that if it was a six-year-old Cuban boy, he might end up a celebrity. They'd take him to Disney World, give him a puppy. My guess was *this* one would get, at best, a trip to the airport. I decided to wait a bit. The required call to the Coast Guard could be made after I knew for certain what this was all about.

I circled around and began slowing the tug several hundred yards out, preparing to pull alongside. I could see now that it was a wooden boat, about fourteen feet long, probably an island fishing boat, but full of water, the gunwales just awash, rising only a few inches above the calm sea. Even full of water, wooden boats will float. The water inside the hull looked dirty and filled with debris. A large pile of bright-colored clothing was mounded up in the stern, and sloshing around in the water were rusty cans, bits of paper, and white plastic water jugs, now empty. Where the hell had they come from? This was not a boat meant to cross oceans—no sail, no outboard, not even oars that I could see. I didn't think it was possible they had come up from down island in this boat. But if not from there, then where?

The child was sitting at the bow of the swamped boat, arms wrapped around a wood post. When I came closer, I saw that her hair was plaited in several short black braids. I realized that it was a little girl, maybe eight or nine years old.

She'd heard the sound of my engine and looked up once, lifted her hand a few inches and waved, then lowered her head again to rest against the post. She was wearing a white dress—or what *had* been a white dress. From her chest down, where the fabric had been immersed in water for God only knew how long and the fabric floated off her legs in the garbage-filled water, the dress was stained a dirty rust-brown.

When I was about fifty feet off the boat and had put *Gorda*'s engine into reverse to bring her to a complete stop, I saw that it wasn't just a lumpy pile of bright-colored clothing floating amid the debris inside the boat.

"Oh, shit," I said aloud. It was a dress and the fabric was stretched tight. I could now see the other side of that mound, and I could make out the head. The bloated body of a woman was floating facedown next to the child.

I've never been seasick in my life, but for just a few seconds I thought I was going to lose it. The birds had been at work on her already, and the bloodless flesh on the side of her head was peeled back, the pink bone showing.

"Hello," I tried, but my voice sounded strangled. I didn't want to scare the girl any worse. "Hello. Hey, kid, are you okay?" Whatever island she came from, she probably didn't speak any English, but I had to say something, to try to get her to raise her head again, to pay attention.

Gorda was now dead in the water, and the child was about twenty feet off the port side, her head still down. She had shifted her position a bit so that her large brown eyes were staring up at me. I expected to see some measure of excitement in her face, a realization that rescue was at hand, her ordeal over, but she simply stared, her eyelids starting to droop, as though she hadn't even enough strength left for hope.

At the sound of my voice, Abaco got to her feet and padded over. She jumped up and saw the girl over the top of the bulwark and began to bark. The girl's eyes snapped open, fear causing her to use what little energy she had. I grabbed the dog's collar, dragged her into the wheelhouse and down to the head.

"Sorry, girl," I said as I closed the door and locked it. "Let me get her aboard first. Then you can meet her."

Gorda was up current, to the south of the swamped boat, and the relentless Gulf Stream would eventually close the gap between us, but I might need the girl to help me, to take a line. If necessary, I'd go in the water myself, but that would be a last resort.

"Hey, what's your name?"

She lifted her head and opened her mouth, but no sound came out—at least nothing that I could hear over the sound of *Gorda*'s idling engine. She was clearly in bad shape, and the exposure to heat and salt and no fresh water had robbed her of her voice.

From *Gorda*'s foredeck I picked up the fifty-foot length of nylon line I had been preparing to toss to *Outta the Blue* and tied a quick bowline in the end, then pulled a loop of line through, fashioning a lasso of sorts. I'm no cowboy, though, so I used the boat hook, and as the gap between the boats had closed to about ten feet, it was easy to reach over with the looped line hanging off the end of the pole.

"Sit up, will you? Get away from that wood post."

She didn't move.

"Hey, kid." I motioned with my free hand. "Move. Move over. Sit up. I want to tie your boat to mine."

Finally, she seemed to understand what I wanted her to do, but she looked from me to the body in the back of the boat and then back at me. Her expression did not change, but she scooted closer to that misshapen thing.

The line dropped neatly over the four-by-four post, and I pulled it tight. Keeping the tension on the line, I rigged my aluminum ladder over the gunwale, down into the water, then began to pull the waterlogged fishing boat over to *Gorda*. It was not easy, not like pulling a boat sitting on top of the water that glides smoothly across the surface. This one had to push aside the displaced water, but slowly I brought in the line, and the submerged hull came alongside and thumped against *Gorda's* aluminum hull.

After tying off the line, I lay on my belly across the gunwale and reached out to the child. "Here, take my hand."

She didn't need to understand my words; my outstretched hand had a universal meaning. She stretched her arm out slowly, and I realized for the first time just how thin she was. I saw the bones of her wrist and elbow protruding beneath the dark skin. There was no return grip in that small hand, but I pulled her up and toward the boat. She reached out with her other hand and attempted to grasp the side of the aluminum ladder, but she didn't have enough strength in her fingers.

It wasn't a pretty rescue. When it became clear that her legs could not support her and the ladder was useless, I dragged her light frame out of the water and across the ladder. She landed on the deck like a boated fish, dripping and breathing hard, wide-eyed and twitching.

I grabbed a towel off the bunk in the back of the wheelhouse and approached her slowly. "It's okay. I won't hurt you. Let's get this towel around you."

"*Gorda, Gorda,* this is *Outta the Blue,* over." The radio sounded much louder with the engine down to an idle. The girl's deep-sunk eyes barely registered my presence, and she didn't resist when I wrapped the towel around her shoulders.

"It's okay. I'll be right back."

In the wheelhouse, I grabbed the mike and we switched to a working channel. I stood in the doorway where I could keep an eye on the girl.

"Listen, Mike, I've got a little problem."

"Hey, Seychelle, we wondered what was going on. We been watching you through the binoculars, and it looks like you're stopped dead. You got engine trouble?"

"No, it's not that." For some reason that wasn't fully formed in my mind, I was not yet ready to announce over the airwaves to all the bored fishermen and yachtsmen who were eavesdropping on our conversation exactly what was now tied alongside *Gorda.* "I've found something here. It's a partially sunk boat and a hazard to navigation. I think I'd better tow it in first."

"Break, break. *Gorda, Gorda,* this is *Little Bitt.*"

I blew a lung full of air out through rounded lips and tapped the radio microphone against my forehead. Damn. I keyed the mike and said, "Hey, Perry, should've known you wouldn't have anything better to do than sit around drinking and listening in on my frequency."

Perry Greene was the owner of *Little Bitt,* a twenty-eight-foot open tow boat that looked like a floating junkyard, piled high with gas cans, rusting engine parts, and greasy fenders, but she had an engine that ran like a watch. I had to grant that Perry was a hell of a mechanic, but I just wished he'd keep his chewing-tobacco-stained teeth and greasy fingernails as far from me as possible. Since the big corporate giants like SEATOW had come into town in the last couple of years and begun eating up the pleasure-boat-towing market, Perry and I were just about the only two independent operators left in the towing business in Fort Lauderdale, and he had taken to visiting me, perched on *Gorda*'s bulwarks, Bud in hand. To make matters worse, he always wore these cut-off jeans that were cut way too short, and he apparently did not own any underwear. I had seen way more of Perry Greene than I ever wanted to.

"Matter of fact, Seychelle, I just dropped a boat off at Lighthouse Point Marina, and I was on my way out to see how you was doing with that sunk Haitian boat, and it turns out you ain't even there."

Much as I hated to ask, I didn't see that I had any other choice. "Perry, I was on my way out to tow in *Outta the Blue,* but something's come up. Could you go pick Mike up for me? He's on this same frequency," I said, as if Perry didn't know. "Mike, you there?" I called.

"I'm here." I could hear in his voice how he felt about this. Mike had about as much fondness for Perry as I did, and in just those two words I could tell that he was furious at my handing him off like this.

"Okay, you guys work out the details, and this is *Gorda* clear and going back to one six."

I felt bad about it, but I had a problem that was going to take most of the rest of my afternoon. I'd be lucky to make it back to Hillsboro Inlet in time. After I set my radio back to the emergency frequency, my hand paused as I was about to hang the mike on the side of the receiver. By law, I was required to call the Coast Guard right about now. I looked at the skinny kid collapsed on my deck. I watched her chest rising and falling under the white cotton as she took short, shallow breaths. Reading the papers about boatloads of immigrants getting sent back home via Coast Guard cutter had always irked me, but never enough to do anything about it. But this was different. This was personal. I'd found her, and somehow that made her my responsibility.

I grabbed a bottle of water out of the ice chest on the wheelhouse floor.

She appeared to be closer to ten years old when I examined her up close. I offered her the sport bottle. She looked at the top but didn't move to accept it. I leaned my head back and squirted the water into my mouth, showing her how, and the first little light appeared in her eyes. She took the bottle and drank eagerly, the water dribbling out the sides of her mouth as she gulped at the stream. Her arms gave out after about five seconds of holding the bottle aloft. The plastic bottle bounced to the deck, and I grabbed it and righted it before too much spilled.

"That's okay," I said. It didn't matter if she couldn't understand what I was saying. I was talking mostly just to soothe her. "You're not supposed to drink too much anyway. You have to go slow. We'll see if you keep it down." During my seven years as a Fort Lauderdale lifeguard, I had treated many drowning victims, but never an exposure victim as severe as this child. I had been trained as an EMT, and I knew the victim needed to rehydrate slowly. The girl's large brown eyes were sunk deep in their sockets, and the skin on her forearms was a dark reddish mahogany. Her upper arms showed a distinct tan line, with the skin peeking out from under her sleeves a much lighter shade of brown. She probably had second-degree burns over a good twenty percent of her body and was suffering from heat exhaustion. I couldn't see any blistering. Her legs were shriveled and bleached-looking from the long-term immersion in salt water, and that might have contributed to keeping her overall body temperature down.

I tried to remember some phrases from my two years of high school French. "*Comment tu t'appelles?* You know, your name? *Ton nom.* What's your name?"

She pointed to the water bottle, and I squeezed another squirt into her mouth. After she swallowed, she licked her lips and whispered something. I couldn't understand her at first.

"What was that?"

"Solange." Her voice was a little stronger and, from the name and the pronunciation, I'd clearly guessed right in trying French first.

"Solange?" I asked with my voice if I had pronounced it correctly, and she nodded, again that faint smile flickering in her eyes.

I patted my own chest. "Seychelle. *Je m'appelle* Seychelle."

Her lips moved, shaping the word, but no sound came out.

At that point I'd about exhausted what little I could remember from two years with Mademoiselle Goldberg. I pointed at her. "You, Solange, Haiti?"

She nodded and said, "Haiti," her voice louder now and pronouncing the name Hi-yee-tee, as though correcting me.

The next question was awkward, but I had to know. I had been about her age when I saw my mother's body on the beach after she had drowned, and I had only recently started to come to terms with that event in my life. And I hadn't had to spend days in a boat with the body. But I had to know. I pointed to the woman in the boat. *"Ta maman?"*

She shook her head and reached for the water bottle. I let her drink a little more but stopped her after a couple of mouthfuls.

The dress she wore had been hand-hemmed with tiny little stitches, and the lace around the collar had been added by hand as well. But either she had lost weight during her time at sea, or the dress had been made for a much larger child. I wondered if it had been her First Communion dress. The thin fabric fell in folds off her shoulders and the skirt nearly ripped as I began to wring out the dirty water. The waistline of the dress could have enclosed two little bodies her size.

She licked her lips and swallowed and pointed toward the swamped boat. "Name Erzulie." She closed her eyes after she spoke, as though the effort had depleted the last of her energy.

"The woman? That's her name? Er-zoo-ly?" I tried to pronounce the name as she had with that musical rhythm.

She nodded. "Yes."

I reached for her arm. "Oh my God. You speak English?"

She nodded, every movement an effort. *"Papa Americain."*

A white American, I guessed. That explained the light skin.

Her thin arm reached toward me, and I thought she wanted another drink, but she wrapped her small hand around my fingers. "You help me." The effort of saying those three words completely did her in; her eyelids drooped again, her mouth opened, her breathing came fast and shallow.

I entwined my big fingers with her tiny brown ones and squeezed softly. "Yes," I said, my throat constricting so that I could barely croak out the words. "I'll help you."

I saw a small twitch at the corner of her mouth. It was almost a smile.

iii

Holding her arm, I helped Solange to her feet, but her little legs collapsed beneath her. I scooped her up and carried her toward the pilothouse. She was tiny, couldn't have weighed more than fifty pounds. I could feel her eyes watching my face, and then she rested her head against my shoulder. Her salty braids brushed against my neck, and I touched the top of her head with my chin, cradling her tight to my chest as we passed through the door. I felt as though a fist had grabbed hold of all the organs in my chest and was holding them tight. I didn't want to let her go.

When I got to the bunk that ran along the rear of the small compartment, I set her down and straightened her dress around her scrawny knees.

"Stay here," I said, motioning with my hand because I wasn't certain how much she understood. She curled up on her side and closed her eyes. I covered her with an old beach towel.

Out on deck, I fired up one of the gas pumps and drained most of the water out of the fishing dory. The hose kept picking up floating debris and clogging the filter, but I soon got out enough water that I could climb down into the boat to tie a good towline on her.

I hadn't been able to smell anything when I'd been up on *Gorda*'s deck, but I was once down in the boat, with the water now pumped out, the stench from the corpse struck me. It was a thick, cloying smell, almost palpable. I felt it would permeate my hair and clothes the way cigarette smoke does. The woman's skin was discolored, turned an ashy green, and though I tried not to look at her, I found myself drawn back again and again for a quick glance at the form that had once been a woman. She wore a bright tropical-print dress with parrots and palm fronds. In other circumstances, it might have looked cheerful. I imagined this woman must have thought so when she chose it, and I envi-

sioned her in an outdoor market in Port-au-Prince, carefully select-
ing the dress she would wear to America, not knowing it would be the
dress she would die in.

Nothing from my lifeguard training told me how long it takes a
body to swell. Had she drowned? I couldn't tell without a closer examination, nor could I tell whether the skin on the side of her head had
been broken by some blow or simply ravaged by the gulls that had been
feeding on her. And I wasn't about to roll her over. I would deliver her
to the authorities as I had found her.

I tied two long nylon lines to the bow bitt and climbed back aboard
Gorda. After securing the towlines at the stern, I put the tug in gear and
got us on a heading for Port Everglades. In the logbook, I made my
entry, noting the time and date and the exact GPS location where I had
picked them up—Latitude 26° 14.29 Long 80° 56.12.

Abaco had been cooped up in the head a long time and I could
hear her whining. I eased her out and introduced her to the girl. She
put her paws up on the bunk, her tongue hanging out the side of her
mouth, breathing dog breath all over the kid. The child's eyes popped
open and she reared back against the bulkhead. But when Abaco licked
her hand, Solange's mouth spread in a tentative toothy smile, and I
knew they would be friends. I opened a bottle of Gatorade this time,
gave her a little, and left them to get better acquainted.

Out on deck, I made a quick check around the horizon for boat
traffic, cleaned up, coiled the lines, and checked on my tow. The fishing boat was riding well, given that the Gulf Stream was like a lake. I was
glad I wasn't towing in a following sea. The weight of the body in the
back of that fishing boat was making it ride very low in the stern. I
checked our progress toward the red-striped stacks of the power plant
that marked the entrance to Port Everglades. We'd be in all too soon,
and I knew I'd better get a hold of Jeannie so she could meet us at the
dock.

I called *Outta the Blue* on the VHF and asked Mike to call Jeannie on
his cell phone and tell her to meet us at the Lauderdale Marina fuel
dock in front of the 15th Street Fisheries Restaurant. I knew I'd have to
get myself a cell phone one of these days, but I was postponing the in-
evitable as long as possible. "Tell her it's an emergency," I said.

"You okay?" he asked over the party-line airwaves.

"Yeah, sure." I tried to make my voice sound light and uncon-
cerned. "You know Jeannie—it's hard to get her moving unless you tell
her it's an emergency." I laughed and held the mike open long enough
for him to hear. When I turned from the radio to check on my passenger, she and the dog were curled up together in the bunk, both fast
asleep.

Jeannie Black was my lawyer and best friend. Though she worked
out of her home, and her six-foot height and nearly three-hundred-
pound figure didn't fit the image of the high-powered corporate
lawyer, I would match Jeannie's brains and heart against anyone's.
Legal entanglements were a given in the world of no-cure, no-pay marine towing and salvage. The client promises you anything to get his
boat off the rocks, but once he's safely hauled at the yard, he often has
second thoughts about the agreed-upon terms. Just recently Jeannie
had helped me settle a salvage claim that paid off my boat loans and
made *Gorda* mine, free and clear. She'd shown me how to use the rest
to set up a college fund for a young girl we'd met on that job. I knew
Jeannie would figure out a way to keep Solange safe.

The rocks at the end of the harbor jetty were abeam before we
passed the first pleasure boat on her way out of the harbor. The
twenty-foot center console open fishing boat was bristling with dozens
of rods and antennae. She was piloted by high school boys. As it was
Wednesday, just past noon, they were probably skipping school. Shirt-
less, they looked like they were wearing white tank tops as their chests
still bore the tan lines from their last time in the sun. They hooted and
hollered at what they must have thought was a drunk, fat lady facedown
in the skiff behind *Gorda*.

Once inside the harbor, I slowed the tug in the turning basin and
pulled my tow alongside. With a small tarp I'd pulled out of the deck
box, I covered the body enough so that when we tied up at the pier at
Lauderdale Marina, the dock jocks couldn't speculate on the contents.

The dock in front of the restaurant parallels the Intracoastal and
serves as fuel dock space for most of its two-hundred-foot length. Late
in the afternoon, the restaurant sends someone out with fish scraps to
feed the pelicans, and hundreds of the birds flock to the dock. The
nearly tame birds often hang out on the pilings, waiting for an un-
scheduled handout, and the antics of the greedy pelicans bring the

tourists. Some days you had to elbow aside the families in matching mouse T-shirts just to tie up your dock lines. Fortunately, there were no tourists on the dock this afternoon.

No one came out to take my lines. The dock jocks recognized the boat and knew that I preferred to handle my own docking, tie off my own lines. Once the tug was close enough to the dock, I used the boat hook to drop a midships spring line over a piling cleat, then I slowly idled the engine in forward, helm hard over, until she eased in and nudged alongside the bleached-wood dock pilings. When *Gorda* was secure, I turned off the engine and checked on my tow. I was considering whether or not to tie a stern line on the fishing boat when I saw Jeannie hurrying through the opening between the 15th Street Fisheries Restaurant and the small bait shop. As always, she was wearing a billowing tropical-print muumuu—today's was decorated with huge red hibiscus flowers; the voluminous straw handbag over her arm had a matching yarn flower sewn on it.

"Seychelle, we're here!" she called, as though I could miss her. Her twin sons, Andrew and Adair, waved to me and then ran to the bait tank and leaned over to watch the fish, their identical blond heads ducking under the wood lids, rumps in the air as they pointed into the water.

I climbed up onto the dock just in time to be enveloped in a Jeannie hug.

"Are you okay? When Mike called, I was so worried! The boys stayed home from school today with the flu, so we came straight here."

My face was pressed against a huge red blossom, and I could barely breathe. "Jeannie, let go, I'm okay." She released me, and I took a deep breath.

"So tell me, then, what's this emergency?"

I knew it would be hard to explain. "Do you think you can get down onto the boat?"

She eyed the three-foot drop to *Gorda*'s deck and gave me an exasperated look. "It won't be a pretty sight, but I can do it."

She was right on both counts. Once she was down on deck, I led her to the wheelhouse, and while I went in, she stopped at the door. Abaco was still curled up with the girl, but the dog lifted her head when she saw us, and her tail thumped against the aluminum bulkhead. The girl awoke with a start and tried to pull away from us, back into the shadowy corner of the wheelhouse bunk.

"It's okay. Shhh. It's okay," I said to the child. "This is Jeannie. She's my friend." The girl's head dropped, chin to chest, as though the effort of holding her head up was just too much for her. I turned to Jeannie. "We've got to get her to a hospital. She needs IV fluids. She's severely dehydrated."

"Wait, wait, wait. Whoa. Time out." She was making referee signals with her hands, and for a moment my mind flashed on the image of her billowing muumuu racing up and down the sidelines of a playing field. "Stop grinning at me." She pointed at the girl. "Where did she come from?"

"I found her out there."

"Oh," she said, not bothering to hide the sarcasm. "You just found her."

"Yeah. I saw what I thought was a half-sunk boat, adrift, and when I went to investigate I found her in it. I have no clue how long she's been out there."

"And apparently you haven't called the Coasties or they'd be here by now."

I shook my head.

"What is it with you, Seychelle? Don't you ever learn? It's not like they're going to send you to jail for it, but why do you always have to start by pissing off the authorities?" She shook her head.

"She's only half of the story, Jeannie. Come on." I led her around the wheelhouse and pointed down at the fishing boat tied alongside.

"That's what I found her in."

"Okay, it's a boat."

"Look again, Jeannie." In the stern, a foot was visible protruding from the tarp.

"Geez, Seychelle, what the . . ."

"That's exactly what I said, Jeannie."

"I take it that person's in a lot worse shape than the girl?"

"You could say that. It's a woman—was a woman. The girl says she's no relation. I wanted you here before the cops came."

"I guess I can understand that. So I'm here. Let's make that call. Now."

"Okay, okay." I crossed the aft deck, then turned back to face her. "You understand this, don't you, Jeannie? I mean the kid, she's Haitian, and you know what they do with illegal Haitians."

"I know. I know this is just you being you. This time, though, you're up against the U.S. government—the INS. You probably don't have a hope in hell of keeping that little girl here. Especially if we continue to delay calling the authorities."

"But she says her father's American."

"You talked to her? She speaks English?"

"Yeah, she speaks a little English—maybe even more than a little. It's hard to tell. She barely has the strength to say two words. I just don't want her to get thrown into a foster family, even for a day or two, and then shipped back to Haiti."

"Seychelle, I'm not an immigration attorney."

"I know that. I just need you to get me some time, that's all. Maybe I can find her father." I climbed up onto the dock, carefully avoiding the dozens of white splotches of pelican poop.

"That's pretty iffy. For all you know the guy won't even want to claim her."

I straightened, brushed off my hands, and paused for a minute, trying to find the right words to express the feeling I'd had ever since looking into those big brown eyes through the binoculars. "Jeannie, there's something about finding a kid like that." I thought about how frail and helpless she had felt when I'd lifted her in my arms and carried her to the bunk, and once again I felt the tightness in my chest. "I just can't turn her over and walk away. I've got to try." I headed up the dock.

Leaning against the side of the bait shop, the pay phone receiver to my ear, I began the second run-through of my story for the 911 dispatcher when I noticed the Coast Guard launch. The hard-bottom inflatable with a center console was piloted by what looked like two well-fed Iowa farm boys in blue coveralls. With their identical builds, Florida tans, and military-style haircuts, they looked like older versions of Jeannie's twins, only one was blond, the other brunette. It was the blond who motioned for his buddy to back the boat closer to the wooden fishing boat. Though their launch was only eighteen feet long at best, the blond waved his right hand in the air, making concise hand signals to back up a little more, speed it up, slow down, stop, as if he thought he was docking a 747 in her berth at the airport.

When the blond reached down and pulled back the tarp, he lost his Florida tan as the blood drained from his face, and then his barracks breakfast when he heaved into the Intracoastal off the inflatable boat's stern.

Over the course of the next couple of hours, *Gorda* **turned into** a rendezvous point for nearly every law enforcement agency in South Florida. Abaco paced the decks and barked at the men and women who came aboard, but soon even she was exhausted, and she retreated to the shade of the cabin. The paramedics were the first on the land side, and I was glad to lead them to Solange. Their uniforms, equipment, and squawking radios scared her, but they had to stick an IV needle in her whether she liked it or not. Solange didn't cry, but the fear in her eyes was naked and raw, and I wished there were something I could do to make it all seem less terrifying. I tried to imagine the world she had known in Haiti. Though I had never been there, I was pretty certain that her former life did not include men in uniforms crowding her, asking her questions, poking her, feeling her limbs.

Several Fort Lauderdale Police Department cars arrived and were followed by a Crime Scene Unit and then the coroner's van. The FLPD Marine Patrol Unit tied their launch alongside the Coast Guard inflatable after a young woman who worked the dock complained that all the boats were eating up her fuel dock space.

Soon there were two sites being worked: the child in *Gorda*'s wheelhouse and the wood fishing boat with the dead woman. A turf war was under way as the Coasties and the sheriffs and the local Fort Lauderdale PD all tried to take control of the scene. Shouting men and women on the aft deck of the tug and on the fuel dock tried to move the wooden boat from where it was tied on the outside of *Gorda* over to the dock so they could begin to collect the evidence and deal with the body. Thus far they were more concerned with all of that than with questioning me, so I sat and held Solange's thin hand as the medics worked on her. Each time something new and strange was thrust at her, those deep brown eyes turned to me with a yearning for reassurance.

Those eyes did something to me. They fired up some deep inner mechanism I didn't know I possessed. I wanted more than anything to wrap my arms around her and protect her from harm. I wanted to tell her it was all going to be okay, as my dad used to tell me when things got bad for my mom. He would hold me and tell me that everything would turn out fine if we'd just give her time, only that turned out not to be true at all. I couldn't be sure that things were going to turn out fine for Solange, either.

The Border Patrol pulled up in a big white Chevy Suburban with green lettering on the side just as the paramedics were pushing Solange on a gurney toward the back of their van. Jeannie told the officers they would have to follow the unit over to Broward General if they wanted to question Solange. I wanted to jump into the back with Solange, but I gave her hand one last squeeze and tried to smile.

A uniformed officer ordered me not to leave the scene until I had spoken to the detective in charge. Jeannie assured me she would follow the ambulance to the hospital and see that Solange got the care she needed, both medically and legally. I thanked her, waved them off, and walked back onto the dock, girding myself to face the grilling I knew was coming.

"Miss Sullivan, over here."

There, standing next to the bait tank, was the last person I wanted to see, but somehow I knew it would be my luck that he would pick up this case.

"Detective Victor Collazo." I bobbed my head in a curt hello. He hadn't changed much in the months since I'd seen him last. Even in this heat, he was wearing black pants and a long-sleeved shirt that was supposed to hide the thick black body hair that tufted out of his collar and around his wrists. His neck was shaved close all the way around. It looked like a firebreak in the black forest. I imagined his barber had to replace his blade after each Collazo visit. In response to the heat, he'd removed his suit coat, and the sweat rings under his arms already reached nearly to his waist.

"You look well, Miss Sullivan," he said.

Typical, I thought. Telling me, not asking. Collazo had a thing about questions. He never asked any.

He carried what looked like the exact same notebook, and I wanted to ask him if there were still notes in there from the first time we'd met, last March, when he'd suspected me of murdering my former boyfriend.

"Collazo, what do you say we dispense with any kind of pretense that we're friends or that we like each other? I know you're here to take my statement, and I've got to get back to work. I've got a tow waiting up in Hillsboro."

"Very well." He rifled through the jacket over his arm and found the gold pen in the inside breast pocket. "You found this boat offshore."

"Yeah, I was up off that Hillsboro Inlet sinking, you know, the Haitian boat that went down night before last." I ran through the rest of it for him, all of it, from getting Mike's call to bringing in the tow to the dock here and calling the police. He wrote very quickly and in a remarkably neat hand. As I talked, I kept focusing on his fingers and noticing how fat they were, like plump, fuzzy caterpillars wrapped around his pen.

"You decided not to call the Coast Guard when you came upon this boat."

"I don't know that it was a conscious decision necessarily," I said, knowing perfectly well that it was. "It was more like I was just too busy at the time."

"Miss Sullivan, as a professional mariner, I'm sure you are aware of the required procedure. By not reporting the incident in a timely manner, you can jeopardize the investigation."

"Detective Collazo, you don't have to lecture me. So, I didn't call it in right away. I just set about getting her to shore as fast as possible. I'm a certified EMT, so I could do just as much as the Hardy Boys over there," I said, pointing to the Coast Guardsmen getting in the way of the police officers working the scene aft of *Gorda*. "I know my tug isn't any speed demon, but I knew I could get her to port in the time it would take another boat to come out to meet us."

He stared at me, waiting for me to continue, knowing that silence between us would make me uncomfortable. I hated when he did that. I tried to be strong, tried to stare right back at him, but every time a figure of authority looks at me like I am doing something bad, I feel guilty. It had been going on since Mrs. Laughlin's first-grade class. I caved.

"It was the kid, Collazo. Did you see her? Skinny little thing? I was just trying to do what was best for her."

"The child is Haitian."

"Part, anyway. She said her dad is American, but yeah, she's Haitian. Her name is Solange. She said the woman in the boat was named Erzulie or something like that. I didn't get much of a chance to ask her anything else."

"She spoke English."

"Not much. She really didn't say much at all. But her knowing some English jibes with her saying her father is American."

"Miss Sullivan, you are aware that there is a great deal of difference between the way our government treats immigrants found at sea as opposed to those who make it to shore."

"Oh yeah, the old wet-foot, dry-foot routine, only if you're Haitian, they don't give a damn about your foot. Collazo, I was only thinking about the kid. She needs medical attention, not a Coast Guard cutter ride back to Haiti."

He stared at me, but this time I held firm, refusing to fill the silence.

"She told you how the woman died," he said finally.

"No. It's like I said, I hardly got a chance to speak to her. She was unconscious most of the trip into the harbor."

Out in the waterway, an air horn sounded a long toot. I looked across *Gorda*'s bow to see *Little Bitt* heading toward the dock with Mike Beesting's big sailboat, *Outta the Blue*, on a short towline.

Mike shouted from up on the foredeck of his boat, "Is it okay if we raft up to you, *Gorda*?" while with one hand, he steadied himself on the rigging. As usual, he was not wearing his artificial leg, and his scarred stump protruded from his jeans shorts. He claimed the prosthesis slowed him down as he tried to maneuver around the tight spaces on a sailboat deck.

"Sure," I called out, and jumped down onto *Gorda*'s deck to take their lines.

Standing next to Mike on the foredeck of the Irwin-54 was a fellow with easily the best pair of legs I had ever seen on a man. Maybe it was just the perspective, my being on the low deck of the tug, and eyeball-to-kneecap with these muscular, suntanned legs, but it probably had as much to do with my recent decision to avoid men. He looked like a fit fifty-something, wearing a crisp white T-shirt that read "Hard Rock Cafe, Cayman Islands" across the front and was tucked into the trim waist of his khaki-colored cargo shorts. He knew enough about boats not to try to throw me the line from too far out as Perry was easing them in alongside with surprising precision. When only about four feet separated us, he tossed me the line and picked up a white fender to cushion the impact as the two boats came together.

Perry idled his boat off the bow of the sailboat and sauntered back to the stern to untie the towline. I hadn't seen Perry in a couple of months, and he was now wearing his greasy hair in a shoulder-length mullet style, long in back, razed close on the sides. He pouched his lips out at me in an exaggerated kiss.

"Just say when, baby. You know you want me." He cackled as he tossed the towline onto the deck of Mike's boat.

"Yeah, like a dose, Perry. Which, given your personal hygiene, probably isn't far from the truth."

Once the sailboat was secure, Mike hopped back to the stern and handed me his shore power cord. That darned cord was nearly the diameter of a fire hose. "Plug that sucker in and we can fire up the AC and cool off that damn cabin down there. It's hotter than a two-peckered goat out here."

I took the cord from him. "Mike, you have got to learn you live on a boat. Flattening your batteries like that should be embarrassing to you."

"Hey, look, it wasn't me, all right? It was Joe. Man, he had to burn every light in the goddam boat all night." Mike waved to Collazo on the dock. "Hey, Vic. What's up, man? Want to come aboard and have a piña colada? Gonna have that blender chugging any minute. What brings you guys down here, buddy?"

Vic? Buddy? Somehow I could never picture either term applying to the Detective Collazo I knew. I plugged in Mike's power cord before one of the dock jocks could object. When I stood up, Collazo was right there, invading my space, breathing on me as he said, "Miss Sullivan. We haven't concluded our conversation." He wiped his brow with an already saturated handkerchief.

"I don't know anything more to tell you, Collazo," I said, taking a step back. "I don't know how she got out there, where she came from, who the dead woman is, nothing." I put my raised palms in the air. "What more can I tell you?"

"You can tell me the exact location where you found her."

"That I *can* do." I jumped back down onto the tug's deck, grabbed the ship's log from inside the wheelhouse, and read off the exact position. I stepped outside the wheelhouse and, looking up at the detective as he wrote in his notebook, described the way the boat had been filled with dirty water and how I pumped it out.

"There is one thing that's a bit strange, Collazo. I don't know how much you know about boats, but I can tell you this: There is no way they came from Haiti in that little boat. It's barely possible a boat like that could make it from Cuba, but from Haiti? With no sails? It's just not possible."

Down the dock, the crowd around the fishing boat opened up and several officers hoisted a bulging white plastic bag up to the dock where a uniformed woman stood alongside a gurney. I climbed back up onto the dock. Mike and his buddy Joe followed me. Another uniformed officer split off from the crowd and came over to consult with Collazo. They stepped aside and murmured just softly enough that I couldn't make out what they were saying.

When Mike got upright on the dock, he asked, "Who died?"

"How about a little courtesy?" I said. "Introductions, perhaps?" I turned to his friend with the great legs. "Hi, I'm Seychelle Sullivan, since it appears our friend is not going to introduce us."

"Joe D'Angelo," he said. "Very pleased to meet you." His hand felt rough and dry, his grip firm and confident. His eyes met mine with a directness, an openness, that I found appealing.

"So you used to work with Mike?"

"Yeah, I was with the DEA. Retired now." His dark hair had been "styled," not just cut, and the only bit of gray was at his temples. He nodded his head toward the far end of the dock. "So, what's going on?"

I shouldn't have expected any different. One thing I'd learned about cops is that little social niceties often aren't on their list of acquired skills.

"Yeah, Sey, that have anything to do with your emergency?" Mike asked.

"The boat I said I found?" I pointed toward the body bag. "That's what was in it. That and a kid, a little girl about ten years old."

Joe turned away from the scene and looked at me. His features were pinched with concern, and I could not help but notice how light his green eyes were. "The kid, she was alive?" he asked.

"Yeah, bad shape, though. Dehydration, sun. On her way to Broward General right now. Who knows how long she had been out there."

Joe shook his head. "Poor kid. It always gets to me when there are kids involved."

"You got kids?" I asked him.

"One. A grown daughter." He paused and his eyes went unfocused, as though looking at something far away, before he turned to look across the Intracoastal. Without turning back to face me, he said, "I haven't seen her in a long time. Too long, I guess."

He stood there, his head turned away, and I didn't know whether to speak or to wait or to walk away and leave him alone.

"This kid," he said, turning to face me and coming back from wherever or whatever memory he had traveled to. "She able to tell you anything about what happened to her?"

"Nope. She could barely talk. She's so thin, she looks like she's been starved for months, not just days. Hopefully, she'll be all right, but then, you know how it is." I shrugged. "She's Haitian, so as soon as she's healthy . . . " I motioned with my hand for them to fill in the blanks.

"Yeah. It doesn't seem fair, does it," Mike said.

"At least she's lucky you found her," Joe said, squeezing and then patting my upper arm. I smiled back at him and nodded, not sure whether or not he was flirting with me and not sure whether or not I liked it.

The officers pushing the gurney with the body bag passed within a few feet of us, and one of them nodded at Mike, left the group, and started toward us.

Mike shook hands with the first officer and several others who followed. Most were big men, either in uniform or plainclothes, and they greeted Mike, shook his hand, and patted him on the back. They gathered around their old friend, and the laughter erupted in sharp, loud bursts, but something about their camaraderie seemed forced. They all tried to look anywhere but at the missing leg.

"Hey, Mike," I said, "some of us still have to work for a living. Think you could move your boat so I can get out?"

He looked up and our eyes met over the top of the heads around him. He didn't say anything, but there was gratitude in his eyes. "Come on, Joe—" he clapped the other man on the shoulder— "let's get ourselves some sea, sun, and rum."

A voice right behind me made me spin around. "That could very well have been valuable evidence, the water you pumped out of that boat." Collazo had walked up behind me, and he now stuck his face about six inches from mine.

"What are you talking about?"

"Collazo, back off," Mike said. "You don't need to pull that bullshit with her. She's not going to hide anything from you."

He didn't break eye contact with me when he said, "Mike, I know you'd never interfere with a police investigation."

"Hey, Joe," Mike said, "I think he's showing off for us." Both men laughed. "Collazo, remember Joe? He worked with us back around, what was it, eighty-two? On that Northwest Lauderdale Task Force? Oh, wait a minute, you were still on patrol then, right? I forgot. Didn't recognize you without your radar gun." Mike and his friend hooted, while Collazo ignored them.

"I *had* to pump it out," I said, "or I wouldn't have been able to tow it in."

"That's why you should have called the experts. The water you pumped out of that boat was probably discolored due to the blood from the woman's body."

"The water was . . . ," I started to say. I'd wrung out Solange's dress, her white First Communion dress, only it wasn't white anymore. And how long had she been sitting in that bloody water?

"Perhaps there was blood there from her attacker as well," he said.

"Her attacker?"

He nodded. "It won't be official until the autopsy, but this wasn't a drowning. She bled out from her wounds. It looks like that woman died from a blow to the head."

It was almost three o'clock by the time I finished with Collazo and could get back to work. Mike got his engine started, and I threw off his lines. Joe stood at the wheel, handling the controls better than Mike ever did. Considering he had claimed on the radio that he had an urgent need to get back ashore, Joe certainly didn't look like he was in any hurry now, with a rum and Coke in the cup holder by the helm and a contented smile on his face. I smiled back at him and waved as they pulled away. His need to get back had probably had more to do with boredom than an appointment. Some guys just don't have the patience or the temperament for the slow pace of sailing. Hell, I'd once had a sailor call for a tow because he had run out of ice.

I got *Gorda* under way and, once offshore, I poured on the speed to get back to Hillsboro. It took me an hour and a half to cover the ten or so miles up the coast. The Gulf Stream usually gave me a little more push than that, but it seemed the current was not running as strong as usual. While en route, I put *Gorda* on autopilot and pulled out the large-scale chart for the Bahamas, Cuba, and Hispaniola. The chart showed the Gulf Stream running at a speed of 2.6 to 3.3 knots at its axis. I thought about Solange and wondered what it was like being alone and adrift, in a boat with a dead woman. How long had she been out there? At the Gulf Stream's usual rate of drift, they would have traveled seventy-five miles in twenty-four hours, and she looked like she'd been out there even longer than that. But there was just no way I would believe they had come from Haiti in that boat. There were times, like right now, when in certain places, the Stream didn't always run at full strength. And close inshore there was frequently a countercurrent. My guess was that Solange had been on a larger boat before being set adrift somewhere to the south. Of course the *Miss Agnes* came to mind, but the timing was off—if she'd been set adrift from that boat, she should have been somewhere up off northern Palm Beach County. If I could find the exact time she got into the small boat, I could calculate the rate of drift and figure out where she started from.

B.J. looked happy to see me as he took my lines to tie *Gorda* back alongside the crane barge. He had been sitting cross-legged on the deck in the shade, his head bowed over a paperback book, when I pulled alongside. I wanted to freeze-frame the image of him sitting there smiling at me and put it away in a special keepsake box before I ruined it. I'd been doing a lot of that lately.

The *Miss Agnes* was afloat and nearly sitting on her lines, while the crane's two huge pumps were spewing water out of her innards.

"So Seychelle Sullivan does it again," B.J. shouted after I turned off *Gorda*'s engine. The noise from the gasoline pumps still made conversation only marginally possible.

"What do you mean?"

"Out saving the world, rescuing small children, finding dead bodies. Everybody's talking about it on the radio. Perry and Mike set off a regular gabfest on channel seventy-two." He pointed to the workers sitting inside the deckhouse. "The guys and I were listening for over an hour while the pumps were working."

The Bahamian cruiser looked even worse out of the water than it had sitting on the bottom. Peeling paint, soaked cardboard boxes, clothing, and garbage littered the decks and what I could see of the interior of the cabin through the fogged-up windows. "I'll tell you about it once we get under way. I'd like to get this boat into the yard before quitting time. Think we can get started and finish pumping her out on the way?"

"I think so. She's still pretty tight, considering."

"Okay, let's do it."

B.J. and I worked well as a team. We always had and, fortunately, the emotional awkwardness of our current romantic separation didn't extend onto the deck. We rigged my pumps on the cruiser's deck, got a good towing bridle secured at her bow, said our good-byes to the Gilman crew, and took off back toward Port Everglades.

Even as late in the day as it was, the heat in the deckhouse was stifling. We set her on autopilot and went up on the bow to catch the breeze we made by traveling at six knots. If it wasn't for our forward speed, there wouldn't have been any breeze at all.

I kept seeing Solange's face, those high cheekbones and big dark eyes—eyes that looked far too old for a child who had lived barely a decade. Though I'd had my share of pain in my childhood, compared to this kid I felt lucky. I could not imagine what her short life had been like.

"You're different," B.J. said, not looking at me but scanning the horizon for boat traffic.

"What do you mean, different?"

"Something about finding that kid, it changed you."

I knew it was true, but somehow his saying it seemed to imply that I had instantly become the maternal type. "Oh, B.J., cut the crap with your pseudopsychological paranormal bullshit. Geez." I ran my fingers through my hair. "She's just a kid." As I turned and made my way aft to check on our tow, I heard his soft laughter.

It was after six by the time we made our way up the Dania Cut-off Canal toward Playboy Marine, the yard that had contracted to haul and store the *Miss Agnes.* The yard workers had quit for the day, but they had left the boatyard travel lift parked over the slip, the slings lowered to the perfect depth for the cruiser. B.J. and I tied the cruiser up and shut down the pumps. If she sank during the night, she would go down no more than eighteen inches and settle right into those slings. They could pump her out again in the morning before they hauled her out.

I climbed back aboard the *Miss Agnes* to take one last look around. B.J. had loaded the pumps back on *Gorda,* and I'd replaced my towlines with some raggedy old dock lines we'd scrounged off the travel lift. Standing on the cruiser's deck, I imagined again the scene of fifty people and the belongings they had brought for a new life crammed into these few square feet of space.

Beads of moisture fogged the window in the aft cabin door. As I reached for the door handle, I wondered again if there was a connection between the two jobs I'd worked that day: a boat bringing in some illegal Haitian immigrants sinks, and a day and a half later I find two Haitians offshore in a half-sunk boat. Had Solange started out aboard the *Miss Agnes*? The problem was that the numbers just didn't add up. The current should have carried her much farther north. Was there a third boat we didn't know about? When I swung the door open and peered into the cabin area, the smell of wet, rotting clothes, ammonia, and dead sea critters hit my face, and the rank sun-heated air flowed out of the enclosed space. Coughing and gasping for air, I stepped back and turned my face away from cabin door.

Abaco growled a low throaty growl from her post aboard *Gorda*. I could hear the sound of her claws clicking on the aluminum decks as she paced, wanting desperately to come protect me.

B.J. looked down at me from atop the cement dock. "Isn't it amazing how ripe people's belongings can get after just a couple of days underwater? After we brought her up, we closed all those windows for a reason, Sey."

"Oh, man." I closed the door to the cabin. "I don't envy the cops who are going to have to go through the stuff in there." The side decks were clear, so I made my way forward and tested the latch on the door to the wheelhouse. It turned, and this time I took a deep breath and held it before opening the door.

"Sey," B.J. said, "you do remember that we had clear instructions from the authorities not to touch anything?"

I ignored him and peered inside.

"You told me that this morning," he said, "and *I* was careful not to disturb any evidence. Anyway, aside from that, there's a bad vibe in there."

Smiling at his comments, I stepped into the wheelhouse, risking the boat's "bad karma." Abaco growled again, and B.J. said, "See? Even she knows."

"Think I'm risking some kind of Voodoo curse, eh, B.J.?" I did not consider myself either a religious or a superstitious person, and, admittedly, I did at times make light of B.J.'s mishmash spirituality, which was made up of bits of Transcendentalism, Eastern religions, aikido, and who knows what all. But deep inside, I knew that he saw and felt things that were totally beyond my ken.

I took a breath, testing the air. It wasn't as bad in here as it had been aft. The inside steering station on most American boats this size would boast a control panel of electronics rivaling that of an airplane cockpit. The *Miss Agnes,* however, had an ancient, pre-digital depth sounder with a circular flasher, and that was it. Not even a VHF radio. The compass had clearly been salvaged from a sunken sailboat. It was mounted on the cabinetry above the helm with wood blocks and nails, and I wondered what those nails did to the instrument's accuracy. That compass had once cost somebody a bundle, but now all the plastic and metal surfaces were covered with bits of calcified shell where barnacles had once grown. It was the helm of the cruiser, though, that really showed the ingenuity of the island people. In place of a steering wheel, the boat was piloted with bicycle handlebars attached to the steering gear that protruded from the cabinetry.

A couple of waterlogged charts were plastered to the woodwork, and other bits of paper and plastic trash littered the cabin floor. Everywhere I looked in the little cruiser's wheelhouse, I saw another jury-rigged contraption that would have thrown most American yachtsmen into a conniption. I don't know if it was real or just the power of suggestion from B.J., but I began to feel there was something creepy about the boat. It was depressing to think about the poverty and desperation of the people who struck out in boats like this to try to get to America, but there was something more. Despite the hot muggy air, I felt a distinct chill.

I turned around, overcome by the desire to get off that boat as soon as possible, and I was about to step back through the doorway when I saw something stuck to the glass windshield. It was a small white rectangle of paper, and when I started to reach for it, something skittered through the trash at my feet. I jumped, letting out a high-pitched squeak.

"Are you okay?" B.J. was squatting on the dock next to the cabin door, ready to jump to the boat's deck.

I pushed aside the wet cardboard on the floor and a small, pale crab scurried for another hiding place. "This place is spooking me out. I just got scared by a crab, for Pete's sake."

B.J. stood up. "Come on, Sey. Let's get out of here."

Leaning over the makeshift helm, I peeled the paper off the windshield. It was a business card. "Racine Toussaint" was written in plain type above a Pompano Beach address. It didn't say what business Racine was in, but I slid it into my pocket anyway, careful not to rip the soggy paper.

It was when I was almost out the door that I noticed the sunglasses hooked under a bungee cord that ran across the top of the steering station. *Miss Agnes*'s crew probably used the bungee to keep charts and equipment from blowing or rolling away out at sea. The shades stood out in that dilapidated cabin because they were obviously very expensive Polarized glasses. That brand started at over a hundred dollars a pair. A beaded string was tied between the two earpieces of the shades to keep them on the mariner's head, and on the wide sides of the frame someone had drawn crude designs in white enamel paint: little skulls with crossbones.

So somebody fancied himself a pirate? I slid the glasses under my T-shirt and tucked in my shirttail to hold them snug. I didn't want any arguments from B.J. about my having taken a souvenir.

The last fingers of pink were disappearing from the western sky by the time I dropped B.J. off at the docks close to the Dania Bridge and reached the mouth of the New River. I had piloted the tug upriver after dark many times before, but every time I appreciated the beauty of the homes as though I were seeing them for the first time. The river took on a different character when the big old oak and sea grape trees were lit by floodlights, and the red and green navigational lights on the occasional pilings marked the river's shallows. Sound carried farther in the darkness, and soft music drifted across the water from the poolside cabana at one of the enormous homes. Many like this one were of recent construction, pseudo-Spanish, and built out to the lot's limits after the nice little Florida bungalows built in the forties and fifties had been torn down. White twinkling lights wound round the trunks of the oaks and illuminated the three party workers slumped on high stools at the outdoor tiki bar looking bored. The party probably wouldn't heat up for another couple of hours. That was one of the few riverfront homes with anyone in residence in June; most of the houses on either side of *Gorda* were shuttered and dark, their owners long since gone in preparation for the coming months of heat, humidity, and hurricanes.

Abaco began to pace the decks and whine. She knew we were nearing home. I lived in a Lauderdale neighborhood called Rio Vista in what had once been a small boathouse, renovated by the previous owners into a tiny, one-bedroom cottage. It was on the property of a riverfront mansion that belonged to a Mr. Lars Larsen, owner of a national chain of muffler shops headquartered up in Milwaukee. Larsen had bought the place as his Florida winter home, and in years past, he'd often had Red tow his various yachts. When Red died, and my brothers and I sold Red's house where *Gorda* used to dock, Mr. Larsen called and offered me the boathouse. He said he'd like to have an on-site caretaker for the months when he and his family were not there. The main house was a huge multitowered, Moorish edifice that dated to the 1930s, when the New River meandered through a Fort Lauderdale that was more of a frontier town, back when fish houses and vegetable docks still stood on the New River's banks. Over the years, a succession of owners had added on rooms and towers, and today, the Larsen house looked like something created by Disney on drugs. The main house was set back from the river, but my cottage was right on the dock, and I could park *Gorda* just a few feet outside my front door.

When I stepped out of the elevator on the fourth floor at Broward General Hospital, it was ten till eight, and the nurse who gave me directions to room 425 reminded me that visiting hours would be over in ten minutes. The forced congeniality and the low hum of machinery were what I most remembered about the weeks I'd spent here with Red before he died. Indoors is *more* indoors in a hospital; even the air tastes artificial. I knew it was the cancer that killed him, but I always felt that being shut away from the sunshine and fresh air had hurried that process along.

Jeannie was sitting in a chair next to the bed, her fingers laced together on top of her stomach, watching the TV screen mounted high up in a corner of the room, while a strange man in a dark green uniform sat on the edge of Solange's bed, speaking to her. The kid looked even smaller in that big white bed, especially because the man sitting next to her had the shoulders of a football player. His biceps stretched the green fabric of his uniform tight and, as he moved, the leather and web belt that held his gun creaked, a continuous reminder that the weapon was there. Again, I felt an odd twist in my gut.

"Well, it's about time you got here, girl." Jeannie stood and tugged at her dress to reposition the fabric around her shoulders.

The man stood up and reached his hand out to me. "How d'ya do," he said. His sandy-colored hair looked a bit shaggy around the ears for a law enforcement type, and the deep tan and white creases at the corners of his blue-gray eyes told me he felt nearly as trapped inside the hospital as I did. "Name's Elliot. I'm with the Border Patrol."

In his voice I heard an accent from someplace not too far north of here, which meant the South.

"Border Patrol, huh?" I looked at the writing stitched over his breast pocket.

"Not many folks recognize the uniform. They mostly think we're park rangers or something."

I nodded. "You do kind of look like Smokey the Bear. You just need one of those hats." I made the shape of the flat brim with my hands. He wasn't smiling at my little joke.

His hand had completely engulfed mine, which doesn't happen often. I glanced down at the card he'd handed me. It said he was Russell Elliot, Senior Patrol Agent, Border Patrol.

"My friends call me Rusty," he said.

"Border Patrol? As in Immigration?"

"Basically, yeah."

"And just what border do you patrol? Georgia? Alabama?"

Jeannie sighed and plopped back down in her chair.

Agent Elliot gave me a look that said that what I thought was a clever line was something he had heard too many times. "Actually, there's plenty of border down here in South Florida. This state has about seventeen thousand miles of coastline—more international border than any other continental state—and yet we've got just one other office on this coast south of Jacksonville. Sixteen people work out of our office, and there's another ten down at the Marathon branch office in the Keys. We're the guys who try to catch the folks who don't come in through normal ports of entry." His eyes flicked a quick glance at Solange, then he pressed his lips together and raised his brows as though to say "Not my fault."

Flashing those baby blues at me all innocent like that made me want to yank him off her bed and push him out the door. I squeezed past him and slipped between the bed and the IV stand. "How are you feeling?" I asked Solange.

She looked more alert now, more focused, and it was obvious she had been listening, trying to understand our conversation. But when I spoke directly to her, she blinked once and then lowered her eyes.

"She's not saying much," Jeannie said. "She slept for about three hours, though, after we got settled in here. I called my mother, and she came and picked the boys up. This little girl ate a pretty good dinner when she woke up, even though it looked god-awful to me, some kind of clear broth, crackers, and Jell-O. Point is, she kept it down. There was a whole room full of folk waiting for her to upchuck." Jeannie heaved herself back up to a standing position. "It's your shift now. I'm heading out."

I reached across the bed and squeezed her hand. "Thanks, Jeannie. I really owe you this time."

"Girl, you owe me so much, you'll never get to even. But today was a pleasure." She turned to Solange. "I'll be back tomorrow. You remember what I told you, okay?" She looked at the Border Patrol agent, then gave the girl an exaggerated wink. To me she said, "I'll call you later."

After Jeannie was gone, Elliot said, "May I speak to you out in the hall for a moment?"

I wanted to get him out of there, away from Solange, and it appeared I was going to have to hear him out to make that happen. "I'll be right back," I told her.

Outside the room, I pressed my back against the wall, and for the first time all day, I felt tired, felt the weight of the day's events pressing me down. I wanted to slide my butt down to the floor and sit. What I didn't want to do was stand out there under those fluorescent lights talking to this big man who had come to send that child back to Haiti.

"Can we get this over with as quickly as possible?" I asked. "I'm pretty damn tired, and I'd really rather be in there with that kid than standing out here talking to you."

"I'll agree not to take offense at that, if you'll agree to tell me what happened out there." There was a definite country sound to his voice. I guessed Georgia.

"Look, I've already talked to the local cops."

"I know that, but this girl isn't really their case. Their concern is the murder victim, mine is this girl."

It was the first time I had heard anyone involved with this case say the word. Collazo had already referred to the woman's "attacker," but this word was powerful: murder. "Okay, look. I'll tell you the story again, but I'm going to tell you right up front, if you're making plans to send that kid back to Haiti, I'm going to fight you every inch."

He pushed away from the wall and slid his hands in his pockets. "This country's policy is pretty clear on that." There was a looseness about him in spite of his size, as though he were incredibly comfortable in his own skin. Under other circumstances I would have found that attractive, but now it merely irritated me. It made me have to work that much harder to *not* like him.

"I don't give a damn about your policy."

"If you would let me finish, what I was going to say was that I am not here this evening to talk about her deportation. Don't get me wrong, Miss Sullivan, we may get to that, but as an unaccompanied minor, we're not going to hustle her off into the night and onto a plane bound for Port-au-Prince."

Yeah, right. The Border Patrol trying to make out like they're really just warm and fuzzy? "But you will get to that point eventually."

"Well" —he shrugged— "if she doesn't have any next of kin here in the States, then, yeah, probably. I'm not gonna lie to you on that."

"So, assuming we don't find any next of kin in the States, how much time do I have before you get there?"

"A week, maybe ten days, max."

I stared straight into those laserlike blue eyes of his. "You are not sending this one back. *Whatever* it takes, she's staying."

"Is that a threat, Miss Sullivan?"

I held his eyes as long as I could, but finally I had to turn my head away. I watched the nurse in the room across the hall as she carried a bedpan to the far patient and drew the curtain around the bed. The sound of the steel rings sliding on the rod reminded me of all the times I had stepped away from my father's bed, both of us feeling awkward about the last days when his body gave out. That was before I finally said "enough" and took him home so he could die in his own bed, and the awkwardness was replaced with a sense of intimacy. I'd often wondered if that sense I had felt as I bathed him and fed him and carried him to the bathroom, that sense of such profound love, if that was the same feeling a mother got as she cared for her newborn child.

"So tell me what happened," he said. "How you found her."

I swung my head back around and blinked at him. I'd forgotten for a moment that he was there. Taking a deep breath, I saw her again sitting in that boat, resting her head just inches out of the bloody water, just staring at me with those eyes. She probably would not have survived another twenty-four hours.

"I've tried to get the story from her," he said, "but she either doesn't understand or she won't talk. The local cops had a Creole translator here earlier. Same thing. She wouldn't say a word."

I knew how that felt; I'd been there once myself. They said I didn't speak for three months after my mother died. I'd gone to some inner place where none of it could touch me. Once you've found your way to that place, it's hard to come back.

"I noticed the birds first, lots of birds, circling," I said and went on to tell him about the boat and the body. The voice I was hearing inside my head was my voice, but it didn't sound familiar. In a flat monotone, I described how weak she was, how, as I'd dragged her aboard *Gorda,* she'd felt so thin and frail and helpless. "In the end, it was really kind of miraculous that I saw her. I don't know how much longer she would have lasted out there."

He put his left hand on the wall next to my head and leaned in closer. "You say she did talk to you. Do you think she understands much English?"

We were close to the same height, our eyes on a level plane, but his shoulders seemed half again as broad as mine, and the muscles in his forearm carved ridges beneath the skin. If his intent was to be intimidating, it was working. "Some, but I'm not sure how much. I believe her when she says that her father is American. That's probably how she learned the little English she does know, and if he's here in South Florida like she thinks he is, I'm going to find him."

"Do you have any idea how many times we hear that? That they have a relative in America?"

"I'm sure that's true, but this case is different. This time you've got me to contend with, and I believe her." I ducked under his arm, then turned to face him from the doorway of her room. "I found her out there, and the way I see it, that means I've got certain salvage rights."

vi

When I went back into the room, a middle-aged black nurse was there with a machine, taking the child's blood pressure.

"How's she doing?"

"A lot better than I would have thought when they brought her in here this afternoon. She looked half dead."

I heard a slight Creole accent in her voice. "Are you Haitian?"

The woman smiled as she unwrapped the cuff from the girl's arm. "That I am, but this little one doesn't seem to want to talk to me, not even in Creole."

When I tried to catch Solange's eye, she deliberately looked away.

"It happens sometimes to kids when they're traumatized," I said. "I'd just like to sit with her for a while. They're not going to kick me out, are they?"

"The other nurses told me you're the one who found her. Family can stay after visiting hours, and I think you are about the closest thing to family this child's got right now."

After she left, I sat down on the yellow plastic chair and tried to make myself comfortable. There wasn't a book or a magazine anywhere in sight, so I took one of the paper towels off her bedside table, got a pencil out of my shoulder bag, and began to sketch. I'd dabbled for years with watercolors and charcoal sketches, having learned it from my mother, so these were all still life scenes I had sketched in the past. First, I drew little pictures of *Gorda,* then a beach scene with palm trees and seabirds, a view of my cottage sitting next to the seawall back in Rio Vista.

I knew she was watching every move I made. Her bed was the one closest to the window and, as there was no patient in the other bed, the only sounds came from outside the room—occasional moans, bursts of laughter, or clicking footsteps beyond the walls of our space. I feared she would grow tired of it, just watching me draw, and fall asleep eventually, but there was an intelligence in those eyes that warned me not to underestimate her. It was as though she and I were engaged in a sort of standoff, neither of us willing to be the first to attempt to cross the space that separated us.

It was when I started to draw the picture of Abaco that I heard her shift her position in the bed, trying to get a better look at the drawing. I sketched my dog lying down, her muzzle between her front paws, her big eyes looking up with that funny, guilty look she gets when she has scattered the garbage all over my cottage to get at some chicken bones or is discovered with a squirrel that underestimated her speed.

"What is dog's name?"

Her voice surprised me, not just because the sound of it broke the long silence, but also because it was strong and clear. She spoke in almost perfect, though accented, English. I found my breathing had gone shallow and sketchy the way it does when I'm nervous.

"Her name's Abaco. After some islands in the Bahamas." Red had continued with the tradition he'd started with my mother—after naming all three of their kids after islands, he had named his dog that way as well.

I reached for another paper towel to start a new drawing and set the sketch of the dog aside. I began sketching the *Wind Dancer,* a lovely little sailboat I had once sailed down in the Dry Tortugas in what often seemed like another life.

"I see Abaco?" She pronounced the dog's name with the accent on the last syllable instead of the first. She made my dog sound like some Parisian show dog, instead of the strong-willed, incorrigible squirrel chaser she really was.

"Sure." I handed her the drawing. She held it up in front of her face, and there was a small smile in her eyes, while the rest of her face held strong. "You can keep it if you like," I said.

She slid the drawing under the covers then, hiding it carefully on the sheet next to her frail body. After she settled the covers back into place, she lifted them one last time to make sure the drawing was still there, then collapsed against the pillows.

"Have you ever had a dog?" I asked.

She shook her head, pressing her lips tightly together.

"Mmmm, it's probably different in Haiti, I guess. I've never been there. I've been to the Bahamas. Never to Haiti, though."

"I been Bahamas."

"Really?" I tried to sound barely interested, didn't even look at her as I said it. I just shaded in the shadows on the hull of the sailboat on the napkin.

"Dogs bad, like Haiti. Not nice dog, like Abaco."

I looked up. "You saw dogs in the Bahamas?"

She nodded. "I work with Erzulie. Bad dog come many day."

I decided to press her a little. "Erzulie, that was the woman in the boat with you?"

She nodded and slid her hand under the bedcovers, feeling for the drawing.

"How did you and Erzulie get in that small boat, Solange?"

She didn't speak for over a minute. I figured I'd blown it, I'd pushed her too hard, and she wasn't going to talk to me anymore.

"Bad man hurt Erzulie."

"Do you know the bad man's name?"

She shook her head.

"He hurt her in the Bahamas?"

She shook her head again. "On boat."

"Oh, you were on the boat that was going to take you to America? Were you coming in that small boat?"

"Big boat."

"Like my boat, *Gorda*?"

"More big. Many people. No dog."

"So you left the Bahamas in the big boat. What happened?"

"Night. Bad man hurt Erzulie."

"So how did you get into the small boat?"

She shrugged and didn't say anything more. Could it be she didn't know how she got there? It was more likely she just didn't want to or didn't know how to tell me.

"Solange, I'd like to help you. I want to find your father. Do you know his name?"

"Papa."

"No, what did other people call him? Other grown-ups?"

"Papa Blan."

"Was he the one who taught you to speak English?"

She bit her lower lip and nodded. "Papa—no Kreyol."

I assumed that meant the father didn't speak Creole, so he must not live in Haiti. He must only have been visiting. "What about your mother? Was she on the boat?"

She shrugged again.

"Do you know your mother's name?"

She scrunched the features of her face into a tight little knot. "No *maman*."

"You don't have a mother? Is she dead?"

Again, just the lifted shoulders, more questions she couldn't or wouldn't answer.

She pointed to herself. "*Restavek,*" she said very quietly, refusing to look at me.

"*Restavek?*" I repeated the word and she nodded. "I don't understand. I don't speak Creole. Can you say that in English?"

She shook her head and then yawned, her wide mouth showing several gaps where teeth should have been. She slid down, pulled the covers up tight under her chin, and closed her eyes.

"Okay, you sleep. I'll be back tomorrow. Maybe we can talk some more then."

At the nurses' station, I couldn't get anyone to talk to me. The nice Haitian nurse was not around, and the busty young woman at the desk was far more interested in her manicure than in helping me. When I finally succeeded in getting her to acknowledge my presence, she told me with a flip of her blond hair that I was not next of kin, and therefore she could not speak to me about the girl's medical condition.

"She has no next of kin," I said. "Does that mean nobody gets to find out how she's doing?"

The young woman stood up and tugged at the hem of her uniform. The pink polyester was straining at the seams to contain the bust that was perched at an unnatural height, somewhere above her armpits. Her name tag said "Jenna." "I have orders from Dr. Louie not to talk to anyone about her, and I have to do whatever Dr. Louie says."

I wondered how far Dr. Louie took that willingness of hers.

I stopped off in the lobby at the McDonald's to grab a burger and fries for the ride home. So many hospitals I'd visited lately had fast-food franchises right on the premises, so I no longer found it ironic to be eating heart-clogging grease a few floors beneath the cardiac surgery suites. I couldn't resist the smell and had just taken a mouthful of hot french fries out of the to-go bag when a perfectly coifed young Hispanic woman approached me just outside the hospital entrance, identified herself as Nina Vidal from Channel 7 News, and asked if I was the one who had found the little girl. I wondered for a minute how she had recognized me, then realized that the salt-stained deck shoes and the Sullivan Towing and Salvage baseball cap were pretty good clues. I acknowledged that I was the one, and I tried to continue on around her. She stepped into my path again.

"We'll be doing a live feed from here when we go on air at eleven," she said as she pointed at the van with the long, extended antenna mast. "Would you be willing to wait around a few minutes and answer some questions for our viewers?"

I swallowed the ball of starch in my cheek. "Sorry. I'm headed home to bed. It's been a long day."

She continued to follow me out toward the parking area. "What do you know about this child? Can you confirm that she was not alone in the boat? We understand there was a dead woman. Do you know her identity? Do you know if she's connected in any way to the other victims?"

I stopped and turned to face her. I was about to tell Helmet Hair what I thought she could do with her extended mast, but I reconsidered. "Lady, I don't know what you're talking about. I only know that there's a sick, scared little girl up there." I pointed to the upper reaches of the hospital. "Just tell your viewers that she's a really sweet kid, she's got the face of an angel, and our government shouldn't send her back to the streets of Haiti. Okay?"

She rolled her eyes and murmured something under her breath as she headed back to the van.

There was nothing left in the bag but some greasy wrappers by the time I pulled my old Jeep into the drive at the Larsen estate. The canvas top on my vehicle was probably the third or fourth one she'd had since her original owners bought her in 1972, but the wind and Florida sun had done their damage, and the back windows always came loose as I drove. An old boyfriend had nicknamed her Lightnin' after watching me try to accelerate and merge onto I-95. Thunder might have been more appropriate, though, given the flapping canvas and the engine's tractorlike rumble. Coming to a stop and shutting her down created a very sudden silence.

I just sat there a minute, too tired to climb out, enjoying the emerging night sounds of insects and far-off traffic. I'd seen the dark brown sedan that was parked on the street in front of the house, and I was certain I recognized the figure sitting in the front seat. I didn't want to talk to him. Not tonight. When I finally climbed out of Lightnin', the sedan's front door swung open and scraped to a stop on the cement sidewalk.

"Miss Sullivan." Collazo made no other movement behind the dark glass. "I need to speak to you for a moment."

I walked over to the car and bent down to speak to him through the open driver's-side window. "It's late and I'm really tired, Detective." The drops of sweat on his face sparkled in the light from the streetlamps.

"Me too," he said. He motioned with his head. "Get in."

He wasn't a bad guy, Collazo, but he had the social graces of a Neanderthal. As I walked around the car, I wondered if he had any kind of life outside his job. I slid into the passenger's seat and rolled down the window. Being in a hot, closed car with Detective Collazo was enough to make me revisit my Quarter Pounder with Cheese.

"You went to the hospital."

"Uh-huh." Tired as I was, I wasn't going to make it easy for him. Maybe it was even a little perverse of me, but I found it impossible to be cooperative with this man.

"The girl's refusing to talk," he said.

"Yeah, I heard you were there with an interpreter this afternoon. You know, I wouldn't say she's refusing, exactly. It happens when you've been through something like this. She's just sort of timed out for a while." I didn't want to lie to him, but I didn't want to tell him that she had spoken to me at the hospital, either. She needed her rest.

There would be time for her to tell more, later, when she was stronger.

Collazo stared out the window at the Larsens' dark, hulking house and didn't speak for almost a minute. I was about to climb out of the car when he finally said, without turning his head to face me, "She was the fourth one."

I didn't know what he was talking about. "The fourth what?"

He didn't answer me for a long time, and I thought it was another one of his waiting games. When he started speaking, his face was still turned away from me, and I had to sit forward on the seat to hear his voice.

"The first one was found on the beach at Pompano just south of Hillsboro Inlet about three weeks ago. A woman. Witness in one of the condos along that stretch said he had seen lots of people on the beach around three in the morning when, as he put it, he 'got up to take a leak.' They were swimming in the surf line, he said. Hundreds of them. Boat must have dropped them off just offshore. Beach clean-up crew found her in the surf line at sunrise." He turned and looked straight at me. "Severe head trauma. Medical report said it was probably a machete—nearly cleaved her skull clean in half."

"Okay, but what does that have to do with—"

He ignored my question and continued talking. "Then tonight, this Border Patrol guy, Elliot, tells me the same thing happened in the Keys last week. Down near Marathon. Some smugglers dropped off a load of Haitians in the early-morning hours, and they found one man walking around, hole in his head so big his brains were hanging out. He collapsed on US-1 and died in the hospital down there. Found the other one on the beach the same night. A man. Monroe County medical examiner says it was the same thing—massive head injuries."

"I haven't seen anything about this in the papers."

"They aren't releasing any of the details to the public. For some reason, the press hasn't put it together yet. They will with this one, though. They will with number four."

I thought about what that woman reporter had said to me at the hospital. She asked me about the *other victims*. Now that made sense. "I think they already have, Collazo."

"We're putting together a task force made up of FLPD, INS, and the FBI. They're calling it the Deceased Alien Response Team—DART."

"Sounds like alphabet soup."

"The child. She may be able to tell us something, but she seems frightened by authority figures. My Haitian translator tells me that's typical for their culture. Elliot says they can't get any of the Haitians to talk about the smugglers. Ever since Papa Doc and the Tonton Macoutes, they don't think much of police or authorities."

"I'm impressed, Collazo. You seem to know quite a bit about Haiti."

Again, it was as though I had not even spoken. "We are operating on the assumption that they were aboard the boat that sank up in Deerfield and they were put off into the smaller boat."

"There's a problem with that theory. The timing doesn't work. The Gulf Stream runs at two to three knots. That boat should have been much farther north if they were dropped off thirty-six hours before they were found."

"There were no other boats in the area."

"None that you *know* of," I said. I'd heard estimates that the authorities stopped only ten to twenty percent of the illegal immigrants flooding into Florida.

"We want you to get close to the child," he said. "See if you can get her to talk, find out what she knows. Anything at all about the people behind this operation and their location in the Bahamas."

I jumped at the mention of the islands. Tired as I was, I suddenly wondered if they had somehow listened in on my conversation with Solange. "Why do you say the Bahamas?"

"The plastic water bottles and the food cans in the boat with the dead woman. The labels were all Bahamian. Get her to tell us something that will indicate *where* in the Bahamas."

"I don't know, Collazo, she's just a little kid. I don't think she knows anything." I wanted to protect her from this mess. She had talked about the "bad man," and I was fairly certain she would recognize him if she saw him again.

"It doesn't really matter what you think, Sullivan. What really matters is what the killer thinks."

That tightness in my chest returned. I felt so stupid. Why hadn't I thought of that? I slid over on the seat and reached for the car door. "Solange, they might try—"

"It's taken care of. There is a guard. She'll be safe. For now."

After Collazo left, I opened the gate and walked behind the Larsens' house to my cottage in such a daze that I barely saw the shrubbery, the path, or the wide yard out back. Abaco seemed to sense my mood, and though she rubbed her wet nose against my hand, she wasn't insistent when I didn't reach down to rub her head. My mind was busy trying to make connections, to draw some kind of lines between the small dots of information I had.

I let myself in and went straight to the fridge, thirsty after all those french fries. A bottle of Corona in hand, I dialed Mike's cell phone. I pulled out the sunglasses I'd found on the *Miss Agnes* and examined the paintings of the skull and crossbones under the light as the phone rang again and again. I was about to give up when he finally answered.

"Mike? This is Seychelle. Did I interrupt something?"

"Nah, I just couldn't find the damn phone. I'm glad you called, young lady, 'cuz I wanted a chance to give you hell for sticking me with that sniveling bastard Perry Greene."

"That's why I'm calling, Mike, to apologize, even though there wasn't much else I could have done under the circumstances."

"Apology accepted."

"Good. And look, promise you'll get that electrical system fixed. I mean, what were you thinking out there all night using all that juice?"

"It was my buddy Joe, I swear. He called me up to shoot the shit, and we got started talking fishing. I told him I lived aboard a fifty-three-foot sailboat now, and next thing I knew, we were motoring out through Port Everglades. We had lots of catching up to do. Joe always did like flash, and my boat impressed the hell out of him. He wanted me to turn everything on. See, he was DEA back in the eighties when he got to go undercover with flashy cars, big houses, and fast women. I think he misses those days."

"Yeah, right. The good old days."

"That isn't really why you called, the apology thing, is it?"

"Maybe not the only reason."

"So spit it out."

"It's hard to explain. I need someone to talk to—about this Haitian kid. Mike, I've got to help her stay in the States, and I don't even know where to begin. What if her father doesn't want to be found? What if he's some married guy who doesn't want his wife to know he has this kid. I mean, doesn't it strike you as a little weird that an American father would bring his daughter to the States on one of these cattle boats?"

"Yeah, you're right. But then again, if there was no birth certificate, no way of proving paternity, he might not have had much of a choice. It's not like the ol' U S of A is exactly welcoming Haitians with open arms these days. She could've died on the streets of Port-au-Prince waiting for a visa."

"Okay, then where is he? Shouldn't he have been waiting for her to arrive?"

"Give it time, kiddo. Tomorrow the kid's story will be all over the papers and the TV. Maybe he'll show up, maybe he won't."

"It seems like after everything she's been through, it's like she's earned it. The right to stay, I mean."

"Tell that to the rest of the people here. You know how crowded it's getting. The last one here wants to slam the door and not let anybody else into Paradise. We may have to rewrite that little plaque on Lady Liberty."

"But the Haitians are getting an especially raw deal. At home there're death squads and starvation. They escape that only to die here in America."

"Like the woman in the boat, you mean."

"She's not the only one. Collazo stopped by tonight. He told me that she was the fourth Haitian found dead. They've all had massive head injuries. Sounds crazy, I know, but somebody is killing off these immigrants. Maybe they do it to set an example for the others, I don't know. Hell of a way to prevent mutiny. Collazo says the Haitians are still protecting the smugglers, even when they're killing off a few on the way over."

"And Collazo's pretty certain all four murders are related?"

"I guess so. He says they've put together a task force with FLPD, Border Patrol, and the FBI. They call themselves DART—the Deceased Alien Response Team." It sounded so silly when I said it out loud.

"Oh, that's good." He laughed, and I could hear the sound of clinking ice cubes as he took a drink. "Sounds like a pilot for a bad TV show."

"They think Solange can ID the killer, but she's not talking. Mike, I don't want to make her any more of a target than she already is."

"Have they got a guard at the hospital?"

"Yeah."

"Then don't worry about her. She'll be fine. They got nothing on the identity of these smugglers?"

"Nothing they shared with me. Collazo sounded 'out there' on this one. He has to be to ask for *my* help."

"Yeah, I'd agree with you there."

After I hung up the phone, I headed back outside with my beer to sit on the dock, my feet dangling over the river. I watched the water swirl past the pilings with the tide. There weren't many stars visible, but the few that could outshine the glow from the city lights appeared as dancing white dots in the black river water.

The thoughts in my head were churning like the ocean caught between a current and a crosswind. And it was creating just as much turbulence. If Erzulie was already dead, why did someone set her adrift in a boat? Why not just throw her overboard? If they were aboard the *Miss Agnes,* how did they wind up drifting off Pompano? And why would people who are supposedly making money off immigrant smuggling be killing their cargo? Why didn't they kill Solange, too? How was I going to find her father? Where would I start?

I was still clutching the sunglasses I'd found on board the *Miss Agnes,* and I wondered if they belonged to Solange's "bad man," the one who had killed Erzulie. The skulls painted on the glasses were in some thick glossy paint, maybe fingernail polish. I could feel the design as I ran my fingers over the plastic, the rounded skulls, eyeholes, crossed bones beneath. Over two hundred years ago, ships had sailed these same waters bearing that insignia. Then, too, the design had signaled that the bearers were dealers of death.

When I'd finished the last of the beer, I had no more answers than when I'd started, but I did feel my eyelids drooping. It took a fair amount of willpower to force my fatigued limbs off the dock and into bed. I felt completely whipped. Seeing a person dead made me feel how fragile human life is. In my bathroom, as I brushed my teeth in front of the mirror, I examined my face, skin over bone and cartilage, brain only a few centimeters below the surface, and I marveled that so many of us live into old age. We are not a well-armored species. With my hand on my neck, I felt the rhythm of the blood pumping through my veins. I thought about the only real armor we humans have—our intelligence and our will to survive.

vii

The night seemed to pass in one quick blink of deep, dreamless sleep. I awoke around 7:30, late for me, but I felt refreshed. A front had moved in overnight, and the dark sky seemed almost to touch the masthead of the ketch moored across the river. The air was thick and heavy with moisture.

I generally tried to fit in some kind of exercise about three mornings a week. Jogging, swimming, paddling—something that was more interesting than using a machine in a refrigerated gym. I pulled on a black tank suit and put the teakettle on the stove for my morning coffee. The wheezing window air conditioner refused to cycle off, so I finally decided to open up and let the humidity in. I gave Abaco fresh water and filled her bowl with dry dog food. In the bathroom, I grabbed a rubber band to pull my hair into a ponytail. This was typical June weather, the start of the hurricane months and the wettest season of the year in Fort Lauderdale.

I grabbed a mug of coffee and my handheld VHF radio and walked out to the dock where I kept my thirteen-foot Boston Whaler up in davits. I began cranking the winch to lower the boat into the water. Abaco made quick rounds of the yard, checking for new smells, adding her own. When the Whaler hit the water, she came over and whined, begging to go. I told her no, and she dropped onto her belly in the grass and gave me her sad-dog look. It didn't work this time.

I motored slowly down the New River, waving to the gardeners and the professional boatmen, the only ones out and about at that hour. Channel 16 was fairly quiet, even considering that it was a weekday morning. The only calls I heard were the occasional charter skipper hailing a buddy and switching to another channel for fish gossip.

Down at the Bahia Mar Marina, I navigated through the northern basin to the finger pier closest to the highway. I tucked the handheld radio into the boat's cubbyhole and locked the Whaler up to the swim step of Jimmie St. Clair's old Chris Craft launch. B.J. would probably be working here later in the day. The interior of the boat had been riddled with termites, and Jimmie had asked B.J. to tear it all out and start over. He was several months into the project and nowhere close to done.

I made it safely across A1A to the beach, then almost got run over by one of the early-morning sand graders, the big yellow monster machines that comb away the previous day's trash and footprints, leaving straight lines in the smooth sand. I started to jog down at the water's edge and kept up a steady pace, the low gray sky doing nothing to slow the sweat that began to drip from my brow into my eyes.

The sea looked about as flat as I'd ever seen it.

I didn't have any jobs on the books for the next several days, although I always kept my handheld VHF radio close by, just in case. I didn't usually chase after the emergency tows. *Gorda* simply wasn't built for that kind of speed, and there was no way I could compete against some of the corporate fleets like SEATOW or *Cape Ann.* On the other hand, the big-money guys who needed to get their mega-yachts up the river to the boatyards didn't like to hire those twenty-something blond boat jockeys in epaulets. Sullivan Towing and Salvage still ruled the river. The business would come, but in the meantime, I was free to see if I could locate Solange's father.

When I'd jogged my four miles round-trip up the beach and back, I dove into the ocean and logged a good two miles of freestyle. I was puffing and blowing more than I would have liked. Back in the days when I used to work as a lifeguard on this same beach, I'd swim five miles both before and after my shifts. I needed to get a more regular exercise routine.

As I settled into a comfortable rhythm, my mind began to wander. The papers had estimated that there had been about fifty people aboard the *Miss Agnes* when she sank. Considering the six who had died, as well as those who had been caught and deported, that still left somewhere in the vicinity of fifteen people who must have made it to shore and now could be tracked down. The article said that the captain of the boat had not been among those picked up by authorities, and it was possible even he could be located. I figured that was where I'd start—

even if it only served to determine whether Solange was ever on the *Miss Agnes* to begin with.

After toweling off, I crossed back over A1A and walked down the sidewalk to my favorite morning breakfast spot, the St. Tropez Cafe. Francine, the French Canadian girl who'd worked there all winter and for some strange reason had not yet disappeared north with all the other Canadians, poured me my café au lait in one of their mixing bowl–sized ceramic mugs and pointed at a gooey apricot pastry with one raised eyebrow. I nodded and she passed me a plate of confection to go with the coffee-flavored milk.

I seated myself at one of the tables outside and picked up the news-paper left by the previous patron. The story about Solange and the dead woman had made the lower left corner of the front page of the *Sun-Sentinel*:

> *Her name, Solange, roughly translated, means Earth Angel. She is ten years old, has big brown eyes and thick black braids. Yesterday morning, when other children her age were going to school and playing with friends, the Earth Angel was found clinging to a half-sunk boat three miles out at sea. Rescued off Fort Lauderdale, suffering from hypother-mia, she was too weak to stand when brought to safety. The little Earth Angel is currently listed in stable condition at Broward General Hospital while Immigration officials decide her fate. A Coast Guard spokesperson stated that the body of an unidentified woman was also found in the swamped wooden boat.*

The author then emphasized the connection between Erzulie and the three other victims.

> *The unusual deaths, and the fact that they coincide with a sharp in-crease in the number of illegal immigrants being smuggled into South Florida, have drawn the attention of several federal agencies. Investi-gators, who are keeping most of the details of the autopsies under wraps, say the deaths could have been accidents. They could have been the result of recklessness on the part of smugglers who routinely over-load their boats to multiply their profits. Or the deaths could be some-thing worse.*

As I was reading, a shadow fell across my newspaper, and in the background, just past the edge of the story, I noticed a pair of sexy brown legs, the thighs wrapped tightly in black Lycra. "Seychelle?"

I looked up and feigned surprise at the sight of Joe D'Angelo's face, although I'd recognized the legs instantly. I quickly chewed and swallowed my mouthful of pastry. "Hi, Joe."

"Mind if I join you?"

"Pull up a chair."

He set down his tray with a small white cup filled to the brim, a double espresso, a glass of ice water, and a slice of papaya with lime. I glanced at the remaining half of my apricot pastry and felt a twinge of guilt, but I felt much better when I'd taken another big gooey bite.

"You're looking exceptionally lovely this morning, Miss Sullivan. You've been swimming, I see," he said, then threw back his double shot of caffeine Latin style. He was wearing a crisp new white tank top that said something about a 10k race.

"Yeah, well, thanks for the compliment," I said, crossing my arms to cover up my midsection where I felt the jellyroll start to grow as soon as I'd swallowed. "I need the exercise, and I find gyms boring."

"Me too." He pointed to a red bike locked to the No Stopping sign out by the curb. It was one of those fancy new mountain bikes, the kind with the alloy or titanium frames that look like they're missing parts. The thing was probably worth more than my Jeep. "I try to log my miles at least three times a week."

"Nice bike," I said.

"Yeah, it's a Klein Palomino. You could call it a *nice bike.*" He stretched his arms out wide, showing the tufts of black hair under his arms and the lovely curves of the muscles in his shoulders and his biceps. I was thinking about how he could be a poster boy for one of those fit-after-fifty diet and exercise plans when I realized he had asked me a question.

"I'm sorry, what was that again?"

"I asked if your father ever mentioned me."

"No, not that I can remember. You knew Red?"

"Well, not all that well."

"How did you two meet? I'm curious to know how a retired DEA agent would know my father."

He laughed. "It's no mystery. I was with the agency for over twenty-five years, most of it here in South Florida, the Caribbean, or South America. This area was real hot in the eighties—lots of smugglers—and whenever we impounded boats and had to move them around, I always tried to hire Red. He was the best. I was sorry to hear from Mike that he had passed."

"Yeah, sometimes even *I* have trouble believing it."

He reached across the table and placed his hand on my wrist. "He was a good man, Seychelle." He paused for a moment, then added, "And one ornery son of a bitch."

I laughed and nodded. "Yup, no question about it. You knew Red."

He leaned back in his chair and laughed out loud. It was good to laugh about Red. I was tired of crying.

"I'll bet he was a hell of a good father," he said.

I pushed away the plate with the remains of the gooey pastry. "Yeah, you know, we were just kids, my brothers and I, and we were always asking for something. In those days my parents didn't have much money, but if I wanted a bike, Red would spend hours fixing up an old one he'd found at some yard sale. It didn't matter that we were poor."

"You think that made you poor? You *got* a bike. My old man? No bikes there. Five boys in the family, and we'd go days without *food.* Then he'd bring home some powdered milk, old dry bread, and Spam. I was sixteen the first time I tasted real milk. And the bastard wasn't just ornery, he was downright mean. Used to beat the shit out of us just because he felt like it."

"Wow." I didn't know what more to say. I'd just met the man and his words seemed too intimate, too soon. Or was it just that it was only okay to talk about a happy childhood in polite company? The growing silence felt even more awkward, so I asked him, "What about your mother?"

He sniffed and grimaced. "She got out when she could. I was fifteen, and it suited me all right. I had a job at a local gas station, and she'd been taking nearly everything I made. Said it was time I paid rent. First time I ever really owned anything of my own was after she left."

I realized then that it wasn't intimacy, his revealing these details about his parents. What felt strange was that he spoke of his childhood matter-of-factly, as though none of it really mattered to him. I felt awkward; he didn't.

"It looks like you did all right for yourself in spite of them. You got your own bike," I said, nodding at his locked-up mountain bike.

He leaned back in his chair and stretched his arms out again, as though laying claim to the space around him. His lips stretched wide in a closed-mouth smile. He said, "You bet, and nobody's gonna take it away from me."

There was something solid and determined about the man. Perhaps it was years of successfully chasing after bad guys that had given him this self-assurance. It wasn't simply that he didn't care what others thought about him, it was that their opinions wouldn't change his idea of who he was. I envied him that confidence.

"So, tell me more about you and Red. Was it like a business relationship, or were you two friends?"

"I wouldn't say friends," he said, then he paused to watch a high-speed ocean racer roar by just outside the beach swim area. He turned back to face me. "He ever tell you the story about towing a Colombian's sportfisherman up from the Hallandale condo?"

"Can't say as I remember that one, no."

Joe chuckled to himself. "We had this kid with us, he was new to the agency, and Red and I had him search the boat while we towed it up the waterway on our way to the River Bend Boatyard. Red and I were on *Gorda,* kicking back and drinking a couple of cold ones, and we were somewhere between the Sheridan and the Dania bridges, when all of a sudden this kid lets out a holler, comes running out of the cabin, and dives overboard. We had a hell of a time getting that tow turned around, then fishing the kid out of the water. Red was cursing up a storm the whole time. Come to find out, the kid had been searching the lockers in the master stateroom, and he'd opened one only to find a twelve-foot red-tailed boa constrictor. Snake was so hungry, he'd tried to coil around that fellow's arm. That sucker's body was yea big around"—he held his hands almost twelve inches apart—"and he could've eaten a good-size poodle." He drained his glass of ice water and wiped his mouth with the back of his hand. "Yeah, your dad was a helluva guy. I didn't know him all that well, but we shared a few of my life's finer moments." He looked out at the highway, focusing those green eyes of his on the cars disappearing down A1A.

I was getting used to it, but I still felt slightly uncomfortable when-ever people talked about Red. There always came this point when they felt the need to share a moment of silence for the dead man. Like he was looking down on them, and he'd appreciate this somehow. I knew better. Red would have thought it was horseshit and, as his daughter, my spiritual leanings weren't far from his. I figured you lived your life and then you were dead—end of story.

"You know, Seychelle, Red used to talk about you all the time. He was crazy about his little girl—everyone could see that." His big hands wrapped around the tiny white espresso cup and clicked it against the saucer in a staccato rhythm. "I have to admit, I was jealous of your dad."

"You? Jealous of Red? Why?"

"Well, I've got a daughter, too. I think I told you." He pursed his lips and stared into the bottom of his empty cup as though he might find the words in the brown sludge there. "Her mom and I split up years ago, when she was very young. You know, I was on the fast track with the agency, trying to make my mark, and I admit it, I was a lousy father. What would you expect with how I grew up? We were all boys and then I have a girl. Didn't know what to do with her. Anyway, by the time I was ready to try, it was too late. I'd missed too many birthdays, failed to show up too many times."

"You're being kinda harsh on yourself, Joe."

"No, just honest. We haven't spoken in over five years now. She's slammed the door in my face." Now the bitterness was apparent in his voice. "'Course, it didn't help that my ex had always been telling her that I was a bastard. Thing is, she's married now. Got a boy. My grand-son. He's mine, and I've never seen him."

"I don't get stories like that. I mean, you're still family."

"You don't even know it's happening when it starts, and by the time you realize it, it's too late. Nothing like the relationship you had with your dad."

"Yeah. He was a good dad. Heck, a great dad. Sometimes I still wake up in the middle of the night and think I've got to tell Red something. Then I remember he's gone."

"Sometimes, it seems as though my daughter is gone, too. Gone from my life, anyway."

"But she isn't dead. You still have a chance to fix things with her."

He leaned back again, so far back that he tilted the chair onto two legs. He bounced his right leg and tapped his fingers on the table. "You're right. And I'm working on it. I intend to see my grandson."

I could tell that just talking about his daughter and grandson was making this otherwise confident man a mess of jangled nerves. "You know, Joe, you're all right. I'll bet if your daughter got to know you, she'd like you. Your grandson, too."

He stopped his twitching, leaned forward across the table, and covered my hand with his. "Thanks, Seychelle. That really means a lot coming from you."

Once again I felt I was getting mixed signals from this man. Was he flirting or being fatherly?

"By the way," he said, "that was quite a day you had yesterday." He let go of my hand and rested his elbows on the table. "Finding that little girl like that. What's her story anyway?" Joe nodded his head toward the pile of newsprint beside my now empty mug. "There's not much there in the papers about her. Is she able to talk?"

"A little, not much. She speaks some English. Some of it doesn't make much sense. Seems she's really afraid of authority figures. She won't say a word to them."

"That's not unusual. I spent some time down in Haiti. Their history has given them good reason to fear the government. But you say she's talking to you?"

"Well, a little. She told me her dad's an American."

"Really? They're going to let her stay, then?"

Questions, questions. I'd forgotten that Joe was a former cop. "I've got to find him first. The Border Patrol guy who came to the hospital last night doesn't believe this American father exists. He says all Haitians claim to have American relatives."

"He's right."

"But I believe her."

"So how do you propose to find this guy?"

"I guess I'll start with the kid. She said a few words to me when I first pulled her aboard *Gorda*. Last night when I visited her in the hospital, she wasn't talking to anyone."

"If there's anything I can do to help out, don't hesitate to ask. It would be my pleasure to spend more time with you, and I'd like to know how things turn out for her. Sounds like that poor kid has seen things we can't even imagine."

viii

The dark clouds were breaking up, and it was almost ten o'clock by the time I hooked the Whaler back up to the davits at the Larsens' dock and cranked her back out of the water. The sun was quickly turning last night's rain to steam. Henri and the three other members of his lawn service crew were working with weed whackers, gas blowers, and hedge clippers. When he saw me, Henri hurried over and waited while I cranked up the dinghy.

"Hi, Henri," I said as I bent down and scratched Abaco's ears. "What's up?"

He looked distressed. Henri was a tall, handsome Haitian in his mid-forties. He was a successful entrepreneur with a thriving lawn service, a good husband, and the father of five beautiful kids. Distress didn't look right on his face.

"A man came. He said he wanted to see you. I told him you were not here, but he insisted and left his things in front of your house."

"What?" I stood and started down the brick path to my cottage. I could see the stuff piled in front of my place: a backpack with dozens of patches sewn on it, an army surplus duffel bag, an old footlocker, and a torpedo-shaped blue Dacron bag.

"This man," Henri continued, "he did not look very clean even though he was very polite. I thought perhaps he was a homeless man. But he claimed he was your brother."

I whooped and grabbed Henri by the arm. "This is great!" It was the windsurfer bag that had left no doubt: My brother Pit had come for a visit. "Henri, it *was* my brother, and don't you worry what he looks like. He's a great guy." Sensing my excitement, Abaco came loping over and started to bark. I knelt down and ruffled her ears. "Pit's come to visit, girl." Abaco sensed the excitement in my voice and began turning circles. I stood and turned back to Henri. "Did Pit say where he was going? When he would be back?"

"He left a note." Henri smiled tentatively. "So it is good your brother comes?"

"Oh yes, very good."

"Then I am happy I did not let Jean-Phillipe chase him off with his machete."

"Yeah, Henri." I laughed. "That is good."

I shoved Pit's things into a corner of my little living room. Surely he didn't travel all over the world on the World Cup Windsurfing circuit with all this baggage. The last thing I dragged in was an old foot-locker, which I recognized as one that used to belong to Red. When we were kids, we used to get into old clothes and U.S. Navy uniforms he stored in the locker. I remembered it being in the garage when we had cleaned out the house after Red's death. I didn't realize that Pit had saved it.

I finally sat down on the couch and read Pit's note.

Seychelle,

In town for 3 days. Thought I could bunk at Tina's but she threw me out—along with my gear that I'd left at her place. Hope I can borrow your couch for a couple of nights. Gone down to Hobie Beach.

See ya. Pit

My brother Pit was the laid-back middle child, the free spirit. Possessions, timetables, careers—they all made little sense to him. Hobie Beach was the windsurfers' hangout down on Miami's Biscayne Bay. Pit was a professional windsurfing teacher and competitor, and while you'd think he'd get sick of it sometimes and want to do something else, it didn't surprise me that windsurfing was the first thing he wanted to do on his first trip home in years.

After a quick shower, I threw on some old jeans and a T-shirt and dialed Jeannie's number.

"Hey, it's me."

"Hey, you. I was just getting ready to go over to visit our little friend."

"I was hoping you'd say that. There's someplace I need to go first, but I'd feel better knowing there will be somebody there with her for the next few hours. Somebody to run interference with cops and reporters, give the kid a chance to rest. At least till I get there."

"You know me," Jeannie said. "I'm damn good at interference."

Ignoring Abaco's forlorn looks, I locked up my cottage and headed out the gate. Henri and his crew had wrapped up their work and headed out, leaving behind trash cans that smelled sweetly of fresh-cut grass. I propped the business card for Racine Toussaint up on the Jeep's dash and pulled a map of Broward County out of the glove box. The address was off Hammondville Road in Pompano Beach. I'd read about that part of the county, but I'd never been up there. Back in the fifties, the area was all agriculture, and the mostly black farmworkers had lived in lousy conditions in farmworker housing on Hammondville Road. There was still a good deal of poverty in what was now called Collier City and Western Pompano, and some people would say I was being unwise to go up there alone.

There was a saying about South Florida: To get to the South from here, you had to go north. There was a small kernel of truth in that, but in areas like Hammondville Road in Pompano, I suspected aspects of the old Deep South were still right here. In spite of the glitz and glamour of Broward County's waterfront and modern facade, racial tensions and segregated neighborhoods were still the norm in much of the county.

Traffic was sparse on I-95 and Lightnin' held her fifty-five-mile-per-hour average in the slow lane. The old Jeep wasn't an expressway vehicle, and given the roaring engine and flapping canvas, I was relieved when I pulled off the interstate at Atlantic Boulevard. In much of South Florida, affluent neighborhoods abut squalid government-assisted housing, so I wasn't surprised to see the new, gleaming, well-lit gas station and mini-mart, the kind that has disembodied voices that speak to you each time you pull up to the pump, while just beyond the fresh black asphalt were dirt yards around small cinder-block homes and businesses of the old district.

The Haitian Baptist Church, a clean and new-looking structure, indicated how this neighborhood had changed in the last twenty years.

This was truly the New South. The huge influx of Haitians and other Caribbean immigrants was apparent in the signs in the stores, the smells of fish and plantain frying, the sound of Creole being spoken on the street.

I located Racine Toussaint's house a few blocks north of Hammondville and fairly close to Old Dixie Highway. I was pleased to see the place looked so well tended and prosperous in comparison with many of the other houses in the area. The house stood alone on almost an acre of land and looked home-built of gray unfinished cinder block, the mortar between the blocks smoothed out neat and clean. Floral-print curtains fluttered between the bars that protected the front windows, and the wood door was painted a bright sea foam green.

When I turned off the Jeep, I could hear the breeze rustling the branches of the tall Australian pines scattered about the dirt lot that stretched between the house and the road. There were no children's toys or old abandoned vehicle parts like those that decorated the vacant lots and the yards of many of the houses I'd passed on my way here. Behind the house, a giant strangler fig tree loomed large, the huge limbs framing the house with prop roots supporting the heft visible around both sides. The tree blocked out all sunlight and looked as though it would engulf the house if the inhabitants dropped their vigilance for only a few months. Aside from a couple of free-ranging chickens that darted behind the house when I drove up, there was no sign of life.

I knocked on the green door, wondering if my decision to come alone had been wise after all. Why would the card of the woman who lived at this address be on board the *Miss Agnes*? But then that is why I was there: to find out if Solange was on that boat. To find out something that would help her stay in the United States.

The place was too quiet. The sound of the traffic out on Dixie and Atlantic was the only noise. For a moment I thought I heard drums from inside the house, but then the amplified voices of angry rappers blasted from a bright orange Impala lowrider that cruised by, the gold rims glinting, the bass booming into the yard and seeming to fill the air with threat. Two muscular young black men in matching white undershirts, flashing gold in their grimaces, glared at me as they rolled by. I faced the street, keeping my eyes on them, refusing to turn my back. There was a slow-mo cinematic quality to the moment, like a high-noon face-off, the only element of speed being my pulse, which had kicked into overdrive.

The door swung inward behind me, and I spun around, my hands rising in the automatic self-defense posture I had learned from growing up with older brothers. The man standing in the doorway was no more than five feet four and impeccably dressed in dark slacks, a long-sleeved white shirt, and a dark bow tie.

"*Bonjour,*" he said, showing a wide mouth of crowded white teeth. His skin was the darkest black skin I had ever seen, but his hair, what little remained in tufts behind his ears, was bright white. "May I help you?"

I stuttered at first, my mind still not disentangled from the menacing Impala. "There was, out there . . ." I turned around and looked at the street, but there was no sign of the car. "I mean, uh." I turned back to face him. He was smiling patiently. "Forget that. Let me start over. The reason I'm here is because I have this boat, a tugboat, and I found this little girl yesterday. You might have heard about it. See, I was looking around the *Miss Agnes* and I found this card." I held out the salt-stiff piece of cardboard. He looked at the card and said "Oh" in a very high-pitched voice, as if he had been startled by something. It was a funny sound, and I let loose with a matching shrill laugh.

"Please," he said, showing me his crooked teeth again, then he bowed his head and stepped back. "Come inside and we will talk." There was music in the way he pronounced the English words. I had heard Creole accents that were harsh and difficult to understand, but this little man sounded more French.

The room I entered was furnished simply, a living room with a threadbare green couch and armchair, and on the far side a yellow Formica dinette set that looked as though it dated back to the *I Love Lucy* era. The walls were painted with vibrant colors, each one different—yellow, teal, and coral—and one wall was covered with paintings. Through a door, I could see the kitchen with an industrial-size galvanized sink and huge pots and pans resting on the drain board. He pointed to the couch and waited until I was seated before settling into the chair. The silence stretched out as we sat, each of us waiting for the other to begin. I turned the card over and over, my fingers holding it gingerly by the outer edges. Finally, he reached out and took it from me and then offered me his hand. His skin felt cool and dry.

"I am Maximillian Toussaint. Please call me Max." He smiled and bowed his head low, revealing the shiny black dome fringed all the way around with delicate cottony filaments. From behind, I imagined his head looked like a dark mountain peak half shrouded in clouds. "Racine" —he held up the card— "is my wife. However, she is very busy today. She cannot see visitors."

"My name is Seychelle Sullivan."

"I am pleased to meet you. Would you like some coffee or a cold drink?"

"No, thank you. I'm fine." I smiled and looked around the small room. On the wall behind him there were primitive paintings of country and city scenes, but each one was crowded with brightly costumed people and animals. There was something about the perspective in the paintings that made them seem very otherworldly. I noticed, too, that some of the people in the paintings wore strange costumes, and masks with horns, and they carried whips. In other paintings, wild animals, from zebras to giraffes and tigers and parrots, all frolicked in big, leafy jungle scenes. Against the wall behind Max's chair was a sideboard covered with a strange assortment of colorful scarves or flags and what looked like large gourds decorated with paint and beads.

"Have you ever been to Haiti, Miss Seychelle?"

His question startled me. I realized that I had been staring past him.

"I'm sorry. No, I've never been."

"It is a very poor place, this is true, but it is also home to some of the happiest people on earth."

"Really? Why do you say that?"

"Because it is so. Americans have so many things, and they are not happy. Haitians have nothing, and yet they still laugh and dance and sing."

"But you live here, not there."

"Ah, yes." His eyes really did seem to twinkle. "I can have a full belly and still have Haiti in my heart." He chuckled but said nothing more.

"I just came to ask you some questions. About this little girl. I promised I would help her. There's nothing for her back in Haiti, no family. She's better off here."

"But of course. I will be pleased to help," he said, scooting forward to sit on the edge of the chair.

"Do either you or Racine know anything about the boat that sank a few days ago coming into the Hillsboro Inlet? You know the one I'm talking about?"

"Yes, yes, I heard about that. Very tragic. Especially for the children, the little girls." When he said those two words—"leettle gerls"—he sounded just like Maurice Chevalier.

I pointed to the card. "Do you have any idea why your wife's card would have been on that boat? That's where I found it."

He shrugged. "Madame Toussaint is very well known in the Haitian community. She is a force, as you say in America, for justice for the Haitian people."

"Are you saying she helps illegal immigrants?"

"*Non,* not at all. Racine obeys all the *lwas.*" He threw back his head and laughed.

His accent was strange, and it grew heavier when he didn't want me to fully understand him. I suspected that Max was not about to confide in me. "Yesterday, when I found this little girl, Solange—uh, I don't know her last name. Anyway, she was floating out in the Gulf Stream in this half-sunk wood boat, and I think she might have come from the boat that sank, the *Miss Agnes.*"

"Yes, yes." He nodded and flashed his teeth. "I heard about this also on the radio. The little Earth Angel girl."

"That's right. I want to see if I can find her family, her father. There was a woman in the boat with her, but she was already dead. Solange says her name was Erzulie, or something like that."

When I said the name *Erzulie* his eyes grew big and round, but it was as though a shade had lowered. He leaned forward. "What did the child say the woman's name was?"

"Erzulie? Maybe I'm not pronouncing it right."

He got up then and began pacing back and forth in short, little mincing steps and then spun around. "You really must talk to *Mambo* Racine. Erzulie? Does the child know what she is saying? What will Racine think of this? She is with her initiates, though. Would she want

me to disturb her?" He was talking to himself, not expecting any answers from me. He continued to mutter, then he stopped abruptly and
faced me. "Can you return tomorrow? You must speak to Racine.
Bring the child with you. In the evening, at, say, seven o'clock?"

I understood only about half of what he was saying. I thought I
might have better luck with his wife. "Yeah, I can try. And if you learn
anything that would help Solange in the meantime, please, let me
know. I don't want to see this kid sent back to Haiti with no parents."

"*Oui,* it is a hard life there for a child."

"She said she doesn't know her mother, but her father is an American. I'm trying to locate him, and I'm trying to find out if she and this
Erzulie woman were on the boat that sank, the *Miss Agnes.* If you or your
wife know any of the refugees who made it ashore off that boat, please,
have them contact me." I took one of my business cards out of my
shoulder bag and handed it to him. "This is my card for my business,
Sullivan Towing and Salvage. You can reach me at that number or just
leave a message, and I'll call you back. Could you ask around for me?"

"Certainly." He stood next to me and was obviously herding me
toward the front door. "I will ask, and you will return tomorrow night,
correct?"

"Okay." I smiled and turned and was almost out the door when I
remembered one more thing. "The little girl, Solange, she said a word
I don't understand. Maybe you can help. She pointed to herself and
said something that sounded like *restavik.* What does that mean?"

Again, a darkness flitted behind his eyes, but he covered it quickly
with a gentle smile. "The word comes from the French words *reste avec,*
which means 'stay with.' In Haiti, many families are very poor, and
they send their children to stay with another family, to work as unpaid
domestics. They are called *restaveks.* Some people think this is very bad,
they call it child slavery, but in Haiti, it is the custom. Your little friend
is how old?"

"I'd say she's nine or ten. She doesn't know anything about her
own mother."

"She probably left home around age six or seven and now doesn't
even know where she used to live. The life of a *restavek* is not good." He
lowered his eyes, and all of the jolliness seemed to drain out of him.
"Some say there are over three hundred thousand *restaveks* in Haiti

today. That is not an aspect of my country that makes me proud." He shook his head and shoulders, as if to throw off a weight, then sat up very straight. "You are right, Miss Sullivan. *Certainement.* She has no home to go back to in Haiti."

When I pulled Lightnin' into the parking lot at Broward General Hospital, it was past noon. Jeannie's van was there in the visitors' parking, as I knew it would be. I was glad to see a uniformed Fort Lauderdale police officer at the nurses' station across from Solange's room, even if he was in deep conversation with Jenna. I would have to thank Collazo.

Solange was sitting up in bed, cross-legged. Spread across the sheets in front of her were what looked like hundreds of colorful Lego blocks. She was so engrossed in her play, she didn't notice me until Jeannie spoke.

"Nice of you to pay us a visit this afternoon." Jeannie was, I assumed, sitting on the same yellow chair, but her bulk hid all evidence of it. Her reading glasses were perched down her nose, and a flowery-covered novel lay on her lap.

"It took me a little longer than I thought." Solange looked up and attempted a shy smile. On the floor, I saw the basket of toys Jeannie had evidently brought from her boys' room. In addition to the Legos, there were trucks, a couple of stuffed animals, and a few picture books. I thought of how nice it would have been if I had thought to bring the girl a toy, too, but it hadn't even occurred to me.

"Collazo's already been here," Jeannie said. Then she chuckled. "He was really pissed off that she still wouldn't say anything to him or his translator. He gave up after about twenty minutes. Said I should tell you he wants to talk to you, wants to know if she's said anything."

"What did you tell him?"

"I said I didn't know if she was talking to you or not." Solange watched Jeannie's face, then turned to wait for my reply.

"That's good."

"Hey, it's also true. And I did pass on the message that he wants to see you, so I've done my part." She reached across and threatened to tickle Solange. "Right, kiddo?"

Solange grinned and covered her sides in self-defense. Evidently she and Jeannie had played this game before.

She looked like an entirely different child from the one I had plucked from the sea just twenty-four hours earlier.

"Have you talked to a doctor? Know anything about how she's doing?"

Jeannie shook her head. "Aside from someone bringing her lunch and taking the tray away, I haven't seen anybody. And, by the way, Solange did eat this morning, and kept it down, even though it was some kind of pukey-looking mystery meat. For what they charge, they could provide better food."

"They probably wouldn't tell us anything anyway. We're not next of kin."

"Ha! You want me to find out?" Not waiting for an answer, she heaved herself up from the chair. "I'll be right back."

I set my shoulder bag down on the rolling table that held a water pitcher, cleared aside some Legos, and sat on the foot of the bed. "Are you feeling better?"

She nodded slowly, her head lowered. She twirled one of her braids and played with the beads on the rubber bands at the ends. Someone had rebraided her hair and added the pretty beads. Everyone else seemed to know what to do for a little girl.

"I want to help you, Solange, but I need you to help me. Do you understand?"

She nodded again.

"What is your last name?"

Her eyebrows came together and her forehead wrinkled. Her lower lip jutted out.

"My name is Seychelle Sullivan. You are Solange . . ." I motioned with my hand for her to fill in the silence.

She shook her head. "*Seulement* Solange." She imitated my motion. "Solange . . . *non*."

"You don't know your last name?"

Her shoulders lifted, but she kept her eyes lowered.

I switched tacks. "Can you tell me about the trip to America? Start with Haiti. Do you know the name of the town you lived in?"

"Cap Haitian."

"Good. And you told me you lived with a family there, as a *restavek*."

She lowered her eyes at the word *restavek*. It seemed to make her ashamed.

"Did you go to school in Cap Haitian?"

She shook her head and still did not lift her head to look at me.

"Who put you on the boat to America?"

"The bad man." Her voice was barely audible.

"The bad man who killed Erzulie?"

She nodded.

"How did you meet him?"

"Water. I bring water to house. Bad man talk to Madame Maillot."

"Who is she?"

"I work in Madame house."

"Had you ever seen this man there before?"

"No."

"So you came back with the water and he was there talking to Madame Mayo. Then what happened?"

"I wash baby Christophe. Madame say no. She send me away with the bad man."

"He took you to the boat?"

Her head bobbed once. "Erzulie was there," she said.

"Anyone else?"

"Bad man. Le Capitaine."

"The bad man, he was the captain of the big boat?"

Her beads bounced as her head bobbed up and down.

I picked my shoulder bag off the table and reached inside to retrieve the sunglasses I'd found on the *Miss Agnes*. "Have you ever seen these glasses before?" I knew before I'd finished speaking that she recognized the glasses from the look in her eyes. "Solange?" She continued to stare at the little white skulls.

"Capitaine *bawon samdi*." She scrambled to the head of her bed, up on her pillows, trying to distance herself from the sunglasses and began making little squeaky, whining noises. She grabbed one of the pillows and tried to hide under it.

I put the glasses back in my shoulder bag. "Shhh. It's okay. I don't understand when you speak Creole, Solange. Did these belong to the captain of the big boat you were on with Erzulie?"

The curved black lashes fluttered several times and a fat tear slid from the corner of her eye, coursing a wet trail down her cheek. She nodded. "He say he take me to Papa, he say Papa want me—" Her rounded shoulders hitched up as she sucked in a quick breath. Her body looked like it was trying to curl into itself.

I slid up the bed, wrapped my arms around her shoulders, pressed her head against the curve of my neck, and rested my chin on her head. Her tiny body trembled with tight, convulsive sobs. As quickly as it had started, it stopped, and her breathing quieted back to a regular rhythm.

"Solange, I promise you, I will find your papa," I whispered into the dark braids, knowing full well that in order to find her father, I would have to find a murderer first.

ix

When Jeannie returned, she opened her mouth to speak, but I raised my finger to my lips. I'd just finished tucking the sheet under Solange's chin, and I was standing there admiring her eyelashes, so long that each one formed a perfect letter *C*. I motioned Jeannie to go out into the corridor, and it wasn't until we were both outside the door that I saw what she had been about to tell me. She had a federal escort.

"Nice to see you again, Seychelle," Rusty said, smiling so broadly that the creases at the corners of his eyes looked like the spokes of a wire wheel.

"Can't really say the same, Rusty." He was in civilian clothes today, faded jeans and black T-shirt, sockless, raggedy-looking boat shoes. It was difficult not to notice the way the T-shirt tapered down from those broad shoulders to his trim waist and how those weathered jeans wrapped his hips neatly in denim. It could have been really nice to see him if he wasn't employed by U.S. Immigration.

"How's our patient?" he asked, inclining his shaggy head toward the door to Solange's room.

"*Our* patient? No, no, no, my friend. You have no claim on her." I turned to Jeannie. "Were you able to find a doctor?"

"Finally, yes, after walking through miles of hospital corridors and continually getting directions that had me following yellow lines and blue lines all over this friggin' hospital. But yes, eventually I found this lovely woman doctor, a little bit of a thing. She said the kid is doing great. Much better than should be expected, the doc said, because Solange was malnourished long before this whole boat trip even started. But there's no need to keep her in the hospital, as long as she is eating and drinking on her own. Doc said she'd be willing to cut her loose this evening."

"Good," Rusty said. "We'll take her into custody. Cases like this we usually send down to Miami to the Girls and Boys Town facility there."

"No way." I turned to Jeannie, my mouth open, but she was talking before I could even ask.

"Listen, Elliot, I am both a court-approved guardian ad litem and a registered foster parent. She can stay in my home. Any judge would see that it would be in the best interests of a child who has been through this kind of trauma to be in a single-family home environment instead of some group home."

Rusty shook his head. "I don't know about that. The police will want to talk to her."

"Exactly. They can talk to her at my home if they need to—and she'll be closer. Don't block this just to be pissy, Elliot. Think of the child."

Rusty raised his hands in submission. "Okay, okay. *I* don't have a problem with it, as long as she stays where we can see her, and"—he turned and looked straight at me—"you work with me on this. I'm not your enemy, so don't try anything stupid."

I tried my hardest to look innocent, to give him a "Who me?" look, but as usual, I felt guilty already. Whenever someone suspected me of something, even if I hadn't even thought of it yet, I felt guilty.

"Also," he continued, "I need to interview her officially, and I'd like your cooperation with that. I can't get her to talk to me."

Now I knew why I'd felt guilty. "It's possible I could help you out there."

"Go on," Rusty said.

"It's just possible she has talked a little bit to me."

Jeannie looked at her watch. "Listen, Sey, I need to take care of some paperwork and buy a few extra things if I'm inheriting a little girl this afternoon. I don't think she'd be thrilled with Spider-Man jockey shorts. You okay here?"

"Not a problem, Jeannie. You go on. I'll see you later."

After Jeannie collected her things and left, I turned to go back into the girl's hospital room. Rusty touched my arm. "You hungry?"

Fifteen minutes later, Rusty returned with burgers, fries, and Cokes. I had been watching Solange sleep and wondering how I was going to keep this promise to find her father, wondering what my next step would be. I forgot about all of it when the room filled with the odor of french fries.

"Lunch is served," he announced.

I held my finger to my lips and pointed at the sleeping child, then said in a whisper, "You're going to drive the rest of the inmates mad with that smell. All they ever get is sugar-free Jell-O and low-fat mystery meat."

Rusty dropped the paper bags onto the vacant bed close to the door, and he motioned for me to climb onto it. "I'll take care of that."

I kicked off my sneakers and snuggled my butt into the covers near the head of the bed as he grabbed the edge of the privacy curtain and drew it closed around us. He smiled and climbed onto the foot of the bed and settled himself, sitting Indian style, not looking nearly as comfortable in that position as B.J. did.

"They'll never know we're here," he whispered as he emptied a mountain of fries onto a paper bag.

I attempted to raise one eyebrow, to give him a look that said "Yeah, right." With the scent of french fries wafting down the hall? I said, "I can't quite figure you out, Elliot. One minute you're 'the man,' and the next minute you're acting like a kid hiding from the nurses."

From another bag, Rusty poured out some two dozen little pouches of catsup. "I like that. I like being complex." He started ripping the catsup pouches open with his teeth and emptying them into a puddle on a waxy burger wrapper. "I hope you don't like catsup. I need every one of these."

When I ventured to dip a fry in his catsup lake, we ended up in a french fry sword fight.

Too bad he was the enemy. He was kind of fun.

After we'd finished off all but the little burnt stubs of fries, I leaned back against the headboard and laced my fingers behind my head. A feeling of contentment settled into my shoulders, relaxing muscles that had been tense for over twenty-four hours.

"How long you been running that tug?" he whispered.

"Full-time for a little more than two years. As a part-timer, all my life."

"Must be nice, working on the water."

I narrowed my eyes. "Looking at you, I'd say fisherman, light tackle, fresh and marine, got about an eighteen-foot Dusky on a trailer you don't get to take out often enough."

He smiled. "You've sure got me pegged. Only the boat isn't on a trailer at the moment, and it's not a Dusky."

I raised both brows this time. "Go on."

"She's in the water at a place I've got in Hollywood on the Intracoastal, and she's a twenty-five-foot Anacapri, built in 1976. Still got the original engines. A classic."

"That boat's not a classic," I said. "It's just old. What do you tow it with?"

"Another classic: a 1971 Datsun pickup."

"Geez, how many miles?"

"Over three hundred thousand. 'Course it's not the original engine."

"Now that's just ancient." I giggled. "And ugly."

He didn't laugh back. He had this deadly serious look on his face. "So what's the difference? Between old and classic. To you," he said.

I couldn't help it. The look on his face. The more I tried to stop, the harder I laughed. Then I began to snort. I hate when that happens.

He was examining the detail in the acoustical ceiling tile. I was about ready to regurgitate french fries through my nose. That was when we heard Solange cry out as though she had been struck.

Rusty was the first one off the bed. He couldn't find the edge of the curtain at first, and he pulled at the fabric and got tangled in it when it didn't slide open as he expected. I saw a pair of sneakers run past beneath the hem of the curtain as Rusty struggled. Once he finally drew the curtain aside, we saw Solange, sitting up in bed, her eyes wide open, staring straight ahead.

"She okay?" I hollered as I slid off the bed and under the curtain on the door side of the room.

"Think so," I heard Rusty say as I went out into the hall. I swung my head, checking both directions. There were several possibilities. To my right, there was a tall black male orderly pushing an empty wheelchair. To my left, a black female nurse and a white male orderly were leaning on the nurses' station, talking. There were patients and visitors walking everywhere. The corridor was crowded with people wearing white sneakers. I jogged right and caught up to the man with the wheelchair just as he turned into a room.

"Good morning, Mrs. Johnson," he said to the large lady in the bed. His Haitian accent was unmistakable. He reached down to lock the wheels on the wheelchair. "Are you ready to go to radiology?"

"Excuse me," I said.

He turned and looked at me expectantly. He was a large man, well over six feet tall, and somewhere in age between forty and fifty. He had a thin mustache and a small goatee.

"Were you just in room four twenty-five?"

"No. Not me. I came from Patient Relations. Must have been some-body else." He smiled and walked over to Mrs. Johnson to help her into the chair. He was very relaxed, and he looked like he was accus-tomed to wearing green scrubs. "How are you feeling today, pretty lady?" he asked the white-haired woman as he pulled back the covers on her bed. I noticed he wore large silver rings on three of the five fin-gers of his right hand. I couldn't make out the designs. "Let's go, dear."

He lifted the heavyset woman from her bed as though she weighed next to nothing. His name tag said "Todd," but he didn't look like a Todd to me. As he swung the older woman around to the wheelchair, he saw I was still standing there. "Is there anything else I can help you with?" He settled the woman into the chair, then turned to look ex-pectantly at me.

I backed out of the room. "No, thanks," I said. I checked down the hall in the other direction, but the nurse and orderly were gone.

Rusty came charging out of room 425, and I headed back down the hall to hear what he had found. By the time I got there, he was stand-ing nose to nose with the cop in front of the nurses' station.

"What the hell do you mean, you didn't see anything? Somebody was just in there."

The female Haitian nurse who had been so kind yesterday hurried into Solange's room.

"Is she all right?" I asked.

"She seems to be okay," Rusty said, not taking his eyes off the other cop.

"I mean I didn't see anything out of the ordinary," the duty officer said.

"Maybe you were distracted by something else." Rusty thrust his chin toward Jenna.

"People have been coming and going all day," the officer said. "I've been watching. Hell, you were in there. Why didn't you see anything?"

Rusty turned away without answering that question. No matter how he worded it, it wouldn't sound good.

I left them arguing and tried to go into Solange's room. The Haitian nurse waved me off, motioning me back outside. She had the blood pressure cuff on the child's arm.

I crossed to the desk and slipped behind the counter. "Jenna, do you know a guy who works here named Todd?"

She rolled her eyes and sucked her teeth. "Yes. What did he say now?"

"Nothing really, I was just wondering, what does he look like?"

"Oh. He's like really old, and he's always telling people I'm his 'honey.' He's too gross."

The Todd I'd seen was no more than fifteen years older than me, but then again, that might qualify as "really old" to this girl. "Can you give me more of a description? Is he tall, short, white, black?"

"He's like this little old retired white guy, and I think the only reason he volunteers here is to rub up against me every chance he gets. Old pervert."

Definitely not my Todd. "Any other guys here with that name? How about an orderly, a tall Haitian guy about forty?"

She shook her head so that her blond hair flew out in a golden arc, then smiled at the cop, who had turned his attention from Rusty back to Jenna. "No, nobody here like that unless he's new," she said to the cop, who nodded as though he understood what she'd just said.

I grabbed Rusty's arm. "Come on." He was striding next to me, trying to keep up without breaking into a trot to match mine.

"Where are we going?"

We rounded the corner into Mrs. Johnson's room. She sat there alone in the wheelchair, nodding off.

"Mrs. Johnson?"

She jerked her head up, startled.

"Where's the orderly who was just in here with you?" I asked.

"He said he'd be right back," she assured me. "I think he might have had to go to the little boy's room, you know. He just left real sudden, like he had to go, if you know what I mean."

"What's going on, Seychelle?" Rusty asked.

I stepped out into the hall and looked in both directions. "Which way did he go, Mrs. Johnson?"

"I'm sorry, dear, I wasn't paying much attention. Is something wrong? I did think it was a little odd. I didn't remember anything about radiology today, but you know how it is, when you come into this place, you just stop asking questions after a while."

"That was him," I said, and slapped my hand against my thigh.

Rusty sighed, shook his head, and started walking back to Solange's room. I followed him. This time we were allowed back in. Solange was now on her side in a fetal position, facing the window, her back to the room. When I got to the foot of her bed, I saw her eyes were open, staring out the window. The Haitian nurse looked very troubled as she placed a moistened cloth on the child's brow.

"How's she doing?" I asked.

The nurse shrugged.

I turned to Rusty. "I thought you said she was okay."

"She was just like that when I got to her," Rusty said. "She doesn't look hurt."

I turned to the nurse. "What happened? What did that guy do?"

"What guy?" Rusty asked.

When I explained about seeing the feet under the curtain, Rusty's face told me what he thought of my story. Typical cop reaction—he didn't want to believe he'd missed something.

"She is right, that Jenna," the nurse said. "We have many Haitians working here, but no one by that name."

I moved in closer, next to the nurse, and asked her, "So what did he do to her? Why's she like that?"

"It is difficult to say."

"We heard her cry out, like he was hurting her."

"I checked her all over, and I cannot find any injuries, no injection site, and the symptoms came on too quickly for it to be something she was given by mouth. I have called for her doctor. She will give her a more thorough examination, but I don't think she will find anything."

"What happened, then? Why is she like that?"

"I think . . ." She paused, as though choosing her words very carefully. "He hurt her here." She pointed to her head. "He said something, and now it is in her mind, and it frightens her. She is from Haiti, and we are very superstitious in Haiti. Our beliefs are very different from yours."

"Are you saying he put a curse on her?"

Her brow wrinkled. "Something like that. We must let her sleep. We hope she will be better when she wakes."

The duty officer stepped into the room and motioned for us to follow him outside.

"Collazo's on his way over. He said to tell you not to leave. He wants to talk to both of you."

I pointed down to the waiting area on the far side of the nurses' station. "I'll be right back. I need to make a phone call."

After scrounging thirty-five cents out of the side pocket of my shoulder bag, I dialed Jeannie's number. Disappointed when I got her answering machine, I left her a message explaining about the incident at the hospital and telling her to keep it very quiet about Solange staying with her. "Somebody out there definitely wants to get to her," I said before hanging up, "and we'd better keep her whereabouts a secret."

Rusty was buying a soda out of the machine, and he held it up to me with raised eyebrows.

"No thanks, I've had enough." The junk food congealing in my stomach felt like an indigestible lump. I sat down on one of the chairs in the waiting area, and Rusty joined me. The silence between us stretched out until I felt the impossible happen. I was actually looking forward to seeing Collazo.

The elevator doors finally slid open, and Collazo stepped out with an attractive light-skinned black woman in a dark suit. She looked too confident and competent and "in charge" to be a local cop.

"Hi, Maria," Rusty said, and he stepped up to shake her hand. Manicured, buffed nails, no polish.

"Rusty, what a pleasure."

Something passed between them, a look or a spark. I could feel the heat. Out of nowhere, I wondered if they had slept together. He turned to me. "Seychelle Sullivan, this is Special Agent Maria D'Ugard, FBI."

Her grip was beyond firm. Her grip said Wonder Woman.

"Sullivan. You're the tug captain who found them." She flashed me a two-second smile showing perfect white teeth that contrasted beautifully with her flawless cocoa-colored skin. Standing in front of her in my jeans, T-shirt, and sneakers, I felt like a kid in the principal's office.

"That's right."

The uniformed officer brought over a couple of chairs and then returned to his post, but not before checking out Agent D'Ugard from head to toe. At least I was glad to see he had moved his chair just outside the doorway to Solange's room. Collazo did not remove his jacket as he and the woman sat down opposite us, but he did take a handkerchief from his breast pocket, ready to mop the sweat. D'Ugard crossed her legs to put her rock-hard calves on display. "Tell us what happened here," she said.

Rusty jerked his head up, and we both started to speak at the same time.

"Go ahead," I said. "You tell them." He gave them a fairly straightforward version of what happened.

Collazo said, "You're certain there was someone in the room who did or said something to frighten the girl."

"No doubt," Rusty said. "The girl's safety was my first concern, however, and by the time I got to the corridor, the perp was gone."

Interesting. When I saw him charge out of the room, there was no indication of his looking for a perp. Was he stretching the truth to look good for Wonder Woman?

"I'd like to have us all put our heads together on this," Agent D'Ugard began. "Miss Sullivan, we are going to share some information that is privileged. I trust you will not share this information with anyone else."

I nodded.

"We"—she made a circle in the air with her index finger—"local police, Immigration, and FBI, together with the Coast Guard, as an interagency group, have been conducting an investigation into an immigrant smuggling ring based in the Bahamas."

"Yeah, Collazo told me. It's called DART, right?"

She flicked her eyes in Collazo's direction, and even I could feel the rebuke. "Yes, well, while we are concerned about the recent deaths, there are larger concerns. From the condition of the boats we've intercepted and of their cargo, we think they have traveled only a very short distance, probably from the Bahamas."

Tough lady, I thought. She can refer to men, women, and children as cargo?

"Originally," she continued, "it was just a local matter, but when these murders started, the FBI was brought in. Assuming they are taking place as this one did, beyond the twelve-mile limit, then they come under the category of 'crimes on the high seas' and only the federal government has jurisdiction."

"The Border Patrol," Rusty said, "became aware of an increase in undocumenteds around March. As the seas calmed down this spring, we've seen numbers like we've never seen before."

"Miss Sullivan, this immigrant smuggling group is highly organized and efficient," Agent D'Ugard continued. "It's not unusual for them to lose boats like the *Miss Agnes*—they don't care, as they have plenty more. At prices ranging from several hundred dollars to seven or eight thousand per head, smugglers are finding that transporting immigrants is as lucrative and less dangerous than the drug trade. If they get caught, the sentences are lighter than they are for drugs, too. We've seen quite a lot of crossover from the one trade to the other."

"I get all that. I've seen the changes in the marinas. I know there are lots of go-fast boats switching over to human cargo. But your whole DART thing is about the murders, right?"

"That is one facet of the investigation, but stopping the entire organization is my first priority. Miss Sullivan, this is more than just an assignment to me. It's personal. My family immigrated to this country from the Dominican Republic." I was surprised when she said that, as she had no accent. "These people are preying on Dominicans, Haitians, Chinese, East Indians, people from all over. The importers are increasingly brazen, and they don't care about the lives of their cargo, as they have already been paid."

"But why kill people? They're in business to smuggle them in. I don't get that part."

"They do it because they can. If anyone complains about the conditions on a boat, they kill one person, and that silences the rest. We suspect that last fall they dumped an entire load of Haitians out in the Gulf Stream when they thought they were being intercepted. A local fishing boat found several bodies, but most of the others were never recovered. Sources in Haiti estimate there had been thirty people on that trip." She leaned forward, over her crossed legs, and looked directly at Rusty. "We believe there is one man leading this group. Although we have not been able to identify him, we know he is extremely dangerous. He has absolutely no regard for human life."

Although it seemed like I was intruding into a personal meeting between Rusty and Agent D'Ugard, I said, "Okay, I get it. There's some really bad guy out there trafficking in human beings. What does this have to do with me?"

All three of them looked at one another as though trying to decide who would speak first. Agent D'Ugard seemed to draw the short straw.

"We believe that this young girl can identify several key players as well as the location of their camp in the Bahamas. Has she spoken yet?"

It had been fairly easy to dodge this issue up until now, but here I was being asked while surrounded by three cops of one sort or another. "Yeah, she has spoken to me a couple of times." They all hitched up on their plastic chairs. "But that was before this incident in her room just now. I'm not sure what happened to her in there, and I don't know if I'm going to be able to get her to open up again. I mean, this morning she was playing with toys and acting like a pretty normal kid. Now, she looks like some kind of zombie."

"You don't really think—" Rusty began.

"No, I'm not talking about Voodoo like in the movies. But let's face it, after what she's been through, she must be pretty fragile psychologically. Think about what she's seen. She was in a boat with a dead woman watching seagulls eat the woman's flesh." I paused for a moment to let that one sink in. "So go easy on her, okay? Here's what I've found out so far. Her name is Solange, but she doesn't know her last name. She was a *restavek,* basically a child slave, in Haiti, in the town of Cap Haitian. A man she refers to as 'the bad man' was the captain of the boat that brought her out of Haiti. He came to her house and took her away to a boat that took them to the Bahamas."

Wonder Woman interrupted me. "She is certain this man was the captain of the boat?"

I shrugged. "She seemed to be. She said they stayed in the Bahamas quite a while, and then they got on another big boat—possibly the *Miss Agnes*—to come here. The same man captained both boats."

"What about the dead woman? Did the child know her?" Rusty asked.

"She said she was no relation, but she seemed to watch out for Solange, even in the Bahamas. Her name was Erzulie, I think. Oh yeah, and the kid says her father is an American, that she learned to speak her English from him. She doesn't know his name, just that everyone called him Papa Blan—that means white father—and she was under the impression she was coming to America to be with him."

"She saw who killed the woman," Collazo said.

"She says the bad man did it. It wasn't really clear whether she witnessed it, or was just told he did it. All I know is she's terrified of him."

Agent D'Ugard said, "Miss Sullivan, if she can identify this man as the captain of the *Miss Agnes* and the killer, then that little girl is in serious jeopardy. I believe we should take her into protective custody."

"Isn't that what you have here?" I pointed to her room. "A cop outside her door? And isn't this where somebody just got to her? Come on. It's not like this is some big mob case. I know she's not going to be high priority to you guys. My attorney, Jeannie Black, has offered to take her in." I told them about Jeannie's background providing foster care and about the security she could provide. To my astonishment, they relented.

We shook hands all around, and then they wanted to see Solange. She was still curled up on her side and her hands were clenched in small fists, resting against her forehead. D'Ugard and Elliot took quick looks, as though they couldn't bear to look at her, and then left to go have a little private tête-à-tête in front of the elevator.

Collazo stopped me outside her room. "There is something more. Something you didn't tell us."

Leave it to Collazo. It was like the guy had a sixth sense and always knew what I was thinking. "Well, there was something, but Mr. Border Patrol thinks it was nothing." I told him then about seeing the sneakers under the curtain and chasing down the dubious Todd.

"We know somebody was in there, and I think he was the guy."

Collazo nodded and took out that little notebook of his and wrote some notes, then stepped in way too close. I could feel the humid heat coming off his body, and I could smell his sweat. "You need to come in to sign a formal statement about finding the body yesterday. Maybe sit with an artist to sketch this orderly. I'll drive you over right now. Elliot can stay with the girl, and I'll have an officer drive you back."

"Okay. I'll ask him."

I turned from Collazo and watched Rusty leaning casually against the wall, his hands shoved in the pockets of his jeans, drawing the fabric tight across his backside, while Wonder Woman leaned in to him, talking with her hands more than her mouth. He had a little half-smile on his face that made him look like he was enjoying every motion she made. I was glad to interrupt them.

x

Collazo wasn't present while a female officer took my official statement. He'd heard the story already and, for once, he wasn't accusing me of holding anything back. When it had been transcribed and I'd signed it, the woman called in an artist, and we ended with an okay likeness of the man I'd seen at the hospital. I was amazed at how little I really remembered of his face beyond the mustache and beard. When it came to the shape of eyes, nose, and ears, I just hadn't paid enough attention.

I went upstairs to Collazo's desk in the back of the room full of detectives' desks. He sat with his jacket draped over the back of his chair, his head bent over a mound of paperwork.

I sat in the chair opposite him. "Hey, does the Fort Lauderdale PD have a Haitian officer?"

He shook his head without looking up.

"You're kidding," I said. "How many people work here?"

"Something like five hundred. The translator I brought with me is a civilian, an outside contractor."

"You mean you don't have anyone who speaks Creole working for Fort Lauderdale PD? Man, you guys need to open your eyes. Look around at this city."

For just a second, he flicked his eyes up at me. "They don't consult me on their hiring decisions."

"Collazo, you are a piece of work." It was kind of nice not to be adversaries, to be cooperating with the detective. He stopped writing and looked up at me. He held his gold pen in front of his face, his hands clasped around it. He seemed to be deciding something.

"You need to get this girl to talk to me," he said.

This was a moment to remember. Collazo needed my help. I could be nasty and rub his nose in it, but I decided it would be smarter to use the moment.

"You got any kids, Collazo?"

"No," he grunted, and went back to his paperwork.

"Me neither," I said.

"Just get her to talk to me."

I leaned across his desk. "There's something about this kid. She gets to me. I've never even *liked* kids before. But this one . . . it's something about how she looks at me, I think. She totally believes that I can help her. Do you think that's what it's like to be a parent? I don't know. It scares me."

He looked up from his paperwork. "Miss Sullivan, we are through here."

"You just want to get to Solange before Miss FBI does, huh?" He shot me a look that was supposed to deny my accusation but had the opposite effect. "I might be able to help you, but I need something from you as well. Can you give me the name of your Creole translator?"

He pulled a yellow Post-it pad to him and wrote down a name and number. "She works for a radio station out in Davie—they do Caribbean shows, reggae, that kind of music. You can usually find her there or leave a message." He tore off the note and handed it to me.

"Okay, the kid has been talking to me. I don't know what's wrong with her right now, but as soon as she comes out of it, I'll call you."

He nodded and bowed his head over his paperwork again.

"So, anyway, nice talking to you. And thanks," I said, standing up and holding out the Post-it note. "This is weird, us working together all nice like this. You haven't even accused me of anything yet. I hardly recognize you." I smiled at the top of his head and turned toward the door.

"We're not working together, Sullivan," he said to my back. "You're not working anything. Go back to your little tugboat."

I turned back at the door. "Ah, there you are, the Detective Collazo we all know and love." I waved my fingers at him. "Bye."

It was after four o'clock by the time the officer dropped me off at the entrance to Broward General. Rusty was gone, Jeannie had returned, and Solange was unchanged. Jeannie motioned me over to the far side of the room. I brought her up-to-date on what had happened. We spoke in whispered tones because of the cop outside the door. Solange seemed more unconscious than asleep.

"There are two ways we can do this," Jeannie said. "I could go out and get the paperwork done legally and get myself appointed as her temporary guardian. That might take several days and then any yahoo who is out looking for her would be able to trace her to me. Or we could snatch her. Personally, since I don't really want any machete-wielding Haitians showing up at my house tonight, I vote for number two."

"Wouldn't that be like kidnapping or something? I'm not up for doing something that might get me sent to jail."

"Nah, not to worry. We'll let Mr. Greenjeans know we've got her, and he agreed to her staying with me. I don't see it as a problem. We just don't want to leave a forwarding address here at the hospital."

"Okay, what do we do?"

Jeannie outlined her plan, which involved me getting Solange to the side door, where Jeannie would be waiting with her van. Out in the hallway, I set about stealing a wheelchair. I headed for Mrs. Johnson's room first and got lucky.

Jeannie had already pulled out the IV and was sticking a Band-Aid on the girl's arm when I wheeled the empty chair into the room. She gave me a brown bag with clothing in it. "We'll dress her and then put the hospital gown back on over her street clothes."

It was like dressing a doll. Her head rolled around as we lifted her frail body, pushing her feet into the legs of the shorts and her arms into the T-shirt sleeves. We slipped yellow Big Bird slippers on her feet. "I know these aren't exactly inconspicuous, but they're the only kid slippers I've got. Andrew loved Big Bird, had to have everything Big Bird for a while there."

"Jeannie, are you sure she's okay? Maybe she needs to stay here in the hospital."

"Some kids are like this, Sey. They sleep the sleep of the dead. You could set a bomb off next to my boys and it wouldn't wake them. She's going to be fine."

"How are we going to get her past him?" I pointed to the doorway.

"There's another set of elevators if you go left and follow the yellow line down the corridor and around to the right. Take the hospital gown off her just before you get into the elevator, in a room if you have to, and then carry her like she's just a sleeping child visiting someone. When you exit the elevators, go right and find the east parking lot exit. I'll be out there in the van. Don't leave the room until you hear me calling for the police."

She took her car keys and then handed me her purse. "I'm about to get mugged," she said.

Solange was propped up in the wheelchair, the basket of toys on her lap helping to keep her upright. I was afraid that some nurse or orderly would show up at any minute to take her blood pressure, change her IV, or bring her another hospital meal. I saw Jeannie get on the elevator and disapper behind the closed doors. It seemed to be taking forever. Every time the elevator doors opened, I strained my ears, listening for some indication of Jeannie's distraction. When it came, I realized there was no way I could have missed it.

"Help! Police!" she bellowed. I heard the chair in front of the door scrape across the linoleum as the officer leapt to his feet. "Help! My purse! He took my purse!"

When I wheeled Solange out the door, all the women in the nursing station were leaning over the counter, staring at the floor of the open elevator. The policeman was bent over, his hand on the back of his neck in a gesture of misery as he contemplated what I assumed was Jeannie flat on her back. It would take some time to get her upright. We scooted down the hall, and no one paid us the slightest attention. Good thing, too, since hanging from my shoulder was the very purse Jeannie was claiming had been stolen.

As I rounded the corner, I saw a group of people at the far end of the corridor waiting for the elevator. No privacy there. I glanced in the rooms on either side of the hall and turned into the first one that had an empty bed. I ignored the moans from behind the other bed's curtain, parked the wheelchair, took the basket of toys off the kid's lap, and slid the hospital gown to the floor. The rigging knife from my shoulder bag cut through the plastic ID bracelet on her wrist. I hoisted her onto my hip, rested her head on my shoulder, and grabbed the basket of toys in my free hand.

I joined the crowd waiting for the elevator and when one arrived I squeezed in.

A little man with a white bushy mustache and a porkpie hat looked up at me. "She looks pretty tired," he said.

I hate it when people want to talk in an elevator. "Yeah," I said, "we were visiting her mom, and the excitement wore her out." The elevator stopped at the next floor down, and two more people squeezed in.

"What's wrong with her mother?"

Geez, what's wrong with these people? "She was in a car accident. Internal injuries, broken pelvis, may be paralyzed." That ought to get him, I thought. Nothing will silence people like saying someone's paralyzed.

"Oh, but you got on at the fourth floor. She's not on the fourth floor, is she?"

The doors slid open at that point, and I nearly fell out the opening. The lobby. Finally. I nodded at the little old guy and headed off down the corridor. For such a skinny kid, Solange sure was getting heavy. I'm a strong woman, but my left arm felt like cooked spaghetti. I saw the sunlight through the glass double doors that led out to the side parking lot, and I picked up my pace.

"Miss, hello, miss . . ." A voice and footsteps were coming up behind me. I tried taking longer strides, but I felt Solange slipping, my arms giving out.

"Miss! Please, stop."

I heard heavy breathing right behind me, and the plaintive note in the voice made me turn. It was Mr. Porkpie Hat. He was leaning over, his hands on his knees, his face so red he looked like a heart attack in the making. He was holding a bright yellow fuzzy Big Bird slipper. "You . . . dropped . . . a shoe," he said, gasping for air.

I took the shoe from his extended hand. "Uh, thanks. Sorry." I fast-walked the remaining twenty feet and was glad to see the doors were self-opening. I wouldn't be required to lift one hand.

Just as I got to the curb, Jeannie's van came around the corner from the north-side parking lot, doing well over thirty miles per hour. At least if she hit someone, it would be a short trip to the emergency room. I threw the basket of toys in through the open passenger-side window and slid the van's side door open. Solange flopped down on the bench seat and, for the first time in our whole ordeal, her eyes opened, but they remained unfocused.

"It's okay," I said as I jumped in and slid the door closed. "We're taking you to Jeannie's house. You're going to live with her for a little while." Jeannie took off a little hotter than was necessary, but she seemed to be enjoying her role as getaway driver. I made sure Solange was comfortable on the seat and buckled her in, then I climbed into the front seat. "How'd you get out of there so fast? Last I saw, you were on your back in the elevator."

"I let that nice young officer lift me to my feet."

That, I would've liked to see.

"And then I said I would go down to the front lobby security desk to report my missing purse. I think he was rather glad, actually. He seemed to be in a bit of pain." She didn't take her eyes off the road, but her body shook as she laughed to herself. "I'd left the van parked in the No Parking area right by the front door."

That explained what had taken her so long to stage her mugging. I jerked my thumb toward the back of the van. "She's awake, but she's just staring. Still not talking."

"Give her time."

Jeannie circled back and dropped me off a block from the hospital so that I could pick up my Jeep. I said good-bye to Solange but got just a blank stare in return.

I was disappointed to find my cottage empty when I returned home. I'd been hoping Pit would be there, lounging on my couch after his afternoon of windsurfing off the MacArthur Causeway, waiting to regale me with stories about his travels and his quest for the perfect combination of wind and wave.

I have two brothers, and they could not be more different. Our parents had this crazy idea of naming all their children after islands, and sometimes it was a struggle as we were growing up, being saddled with these weird names. Pitcairn's name fits him, as he's spent his life roaming from island to island. Pit is the brother I get along with best, the brother I adore. Madagascar, the oldest, is, well, Maddy. When we were kids, if we were eating cookies and I had finished mine first, Pit would share his last cookie with me. Maddy, on the other hand, would snatch the halves out of both our hands and laugh. In school, Pit was the athlete; Maddy was the fat kid. The girls were all crazy about Pit even though he was more interested in the daily surf report. Maddy tried to bully the weaker kids to get the girls' attention. Pit seemed to glide through life effortlessly, while Maddy was always suffering from demons—most recently his addiction to gambling. I love both my brothers, but even when you're related, some people are more difficult to like than others.

Abaco was giving me the look that all dog owners know, the one that says, "You've been neglecting me, you don't love me anymore." The great thing about dogs is that they have such blessed short memories. I reached for the leash, and all was forgotten and forgiven. She leapt and spun in midair, full of pure doggy joy.

I'd just snapped her leash onto her collar when the phone rang.

"Hey, Seychelle, it's Joe here. I just thought I'd call to see how you're doing."

"I'm fine."

"That's good to hear. It was nice seeing you at the beach this morning."

This guy was more than twenty years older than me. While I found the attention flattering, and I did consider him attractive, I felt the need to change the subject—fast.

"Joe, I just got home from the hospital and my dog is desperate to go out."

"You were visiting your little friend? How is she?"

"Physically, she's fine. The doctors say that in spite of how skinny the kid is, she's in good health. She's bounced right back from the exposure."

"You know, if there's any way I can help, I'd like to."

"Well, that's really kind of you, but—"

"I'm serious. At my age, you want to be helping the next generation. It's the least I can do for Red's daughter."

I liked hearing that. It had been a while since I had thought of myself as a daughter. Maybe I was misreading Joe. Maybe he just needed to feel like a father as much as I yearned to be a daughter again.

"You know I'm retired," he continued, "and sometimes I get kind of bored. I don't have enough to do. I know people, I've got access to information, and maybe I can help you find her dad. I'm just offering."

I thanked him and promised I would call him if I needed assistance. In fact, I doubted I would ever make that call. Maybe it was a result of having grown up, from age eleven on, in an all-male household, but I had a very difficult time asking for help.

Abaco and I were about halfway down my block, going very slowly as Abaco sniffed every single bush and tuft of grass, when B.J.'s black El Camino pulled up alongside.

"I was hoping you'd be home," he said. "I brought dinner." He pointed to several white paper bags resting on the seat next to him.

"Great." I tried to sound enthusiastic. It's not that I wasn't happy to see him, but after living with him for a couple of months, I knew what his version of dinner might be. Granted, after two days of burgers, it would probably do me good, but why did B.J.'s version of good have to taste so yucky? "The cottage is open. I'll just let Abaco sniff a while longer, and I'll see you back there."

When I returned and let Abaco off the leash in the backyard, she ran straight back to the dock where B.J. sat with legs dangling over the water. She licked his ears, and he scratched hers. She soon began groaning in pleasure as his magic fingers did their work. I smiled as I sat next to them. I could relate.

B.J. handed me an icy Corona. He was drinking from a plastic bottle of Florida spring water. "The food's all ready, I just wanted to sit out here for a bit. Enjoy the river. How's the little Earth Angel doing?"

"Not good. I mean, she's recovering from the exposure at sea faster than expected, but something happened at the hospital today." I hesitated, reluctant to tell the story again, but B.J. just waited quietly until I was ready to start.

We watched a small outboard chugging its way up the river as I talked. An older black man and a boy were in the inflatable dinghy, but with a mere eight horsepower, the craft was barely able to make any headway against the current.

"I followed this one guy, a tall Haitian who was dressed and acting like an orderly. He seemed normal enough at the time. I even spoke to him, but I didn't realize until later that he was probably the one who did it."

"Did what, exactly?"

"Well, I don't really know for sure. That's where it gets weird. None of us saw it, and he was with her for only a few seconds. They couldn't find any evidence that he had fed her anything or given her an injection, but she acts like she's drugged or in a trance. There's a Haitian nurse who works there at Broward General. She as much as said that she thinks this guy put a curse on her. The kid won't talk. She just stares straight ahead. She acts like a zombie." I watched his face to gauge his reaction.

"Hmm. Zombies. Everybody in America hears 'Haiti' and thinks Voodoo and zombies."

"I said *like* a zombie. I don't think he really turned her into a zombie. I don't believe in that stuff."

"You don't?" B.J.'s eyebrows arched high.

"Hell, no."

"You might be surprised at what goes on down there. Don't be so quick to write it off as silly superstition. There's a great deal about this world that we still don't understand, that our science can't explain."

"Come on, B.J., zombies?"

"Haiti is so close to the United States, and yet we know almost nothing about it. Did you know, you can do graduate work in world religions in this country and never study Voodoo? Yet they're right there," he said, extending his arm out in front of him, his flat palm indicating how close. "Like six million of them, and nearly all of them are Voodoo practitioners. There's a saying: 'Haiti is ninety percent Catholic and a hundred percent Voodoo.' "

I knew one of B.J.'s degrees was in comparative religions, but I didn't know his expertise extended to Voodoo. "How much do you know about it?"

"Not that much. I've read some. I know that it is a real religion, even if to most Westerners it sounds like a bunch of superstitious mumbo jumbo. But if you think about it, Christianity would sound that way if you were hearing about it for the first time."

"Okay, but we don't go poking little pins in dolls."

He rolled his eyes at me. "Sey, Voodoo is a monotheistic religion, which means its followers believe in one supreme being. Not so different, right?"

"Okay." I smiled. It was really fun sometimes to poke at him when he got all serious. "But what about the zombies and the dolls?"

He ignored my question. "Voodoo originated in West Africa, and in the last three centuries, a lot of Catholicism has been blended into the mix. Voodooists believe in over two hundred different spirits, and many of them are now intertwined with Catholic saints. For example, an altar to their mother spirit—I forget her name—might include photos or statues of the Virgin Mary. They call upon these spirits much as Catholics call upon their saints."

"Geez, B.J., should I be taking notes?"

He squinted. "You're making fun of me."

"No. It's just that you're very cute when you lecture."

He smiled. "Sorry. Didn't mean to get carried away. Sometimes I can't help it."

"I know."

"I've just always felt that Haiti and her culture have gotten a bad rap. Like you said, you thought this child was acting like a zombie. That's how most Americans see Haiti: black magic, Voodoo dolls, witchcraft, zombies. It's not your fault. You've been fed that image. When a Voodooist enters into a trance—or is 'possessed'—it is an absolutely amazing thing to see. I've only seen it on video, myself. These people are in altered states brought about by their spiritual beliefs. You said this girl Solange has had a curse put on her. Whether you believe in such things or not doesn't really matter. We may not share her beliefs, but she is in an altered state, and she needs a *hougan* or a *mambo* to help her get out of it."

My head jerked up. "What did you say?"

"That's what you call the priests and priestesses of Voodoo. The men are called *hougans* and the women are called *mambos.*"

"This morning I visited this woman, Racine Toussaint. Remember? From that card I found on the *Miss Agnes?* I met her husband, but I couldn't see her, he said, because she was too busy. I liked him, but there was something creepy about the house and how he acted. But he referred to her as *Mambo* Racine. He asked me to bring Solange back to see the *mambo.*"

"It could be your best bet for this kid. If it is Voodoo that has caused her to be in this state, it's going to take Voodoo, not Western medicine, to cure her."

I brought my heels up to the edge of the dock and wrapped my arms around my legs. Part of me wanted to curl into a ball and make all this go away. "B.J., I don't know what to believe. It was pretty strange today up in Pompano. I wish you could have been there. This house, this man, the way he talked about stuff I didn't really understand. And then he got all agitated when I told him about the body of that woman who was found in the boat with Solange. He kept repeating her name over and over. He said, 'Erzulie, Erzulie, I wonder if *Mambo* Racine knows' or something like that."

B.J. snapped his fingers and pointed at me. "That's it. That's the name I couldn't remember. Erzulie is the name of the Voodoo mother spirit."

—

B.J. had already set the table with place mats and napkins and little paper packets of wooden chopsticks. All the junk that had been on the table was neatly stacked on the bar that separated my kitchen from the combination living room/dining room. In the center of the table was a plate that contained what looked like an assortment of colorful little packages, like a miniature birthday party. None of it looked like anything I would refer to as food.

"What's that?" I pointed to the pile of presents.

"Sushi," he said with a mischievous smile. "You're gonna love it."

That was B.J. He knew very well that I was not going to love it. I don't like being forced to try new things. Especially pretty things. Food was not supposed to be that pretty.

I piled twin peaks of white rice and some kind of noodles onto my plate and then took the smallest, least fancy-looking little package. B.J. just sat there beaming.

"Aren't you going to eat?" I asked him.

"Yeah, eventually. I just don't want to miss any of this." He nodded in the direction of my plate.

With the wooden chopsticks in hand, I grasped the sushi roll and nibbled a little off one end. It wasn't half bad. B.J. looked so expectant. He didn't think I could do it. Just to show him I wasn't a total wuss, I chomped off a big bite.

The heat started to grow in my mouth. In an instant, my tongue felt like it had turned into glowing charcoal briquettes. After nearly tripping over my chair, I made it to the fridge, grabbed a beer, twisted off the top, and began to chug-a-lug.

B.J. almost fell out of his chair, he was laughing so hard.

"What the hell was that?" I said before taking another swig of beer.

"You picked the one that Sagami's refers to as the kamikaze roll." He took a deep breath and tried to make his face look serious. "They're not all hot like that. Try another."

"Oh, sure," I said.

B.J. was trying so hard to control his laughter, but his chest and shoulders kept bouncing as more chuckles burbled to the surface.

I finished the beer, then crossed back to the table and proceeded to drown the rice and noodles on my plate in soy sauce. I pushed the grains of rice around my plate, not eating and not talking. I refused to look up, even when I heard his chair scrape back and B.J. came up behind me and put his fingers on my shoulders. Ever since I was a little girl with two older brothers, I've turned very cranky whenever anybody teased me, which was fairly often.

His fingers pushed deep into the tense muscles on either side of my neck, and I tried, unsuccessfully, to suppress the little shiver that ran up my back. The heat from his touch traveled down my arms and made my fingers tingle. Actually, my fingers weren't the only part of me tingling. He alternated deep muscle massage with a feather touch on my neck. I knew I should tell him to stop. He wasn't playing fair. We were supposed to be taking a break, but when I opened my mouth to speak, he ran his hands down my arms, and all that came out were two sharp little gasps for breath. I turned, looked up at him, and then closed my eyes.

I was the first one to push back and break away from the kiss.

"B.J., I—"

He walked around the table, sat, and, smiling, filled his plate with the colorful rolls and began to eat with those precise bites of his, the careful chewing. He was wearing a bright yellow T-shirt with some kind of surfer logo on the front. The fabric set off his teak-colored skin. I watched him fork the last bite of a roll into his mouth, watched his full lips as he chewed.

I was still trying to catch my breath and make the aching go away, and he acted as though nothing had happened.

"Good sushi, huh?" he asked, his eyes sparkling with the message that he was enjoying every moment of my misery.

Why was I pushing this man out of my life? Okay, so he ate weird food. But otherwise, what was the problem? That he wanted to start a family? I thought of Joe, yearning to retrieve his lost family. And then there was Collazo. Geez, I sure as hell didn't want to end up like Collazo. Was my life alone with my dog and my boat really such a great life?

That was it: The answer was yes. I enjoyed my river, my routines, my rhythms. That was how I defined myself. Sometimes, when making love to B.J., it felt as though *I* disappeared, *I* became pure sensation—

and it scared the hell out of me. What if I gave in to that, and the me I now know turned into something else? And worse yet, if I let that happen, and B.J. did as B.J. had always done, what would I have left after he went away?

He wiped his mouth carefully with his napkin, crumpled it, and tossed it onto his plate. I glanced down at my still-folded napkin on the table. Oh yeah, I thought. I kind of forgot about that. It's not something I worry about when it's just me and Abaco. I wiped my own mouth.

"What's all that stuff?" B.J. pointed at the gear in the corner of the living room.

"Pit's in town," I said, glad that we had found a neutral subject to discuss so my heart rate could ease back to normal. "He dropped that off here this morning, talked to the gardeners, and left me a note. Then took off to go windsurfing. Typical, huh?"

He nodded. "It'll be good to see him. How long is he going to stay?"

I shrugged. "You never know with Pit. I'm sure it won't be long, though." I got up from the table and walked over to the pile of gear. "I have a feeling he'll be asking me to store some of this stuff." I pointed with my shoe at the green footlocker. "Like this, for example."

"Yeah, too much for traveling the way he does. Not his style." He got up from the table and began to clear the dishes.

I dragged the footlocker out into the middle of the room and sat on the floor next to it. "He said he'd been storing this over at his old girlfriend's. I think she got tired of having his junk around." I ran my hand over the top of the trunk. "I haven't seen this trunk in years. I remember it was in the garage at the house after Red died, but I didn't know Pit had taken it. There was so much stuff to be dealt with, I guess when this disappeared, I never even noticed."

B.J. came over and sat on the floor next to me. He rested his hand on my thigh, and I jumped a little. "This was your dad's?"

I nodded, started to say yes, but my throat seemed to close on the word. It's funny how you just never knew when it was going to hit you, that feeling in the center of your chest of missing someone so much. There were lots of times I could talk about my dad without feeling the slightest bit of sadness, and other times when I just wanted to see him again and couldn't speak without my voice getting tight and my eyes going all blurry. I swallowed and blinked and started again. "When we were kids, Pit and I used to sneak out into the garage and pull this trunk down and get into it even though we weren't supposed to. Mostly, Red kept his mementos from the navy in here, uniforms, old letters, and photos and stuff. He didn't really want his kids getting into it, which, of course, only made it all that much more attractive to us. One time we even tried on Red's uniforms."

I reached for the brass latches and tried to loosen them. The metal was corroded, green with flaking brown bits. The hinges screeched as they gave way and both latches opened. The smell of musty books, damp wool, and mothballs triggered another montage of memory as I closed my eyes and inhaled deeply. I saw my father, back when he seemed so big, bellowing at us, telling us to stay out of the garage, out of his trunk, away from his tools and all his gear. My father, who fell apart after Mother died, until one day when there was no more food in the house and Pit was crying because Maddy was beating on him. That day Red had come into my room and taken me and my brothers to the Winn Dixie and bought boxes of macaroni and cheese and cans of soup. He learned to cook and clean and wash and made us do our share and brought some order to the house and our family and our lives. And then I saw the three of us, his grown children, so lost that morning after his death. When, by two in the afternoon, all the paramedics and cops had gone, and they had taken his body away, we didn't know what to do with ourselves. We wandered from room to room, out to the dock and then to the garage, and back into the house, not one of us knowing what to say or do for the others, each of us so alone in our loss and unable to imagine our lives continuing without Red.

The footlocker was only about half-full, just as I remembered it. It didn't look as though Pit had disturbed the contents. I wondered if he had ever opened it or if he just took it out of the house and stored it at Tina's, unopened.

I reached in and ran my fingertips over the navy wool of the peacoat, remembering how silly Pit had looked wearing the huge thing. He'd never had the shoulders of his father. Maddy was built more like Red, while Pit had the slim build of our mother.

"You're lucky," B.J. said. "I never knew my father. When I was young,

I used to make up stories about him—my father, the hero. My mother was a Polynesian dancer, and I spent lots of time in dressing rooms reading books, making up my own stories." He pointed to the contents of the trunk. "Your dad really was a hero in the navy, and then saving boats and lives with his tug."

"Yeah, he was." I paused to get my voice under control.

The way we were sitting, our knees nearly touching, made it easy for him to reach up and give my shoulder a reassuring squeeze. Then he pointed into the trunk. "What are those pictures?"

Some were scattered loose and others were bound into packets. A yellowed envelope contained a few dozen slides. Reaching for a packet of photos, I explained. "Mother was into photo albums and organizing pictures into books and all that. Each of us kids had a baby book. I remember she used to ask Red to give her these photos so she could put them into a book, and they argued about it. He didn't want her to touch them. I was just a kid, I may not have even understood what the arguments were about, but I knew it was a big deal. It would usually send my mother into one of her bad spells."

My mother had her good days and her bad days. Today, she probably would be diagnosed with bipolar disorder, but back then Red just told us our mother had her moods. When things were good, she laughed and painted and took us on adventures and picnics, and she made the world seem a brighter, more wonder-filled place. When she was having her bad spells, however, we had to tiptoe around the house and take meals to her in bed. I remembered feeling that I wanted her to be the mom, to take care of us, and the fact that it was often the other way around didn't seem fair. I was eleven years old the day she just walked out into the water and drowned on a calm day off Hollywood Beach. I was the only one of the family with her that day, and I failed to stop her, failed to save her.

I picked up the packet of photos. When I pulled on the rubber band, the old rubber snapped and fell in a limp tangle onto the blue wool jacket. The photos spilled across the contents of the trunk, and several fell to the floor outside the trunk. They were all color photos, but most of them had a greenish tint, as though they had been exposed to too much heat before developing. They were boating pics, shots of people standing around on a sailboat, working the sails, talking on the docks. I didn't recognize the place, but as I picked them up and stacked them on my lap, I did recognize in one photo a much younger version of my father.

I angled the photo toward the late-evening light slanting through the cottage's kitchen windows. Instead of the big square man I remembered, the man in the photo had broad shoulders that narrowed to slender hips. He was wearing swimming trunks that showed his well-muscled legs. He still had the red beard, but his hairline was different, his forehead less broad. I had been looking so intently at this younger version of my father, I had not paid much attention to the other man in the photo. It wasn't until I turned the photo over and looked at the back that I realized why he looked familiar. In pencil on the back, Red had scrawled, "With Joe D'Angelo, Cartagena, 1973."

I flipped the photo over and looked more closely at the man standing opposite my father. He, too, wore a mustache and beard, brown, streaked with blond, like a golden halo surrounding his mouth. I recognized the eyes, and then the legs, of course. Where Red looked like he was in his late thirties, Joe looked like he was ten years younger. They were horsing around, acting as though they were fighting over a dock line, but they were smiling. The yacht in the background was a classic wooden schooner, gleaming white hull, pristine bright work, the name *Nighthawk* in gold leaf on the bow.

My mother had often talked about this trip. She brought it up several times when she was arguing with Red over something, and she'd asked him why he didn't go into the yacht delivery business because he had made so much money on that *Nighthawk* trip. I had no memory of his leaving—I was only three years old in 1973—but I seemed to remember hearing that he had been gone for two or three months.

The way I'd heard it, he had been just over halfway through the building of *Gorda.* I'd seen photos of the aluminum hull, deck, and deckhouse all taking shape over time amid the sheds and changing backdrop of boats at Summerfield Boatworks. He eventually got to the point of nearly finishing, but he still needed to power his new boat. He was out of money and in danger of never finishing, of having to go to work for somebody else. He had thought his pension from the navy would stretch further than it did. That was when he got this offer to go down to Colombia and help a friend deliver a schooner back to Fort

Lauderdale. When he got back, he'd made enough money to buy the engine and finish off the boat. *Gorda* was launched in early 1974.

When Joe said he and Red had worked together, why hadn't he mentioned this adventure?

"You know that guy?"

"Huh?" I looked up and blinked, tried to focus on B.J.'s face. The last of the light was leaving the room; I would need to turn on a light soon.

"You're staring at that picture as if you know that guy."

"Yeah, well, it's pretty weird. The guy in this picture is Mike's buddy. You know, the guy from yesterday who was on the *Outta the Blue,* who'd been out fishing with Mike all night? Mike tried to make out like the dead battery was this guy's fault. He said the guy wanted to turn on every light on the boat." Mike had made it sound like Joe didn't know much about boats. Had that been Mike's way of shifting the blame? Joe knew a hell of a lot more than Mike if he was on a delivery crew back in the seventies.

B.J. leaned in close to examine the photo. "Odd coincidence, huh?"

"I'll say. But it gets weirder. I ran into him again this morning down on the beach. He told me that he knew Red, but he didn't mention that they'd been on this." I pointed to the photo. "He said back when he was with the DEA, when they used to impound drug boats, he'd hire Red to move them around."

B.J. picked up the photos that had scattered when the rubber band broke, and he was leafing through them. "He's in a quite a few of these other photos, but there aren't any more of the two of them together." He straightened the photos into a neat pile and handed them to me. "Do you think this Joe guy was with the DEA back when these photos were taken?"

"How should I know? He was pretty young then."

"I don't mean to belabor the obvious, Seychelle, but think about it—DEA, Cartagena, *Colombia,* you know. What do you know about this trip your dad was on?"

My mind was still trying to comprehend that Joe and my father had been more than just client and captain. It took me several seconds to get what B.J. was hinting at. "B.J., you are out of your mind! You knew

Red. Just a minute ago you were calling him a hero. Do you think for one minute that he would get involved with something like that?"

"Money makes people do the unexpected. You know that."

I dropped the photos back in the trunk and slammed the top closed. "We're not going to talk about this any longer." I stood up and looked at the clock on the wall over the kitchen stove. "It's almost nine o'clock already. Where the hell is Pit?"

B.J. came up behind me and placed his hands on my shoulders. "I didn't mean to offend you, Sey."

"I don't want to talk about it," I said, jerking my shoulders and walking away, out of his reach. "I'm tired, B.J. I just want to go to bed." I opened the front door for him. "Tomorrow I've got to start looking for this kid's father, and I don't even know where or how to start."

He stopped in the doorway and turned to face me, our bodies less than a foot apart. "Seychelle, please. Don't push me away." I looked past him at the trunks of the oak trees barely visible in the starlight. I knew if our eyes connected, something inside me would start to collapse, to go soft and cave in.

"B.J., don't. Not tonight."

"You know, Seychelle," he said as he reached out and tucked a strand of my wayward hair behind my ear, "what happened between us these past few months has been extraordinary. You're feeling it, too, and it scares you. I can see that. That's why you wanted to step back for a little while. You need to breathe. You are a very independent woman. That's a large part of what I find so attractive about you, and I want you to know, I'm not trying to change you. It's just that I've known many beautiful and amazing women in my life, but not one of them has ever felt like family. Everything's different with you. When we are together, I feel like I am home."

My heart had just gone from zero to sixty in under ten seconds, and I felt light-headed. Family! That meant a mommy, a daddy, and one point two children. I didn't fit in that picture. What kind of mother could I possibly be? I didn't even know what to do for a ten-year-old girl, much less an infant. And when it came to mothering, what kind of chance did I have? Look at the role model I'd had.

He was going to outwait me. Silence had never bothered B.J. He was just going to stand there, waiting for me to say something. I inhaled the smell of his sweat, his coconut soap, and the faint lingering odor of the Japanese food. Damn him. More than anything I wanted to mold my body against his, take him into my room, rip off his clothes, and lose myself in our lovemaking. And I knew if I did, it would mean I had made a decision I was not yet ready to make.

"B.J., just go. Okay? This is not a good night for this. Tonight, I just need to rest. I can't—" I couldn't what? Look at his eyes? "Night," I said.

I closed the door and leaned back against it, and when I heard the gate close behind him, I wondered if I would ever have a really good night again.

xii

About the time I figured out that the ringing sound was the phone, and I realized I had better pull myself out of the depths of sleep to answer it, the answering machine clicked on, and I heard myself saying, "I'm either not home or out on the boat, so call me on channel sixteen or leave a message here. Bye."

After the beep, I heard Perry Greene's voice. "Seychelle, get your butt out of bed, honey. I know you're there."

I wanted to bury my head under the pillow and make him go away, but since the only reason Perry would be calling me at home at that hour would be for some kind of work, I reached over and lifted the phone on my nightstand.

"Shit, Perry, what time is it?"

"There's my darlin'. It's what, five-thirty? Hell, the sun'll be up any minute now. I knew I could call you 'cuz I bet a foxy chick like you is up at the gym every morning making your hard little body even harder."

"Perry, this little body of mine is two inches taller and about the same weight as your scrawny ass. What do you want?"

"I'm offering you an employment opportunity, sugar."

As much as I detested the thought of working with this sleaze, I couldn't afford to turn down a job. That *Miss Agnes* job had been my only work in the past week. "When, where, and how much?"

"I got a job moving some eighty-foot Eye-talian motor yacht from Port Everglades up to River Bend. This is an important dude. We're talking future jobs here. It's gonna need boats bow and stern. My cousin Leroy was gonna handle the aft end with his launch, but I just found out he got into a little trouble at Flossie's last night."

I sat up and swung my legs over the side of the bed. The size of the boat told me the paycheck would be enough to make working with Perry worth it. "A little trouble?"

"Well, Leroy didn't know the guy had a knife! Anyways, it's not so bad 'cording to my auntie, just a few slashes. He's over at Broward General now, but we're coming up on slack high water at nine this morning."

"I'll only do it if you'll go fifty-fifty."

"Damn, girl. It's my job."

"And you need me. Take it or leave it, Perry."

He barely paused a beat. "All right. The boat's called *O Solo Mio*, and she's berthed between cruise ships right on the commercial dock. You can't miss her. Be there by eight."

He'd given in too easily. That could only mean he was hiding something.

I was famished after last night's sushi, but I didn't feel like driving anywhere. I had no fresh milk for cereal and no bread for toast. When all else fails, I turn to a supply of toaster waffles I keep in the freezer. I knocked the clumps of frost off a couple of waffles by slamming them into the side of the sink half a dozen times, then dropped them into the toaster. With the coffee water heating and the waffles sizzling, I walked over and lifted the lid to Red's trunk and took out the stack of photos. While I ate the waffles with my fingers, licking off the syrup and washing it down with two cups of coffee, I sorted through all the photos in the trunk, dividing them into two piles—those taken on the yacht delivery trip, and all the rest. If I'd had more time, I might have been interested in some of the old pictures of my parents hanging out together before they became my parents, or the photos of Red with his navy buddies, but right now, I just wanted to learn what I could about that trip back in the spring of 1973.

There were six photos of the trip, and I counted four recognizable characters. Besides Red and Joe, there was a young woman and another man with a big black walrus mustache and one of those awful boxy seventies hairdos. There was something odd about his face, as though it weren't quite symmetrical, but I couldn't really identify what was off.

He was shorter than Red and bowlegged. He looked a good deal like that character in the cartoons—Yosemite Sam. He seemed to be the head honcho. Maybe he was the hired captain of the boat, maybe the owner. I doubted that last, though. He didn't look much older than thirty, and even back in 1973, a schooner like the *Nighthawk* was very expensive to buy and even more to maintain. Trying to keep a wooden hull in that kind of shape in the tropics was like fighting a constant war against marine borers, termites, dry rot, the tropical sun, and electrolysis. Classic boats were beautiful to look at, but I sure as hell was glad that there were other people out there working on them, not me.

One of the photos showed a close-up of Yosemite Sam's face, and I noticed that a wide scar cut through his left eyebrow and the two halves of the eyebrow didn't align quite right. Whoever had stitched him up had left him with a zigzag look. His nose had been broken as well, and the skin of his face was deeply pockmarked, probably from acne.

I slid the photos into my shoulder bag with the idea that, at some point in the day, I would head over to Mike's and ask him what he knew about his buddy Joe. Then I dug around in my bag for the Post-it that Collazo had given me with the name of the Haitian translator. The number was for the radio station where the police translator, Martine Gohin, worked. When I dialed it, an answering machine picked up. I left a message explaining to Ms. Gohin that Collazo had given me her name and that I wanted to ask her some questions about Solange.

Perry's boat, *Little Bitt,* was already tied up astern of the Italian mega-yacht when I throttled *Gorda* down in the Port Everglades turning basin. Perry was on the bow of *O Solo Mio,* readying the towlines. As I knew he would, he motioned me to tie up off the bow. This meant I would end up the head boat, and what had started as Perry's job was now mine. Not a problem. *Gorda* had more power than *Little Bitt,* and I had more experience than Perry at this type of work.

The tricky part of towing yachts this size up a narrow river is that boats get steerage only from moving at a certain speed through the water. If there is no water flowing past her rudders, a boat cannot turn. With the help of twin screws and bow thrusters, some boats are able to spin in their own lengths, but a boat like *O Solo Mio* still did not have brakes. The regulations required that vessels of a certain length and draft be assisted by a tug when going upriver. So, with five drawbridges standing between Port Everglades and the upriver boatyard facilities, as well as riverbanks that were lined with millions of dollars' worth of yachts and properties, there was always plenty of business for *Gorda.*

For three to four miles inland, the river remained tidal so that it reversed its flow with each change of the tide. When towing a vessel, it was always preferable to tow against the current so that *Gorda* and her tow could be moving at five knots through the water, but actually only be moving at three knots over the bottom and past the riverbanks. I also had to be concerned about depth because there were spots where the river shallowed up to six or seven feet at low water. The trick was to tow upriver just after high tide while the water was still deep but the current was flowing downriver.

After I tied up *Gorda,* I went to check Perry's work with the towing harness. Not that I didn't want to trust him, but, well, I couldn't afford to trust him. With every job, I put the name and reputation of Sullivan Towing and Salvage on the line. I could get away with an occasional screw-up in many other aspects of my life, but when it came to towing somebody's multimillion-dollar vessel, that's where I became a perfectionist. And my insurance agent appreciated it.

Up on *O Solo Mio*'s bridge, I introduced myself to the yacht's captain. An Italian in his mid-forties, he had the classic good looks—strong chin and alert eyes—of many yacht captains. I swear they must ask for photos when they advertise for these positions. I'd never seen an ugly one. Apparently, if you are going to drive the yachts of the rich and famous, you must be one of the beautiful people yourself.

He told me to call him Salvatore instead of Captain Lucca, and he asked me if I wanted a tour of the boat. That is one of the best parts of my job—getting to see how the other half lives. Through the main salon with the sleek, mirrored, and brushed-stainless built-in furnishings—including wet bar, stereo, and large-screen TV—he took me through to the owner's stateroom. I half expected a sound track of jungle animal noises to be playing. The whole room was decorated in exotic animal prints, and in the middle of the cabin was a perfectly round bed that sported a mosquito net draped from above. On the walls were dozens of pictures of the owner and his friends. I was admiring the photos—one with former president Nixon, another with Frank Sinatra. Then I recognized a face.

"Salvatore, who owns this boat?"

In the photo I was examining, a group of ten men, all smiling for the camera, sat around a table in a brick-walled restaurant. One face stood out. I recognized the big handlebar mustache, the zigzag eyebrow. An older version, by maybe ten years, of Yosemite Sam from the *Nighthawk* photos.

"He is a businessman in New York City."

"What does he do?"

"I've been with him for eighteen years—precisely because I don't ask exactly what he does."

He was smiling at me, a twinkle of humor and flirtation in his eyes. I was beginning to understand what Perry hadn't told me about this job.

"I see."

"I believe you have been on the water long enough," he said, "to know exactly what I am talking about."

Perry's face appeared in the stateroom's doorway. "What are you guys doing farting around down here?"

"Captain Lucca here was just showing me around the boat. We were talking about the owner."

"Hell of a guy," Perry said, and he gave me an exaggerated wink. "I hear he's an importer."

Behind Perry, I saw Salvatore frown. Obviously, Perry did not share his discretion. But he had kept the yacht owner's affiliations secret from me long enough to get me on the job. Perry knew I usually chose not to work on these yachts.

Perry came up behind me and peered at the photo I had been examining. "Hey, I know that guy." He pointed to the man with the handlebar mustache. "That's Gil." Then he snorted and pulled at the crotch of his pants. "Man, he was just as ugly back then."

"How do you know him?" I asked.

"Huh?"

Perry had a habit of spacing out in the middle of a conversation. Though he generally wasn't under the influence when he was working, even when he wasn't high, Perry wasn't all that coherent.

"The guy in the picture," I said. "How do you know him?"

"Oh, yeah, me'n him done some drinking in Flossie's a time or two. That's all. Was nothin'." There was clearly more to that story. Perry was a lousy liar.

"Do you know his last name?"

"Nah, just Gil. Dude's been around forever."

I turned to the captain and asked him if he knew the man in the photo.

He shook his head. "No, that photo was from many years ago. Before I came aboard."

Perry pulled at the front of his pants again. I was about to ask him if he had to go to the bathroom, the way my brother Maddy always asked his son, Freddy, before getting into the car, but then Perry said, "We gotta get going, you guys. Tide's turnin'." He was right.

After a quick peek into the engine room and a check on deck, Perry, Salvatore, and I met to go over the plan. The deckhand was given his instructions. We all decided to monitor VHF channel 72, and then we got underway. Red had taught me that the trick to maintaining control of a large yacht was in using two short towlines or hawsers. *Gorda* had port and starboard towing bitts located in each corner of her stern. With the short hawsers that ran from those bitts up through the chocks on either side of the bow of the Italian yacht, I could quickly and efficiently turn the ship as we made our way upriver. As we negotiated each bend of the river with *Gorda*'s Caterpillar engine revved up, pulling the more than fifty tons of aluminum, and *Little Bitt* pulling the yacht's stern around, I went through the motions on mental autopilot, all the while thinking about a trip down island back in 1973. Whoever this Gil character was, he clearly had connections with some serious New York wise guys.

xiii

As soon as I finished adjusting the spring line and getting *Gorda* safely secured to her dock back at the Larsens' place, I glanced toward my cottage and saw the Windsurfer board and sail spread out to dry on the grass. I gave a whoop and started running. Pit must have heard me because he stepped out the front door and threw his arms around me just as I arrived.

"Hey, little sis," he said, and stepped back, putting his elbow on my head to show me how much taller he was than me, just as he had when we were kids. "Great to see you."

I pushed him away and held him at arm's length. "Where the hell have you been? You drop your stuff off here and then disappear for days. What kind of way is that to treat your baby sister?"

He just grinned that lopsided grin of his and shrugged. "Didn't know you were going to try to be your brother's keeper. I'm not used to telling anybody where or when I go."

"Man, it's good to see you." I hugged him once more, then slipped past him into the shade of the cottage's cool interior. "Come on in and tell me what's been going on in your life."

I grabbed a couple of cold beers out of the fridge. It was early, but seeing Pit was worth celebrating. We sat at opposite ends of the couch as he told me a little about what it's like to be an ocean nomad. He had crewed on the delivery of an eighty-foot racing sailboat down to Rio, flown over to South Africa for some world championship windsurfing tournament, then spent six months in Europe windsurfing the Med's mistrals. Finally, he'd come back here via the Caribbean and another yacht delivery into Fort Lauderdale.

"So," I said, "I take it I'm not to expect you to settle down and produce a sister-in-law or any nieces or nephews any time soon?"

He smiled and rubbed his chin for a moment as if he were thinking real hard. "Nope."

"You goofball," I said, and kicked him lightly in the shins.

He set his beer down on the end table, turned to me, and narrowed his eyes. "That a challenge?"

"No way," I said. "Our years of wrestling are over." But knowing my brother, I placed my beer bottle safely on the other end table. "We're supposed to be grown-ups now, you know."

I had barely gotten the last words out before he pounced on me, rolled me off the couch, and had me pinned with my arm twisted up behind my back. "Gonna say uncle?" he shouted.

What he didn't know was that his little sis had been taking some aikido lessons from B.J., and with a simple twist and roll I was out of his grip and standing on the other side of the trunk that still rested in the middle of the living room. He looked up at me from the floor.

"Damn. Not bad." He crossed his arms behind his head and, looking up at me, said, "So, what about you? You and B.J. going to be ringing the wedding bells soon?"

I waved my hand in the air as though to dismiss the question. "Let's not go there. That's a bit of a sore spot these days."

He laughed. "Hell, we Sullivans make damn lousy spouses, eh?"

"Just look at Maddy," I said, and we both giggled.

Pit's laughter stopped abruptly, and he got to his knees and crawled over to the trunk. "You opened it," he said, suddenly solemn.

"Yeah. You just left it here and disappeared."

"I wanted to open it, you know. But something stopped me."

At that moment, I didn't want Pit to know about the Cartagena trip and all the questions it had raised. I didn't want him to feel what I had been feeling, wondering if Red had been involved in drug smuggling. "Yeah, it's just a bunch of old stuff." I grabbed the stack of photos off the counter, dropped them into the trunk, and started to close the lid.

"Wait, I'd forgotten all about this old jacket." He reached in and pulled out Red's old navy peacoat. The musty smell of the wool filled the room when he stood, shook the coat out, and slid his arm into one of the sleeves. It still didn't fit him.

"Remember?" I asked.

"Yeah," he said, "that afternoon in the garage." His eyes seemed to be looking across the living room, but they weren't really focused on anything in that room. He grinned. "I can still hear him yelling at us."

I touched the sleeve of the coat. In spite of having been closed up in that trunk for years, it still harbored a faint hint of Red's smell. I stepped toward Pit and pressed my nose into the rough fabric of the coat's sleeve and tried to remember my father as he was when he was healthy. I put my arms around my brother and inhaled deeply the odor still living in the wool.

"Some days I miss him so much," I said in a half-whisper.

"I know," he said. "Me too. Sometimes I wonder if that's why I keep moving all the time. Keeps me from thinking about what I don't have."

I pushed back and took hold of his hands. "Hey, you've still got a family. I'm here. Maddy is, too."

"Do we have to count him?" he asked, and we both laughed again.

"We really lucked out in the father department," I said, "but how Red could have sired Maddy, I'll never know."

Pit started to take off the jacket. "You know, it's not nearly as much fun making fun of him when he's not here to turn all red and get pissed off. What do you say we go down to see him and torture him like we used to?" This time when he laughed, it helped make the tightness in my throat ease off. God, I'd missed Pit.

"I'm afraid Maddy wouldn't exactly be happy to see me."

"Why do you say that?"

"It's a long story, but a few months back he got down several thousand dollars at the track, and some not-so-nice guys I'd been involved with kinda took it out on him. Really did a number on his face. Later, when I bought him out of *Gorda* and he paid off his bookie, he didn't cut me any slack. Still maintains the whole thing was my fault."

"Sounds like my bro."

When we'd first come in, I had noticed the red light was blinking on my answering machine, but I had wanted to take these few minutes to catch up with Pit first.

"Hope you don't mind, but I've got to check this." I pushed the button and a female voice, slightly accented, started to speak.

"Allo. This is Martine Gohin." I sat down on the couch and lowered my head over the machine, anxious to hear every word she would say. "I heard about this Earth Angel child on the television, and I would like to help you very much. I am working on my radio show this morning, but if you could join me at my home for lunch, that would be very nice." She went on to give her address and cell phone number. I checked my watch. I had about an hour to spare—just enough time to swing by and check on Jeannie and Solange.

When the machine clicked off, Pit asked, "Earth Angel? What are you into now?"

I told him the most abbreviated version of the story that I could manage.

"Is there anything I can do to help?"

"Might be. How are your navigation skills?"

"Great. I was the navigator on the last delivery up from St. Maarten."

"Okay, then, here's the problem: I want you to find out how this kid and the dead woman ended up in that part of the ocean. If they weren't on the *Miss Agnes*, then I'm spinning my wheels trying to find folks who were aboard that boat. You'll find the position where I picked up the dory entered in *Gorda*'s log. The pilot charts are here in the cottage somewhere—probably at the top of my closet. I think Solange and that woman were set adrift from the *Miss Agnes* as she was making a run across the Gulf Stream. Problem is I can't quite make it all fit in my head. The *Miss Agnes* sank more than a day before I found the kid. Why hadn't they drifted much farther north if they were riding the Stream? Was there some kind of cross current? It would be great if you could find that out for me. Check the Gulf Stream stats for that date, call NOAA if you have to. Let's see if we can figure out where the boat set them adrift, and then where they might have their camp."

"Will do." Pit saluted me, then headed to the kitchen for another beer.

After changing from my work clothes into a clean pair of jeans and a Hawaiian print shirt, I jumped into Lightnin' and took off.

Jeannie lived in a neighborhood called Sailboat Bend, upriver from my house. Sprinkled throughout Sailboat Bend are some of the oldest houses in Fort Lauderdale, pretty little Key Westy Conch cottages, half of which were undergoing some form of rehab. The rest of the neighborhood is dominated by bleak cement blocks of government-subsidized housing, and the place Jeannie lived fell somewhere between the two extremes. Her apartment was on the second floor of a concrete-block building that dated back to the fifties. There were only four apartments in the building, and it was set back on a lushly landscaped lot and shaded by a huge hundred-year-old oak tree. The oak's trunk split into three parts right at ground level, and the nail holes throughout the branches were from all the different tree houses folks had built through the years. Hurricane Andrew had destroyed the last tree house, and Jeannie was petitioning her landlord to allow her to build a new one. Even without a tree house, the tree was her boys' favorite playground, and I was surprised, when I pulled into the yard, not to see them up there hanging from its branches.

At the top of the exterior staircase I called Jeannie's name through the screen door, hollering to be heard above the blasting TV. I recognized the music from *Sesame Street*. Assuming the kids were watching that TV in the family room, I imagined that someone could easily walk right in the front door and snatch a kid without being seen or heard. So far, I wasn't impressed with Jeannie's security.

"Morning!" shouted Jeannie. "Welcome to our madhouse." She punched several keys on an electronic keypad, then opened the door and waved me in.

"Geez, Jeannie. Wouldn't it be pretty easy for some crazed kidnapper to punch through that screen and snatch the kid?"

She smiled and pointed to the screen. "See that thread, how it's different? It's wired into the alarm system. I installed these screens last winter after an irate client's husband came gunning for me one night over a divorce I was working. I needed security, and I hate air-conditioning, so I wired the screens."

"Okay, I guess that'll work. So how is she?"

"Not much change. Come on and see for yourself."

She led me back to the apartment's third bedroom, which she had made into a family entertainment room with a big TV, video games, stereo, and shelves covered with children's books, toys, and puzzles. Jeannie's two boys sat cross-legged on the rug in front of the TV, chuckling at the antics of Cookie Monster. Behind them, Solange sat on the couch, limp, staring at the TV with unseeing eyes. Her eyes didn't even flicker when we came into the room.

I sat down on the couch next to her and put my arm around her thin shoulders. "Morning, kiddo." She didn't flinch, blink, or react at all. I could feel the bone and muscle through the thin white T-shirt, and her body felt stiff and rigid. It was as though there were something inside her, and she was holding on to keep it deep within. I looked up at Jeannie. "Has she eaten anything?"

"Not much. I spoon-fed her some applesauce, and I think some of that got down. She goes when I put her on the pot, but she won't get up and go by herself. I've never seen a kid in a state like this. It's kinda creepy."

I pulled her to me and rested my chin on her head. She smelled of Johnson's Baby Shampoo. Bill Cosby was on the TV making faces at Big Bird, and the boys on the floor were laughing. Jeannie disappeared down the hall.

I closed my eyes and squeezed her rigid, thin shoulders, trying to make her understand that I would do anything I could to make her pain go away. Even at twenty-seven years old, I had felt terribly abandoned when Red died, and I realized the term *orphan* applied to me. What would that feel like at her age? I had to find her father. I whispered into her hair, "Remember what I said before. Whatever it takes, I promise."

The phone started to ring as I walked out of the family room. Jeannie came out of the kitchen and handed me the portable. "It's for you."

"How do you know?"

"Trust me."

I pushed the button. "Hello?"

"What the hell were you thinking?"

"Good morning to you, too, Rusty."

"The hospital called the cops, you know. You're lucky you're not in jail right now. Only reason you aren't is because your lawyer called me, and I was able to give the cops a plausible story."

"Your concern is touching."

"I'm not kidding, Seychelle."

"Neither are the people who want to hurt this child."

"And you two think you can protect her better than the cops?"

"They got to her yesterday when she was under your protection, right?"

He sighed. "How is she this morning?"

"No different. Still looks like she's catatonic. But she's no worse, and nobody else has been able to get to her. We told you we would be bringing her to Jeannie's, and you agreed. What, you think we should have waited for you guys to churn out more paperwork and then leave a forwarding address with the hospital?"

"No, we don't work that way. You need to trust me a little more here, stop thinking you need to do this on your own. And I sure as hell don't like getting blindsided by cops asking where she's disappeared to. I look stupid if I don't have the answers."

"Well—"

"Hey, watch it."

"Leave me an opening like that, and I just can't resist."

"Yeah, yeah, that's what all the women tell me."

"Well, maybe I'd be nicer to you if you had offered to share your catsup with me."

On the other end of the phone I could hear someone talking to Rusty, then more muffled voices as he covered the phone with his hand and talked to someone who was, presumably, in his office. The conversation ended and Rusty came back on the line.

"Sorry about that," he said, his voice deep and serious. "Seriously, Seychelle, you've just got to stay in touch with me."

After our earlier conversation, I was tempted to ask him what part he wanted me to stay in touch with, but from the sound of his voice he was no longer in a mood to play.

"For now, she's in good hands here with Jeannie. What about you guys and the DART board? What have you and your friend Miss D'Ugard found out about who was behind the *Miss Agnes*?"

"We're working on it. That's not your concern." I wasn't sure whether he meant the working of DART or his friendship with Miss D'Ugard. He sounded peeved all of a sudden. "In fact, aside from the fact that you found her, what *is* your concern in this? Why not just turn her over to the authorities and get on with your life?"

Damn this man. One minute he wants to play, the next minute he's on the attack? "Rusty, if I were to walk away right now, what are her chances of staying in the States?"

"Honestly? Not good, unless someone can find a relative."

"And I'm working on that. That's your answer."

I found Jeannie in her study sitting at her computer, and I handed her the portable phone. "Mr. Rusty Elliot is not going to be much help in the Save Solange project."

"Typical bureaucrat."

"I don't know. I can't figure him out. One minute he's flirting and seems like he's going to help me out, the next minute he's Mr. Immigration drawing the line on 'undocumenteds,' as he calls them. Anyway, I've got to run around and see what I can find out about Solange's dad."

I hesitated before turning for the door, listening to the sounds of canned laughter from down the hall. "Collazo really thinks she's in danger, Jeannie. Maybe we should just let the cops look out for her. Are you sure you're all going to be okay here?"

Jeannie stood up to her full height and reached up to the top of the bookshelf in her den. She glanced at the door to make sure no kids were watching, then lifted up a shotgun. "I normally keep this baby locked up because of the kids, but I got it out last night. Nobody's gonna touch that kid."

I smiled at her. "And God help them if they try, right?"

Jeannie turned her head and winked at me. "Exactly."

Martine Gohin lived in Victoria Park, where most of the homes had been built in the fifties or earlier, little cinder-block two-bedroom, two-bath, tile-roofed bungalows. Since the early 1990s when the area became very popular, those little homes had sold for well over $200,000. Martine Gohin's house stood out on the street because of the color—a light salmon with cornflower blue shutters and a bright yellow door. She seemed to be making a statement with her colors, proclaiming her Haitian heritage in this mostly Anglo neighborhood.

A minivan was parked in the driveway, so I assumed she was home from her radio job.

The girl who answered the door smiled shyly when I told her who I was. Her hair was plaited like Solange's. She wore a simple white cotton shift, but her body had the ripe roundness of budding puberty. I guessed she was about thirteen years old. She motioned me to come in and kept her head lowered.

"Are you Mrs. Gohin's daughter?"

She shook her head and walked down the hallway, then pointed through the dining room to open French doors that led out to a wood deck. A very short black woman leaned over a glass table, arranging flowers in a vase, and she looked up when my sneakers squeaked on the dining room tile.

"Oh, allo. I did not hear the doorbell." She gripped my hand hard with her fat fingers. "I am Martine Gohin, and you must be Miss Seychelle Sullivan. I thought we would eat lunch out here on the deck." She swept her arm around in a 180-degree arc. "I love the fresh air."

The wood deck was elevated a couple of feet above the green lush foliage of her backyard. Huge fronds of elephant ears arched over the water of a pond full of colorful fish. I recognized banana and papaya trees, heliconias, orchids, birds of paradise. Her yard looked like something out of a magazine. "Wow, it's beautiful out here."

"I enjoy gardening," she said. She pointed to a cute little shed made to look like a cottage in the back of the yard. "I find it very relaxing to work out there. I have everything I need to pot and germinate many of my own seedlings. It is my passion."

The girl still stood at her side with her eyes downcast. When Martine turned to speak to the girl, she had to look up at the child. "*C'est tout,* Juliette."

Though Martine Gohin stood less than five feet tall, there was a sense of power about her. Her body was thick, and she wore dark glasses with heavy frames. I settled in the chair she indicated and accepted the tall glass of iced tea.

"So what can I do for you, Miss Sullivan?"

"I assume you know that I am the one who found the little girl they're calling the Earth Angel."

"Yes, the little Solange. I read about it in the paper."

"Let me explain what I'm trying to do, and then maybe the rest will make sense to you. See, when I found that girl two days ago, I told her—promised her, really—that I would do whatever I could to help her stay in this country."

"I wish more people felt as welcoming to Haitian immigrants."

"I know what you mean. But now the Immigration people tell me that the only way she can stay is if I find a relative. And since the girl told me her father is American, I'm determined to find him."

"She spoke to you? In English?"

"Yes."

"That is very strange. I saw her at the hospital. Twice, actually. I guess you know I work for the police sometimes as a translator, but when I saw her, she refused to speak. No Creole, no English, nothing. The police need to interview her if she is speaking now."

"Well, there's a problem." I told her there had been an incident at the hospital. "I'm afraid she's not talking to anybody right now. She's clammed up again. But that doesn't change anything about her status with Immigration. I need to find her father as soon as possible."

"How do you think I can help?"

"I want to talk to someone who came over on the *Miss Agnes,* the boat that sank off Deerfield. We know that quite a few people made it ashore, and we think Solange may have started out on that boat. Maybe one of the people aboard knows something about her or her family. I was hoping you could get my message out to the Haitian community on your radio show. If someone is willing to give some information, they can stay anonymous, I don't care, I just want to find her father—if he is, in fact, here."

She took a long drink from her iced tea, then called out, "Juliette." The child came scurrying out of the house with a platter of fish in one hand and a bowl of rice and beans in the other. Martine pointed to the food and said to me, "Please, help yourself."

For the next few minutes, she explained to me how Juliette had cooked the fish according to Haitian custom, and while this meal had been cooked on her electric stove, back in Haiti they had grown up eating the same food cooked over an open charcoal fire. As she spoke, the girl moved silently in and out, serving the food, clearing dishes, bringing more bread, filling our iced tea glasses. Through the French doors, I could see framed photos on the wall unit in the dining room. All were of two parents and a young girl about three years old.

"Is Juliette a relative of yours?" I noticed the girl shot a quick glance at Martine.

Martine wiped at her mouth and swallowed. "Yes, she is my niece. Her mother is still in Haiti, but I brought her here a few years ago so she could learn English and get an American education. I have a young daughter, Camille, who is away at her playgroup right now. Juliette is a great help with her, as well."

"Is that Camille in those photos?" I nodded toward the dining room.

"Yes," she said, and smiled broadly, showing very white straight teeth. "She just turned four last week."

"You are very lucky to have such a family. Two beautiful girls. Why doesn't Juliette pull up a chair and join us?" The girl slipped through the French doors into the house.

"That is not our custom in Haiti," Martine said, and then took an enormous mouthful of rice and beans that made further explanation impossible.

The fish was excellent, flavored with lime and some fiery spices. I waited to see Juliette again, to compliment her on her cooking, but she never reappeared.

By the time I left her house, Martine Gohin had agreed to broadcast a request for more information from anyone who was aboard or who knew anything about the *Miss Agnes* and her fate. She would ask her listeners to call the radio station, and she promised to pass on to me any tips that came her way.

When I walked out the finger pier next to *Outta the Blue,* **I saw** Mike down in his inflatable dinghy off the stern of his boat, staring up at his outboard where it rested on a flatbed dolly on the dock.

"Hey, buddy," I said, smiling. "Looks like you could use a hand getting that beast on your dink." The outboard was a twenty-five-horsepower four-stroke Honda, and it probably weighed over a hundred pounds.

"Whew, Seychelle, am I ever glad to see you. I could sure use an extra hand right now. An extra leg, too." He chuckled at his own joke.

"Don't tell me you've been considering trying to get that thing into your dinghy all by yourself?"

He grinned and shrugged. "Well, I guess I was. Joe helped me get it off the dink the other day and into his truck. We took it back to the dealer because it was running kind of rough. Anyway, I hated to have to call somebody and beg for help."

"Listen," I told him, "you've got to stop trying to think strong, tough guy on a boat. It doesn't work. I'm nowhere near as strong as most men in this business, but I can do it because I think smarter, not stronger."

In a few minutes, I had shown him how to use his sailboat's main boom as a crane and his mainsail sheet as a come-along. We used sail ties made of nylon webbing to fashion a harness around the outboard and winched it into the air. I swung the boom across the cockpit, then lowered the outboard over the side of the big sailboat and into the waiting dinghy. Mike slid it onto the transom of the inflatable as I fed out the line. Twenty minutes later, the job was done and we were tidying up the cockpit.

"Thanks, Seychelle. Come on below. I owe you a cold one for that. Then you can tell me why you really came over here today."

Dry, cool air tumbled out the passageway doors and chilled my ankles as I followed Mike down the companionway ladder. I slid the teak hatch closed and latched the clear Plexiglas doors. Down below, *Outta the Blue* resembled an air-conditioned condo more than a seagoing vessel. Back when he bought the used Irwin-54 with his generous retirement settlement, she had been neglected and needed a complete refit. Mike had refurbished her to suit his tastes. Since he had never had any boat bigger than a trailerable flats skiff, he had no idea what he was doing and the result was a vessel interior that looked something like a man's basement hideout. The TV sported video game controllers, and large speakers hung from the overhead in the four corners of the main salon. The chart table was weighted down with a full-size desktop computer with a seventeen-inch monitor. Where most boats use small portable electronic gear, Mike had installed household versions of everything from microwave to VCR. Then he'd allowed the old generator to seize up from lack of use, since he rarely if ever left the dock in those days.

He reached down into the top-loading refrigerator and offered me a frosty Corona. I waved it away.

"It's still a bit early for me, Mike." For a second beer, I thought, smiling at the memory of seeing Pit.

He poured himself some dark rum over ice. "So what's on your mind?" he asked when he finally settled into the other side of the dining booth in the main salon.

"I don't know where to start."

"I assume this is about the kid. The Haitian girl."

"Actually, no." I watched him finish that rum and pour himself a second. "How well do you know Joe D'Angelo?"

"Joe? What do you want to know about him for?"

I lifted my shoulder bag off the floor and unzipped the side pocket. I slid the photo across the table. Mike reached over to a small cubby by the chart table and retrieved some reading glasses. After adjusting them on his face, he examined the photo.

"Hmmm," he said as he held the photo far from his face and tried to focus. "Well, I'll be damned." He looked up over the top of the reading glasses. "What year was this taken?"

"Nineteen seventy-three. Do you know where it is?"

"I don't recognize it as any marina around here." He looked up, slid his glasses to the top of his head, and squinted his blue eyes at me. "Why is that important?"

"Look on the back."

He flipped the photo over and slid the glasses back down onto his nose. He let out a low whistle. "Cartagena." He rolled the *r* when he said the name of the city. He ran his fingers through his stubble, and I could hear the scratchy, sandpapery sound over the low hum of the air conditioner.

"So what do you make of that, Mike?"

"I don't know what to tell you, Sey. This is the first I've heard about this. Joe and Red? Hell, I didn't meet Joe until about eighty-five. Don't know for sure when he started with DEA. What do you know about this?"

"I found this picture and some others in Red's old trunk. I have very vague memories of that time, as I was only about three years old. I don't know if I remember Red's being gone, or if I just heard my folks argue about it so many times afterward that I think I remember it. Here's what I do know: My dad had just about finished building *Gorda* when he just plum ran out of money. Somebody offered him the opportunity to make a delivery on this big fancy yacht. The pay was going to be enough to buy the engine for the tug, and he'd only have to be gone a couple of months. Even as adults, Red and I never talked about it. When they used to argue, my mother would say that he made a better crew than captain. He would have made lots more money working on rich people's yachts than he ever did owning his own boat. Which was true, of course, but Red was never about making money. He just loved that tug." I had been listening to my own telling of the story. "I know it doesn't sound good, but I don't think either Red or Joe would have been involved with anything illegal."

The look on Mike's face worried me. He wasn't looking me in the eyes, and his lips were stretched thin. "Sey, I've seen too much of what people are capable of. Are you sure you want to go digging into this?"

I didn't say anything for a moment. Was I sure? How would I handle it if I found out my father had been involved with something illegal? No, the doubts were worse. I had to settle it.

"Mike, I need to know what really happened down there. Not knowing is the worst."

"Okay then, if that's really what you want, I'll be glad to help."

Mike sounded less convinced than resigned.

"First," he said, "I suggest we stop speculating and go talk to these fellas. See, the thing is, I know who this other guy in the picture is, too."

"The guy with the big mustache?"

"Yeah. And, Sey. The news is not good."

Mike had been planning on taking his dinghy out for a run to test the outboard that afternoon anyway, so we decided to run down the Intracoastal to the Dania Cut-off Canal and then up the canal inland to Pattie's Ravenswood Marina. I figured we'd be gone a couple of hours, and there wasn't much I could do for Solange at this point. Either that or I was rationalizing this trip because I wanted to know what had happened down in Colombia all those years ago.

Mike had tried to call Joe on his cell phone, but he got no answer. He left a message saying he'd just called to say hello, then he told me we'd try Joe again later. That gave us time to check out Gil first.

Mike's was a rigid-bottom inflatable with a center console. He was standing at the controls, his artificial leg strapped on below his knee and worn-out Topsiders laced onto both feet. I was holding on to the stainless-steel bars around the center console as he told me what he knew about Gil's background. The inflatable leapt onto a plane when we reached the Intracoastal Waterway, and I flexed my legs to take the pounding as we flew over boat wakes and the small chop from the southeasterly breeze.

According to Mike, the man's real name was Gilbert Lynch, and he had been a highflier in the drug trade in the 1980s. He had come to Florida from Georgia in the seventies, right after his return from Vietnam, and he had always retained his accent, beguiling his enemies with his slow country boy act and then brutally stomping them out. In his heyday, he used to fill his riverfront estate with his army buddies, and he liked fast motorcycles and faster women. Back in those days, Gil knew everybody in the importing business. He was a real player.

Like many dealers, however, Gil had sampled his own product a little too freely. He started a downhill slide after he fried a few too many brain cells. Mike explained that Gil kept getting busted and eventually lost everything, but he avoided any serious jail time by pleading that he was a psych case. The really big guys in New York never bothered to get rid of him, because, even with all the time he spent in jail, he never talked about their business. Mike said that just proves he's not as crazy as everybody thinks.

"Today, though, a lot of that has changed," Mike said as we passed the cruise liners and freighters in Port Everglades. "Several of the detectives have been using him as a snitch. Most of the people Gil hangs around think he's just another waterfront derelict. They say stuff around him, thinking he won't understand much. But as long as he keeps taking his meds, he can hold it together, and he's pretty smart. Well, crafty anyway. I don't even know if Gil's gonna remember anything from when those pictures were taken, but if he does, he'll probably tell you everything he knows for about twenty bucks."

Mike had heard that Gil hung out at one of the marinas along Ravenswood Road, so we headed south past the entrance to the harbor.

After traveling about a mile up the Dania Cut-off Canal, we pulled into Pattie's Marina and tied up to the fuel dock. The only other boat tied to the dock was a twelve-foot wooden punt covered with multihued paint splatters. It was obvious that this year's most popular boat colors were yellow and green. Pattie's had a small travel lift and boatyard, and the big outboard on the ugly punt meant they used it as a mini boatyard tug as well as the waterline paint boat. Painting a boat while in the water was heavily frowned on by OSHA, but one got the idea that Pattie's Marina broke more than a few regs.

Several locals were sitting around a table under a thatched Seminole Indian chickee hut, drinking from beer cans and watching us. Mike looped our line over the cleat on top of the marina dinghy's line, then he ran a cable and padlock around the piling. The group under the hut included two men wearing baseball caps, T-shirts, and jeans. The only distinguishing characteristic between them was that one had long straight hair hanging both in front and back of his big jug ears. Of the three women, two wore halter tops and the third, an older woman, wore a faded Pattie's Marina T-shirt that stretched tight around her ample bosom and hips. It was hard to tell if the couples lived in Pattie's Trailer Court or if they lived aboard some of the barely floating homes in the marina. Laundry hung from lifelines, bikes rusted away on decks, barnacles grew along the waterlines, and rotten lines, fenders, toolboxes, and garbage bags littered the decks of Pattie's live-aboard community. I guessed that the older woman sitting with the group was probably Pattie herself. Though Pattie's was only five miles or so from the glittering marinas of Bahia Mar and Pier Sixty-six, in other forms of measurement the distance was incalculable.

Mike lifted his hat when he ducked into the shade under the chickee. "Afternoon, folks."

One of the men murmured something that sounded like "good afternoon," but the others just stared at Mike's artificial leg, the stainless-steel knee and ankle joints, and the smooth pink "flesh-colored" plastic calf that protruded below his cut-off jeans. He ignored the stares and pushed on.

"We're looking for a fellow by the name of Gil Lynch. I understand he lives round here."

The older woman had been lifting her beer can to her lips, but she stopped, left the beer hanging in midair. "Who's asking?"

I dropped my business card on the table in front of her. "I'm Seychelle Sullivan. I own the tug *Gorda*. My business is Sullivan Towing and Salvage." I didn't think Mike's credentials as a former FLPD officer would go over big with this crowd.

The gray-haired woman drank from her beer and then slid my card into the front pocket of her T-shirt. "I seen your boat around." She reached for a pack of cigarettes on the table and shook one out. With the cigarette dangling from her lips, she asked, "Red's your pa?"

"Yeah. He died a couple of years ago. I'm running the boat now."

"Sorry to hear that," she said, struck a match, and inhaled long and deep.

I nodded. "I understand Gil used to know Red, and I just wanted to ask him some questions about my dad."

She took the cigarette from her mouth with two cracked, callused fingers, then she thrust her other hand out to me. "I'm Pattie Dolan." I tried to shake her hand with the same strength and assertiveness that Wonder Woman had used on me, but Pattie's grip turned mine to putty. She turned from me and spoke to the man with the jug ears. "Go

git the truck." He slid back his chair and started for the once white
Ford Ranger parked in the dirt lot opposite the trailer that served as an
office.

I rested my hand on Mike's shoulder. "Pattie, this is my friend,
Mike Beesting." They, too, shook hands. Pattie made no attempt to
introduce the others at the table.

"Odds are Gil's down at Flossie's this time of day. Jack'll run you
down there. It's only 'bout a quarter-mile down the road."

"I know where it is. Thanks."

The truck pulled up, and out the open window Jack jerked his
thumb toward the back. Mike pulled down the tailgate, and we slid into
the truck bed. After a short drive down Ravenswood Road, the truck
pulled into a parking lot that stretched along the side of a drab-
looking two-story cinder-block building. Downstairs was the dirty
glass entrance to Flossie's Bar and Grill. Upstairs, an outdoor corridor ran the length of the building where the late Flossie had sometimes
rented rooms out to her patrons. The parking lot was half-filled with
older pickups and a handful of bikes, mostly Harleys. Leaning against
the wall of the building was a rusty old beach cruiser bicycle with high
wide handlebars and a plastic milk crate tied behind the seat with a
sun-faded polypropylene line.

We slid out of Jack's truck and waved our thanks as he headed back
to Pattie's. "I'm sure glad I locked up the dink and outboard. I don't
think any of them back there would be above helping themselves."

"I'm sure you're right about that," I said as I pushed open the door
and nearly gagged on the cigarette smoke. My ears were assaulted by the
sound of Garth Brooks singing about how much papa loved mama.
The bar was so much darker than the bright sunlight outside that I
stood in the doorway a few seconds, waiting for my eyes to adjust. Mike
came in behind me, hooked his arm in mine, and led me past the couple of pool tables to a pair of empty stools on the far side of the bar.

I'd driven by Flossie's probably a hundred times in my life, but I'd
never been inside. I knew about the place because it had been a landmark for thirty-some years, and both my brothers had boasted to me
when we were in high school that the bar's owner, Flossie, never
checked IDs. They often came over here to drink and practice being

men. The dominant decorating themes went from Nascar to Bud-weiser, from neon signs to inflatable oil cans to a full-size picture of Dale Earnhardt on the storeroom door. The place was very crowded, although I counted only two women other than the bartender.

I didn't spot Gil as I surveyed the crowd, but I wasn't surprised to see Perry Greene sitting at one of the bar-height tables by the door. He was wearing a white mesh baseball cap stuck backward on his head, the straggly ends of his long hair curling around from the back of his neck. Smoking a filterless cigarette no more than an inch long, he squinted across the bar and sucked on the butt, and I was surprised the red glow didn't burn his fingers.

After Mike secured us a couple of beers, I pointed Perry out to him.

"Check out my competition over there." I squeezed the lime down the neck of the bottle and took a couple of swallows.

"Interesting," he said. "Think we ought to mosey over and see who's smoking that other cigarette burning in his ashtray?"

I hadn't noticed the smoke rising from the ashtray. "Think he'd tell us if we did?"

"Probably not."

I told Mike about the tow of the Italian yacht *O Solo Mio.* "Perry seemed to be very proud of his connections to those big boys. I've always thought of Perry as just a sleazeball—a user, yeah, but not a dealer. A guy not above some small-time crime if the chance presented itself, but not a big criminal. Do you know anything I don't know?"

"Not really. I know he's been busted for drunk and disorderly a few times, and he does sell a little weed to his friends. That's it, far as I know. I think he's probably just bullshitting, but then again, I wouldn't put it past him, trying to hook up with some kind of big-time score."

"That's just it. I don't think *anything's* beneath Perry."

Mike laughed. "Yeah, he's definitely a bottom-feeder."

The beer tasted fresh and clean. My throat already felt scratchy from the cigarette smoke and from trying to shout over the noise coming from both the jukebox and the inebriated crowd. I turned around on my stool and watched the game of pool at the table behind us for a few minutes.

"Doesn't look like Gil's here," Mike said, and I could tell he understood how disappointed I was.

A heavyset, ponytailed white man at the pool table was accusing a younger black man of having cheated by moving the cue ball. Ponytail was a biker type with a huge gut and various chains hanging off his belt. On the table, the striped balls grossly outnumbered the solids, and I suspected the accusation was a way of trying to make up lost ground.

I turned around and reached for the last of my beer. "Let's get out of here."

At that moment the door to the men's room opened and a large man walked out, his hands still fumbling with his fly. His belly, stretching the fabric of the faded black T-shirt, was third trimester size, and his head bobbed as he struggled to get things situated in his trousers. When he stepped into the red glow of the neon Bud Light sign, I saw the wide handlebar mustache and the scarred, off-kilter face. Although the skin was etched with deep crevasses, there was now more to the unbalanced look than just the eyebrow. In person, Gil Lynch looked positively insane.

Gil saw us just as he came abreast of our bar stools, and when I opened my mouth to speak to him, he bolted for the door. The move caught me off guard, his quickness remarkable for such a heavy man.

Mike was off his stool and heading for the door before my brain was able to process what was happening. He turned to me and shouted, "Come on," his cop instinct just like a dog's—the sight of a man's back only whetted his appetite. As my feet hit the floor, I identified the source of my confusion: I couldn't comprehend why or how Gil would know that we were looking for him. To my knowledge, I'd never met the man before.

I was no more than a few seconds behind Mike, but he had stopped and was holding the door, staring out toward the street. Just before I went through the door, I saw Perry cover his face with his hand. Seemed nobody wanted to have anything to do with me today. Outside, I looked to my right and saw the bike and its rider in a faded black T-shirt turn south in the direction of Pattie's.

"We'll never catch him by running, leastwise I never will," Mike said.

"Think he's headed back to the marina?"

"Probably." He stretched out his hand in front of me. "After you."

The dinghy was still where we'd left it, a fact that caused us both to sigh with relief when we walked down the gravel road in front of Pattie's office and saw it still floating along the fuel dock. The chickee hut was abandoned, the only sign of its recent occupants an overflowing ash-tray and one still smoldering butt. Gil's bike lay on its side in the weeds next to the office trailer.

"Come on, let's have a little talk with the folks here." Mike stepped up and opened the door.

Pattie sat in an aging office chair on the far side of a low counter. From where we stood, the counter hid nothing, and I had to stifle a grin when it struck me how much her body looked like one of Abaco's chew toys—a round piece of red rubber that bulged with multiple rings of ever-widening widths. She sat with her legs spread, her capri pants showing her thick, vein-riddled ankles.

"Howdy," Mike said, once again removing his hat for the lady. "Seems we just missed Gil over at Flossie's. I seen his bike out there. Any idea where he got to?"

I was amazed at how well Mike spoke the lingo of those he questioned. The man was a veritable chameleon, but Pattie wasn't smiling at him this time.

"Shoulda told me you was a cop."

"Me?" Mike looked absolutely injured. "I'm not a cop." Then he ducked his head and looked apologetic. "Well, it's true, I used to be a cop, but not no more. Hell, you ever see a one-legged cop?"

That stopped her. Her face seemed to fold in on itself, eyebrows lowered, chin up, as she mulled that one over. "Yeah, okay. Well, Gil said you was a cop."

"He musta recognized me from the old days."

"He's not so right in the head sometimes," she said. "He took the marina launch. It's got a twenty-five-horse engine. I don't know where he'd be headed. Think he's got someplace he sleeps up the canal some-where. You know, he's good on the water. He don't want you to find him, you ain't gonna find him."

On the fuel dock, we saw that, though the dinghy floated where we'd left her, she was no longer tied to the dock. Gil had thrown off our line to untie the marina boat, and the dinghy painter now trailed into the depths of the brown, oily water. It was Mike's cable around the piling that had prevented the boat from drifting off.

Once he got the outboard started and we were idling out toward the canal, Mike said, "Pattie's probably right. We'll find him another day. I sure as hell would like to know why he's running, though."

From Pattie's marina, we could get back to Mike's dock by turning either left or right since we were on a big circle made by the New River and the Dania Cut-off Canal. We headed left, west, up the canal, inland. Joe D'Angelo's house, our next stop on our way back to Mike's, was far up the New River, and eventually the canal we were on would connect with the river. Mike explained to me that Joe had bought his house in the Riverland neighborhood back in the eighties when a DEA guy could afford those places. His point lot home not far from the Jungle Queen's tourist compound was the smartest investment the guy had ever made.

As we entered the stretch of the canal that passed through Pond Apple Slough, the canal banks changed from neat lawns to twisted mangroves. The evidence of civilization slipped away. Except for the occasional channel marker, we could have been deep in the Everglades. The Slough was one of the last remaining freshwater swamps on the southeast coast of Florida, and environmentalists had managed thus far to prevent its total destruction. It remained an isolated island of wilderness in the middle of Fort Lauderdale's urban sprawl.

Mike pushed the throttle forward and the inflatable jumped into a plane. While I would have preferred to dawdle along at five knots, watching for birds and fish and raccoon, I had more important things to do—like find Solange's father. A snapshot of her face kept popping up in my mind, even as I watched the flocks of cattle egrets take off from the mangroves as our outboard sped by. Occasionally, narrow passages branched off from the main waterway, and I glanced down them, yearning to explore. I'd forgotten how pretty it was up here. I told myself I'd have to come back here someday in one of the Larsens' kayaks. Maybe bring Solange once this whole mess was worked out.

"Slow down, Mike." I'd seen a flash of bright yellow and green.

"What's up?" he asked as the boat settled back down into the water and our wake splashed into the mangrove roots ahead of us.

"Turn around." We had just passed a little creek or something off the west side of the canal. "I saw something."

He swung the boat around and motored back the hundred yards or so, then slowed and turned into an opening in the trees. There was a small barge aground about five hundred yards into the swamp where the narrow passage dead-ended. The rust brown sides of the barge blended into the brown and green of the mangroves. I never would have spotted it if Pattie's paint-splattered boatyard punt had not been tied alongside.

"What do you know," Mike said. "I think we found Gil's little hidey-hole, after all."

"Think he's there?"

"Naw. He'd have to be deaf not to hear this outboard out here. Like Patty said, he doesn't want to be found." Mike shrugged. "He's probably slithered off into the swamp. Want to go aboard and check it out anyway?" He bobbed his head in the direction of the barge.

"We could take a quick look, I guess," I said.

The old iron barge appeared to be no more than sixty feet long. They'd used such barges to haul out the muck back when many of South Florida's canals were dredged. This one was now holed by rust and waterlogged, resting on the mud bottom in what I guessed was about two feet of water. Even in water five inches deep, the bottom wouldn't have been visible. The swamp water resembled strong tea, stained as it was from the tannin in the mangroves. A small plywood-and-epoxy deckhouse, no more than ten by twelve, had been erected on the flat surface of the barge in what appeared to be the aft end of the derelict. Small plants, grasses, and mangrove shoots grew out of holes in the iron sides where rust had caused the metal to cave in and enough organic material had collected to allow seeds to root. What had once been a huge metal structure was rapidly being reclaimed by the swamp.

Mike tied the dinghy to an area that looked relatively free of sharp protuberances, and we climbed aboard. Polyethylene plastic sheeting was duct-taped over what had once been the wheelhouse windows. It was difficult to see through the plastic film, but Mike was right—it wasn't likely that Gill was still around. Still, I was happy to let Mike enter the deckhouse first.

"It's okay, Sey. No bogeymen in here," he shouted, his voice sounding muffled through the plastic sheeting.

"Hey, I'm not scared."

He poked his head out the doorway. "No, that's why you're standing out there, twenty feet away, looking like you're ready to bolt at the slightest sound."

"You've got to admit, this place is creepy."

"You want to be grossed out, come in here."

The smell in the deckhouse touched off some faint memory I could not place. Human sweat mixed with fishy iodine and the sickly smell of dead things. Rotting leaves and food and papers were strewn around the inside of the structure. A single twin mattress, wet by the smell of it, rested on the floor, and the inside walls were covered with newspapers taped up with wide strips of duct tape. An ornate end table that had probably once sat in a Fort Lauderdale family room now rested between the mattress and the wall, the brass drawer handles rusted to greenish lumps and the wooden top now warped from the damp of the swamp. On the table was an ashtray that held a couple of roaches—evidence that Gil still smoked some weed when he could find it.

While Mike was pulling out the drawers and looking for anything of Gil's that might tell us something, I noticed the newspaper on the bulkhead closest to the door was newer than the others. The front page of the *Miami Herald* had a small headline in the lower left corner, "Haitian Boat Sinks in Hillsboro Inlet," and in the first paragraph I saw the name *Miss Agnes*.

"Well, would you look at this?" Mike held up a flashy new handheld VHF radio and a Nextel cellular phone. "I wonder where our friend picked up these little items?"

"Pretty expensive gear for a guy who's homeless," I said.

"Yeah, I think it's more likely our buddy Gil has sticky fingers than a major credit card." He pulled out the drawer where he had found the electronics and felt around inside for anything that might be taped to the underside of the cabinet. When he didn't find anything, he slid the drawer back in place, adjusted his leg, and pushed himself to his feet.

"Take a look at this," I said, pointing to the newspaper. "What do you make of this?"

"What? That Gil uses newspaper for wallpaper?" Mike leaned in closer to the newsprint and tapped his finger against the headline. "Interesting, but probably just a coincidence." He held up the phone and radio. "This, however, this intrigues me. I know Gil Lynch is not as loony as he pretends to be." He handed me the phone and took a scrap of paper and a mechanical pencil out of his pocket. "Read me the number off that phone. I'll have somebody run it and see who it belongs to."

After I'd read him the number, he placed the items back in the drawer. "Let's get out of this stink hole."

We both managed to climb back down into Mike's inflatable without falling into the canal or tearing any clothing on the rusty metal edges of the barge. I continued to be surprised by Mike's agility with his artificial leg.

He cranked up the outboard while I untied our line and pushed the inflatable away from the rusty old derelict. "Tell me what you're thinking," I said as we idled slowly out of the little side creek.

"Okay, let's look at what we know. Gil Lynch is a burnt-out dealer turned snitch. He might get Social Security, but he's dirt poor, living on the streets, and sleeping in shitty holes like that." He jerked his thumb back at the barge. "As far as I know, the guy usually doesn't mind seeing the cops come along. He normally tries to sell some tidbit of information."

He turned the corner back into the Dania Cut-off Canal and pushed the throttle forward. The outboard noise climbed, and Mike continued by shouting.

"Two things are weird. First, if Gil knows something, why didn't he try to sell it to me? And second, if he stole that stuff, why's he hanging on to it? Guys like him usually head straight for the nearest pawnshop when they lift something like that."

I wasn't up to trying to shout over the outboard, so I just watched the riverbank flash by, and I let my thoughts blur in the same way. There had once been cypress trees in the freshwater swamp we were passing through, but when developers tapped into the aquifer to water all the green lawns they were planting, the water table dropped and Pond Apple Slough suffered as the saltwater seeped in. The twisted branches of the dead cypress trees still provided nesting space for hawks and osprey, though. I pointed a nest out to Mike. "Osprey," I shouted.

"Cool." He nodded.

Red had known Gil for about twenty-five years, and in all the time I had worked for my father on board *Gorda,* I didn't remember Red ever mentioning him. Had they stayed in touch after the delivery, when Gil became a big-time drug dealer?

We rounded a bend in the waterway, and I saw we were exiting the swamp. More boat traffic and the bridges of the interstate were just ahead. Mike slowed the dinghy. Finally, he was able to talk in a more natural voice.

"We're not far from Joe's house now."

"What do you think Gil's connection to Joe is?"

"That's just what we're going to ask him," Mike said.

Joe D'Angelo's house stood out from its neighbors. The canal that stretched back from the river along the side of his property was lined with simple suburban homes whose backyard embellishments consisted of barbecues and swimming pools. Joe's house was anything but simple. The large corner lot fronted about seventy feet on the river and another hundred feet along the canal, so you could not miss the elaborate patio and swimming pool with a huge artificial rock waterfall, the built-in waterslide, and the raised Jacuzzi that spilled into the pool. A covered redwood bar adjoined the Jacuzzi so that the bartender could easily deliver drinks to those basking in the bubbles. The pool cabana house had a small satellite dish on the roof, and the ranch-style house had been modified beyond recognition with a raised roof to accommodate the cathedral ceilings and glass walls that fronted the pool area. Davits at the far end of the dock held a black Jet Ski suspended over the water. The only boat tied to his dock was a sleek white

Donzi ocean racer, maybe forty-five feet long, with a large cabin forward and room for half a dozen bikinied babes on the large upholstered transom. Judging from the dirt and leaves on the white fiberglass, Joe didn't take her out much.

Mike slid the dinghy alongside the dock in front of Joe's boat and killed the engine. After all his shouting and the constant whine of the outboard, the quiet seemed almost unnatural. From up the canal somewhere, the smell of grilling meat mingled with the sound of children laughing and shouting.

Mike took a deep breath. "Hmm. Smells good. Didn't realize just how hungry I am." He smiled at me. "No lunch." He held his stomach. "I'm doing Weight Watchers."

"What? With all the piña coladas you drink?"

He grinned. "That's what I like about Weight Watchers. I can drink all my points."

I shook my head and hopped up onto the dock. "Do you think we should have tried to call again?"

"Nah. When you want information, you don't let 'em know exactly when you're coming. Much better to just drop in."

Looking around at the elaborate pool and patio setup, I said, "Wow, this is some property. Joe didn't do too bad as a DEA agent."

"Like I said, he bought this place twenty years ago when they were affordable, and this particular property was a real dump, I heard. He says he did lots of the work himself."

We were walking around the Jacuzzi when the sliding doors opened and a stunning, smiling black woman waved to Mike.

"Mister Mike. Hello." Her head was wrapped in a bright blue headscarf, and she stood in the doorway with one hand at her hip, the other shading her eyes from the sun. The pose was casual, but a photograph of her at that moment could have sold any product. Although her English was almost unaccented, I detected a bit of Haiti in there.

"Hey, Celeste, is Joe around?" Mike asked as we rounded the pool.

"He is not here right now, but he'll be home soon." She stepped out of the opening in the sliding door and waved her hand toward the interior of the house. "Would you like to come in and wait?" Her movements were like those of a dancer. Though she was wearing a simple cotton dress and no makeup, her figure and face were striking.

Mike turned to me with raised eyebrows. "Your call, Sullivan. You got the time?"

I shrugged. "We can wait a while. If he doesn't get here in twenty minutes, though, we'd better take off. I have to meet someone tonight."

"Fair enough." He waved his arm in the direction of Celeste. "After you."

Celeste brought us glasses and bottles of St. Pauli's Girl beer. She set us up at the indoor bar in the study that overlooked the pool. Clearly, Joe was into bars. I was trying to discern if Celeste was a housekeeper or girlfriend. Or both. When she disappeared and did not come back, I decided on housekeeper.

The decorating scheme for the house could only be called eclectic, but, somehow, it all worked. Along one wall, a narrow section of bookshelves stretched to the ceiling while the rest of the wall was covered with lighted nooks that held sculptures or photos or antiques. A wheeled library ladder reached up twenty feet to a rail that ran just below the ceiling. An antique barber's chair was bolted to the floor just inside the window where it would have the best view of the river.

As promised, Joe was home in less than ten minutes. We heard the car, followed by a loud greeting, then the hushed tones as Celeste told him we were there. His whispers sounded loud and harsh, angry about something. I wondered if it was us. But when he came through the doors, he was all smiles.

"Mike. Seychelle." He shook both our hands. "So good to see you both. What brings you by the old hacienda?"

In his white shorts and lime green polo shirt, Joe looked the part of the retiree. I doubted the ensemble was a biking outfit. Maybe golf?

"Hey, Joe. Sorry to barge in on you like this," Mike said, "but I'm going to get straight to the point. Sey came by to visit me today, and she found some old photos among her dad's things. She wanted to find out more about the history behind those pics."

I had already retrieved the photos out of my shoulder bag, and I spread them out on the bar. "I'm more than a little confused, Joe," I said. "Yesterday morning you said that you and Red used to work together when you were in the DEA, and he used to tow boats for you."

Joe picked up the picture of the three of them. He had a peculiar little half-smile on his face.

"You never said anything about knowing Red over twenty years ago," I added.

He didn't say anything for over a minute. None of us did. We just sat there and watched the shadows in the room stretch out.

"I haven't talked about that trip in years," he began. He climbed onto a bar stool on the far side of me. Mike rested his hand on my shoulder. Joe looked up from the photo in his hand. "You have grown up to be such a beautiful young woman, Seychelle. I would never say or do anything to hurt you. I didn't lie to you the other day, I just didn't tell you everything. That was the way we always handled it. When Red and I began working together again in the eighties, we never discussed the past." He looked back down at the photo. "Seychelle, I think this is something you should just forget. Destroy these photos, forget you ever saw them, and get on with your life. Trust me when I tell you there are some things you are better off not knowing."

"I can't do that, Joe."

"Then you need to try to understand those times, Seychelle. Everyone was doing it, and your dad was in a bind, as I understand it. Financially."

"But that doesn't mean he would—"

He raised his hand palm up. "Hear me out, then, if you insist. I was there as the delivery skipper, already down in Cartagena, and some guys I knew up in Lauderdale recruited your dad. It was a long time ago. I was only, hell, what, twenty-seven, twenty-eight years old."

"Were you working for the DEA then?" I asked.

Joe's eyes flickered, sought out Mike, then looked across the room, out the window. He ran his fingers through his hair and sighed. "You're not making this easy. Yes. Yes, I was. I was pretty fresh, only nine months on the job when they asked me if I wanted to go undercover as a yacht delivery captain. Shit. Nobody's even supposed to know we were doing that back then."

Part of me wanted to stop him. If it was even remotely possible, I didn't want to know about it. But it wasn't possible. Not Red. No matter what Joe said.

"The guy who owned the boat had been under surveillance for quite some time. He had lots of toys and no identifiable means of support. Turned out it was easier than I thought getting hired on as the captain of his yacht. And, eventually, he brought me in on what was really happening. He had this crewman working for him. The guy's still around."

"You mean Gil Lynch?" Mike asked.

"Right. Of course, you'd know him, Mike. Forgot about that." Joe pointed to Gil in the old photo. "That's him there. This was the early days, before he was known much here in Lauderdale. He became a much bigger player after that trip."

"You see much of Gil these days?"

Joe grunted a half-laugh. "I'd be surprised if he's still alive."

"Oh, he's alive all right. Sey and I saw him just a few hours ago."

"Really? Did you talk to him?"

"No. I've used him as a snitch in the past, but today he ran from us. Don't know why."

"Hmm. Well, it was Gil back then who set up the buy, did all the legwork down in Colombia. But I didn't bust either him or Red. My bosses were after the yacht's owner, the bigger fish. I probably shouldn't have done it, but I protected Red. Hell, you know what I'm talking about, right, Mike? The guy had a wife and kids back in the States, it was his first time getting into something like that."

"Sure, I know what you're saying," Mike said.

My elbows were propped up on the bar, and I rested my forehead against the heels of my hands. I began to shake my head. "No way. I don't buy it." I lifted my head and turned to face Joe. "Red did not knowingly get on a boat that was smuggling drugs up from Colombia." I swung my head back and forth, looking first at Mike, then Joe. Neither would look at me.

No one said anything for several seconds. Mike's hand rested on my shoulder, massaging the flesh in a little circling motion. I wanted to reach over and smack his hand away.

Finally, Joe said, "Listen, honey, I know you don't want to think of your daddy—"

I stood up. I wanted to break something. I wanted him to stop calling me "honey." "Red didn't know," I said. "He couldn't have." I could hear that my voice sounded whiny, and it made me even angrier. I slid off my stool and stomped out of the room.

Celeste was standing in the hall, just outside the doorway. As I passed her I asked, "Bathroom?" She motioned for me to follow her.

I sat down on the closed toilet lid and gave myself about three minutes to just let my emotions go. It wasn't long enough to turn my eyes and face all red and puffy, but it was just enough of a little *pfft*, like a pressure cooker's jiggle, to make sure I wouldn't blow when I went back into that room with those guys. They were undoubtedly talking about me right now—some "poor kid" scenario, where they were painting themselves as the big tough cops who knew how bad folks could be.

But Red was different, and they weren't used to people like Red. He was a man whose morality was absolute. He would not bend, nor did he ever struggle over a moral issue, much to the chagrin of his teenage daughter. Red would never have willingly smuggled drugs—not even to finish *Gorda*. That was a truth. I felt it in my gut. I was not sure whether Joe was floating this tale out of ignorance or deceit, but I intended to find out.

After splashing some cold water on my face and relishing the soft, Egyptian cotton towels, I unlocked the door and ventured out. The men's voices and loud laughter carried from their end of the hall, but I turned in the opposite direction. I decided to explore a little before returning to the boys' club.

I saw three doors down the hall. The guest bedroom was located diagonally across from the bathroom. The furnishings were expensive and tasteful, but the room had all the personality of a model home. The next door led to the master bedroom, a huge room, nearly twenty by twenty, with French doors that opened onto the pool deck. When I came to the last door, I nearly collided with Celeste.

"Oh, pardon," she said, looking startled and then lowering her eyes.

"No, I should be saying that."

Over her shoulder I saw a room that was small and spartan, containing a twin bed, a dresser with a small mirror, and a single chair. Unlike the other two rooms, this one had personal items, a lovely brush-and-comb set on the dresser, a hand-stitched quilt on the bed, a small bright painting on the wall.

"Really, I'm sorry. I was just being nosy. I wanted to have a look at the house. Is this your room?"

She nodded and lowered her eyes.

I pointed back down the hall. "I kinda got in an argument with those guys back there. Do you mind if I just sit here for a while? I could use some female company."

She smiled and stepped into the room, offering me the chair. After we'd settled ourselves, neither of us quite knew what to say. I could sense her awkwardness. After a while, she began to hum a tune.

"That sounds very pretty. What is it?"

"Oh, it's a song we used to sing in Haiti. To make children go to sleep."

"Can you sing it for me?"

She smiled shyly and began to sing softly, but in a strong and pleasant voice.

Dodo ti pitit manman'l
Do-o-do-o-do ti pitit manman'l
Si li pas dodo
Krab la va manje'l

Her voice cracked, and she stopped singing. She stood suddenly, then crossed the room and stared out the window.

"You miss Haiti, don't you?" She did not move to respond to my question, so I tried a different one. "How long have you worked for Joe?"

"Five years," she said, so softly I could barely hear her.

"That's when you came from Haiti?"

She nodded and spoke without turning around. "Mister D'Angelo brought me over, and he sent me to school to learn English."

"Your English is very good."

She turned around and smiled, then crossed to the bed and sat next to me. "Thank you," she said. "I cannot read yet, but I will learn." She sat with her head down, her fingers tracing the floral design on her dress. I had never seen such a beautiful woman behave so modestly. Was it possible, I wondered, she didn't know how lovely she was?

"So you met him in Haiti?"

She nodded without looking up.

"What was he doing there?"

"He was a drug policeman. There were lots of drugs in Haiti. He help the Haitian people."

"Hmmm. I've met so many Haitian people lately. I didn't realize there were so many Haitians in Florida."

She smiled. "Yes, this is true. Haitians are in the supermarket, restaurants, shopping malls. Every year more and more. It is because it is so bad at home."

"Do you still have family there?"

She frowned and appeared to struggle with her reply. "No," she said, her voice barely more than a whisper. "All dead."

"I'm so sorry." I looked at the top of her bowed head. She looked so young to have known such loss. "How old are you, Celeste?"

"I am twenty-three."

"Joe brought you here when you were only eighteen?"

She looked up quickly. "Yes. I love my country, Haiti, but it was bad there for me. There are many beautiful things in Haiti, many wonderful people. But this is my new country. There is nothing in Haiti for me now."

Joe appeared in the doorway. "What are you doing back here?" There was something in his voice, some undercurrent of threat that made me feel like a kid who had been caught rifling through her parents' belongings.

"We were just visiting." I patted Celeste's hand. "It was nice talking to you."

Joe walked us out to the dock, where Mike untied the dinghy line while I prepared to climb down the dock.

"Seychelle, I want you to know—" Joe said.

"Joe, stop." I held up my hand like a traffic cop. "I came here looking for some answers about my dad, about who he was. And you know what? I found out that I've known that all along. I've always known who Red was. Nothing you say can change that."

"I'm glad. I hope you understand that I would never intentionally say or do anything to hurt you. Are we still friends?"

I nodded once and he leaned in and kissed me on the cheek.

Mike and I didn't talk much on the ride back. As we cruised through the heart of the city, the late evening sunlight was turning the downtown buildings into golden towers. I sat up on the bow of the inflatable and tried to enjoy the beauty of the river, but my mind kept spinning images: Red, Gil, and Joe dockside in Cartagena; Perry waiting for someone in Flossie's Bar; Gil's photo on Perry's Italian tow; new cell phones and radios. Joe had given me one version of what had happened down there over twenty years before. I needed to hear Gil's version.

By the time we secured the dinghy and I'd turned down Mike's dinner invite, it was approaching five o'clock. I drove straight to Jeannie's to pick up Solange.

$\mathcal{X}\mathcal{V}\mathcal{I}$

When I pulled Lightnin' into Jeannie's yard, I saw B.J.'s black
El Camino parked on the far side of her van. I had hoped to just grab
Solange and take off for *Mambo* Racine's, so this was an unwelcome
complication.

I saw him through the screen door when I reached the top of the
landing. He was sitting on the couch talking to Jeannie, and in the few
seconds before I knocked, when neither of them knew I was there, I
watched him. He still gave me that shivery feeling—the way his biceps
stretched the fabric of his white T-shirt as he raised his arm, his brown
thighs showing beneath his khaki cargo shorts. His back was angled toward the door, and I could see his sleek black ponytail and his neck
hairs pulled up into that rubber band. I had a sudden urge to kiss him
right there, on his neck, just behind his ear. I shook my head and
knocked.

He was smiling when he unlocked the screen door. "We were just
talking about you," he said.

"Great," I said as I walked through the door. "Hi, Jeannie. I came
to pick up Solange."

"Hey. I think taking that girl up to some Voodoo lady is nuts, but
I can see you've got your stubborn heart set on it." She rocked back and
forth a couple of times to build momentum and then lifted her bulk
up into a standing position. "I'll go get her ready. It'll take me fifteen
minutes or so. She's not dressed."

I had the distinct feeling that she was giving B.J. time to talk to me.

"I wanted to see you," he said. "I felt bad about the way we had left
things yesterday."

"Listen, B.J., I really don't have time to get into this now. I'm supposed to have this kid at Racine's by seven, and I've just been on this

ridiculous dinghy trip with Mike." I was still in a bad mood from the conversation with Joe.

"What dinghy trip?"

"I was trying to find out something about my dad. It's hard to explain. I don't really want to talk about it."

We sat in silence for a while then, the only sounds in the room those of the wall clock ticking and, through the screen, the city sounds of traffic and sirens and the far-off music of an ice cream truck.

B.J. took a deep breath. "Sey, I know what it is like to hear stories about your father. Stories are all I've ever had about my dad."

I knew that B.J. had been raised by a single mother in Southern California and that he had absolutely adored her. She'd died when he was only a few years out of graduate school. It was then that he abandoned the corporate lifestyle, moved to Florida, and started working as a boat carpenter. He rarely talked about his life before Florida, only occasionally letting loose with little tidbits.

"Even though I never met my dad, by his very absence, he played a part in my life. I would imagine he was this very powerful man, and it was the people around him who were preventing him from ever coming to visit his son. When I was in high school, my mother told me that he came from a wealthy Hawaiian family. He had been slumming in Southern California before going back to school up at Berkeley. She was seventeen and dancing in a Polynesian restaurant, and when he found out she was pregnant, he offered her fifty thousand dollars to get an abortion. She refused, he left, and that was the last she ever heard of him."

"I'm sorry, B.J."

"Don't be. I had the greatest mom. No complaints. I just know that I want the chance to do the fatherhood thing right. Sey, being a family doesn't have to mean polyester clothes and a minivan. Look at me. I was raised in women's dressing rooms in a handful of Polynesian restaurants."

I rolled my eyes. "That explains a lot."

His mouth spread wide, showing his incredibly white teeth. "So I love women. But Sey, of all the women I have known, I've never felt like this. I miss you when you're not there. I've never ever missed anyone before." He took my hand.

Jeannie appeared in the hallway with Solange at her side, and she clutched at her chest and gasped. "Oh, my God. He didn't propose to you, did he?"

I pulled my hand back and stood up. "Of course not, Jeannie. B.J.? Propose? You've got to be kidding. The man *loves women*. Plural. He'll probably have a new girlfriend by the end of the week."

The street where Max and Racine lived looked even less inviting in the dark than it had in the daylight. I was acutely aware of how little protection the Jeep's soft top afforded us as I rounded the corner and began peering down the unlit street, trying to recognize the cinder-block house that was set so far back from the street.

Jeannie and I had argued just before I'd climbed into the Jeep, just after B.J. had smiled sadly and left the house. I hadn't been nice to him. He deserved better than that. Jeannie told me all that and then some, and I knew she was right. Then she called me irresponsible for taking a child into Collier City after dark to see some kind of Voodoo priestess. When she put it that way, it did become difficult to defend. Then I thought of B.J.'s words on the topic, how he had explained it to me the other night, and I tried to tell Jeannie that she needed to step out of her middle-class American point of view and accept the fact that there were alternative religions, alternative ways of healing. She looked like she wanted to slap some sense into me. It had all sounded so much more convincing when B.J. said it.

It wasn't the house I spotted finally, but rather the number of cars parked in front of the house. What had been a wide, empty dirt yard was now covered with a varied collection of cars, everything from huge sport utility vehicles with dark tinted windows to older-model sedans and shiny new imports.

I parked the Jeep close to the street, so as not to get blocked in by any late arrivals. Solange was sitting up, her eyes open, but she took no more interest in these surroundings than she had taken in me or anything back at Jeannie's house. She simply stared ahead as though she had retreated to some place deep inside. I helped her out of the car and held her hand as we walked to the door.

Still a few feet from the front door, I hesitated. The front porch was dark, but colored lights behind the house illuminated the branches of the huge strangler fig tree. Loud island drumming and the sound of people laughing and talking drifted over the top of the house, intensifying the stillness in the front yard. I felt like a voyeur about to peep through a window.

I leaned down, closer to Solange's face, concentrating, trying to see her features in the darkness. "Solange, I wish you'd help me out here, kid. Is this right? I've got to find somebody who can help you." As usual, she showed no reaction. "Do you want to go in? I want to help you, but you probably know more about what's going on here than I do."

Nothing. She stared straight ahead. I had no idea if she could hear me or understand me. I didn't know what else to do, so I took her small hand in both of mine, squeezed it, and walked forward.

Max opened the door. He was wearing a formal black suit and black bow tie. *"Bon soir! Bienvenue!* I am so glad you have come, both of you." He bent down and peered into Solange's face. "This is your young friend?"

"Her name is Solange."

He said something to her in Creole, which I didn't understand, and for all the reaction he got out of her, it was as though she didn't understand, either. His eyes crinkled at the corners when he looked at me again. "She will be fine," he said. *"Ne t'inquiet pas.* Don't worry. *Mambo* Racine will take care of the child."

Max led us through the house, and when we stepped into the backyard, it was like stepping into another world. All my senses were immediately under direct assault. At least fifty people stood around the yard, clustered in groups, talking, drinking, laughing. No one turned or paid any attention to us. The women all wore scarves on their heads, and most wore bright, colorful dresses, although a few were dressed entirely in white. Many of the men wore their work clothes, while others were dressed in white with red sashlike belts.

The high thick branches of the strangler fig tree made a ceiling over the fenced-in yard, so it was like stepping into a massive room. The branches of the tree completely obscured the sky, but it was the trunk of the tree that startled me most. Strangler figs start as vines that surround and eventually kill the host tree, leaving a trunk that looks like dozens of roots all tangled and woven together. This tree had been painted with colorful designs that used the natural shape of the twisted roots to form pictures and patterns. There was one especially thick root that twisted around the rest of the trunk, and this root had been painted to look like a rainbow-colored snake climbing the tree. As we stepped down from the back door, I looked up and saw the head of the snake, his tongue and fangs painted on a large gnarled stump of wood in the branches just over our heads. Bits of ribbon and rags were tied among the upper branches of the tree, and other strange artifacts like gourds and beads and dried flowers dangled there on strings. A low, foot-high wooden bench had been built around the base of the tree, and it, too, was painted with vivid designs.

The light in the yard was dim, just one small spotlight at the base of the tree. Beyond the tree, at the very back of the yard, I could make out two smaller buildings, and it looked as though one had designs and human figures painted on its side. The other with its thatched roof looked more like a Seminole Indian chickee hut.

The air was pungent with the smell of wood smoke, though I didn't see the fire anywhere. A group of three musicians pounded on different-size handmade drums, and the drumming seemed to drive the crowd to laugh and talk louder and louder. Everything in the whole tableau moved to the rhythm of the drums.

"Max . . . " I turned to ask him where Racine was, but he had gone. The back door to the house was closed.

I knelt next to Solange and watched her face. "Solange." I stroked the side of her face and moved my lips close to her ear. "Can you hear me?"

Nothing. She stared straight ahead, her body even more rigid than before.

A hand touched my shoulder and I jumped, nearly falling on my butt in the dirt. When I stood and turned around, I was facing a woman who was taller than me. She had to be more than six feet tall, though from the look of her sharp, jutting elbows I probably outweighed her significantly. Her skin was exceptionally dark, a match in hue to Max's, but she was so thin that her cheekbones protruded above deep hollows. She wore a bright red dress and an elaborately embroidered straw hat.

"You are Seychelle Sullivan?" she asked, grasping my fingers in her dry, bony hand and shaking it vigorously. Her voice was deep and raspy, as though she had smoked cigarettes her entire life, but she spoke so low I could barely hear her over the pounding drums. "I am Racine Toussaint. I understand you have come here to speak to me." Her English revealed only the mere hint of an accent.

"Yes, I brought this child," I said, wrapping my arm around Solange and pulling her close to me.

"I know about the child. Follow me."

She led us through the crowd. Many of the people had started dancing. Those not dancing were moving off to the perimeter of the yard, while the dancers marched slowly around the tree, undulating to the rhythm of the drums.

We passed a man who was kneeling on the ground, drawing curly designs with sand in the dirt yard. The fine white grains trailed from his fist as he added a final flourish to what looked to me like a large stylized compass rose.

Racine stopped in front of a door to one of the outbuildings. Up close, I could see that the paintings on the walls were far more elaborate than I had originally thought. The style was unusual, what fancy art critics called *primitif,* but the subject matter was clearly religious—from the black Madonna and child on the right of the door to the intricate black cross adorning the door itself.

"Miss Sullivan," she said, "I understand this must all seem very strange to you."

I nodded and smiled. While it was easier to speak out here farther from the drums, I still found myself overwhelmed and not sure what to say.

"We Haitians practice a form of Christianity that has blended with the African religions of our ancestors. We call this religion *Vodou.*" She directed her gaze over my shoulder at the dancers back in the yard and smiled. "Most Americans, when they hear that word, they think of black magic. They have all those images of zombies, curses, and Voodoo dolls from their films. In reality, *Vodou* is a way of seeing the universe, of being connected to our ancestors, of using nature to heal. I hope you can keep a more open mind."

I nodded. "I'll try. But I've got to tell you, all this"—I swung my hand in an arc toward the drummers and the people who were starting to dance—"I've never seen anything like it. It's very beautiful, but a little frightening as well."

She smiled. "I appreciate your honesty. But there is no reason to be afraid. One of our rituals is a sacred cleansing ritual called a *lave tete*," she said, pronouncing the words *lavay tet* with a beautiful French accent, "because we wash the hair several times with special herbs. This clears the consciousness of the individual. This will help the child wash away her fears and bring her back to us. Can you trust me?"

"You're just going to wash her hair?"

Racine took my hand in hers. Her skin was cool and dry, and her palms felt almost like crepe paper. As she spoke, her dark eyes locked on mine. "I would never do anything to hurt this child."

I believed her. "Okay. I just want her to get better. I don't know what else to try."

"When we are inside," she said, "I don't want you to say anything. You may watch, but I ask you not to speak."

Racine took Solange's hand and led her into the small room. An involuntary shudder shook my shoulders as I watched Solange pass through that doorway without me. I was seized by an overwhelming urge to grab her, run for the Jeep, and get the hell out of there. Instead, I followed them inside.

The only light inside the room came from dozens of candles on an altar that ran along the right side wall. Scraps of cloth bearing a variety of patterns covered the base of the altar. It was difficult to make out all the paraphernalia that crowded the shelf. There were bottles and jars made of colored glass, a big wooden cross, a stone bowl, terra-cotta pots, and what looked like little packages wrapped in colored paper with ribbons tied round the paper to form long necks. Two low chairs had been placed directly in front of the cross in the center of the room, one in front of the other.

Racine led Solange to one of the chairs and began to undress her. When she pulled the T-shirt over the child's head, her arms flopped down and dangled loose at her sides. The term *rag doll* popped into my mind. Solange was flesh and bone, but she seemed to have lost all control of her body. She was wearing only her new white underwear, and I realized again just how skinny she was. She looked so small and vulnerable.

I held my breath, and I was certain my hands would shake if I held them in front of me. What was I doing here?

A woman in white entered the room carrying a small white dress. Racine pulled it over Solange's head. The skirt nearly touched the dirt floor, and I thought of the white dress Solange had been wearing the day I pulled her from the sea. Racine eased Solange into the front chair, then sat in the chair behind. She gently removed the beaded bands and combed out the braids in the girl's hair. Two more women dressed in white came in, carrying between them what looked like a huge galvanized soup pot and ladle. As they placed the pot behind the chairs, gentle steam rose from the water inside. The smell was earthy, almost musky. It reminded me of when, as kids, my brother Pit and I used to make "tea" by mixing sticks and leaves from all over our yard.

Racine stirred the pot, then tested the liquid on her wrist, like a mother testing the temperature of her baby's milk. She nodded, then lifted the child's chin, tilting her head back, and ladled the steaming water over her head.

Solange showed no reaction to what was happening. I looked around the room. My eyes had adjusted to the darkness, and I noticed for the first time that there were other observers leaning against the walls. I couldn't make out the features of a tall man on the far side of the room, dressed all in black, but closer to me, slouching and sucking on three fingers, was a girl not much older than Solange. When she turned to look at me, I recognized her. It was Juliette, the girl from Martine Gohin's house. She pulled her fingers out of her mouth and pointed first to her lips and then to me.

Did she want to talk to me? I pointed at her and then at myself and lifted my hands and shoulders as if to ask "What?"

She ignored me, walked around the head-washing ceremony, and slipped out the door.

I assumed she wanted me to follow her. I looked back at Solange and was surprised to see her smiling. Racine was saying something in

Creole that I could not understand, but the child seemed quite safe. I would step outside for just a minute.

It wasn't until I opened the door that I realized how well sound-proofed the room had been. The noise of the drums hit me, and I could feel each beat pounding in my body. The dancing in the yard had grown more frantic. Nearly everyone was involved now. Some of the dancers were writhing on the ground, and others were jumping around in bizarre contortions that made them look double-jointed. One woman fell to the ground, flopping around like a snake that had just been run over by a car. Three people surrounded her and helped her to her feet, but she seemed to struggle against them. They dragged her from the dance area toward the building that looked like an Indian chickee hut.

"Pssst." Juliette's head poked out, then disappeared into the shrubs at the side of the building I'd just left. I started in her direction.

"Seychelle Sullivan? Is that you?"

When I turned around, a short woman in a bright blue-and-yellow dress was coming toward me from the center of the yard. Like all the other women, she wore a colorful headscarf. I used my hand to shield my eyes from the spotlight behind her and attempted to make out the features of her face. She wore heavy, dark-tinted glasses.

"Martine?"

"*Mais oui.* Seychelle, what are you doing here?"

I pointed to the door. "I brought Solange. You know, the little girl? The Earth Angel? She's sick. It's a long story. I found this card on board the *Miss Agnes*—it had Racine Toussaint's name and address. They're washing her hair in there."

"Ah, the *lave tete.* Yes, that will help."

"You practice Voodoo?"

She shrugged. "I am Haitian, *non*? Come, follow me."

I glanced over my shoulder. There was no sign of Juliette. Martine led me closer to the dancers. She motioned for me to bend down, so that she could talk over the drums and into my ear.

"Some of these dancers have been mounted by the *lwa.*"

"What does that mean?"

"The *lwa* are spirits who can enter the body of a living person and possess him in order to communicate. We call that mounting, just like

a rider mounts a horse. You see the tree in the middle of the *peristil*?" She pointed to the strangler fig trunk. "That is called the *poto mitan,* or center post. It is hollow, and that is how the spirits pass the Crossroads and travel from their world to ours. Usually it is truly a pole, but *Mambo* Racine has chosen a tree. It seems to work well enough." She shrugged again.

At that moment the door to the chickee hut opened, and the woman who had been taken from the dance area emerged wearing a bright red dress. It was difficult to recognize her as the same woman who had been writhing on the ground. Her face was made up, her lips bright red, her hair combed loose, and now *she* was leading the people who just moments before had been dragging her. She strode onto the dance floor, commanding the attention of all the men, and began a slow, seductive dance. Although she was more than fifty feet away from me on the far side of the yard, I was sure I could smell her perfume.

"That's Erzulie. She is the spirit of love."

"You said 'Erzulie'?"

"Yes, she manifests herself in several different forms—from the gentle seductress to the fierce protective mother. This is Erzulie Danto, the mother. She may have come because of the child. You see that man with the cane? That is Legba."

Martine continued to talk about many of the other *lwa* who had possessed the people who were dancing before us, but I ceased to hear as I tried to sort out what all this meant. Why had that woman in the boat told Solange she was Erzulie? Was that her real name? Did Solange think the woman on the boat was a spirit or possessed by one? I had told Racine I would keep an open mind, but it was growing more and more difficult.

My attention was jerked away from the dancers when the door opened and Racine Toussaint marched out and crossed the yard to the thatched hut. Who was with Solange?

"Martine, excuse me," I interrupted her. "I have to get back to see how Solange is doing. I get worried when I can't see her."

"She'll be fine. In fact, she will be very much better after this. You will see. There are not many children like her who get a *lave tete*." She took hold of my arm and held it fast.

I jerked out of her grasp. "What do you mean?"

She exhaled a puff of air. "Seychelle, she is a street child. A *restavek*. There are thousands of them in Haiti." There was something about the way she said the word *restavek*, spitting it out, as though she despised even the word.

"So what? Is that supposed to make her less human?"

Martine pursed her lips and turned to watch the dancers.

"Martine, I'm going back inside."

"Okay," she said, and blew out air through her mouth in disgust. "Go on. And if you see that empty-headed niece of mine—Juliette—tell her to get out to the car and wait for me."

For such a stocky woman, she was fast. She took off and disappeared into the dancing crowd, leaving me certain that I had offended her somehow.

Just as I reached the door with the black cross, I saw Juliette frantically waving me over.

"Juliette, your aunt wants you to go to the car." I felt like an idiot talking to the ficus hedge.

"Please, come."

I dropped my head and sighed. After a quick check to see if anyone was watching, I plunged into the bushes.

On the other side of the hedge, a chain-link fence bordered on an alley. We were standing next to Racine and Max's plastic garbage cans, and it didn't smell like Erzulie's perfume anymore. "Okay, what is it, Juliette?"

"The boat *Miss Agnes*."

With that, she had my total attention. "What about it? Do you know someone who was on that boat?"

The girl appeared frightened. She kept tugging at her dress and glancing at the building next to us as though she were afraid she might see someone peering around one of the corners. "I know a girl," she said in a stage whisper. "She is now *restavek* with friend of Madame."

"She's a *restavek* here? In the U.S.? But I thought that was only in Haiti?"

Juliette lowered her eyes and breathed deeply, her nostrils flaring. "*Non.*" She said it so softly I almost could not hear her over the drums. "*Restaveks* are here, too."

As the realization settled in, I began to feel nauseated.

"Juliette, how can I find this girl? I must talk to her. Can you arrange for us to meet?"

She lifted her face and there was an eagerness in her eyes, as though she expected something from me.

"Tomorrow. In the Swap Shop. The booth is Paris Kids."

"What time?"

"Anytime. She work all the time."

"How will I know her? What's her name?"

She shook her head. "You will know. Now I go. Madame waits."

"Juliette." I had to ask, even though I was fairly certain of the answer. "Martine . . . she's not your aunt, is she?"

She looked down again, refusing to meet my eyes.

"But where is your family?" She shrugged her shoulders very slightly but still did not look up.

"Does Martine let you go to school?"

The young girl raised her eyes slowly and smiled with her lips, but in those eyes there was something old and tired and angry. A fat tear pooled and slid down her smooth cheek.

"Juliette, I'm so sorry."

I reached out to her, but before I could touch her, she turned and slipped through the hedge.

xvii

I had been leaning against the side of the building, deep in thought, when I heard a child's scream.

A branch of the ficus hedge caught on a button of my shirt, ripping it. The door flew open as I came around the corner, and a huge man, dressed in black and wearing a black top hat, ran out, raised his left hand, and pushed me hard. I fell to the ground, dazed. When I sat up, he was gone. I'd gotten only a brief glimpse of his face, his mustache and goatee. My eyes had been drawn to the sequined design that adorned his hat: a skull and crossbones.

I pushed myself to my feet and ran into the dark room.

The chair was empty, the pots gone, but on the floor, glistening in the candlelight, was a pool of what looked like blood. There was no sign of the child.

I turned and ran out into the yard.

The drummers' bodies were slick with sweat as their hands danced over the skins stretched taut across their drums. The pounding beats bounced inside my head, and the rhythm became almost painful. I wanted to yell at them to be quiet, but a part of me was afraid.

The dancers ignored me as I pushed through them, searching for Racine or Max. One man tipped back a bottle of rum, filling his cheeks, then sprayed out the liquid and lit it with a disposable lighter. The ball of fire jumped out of his mouth and seemed to come straight for my hair. I leaped away and fell backward into the arms of a man who was jerking and twitching, his eyes rolled back in his head. He kept in perfect beat with the drums. I pushed myself away from him only to feel something smack me on the backside. When I reached around, my fingers closed on the shaft of a cane. Holding the other end was a strange man dressed in raggedy clothes and dancing a silly jig. The other dancers were laughing and pointing as he mugged and joked in

Creole. I let go of the cane when I felt a hand on my forearm. The lady in red, the one Martine had called Erzulie, was speaking to me in Creole. I couldn't understand a word, but when I shouted Racine's name, she stroked my hair and my face, then put her arm around my waist and led me out of the crowd of dancers. She pointed to the hut and said something in Creole, the only word of which I understood was Racine's name. I ran across the dirt yard and burst through the door.

"Racine," I shouted. The tall woman stood alone in the room before an altar with a painting of the Virgin Mary and dozens of candles, bottles of perfume and rum. The altar was decorated with garlands of Christmas tinsel, beaded flags, and pink silk roses. "She's gone."

Racine put her fingers to her lips, indicating quiet.

"There's blood all over, and Solange is gone."

She placed her hand on top of my head as though I were a little child. "Calm down. Solange is fine. She is resting." Her gravelly voice was soft and quiet.

"I heard her scream, Racine. Then this huge man in a black suit and hat ran out. He had a skull and crossbones on his hat."

The look on her face changed to one of concern. *"Bawon?"*

"I've seen that skull before. On dark glasses I found on the *Miss Agnes.*"

"Come," she said, nodding her head. "We will see." She put her hand in the small of my back and pushed me toward the door.

We crossed the yard at a pace that required me to trot to keep up. She walked past the bloody chair without concern and led me to the back of the room. There on the floor, a small mattress and bedding had been laid out. The white sheets were streaked with bloodstains. "We left her here, asleep. She must sleep after the *lave tete.*" She shook her head. "It was the *bokor.*"

"*Bokor?* What's that? I don't understand. Where's Solange?"

The sound of breaking glass caused us both to turn. One of the bottles had fallen off the altar, and the smell of rum filled the room. Then a section of the curtain beneath the altar moved, and a small hand poked out.

"Solange," I yelled. The broken glass crunched beneath my sneakers as I reached her side. Her eyes looked huge beneath the white scarf that wrapped her head, and I slid my arms under her and lifted her up so her bare feet would not touch the glass. Her white dress was splattered with blood. Until I felt the tears on my cheeks, I had not been aware I was crying.

I set her down on the bed to check her wounds.

Racine, who was standing behind me, said, "She is fine. She is not hurt."

"But the blood."

"It is part of the *lave tete*. We kill a white chicken. It is a gift for the *lwa*. The blood is not hers."

Then Solange pushed her head back and looked up at me, her brown eyes focused. "We go now?" she asked.

My whole body sagged, limp with relief. She was talking again. I wrapped my arms around her and held her. I looked at Racine over the top of her head and mouthed, "Thank you." She smiled and nodded as though she had never had a doubt that things would turn out this way.

Most of the time I'd felt so awkward not knowing what to do for this child, but hugging her skinny little frame at that moment felt just right. I didn't care if they had used dead chickens, magic herbs, visiting spirits, or whatever. Solange was back from that place deep inside herself.

"Sure, kiddo," I said. "We'll go now."

Racine accompanied us across the yard, which was still filled with dancers. I carried Solange on my hip, afraid to let her go. Inside the house, Racine put her cool hand on my arm.

"Wait one moment, please," she said. She motioned toward the couch. "Set the child down a moment. We need to speak."

"Racine, I just want to get her home."

"You are looking for this child's father, *non*?"

"Yes." I sat Solange down on the couch and joined her. "Can you help me find him?"

"Perhaps. We are both searching for the same answers, you and I."

"I don't understand."

She took my hand in hers again. "Now it is my turn to trust you." She paused, as though trying to decide whether to continue. "Many Haitians try to come to the United States. Some make a cooperative and build their own boats. They work together for their freedom, but it can take many years. Others, they pay the smugglers, money-hungry men who sometimes dump their human cargo rather than be captured. People go with smugglers because they feel they cannot wait any longer."

"But Racine, what does this have to do with Solange?"

"There are people here who get word when a boat has left Haiti. A watch is kept and when the boat comes ashore, people drive down to help any make it safely ashore. I was there that night, waiting for someone, when the *Miss Agnes* sank."

"You were there? Can you put me in touch with anyone who might know her father?"

"No. And Haitians will not be willing to talk to you, but perhaps they will speak to me. I will see what I can learn. People are very frightened now. It is the *bokor*. It is very dangerous for you to be asking these questions." She squeezed my hand, then let go. "I have something for you."

She stood and walked into a room at the back of the house. Solange had fallen asleep leaning against my arm. The house was quiet, though the sound of the drums outside grew ever louder. I wanted to get out of there, and I was tempted to just get up and leave. Finally, Racine returned with a small sachetlike bag on a leather thong. She placed it over my head.

"Do not take this off. This is from La Sirene. She will help you, protect you from the *bokor*."

I held the bag to my nose and sniffed. It smelled like old seaweed, and I made a face. "What's in this?"

"Just wear it, and La Sirene will be watching."

I shook my head. "Who is La Sirene?"

Racine smiled. "La Sirene is the spirit in the sea, and she watches over you. She will protect you from the *bokor*."

"And what the heck is a *bokor*?"

"Americans think *Vodou* is about black magic. This is not so for *mambos* and *hougans*. We are healers. But the *bokor* . . ." She looked away and lowered her head. She spoke very softly. "He is not a healer."

I rubbed my hand over my eyes and then thought about Racine's kindness and concern. "It's a lot to digest in one night, you know," I said. "People possessed by spirits, animal sacrifice"—I held up the pouch—"and magic seaweed." I shook my head and attempted to smile.

She pointed to a painting filled with bright-colored animals standing around a large wooden cross. "Many years ago, when the missionaries in Haiti asked the African slaves to worship the cross that Christ died on, the Africans saw it as symbolic of the Crossroads—the divider between the spirit world and ours. The Europeans were pleased when the Africans accepted the cross, but what they did not realize was that though they and the Africans were looking at the same cross, each was seeing something profoundly different." She stroked my hair, as if I were a child like the one sleeping between us. "Always remember, Seychelle, you will see what your experience has prepared you to see."

All the way to the car, Racine kept insisting that Solange was supposed to sleep in the *peristil* overnight, that the child needed to stay for the full benefit of the *lave tete* ceremony. The *lwa* would protect her, Racine said, and she argued it was too dangerous to take her away.

I thanked her profusely for helping the girl, buckled Solange into the Jeep, then turned back to face her.

"Racine, you said you were going to meet someone on board the *Miss Agnes*. What happened?"

I could barely make out her features in the dark yard, but I could sense how her body tensed. After several seconds of quiet, I thought she wasn't going to answer my question. When she spoke, finally, her voice was tight with emotion.

"It was my sister. She never made it to shore."

At the stoplight, waiting to turn onto I-95, I saw Solange staring into the darkness, the fear raw on her face.

"What happened back there?" I asked. "Why did you scream?"

She turned to face me. "I saw him," she said.

"Who?"

"Le Capitaine." She turned her head to stare out into the night as the light turned green.

XVIII

As I pulled the Jeep into Jeannie's yard, I cursed at the sight of the white Suburban with the green lettering. I checked my watch, then winced. It was after ten. I didn't want to give Rusty Elliot any reason to think I wasn't taking care of Solange properly, any reason for him to take her away. How the hell was I going to explain bringing her home in a dress splattered with blood?

Racine had handed me a plastic bag with Solange's shorts and T-shirt as we had passed through the house on our way out, and now I dug around in the back of the Jeep to find them. I figured I would change her clothes before taking her upstairs. It wasn't only that Rusty was here; Jeannie hadn't been all that thrilled at my taking the child off to that Voodoo house at night, either. She'd go ballistic, too, if she saw her now.

As I helped Solange unbuckle her seat belt, the porch light went on upstairs, and Jeannie appeared on the landing. "Hey, you. What took you so long? I've been trying to entertain Mr. Wonderful up here for a couple of hours now, and he's been getting more and more charming by the minute. Get yourself and that kid up here."

Damn. My chance to cover up the evidence had just evaporated. "Okay, we're coming."

Rusty came through the door just as we reached the top of the landing. I saw something in the way his face lit up when he saw me that told me he hadn't come only on business. I was sorry that I was going to disappoint him.

In his green work uniform, with its patches and badges, leather belt and gun, he looked more intimidating than he had in his shorts. This was not a man to play around with.

He looked at Solange. "What the hell happened to this child?" he asked.

She was walking on her own, awake and alert, but in the bright glare of Jeannie's porch light, it was clear her white dress had red polka dots.

"Calm down," I said, and as I said it, I couldn't help but think that those were the exact words Racine had told me less than an hour earlier. "Look at her." Solange smiled up at me. "See?" I pointed to her smile. "It worked, so don't gripe." I smoothed her loose clean hair back from her brow, tucked it into her white headscarf. "And as far as I know, they're going to eat the chicken." Rusty's jaw dropped.

Jeannie pushed Rusty out of the doorway and stood on the landing with her hands on her hips. "What chicken?"

I ignored her, tried to act like it was perfectly normal to come home after ten o'clock at night with a ten-year-old covered in blood. "It's not really that different from your going to Winn Dixie, when you think about it, except when you buy the chicken you don't risk getting the blood on you."

Rusty hadn't moved, he just continued to stare at me. Finally he said, "You took this child to some kind of animal sacrifice?"

"Well—"

Jeannie shook her head, took the girl's hand, and said, "I'll go wash her up and get her into some clean pajamas." She fixed me with a stare over the top of Solange's head and said in a soft voice, "You and I will discuss this later."

"You didn't answer me, Miss Sullivan," Rusty said when Jeannie had disappeared through the door and down the hall. "Did you or did you not take that child to a place where they were engaged in animal sacrifice?"

"Oh Rusty, yes. Yes, I did. Okay? This *is* South Florida, though. Come on. You'd have a right to be that shocked in Omaha or Wisconsin or somewhere, but not here."

"She's got blood on her!" he yelled.

"And she's Haitian," I yelled back. "For Pete's sake, man, down in Miami they've got a guy at the courthouse whose job it is to go out and pick the dead chickens up off the sidewalk every morning. Family members leave them when the prisoners are transferred from jail to court. Wake up, man. You're not in Kansas anymore."

He crossed his arms, his lips stretched thin. He stared at me for several seconds, letting the silence stretch out. "Are you finished?"

"Yeah, for now." I stepped around him and walked into Jeannie's living room.

Rusty followed me. "Seychelle, you don't seem to understand that I am stretching the regulations very thin even to allow this child to stay in this home." He reached out and put his hand on my shoulder. "What were you thinking?"

"You are so out of your element on this one, Rusty. Hell, we both are." I spun away, out of range of his touch. "I'm not sure you and I have an explanation for what happened to her at the hospital the other night or out at *Mambo* Racine's tonight. But didn't you hear what I said? *It worked.* She's talking again. And one thing I do know is that those people were not faking it. What I saw tonight—" I paused, not knowing how to explain it to him, how to give it the reality and the dignity I had seen. "Rusty, they *believed* completely. I'm not sure *I'm* ready to believe they were possessed by spirits, but it sure as hell was every bit as real as what your cousins up in the Georgia mountains do when they handle snakes and speak in tongues." I crossed the living room and plopped down on the couch, leaned back, and closed my eyes. "Man, am I tired." My stomach gurgled, and I pulled my arm across my belly to try to muffle the sound. "And starving. Haven't eaten anything since about noon."

Rusty walked over to the front door, crossed his arms again, leaned against the doorjamb, and stared out into the yard.

Jeannie had one of those couches with tons of throw pillows and cushions, and the cushions seemed to be pulling me down, relaxing me. I'd just about nodded off when I heard Rusty say something.

"What?"

"They'll still be serving over at the Downtowner. Do you want to go over and grab a bite? I'll buy if you'll stop yelling at me and tell me what's really going on with this kid."

I opened one eye and looked up at him. I wasn't thrilled about being seen with him in that uniform. Could scare off some of my clients who sometimes tread lightly on the wrong side of the law. But I was starving. "Conch fritters and fries?"

He lifted his cell phone off his belt and dialed a number. "Hi, it's Rusty. Think you could pick me up at Cooley's Landing in about ten? . . . Thanks." He put away the cell phone, then reached for my hand to pull me up off the deep couch. "Let's go. The Water Taxi'll pick us up at the marina."

I took his hand but let my body remain a dead weight. He had to strain to lift me up from those deep cushions.

"Man, you are heavy, Sullivan."

"Wimp," I said, and smiled as he pulled me to my feet and I bumped into his left side, where the cold steel of his gun brushed against my arm. "Seeing as you are wearing a gun, however, I guess it's Mr. Wimp."

"Damn right."

I stopped briefly to tuck Solange in like my mother used to do for me and wondered, as I kissed her forehead, why I was flirting with Rusty. As I passed by the master bedroom, I told Jeannie we'd be gone for about an hour.

Rusty came down the hall and motioned to me with a "let's go" signal. I turned back to Jeannie.

"Thanks again, Jeannie. I know she's better off with you than anywhere *he* wants to send her." I cocked my head in Rusty's direction.

"So I'm the bad guy, eh?" Rusty said over my shoulder.

"Yes," Jeannie said. "Get over it."

"Jeannie," I said, "I've got a connection to the *Miss Agnes* from my visit to Pompano tonight. I'll tell you all about it in the morning."

"Sounds good. Animal sacrifice, Voodoo, secret meetings. I can't wait." She winked.

The walk to Cooley's Landing Marina was only about three blocks, but being tired, I began to wish we'd taken the car. The Downtowner was on the other side of the river, and they had a large parking lot, so the car would have been easy. I feared we'd have a long wait for a Water Taxi.

Rusty sensed that I was not in a talkative mood. The streets were dark under the heavy canopy of old trees that covered most of Sailboat Bend.

"Over there," Rusty said when we reached the marina parking lot, and he pointed to the boat idling at the dock next to the launch ramp. There were no other passengers aboard. "Hey, Carlos," he said to the captain, a kid about twenty years old. "Thanks for the lift. This is Sey-chelle Sullivan."

"Sullivan Towing? *Gorda?*"

I nodded.

"Thought I recognized you. Seen you go by on your boat a lot."

"Carlos's dad works with me at the Border Patrol." He clapped his hand on the young man's back. "We've been fishing together since this guy was in diapers."

I leaned back and watched the lights of the parks and businesses downtown as we motored downriver. Too often lately, the river became just the place where I worked. It was pleasant being a passenger for a change, enjoying the view without worrying about bridges or currents or traffic.

The restaurant and bar were nearly empty inside. I waved hello to Pete behind the bar and his one customer, Nestor, a charter-boat captain. Pete raised his eyebrows at me when he saw I was with a guy wearing a gun.

"You want to sit outside?" I asked Rusty. The privacy of it would make it much easier to tell him about the evening's events—the story still sounded weird even to me—and more difficult for the guys inside to eavesdrop.

I waited until the server had taken our orders and brought us our cold draft beer.

"So tomorrow I'll go see this friend of Juliette's at the Swap Shop. I'm fairly certain that this girl actually came over on the *Miss Agnes.*"

"I don't think it's a good idea for you to get involved like this. You should leave this to the professionals. We could round up the people who work in this Swap Shop booth and question them all."

"Come on, Rusty. From the first minute I saw that kid's face, I've been involved. Do you really think these Haitians are going to say anything to Immigration? In their eyes, you guys are worse than the smugglers—even if the smugglers are bashing in a few heads."

He took a long swig from his beer, then reached for my hand. "I worry about you. I don't want anything to happen to you."

"That's nice, but I'm just meeting a kid at the Swap Shop—one of the most populated tourist attractions around here. I'm not walking into some den of bad guys. Not this time."

He shot me a questioning look, and I hurriedly changed the subject. "On the way home tonight, Solange said she saw 'Le Capitaine' at the Toussaint house. The guy on the boat that brought her here. He must have been the guy who knocked me down running out of the altar room. I didn't get a good enough look at his face to say whether or not he's the same guy who was in her hospital room, but the height, build, and facial hair were about right. And I remember seeing rings, several of them on the left hand, both times." I thought about mentioning the skull and crossbones on the sunglasses I had found on board the *Miss Agnes* but thought better of it. I didn't want to be accused of tampering with evidence. "It's got to be the same guy, but I don't know that I could pick him out of a lineup."

"Here's a question," Rusty said, and he hitched forward in his chair, now grasping my hand in both of his. "What was he trying to do to her tonight, and why didn't he succeed?"

"I assume he was going to shut her up—permanently," I said. "As to why he didn't succeed, well, according to Racine Toussaint, he couldn't do it because the *lwa* protected her. Racine wanted me to leave her there overnight. She said it was the only place Solange would be safe." With my free hand, I fingered the pouch Racine had given me that I had tucked inside my T-shirt.

"I'm sorry, Seychelle, but that's bullshit. I hope you don't believe that."

I pulled my hand back out of his grasp and finished off the last of my beer, feeling light-headed and confused from the combination of beer, exhaustion, and an empty stomach. "You know, Rusty, I don't know what to believe." Looking around me, at the glamorous yachts docked along the river, and above me at the blue and white lights of the downtown high-rises, I found it hard to believe what I had seen in that yard in Pompano just hours before. "I'm not going to just dismiss this as hocus-pocus, though. I can't. I was there and something very powerful was going on," I said. "Just because we don't understand it doesn't mean it isn't real."

"You're more open-minded than I am."

"Trust me, open-mindedness doesn't come all that easily to me. I'm having to work at it. This guy, though, this Capitaine, he scares me. He's so persistent in going after this kid." I leaned forward and put my arms on the table. "Let's just say Solange did see him kill that woman. What can she do to him? She doesn't know his name. She can't do anything except maybe pick him out of a lineup. So what's he doing still hanging around here? Why hasn't he gone back to the Bahamas? And here's another thing: If we assume that this guy is the one who killed the other three, then there have been witnesses before, and there are probably more witnesses among the people who came on the *Miss Agnes*. What makes this kid different?"

"You're right. And I don't buy that business about some kind of spirits protecting the kid. He had the chance to kill her tonight, and he didn't. That means he didn't intend to. So what does he want with her?"

The waitress brought our food then, and I didn't say another word as I filled my mouth with conch fritters. The ground conch was sweet and chewy and drowned in fresh lime juice. Rusty had ordered chicken wings, and I found I was unable to look at his plate without my stomach twisting in a little queasy twinge. It might be a while before I felt like eating chicken again.

"I hate all this," Rusty said, pointing a chicken bone at the brightly lit buildings across the river from us. "Look at that skyline. Have you counted the construction cranes lately? Seven. I counted seven the other day. What are they doing to our town? Remember what it was like when we were kids?"

I smiled. " 'Course I do. But I also remember when downtown was dead, the storefronts were mostly empty, and there were homeless guys wandering all around here. There was good and bad in those good old days."

He gnawed on his last wing and began licking the sauce off his fingers. I watched each finger slide between his lips and then slip out, making the sound of a kiss. It took every bit of energy I had left to concentrate on what he was saying.

"Nowadays, everywhere's changed. They're building on every last scrap of land. And places where there is no more land, they're just building straight up." He finished cleaning his fingers and drank off the last of the beer in his glass. "Everywhere you go nowadays, the person serving your food, bagging your groceries, cutting your lawn, or cleaning your hotel room arrived here just a few months ago. And they got here by slipping past me." He leaned back in his chair and pushed his plate of bones away. "They're changing this place I call home, and I can't stop it. I hate it."

"So get over it, Rusty. All these immigrants make this place the town I love. The cultures, the languages, the religions, mix together here. Sure, Fort Lauderdale is no longer a little dusty, white-bread, cracker town. But hey, some of us happen to think that's a good thing."

He grumbled as he waved at the young Latina waitress, signaling her to bring our check.

Rusty and Carlos talked fishing on the way back to Cooley's Landing. Carlos was saying how he and his dad had chartered with this great fishing guide, fellow by the name of Bouncer, who worked out of Miami. Carlos was saying it was like Bouncer had some amazing sixth sense—he just knew where the fish were, and with Bouncer's help, Carlos and his dad had won some big-deal tournament down in Key Largo.

I thought about how it was okay for a fishing guide to have a little inexplicable magic, but if it was a Haitian doing it, we called it hocus-pocus. I felt the weight of the leather pouch around my neck. What did I believe? I wasn't sure, but I didn't see the harm in a little extra insurance. I did not intend to remove the pouch any time soon.

I was jerked out of my reverie when the boat bumped up against the dock and the fenders squeaked as the air was squeezed out of them.

"Time to head for home," Rusty said, hopping out of the boat first and reaching back to offer me his hand. Once on the dock, he didn't let go. We both said good night to Carlos and started the walk back, still holding hands like a couple of kids.

"Thanks for dinner," I said.

He didn't say anything. We walked across the asphalt, listening to the sound of our shoes crunching bits of barnacle from the launch ramp. Just as we reached the grass on the far side of the launch ramp, Rusty pointed to the river on our left. "Look, a manatee." He let go of my hand, put his arm around my shoulder, and pointed through an empty boat slip. "See those rings in the current midriver?" Just then the fuzzy snout surfaced, and we saw the black nostrils and the little cloud of mist around them.

"It's late for a manatee here," I said.

"Uh-huh," Rusty said, and from the sound of his voice in my ear, I knew he was looking at me, not the manatee. Then he said, "I'm not very good at this," and he placed a hand on the side of my face and kissed me on the mouth. While I would have to agree with him that his technique for getting there was rather abrupt, when it came to the actual kissing, he wasn't half bad.

An alarm sounded several blocks over in the neighborhood, and we broke apart, taking an air break. The alarm continued to whoop, and I said, "Sounds like somebody can't remember their code."

"Damned gadgets," he said. "What the hell good are they when everyone ignores them?"

I didn't get to answer him. It was then I heard the shot. It wasn't a little pop like they say gunshots make, and not a *whomp* like an explosion, either. It was a muffled *boom*. Like it had come from inside a house. We both started running.

xix

I leaped up to the second step, and my sneaker slid in a puddle of something wet. Blood. I didn't stop to examine it but took the rest of the steps two at a time, calling out Jeannie's name as soon as I hit the landing. The alarm was still whooping, but I heard Jeannie's voice inside.

"I'm in here," she shouted.

The screen door was shredded and part of the wood frame hung in splinters. Where was Rusty when I needed him? I wondered if Jeannie was alone in there or if somebody was with her holding a gun to her head.

"Everybody okay?" I called out before approaching the door.

"Yeah, we are," she said. "Not sure about the other guy, though."

When I went to reach for the handle to open the door, I realized there was no handle left. I grabbed a piece of the dangling wood and made an opening between the screen and the shredded door frame big enough to climb through. Just inside, to the right of the door, the plaster was blown off the wall, the bare cinder block exposed. Jeannie was standing on the far side of the room, staring at the alarm system's control panel, the shotgun still cradled in her arms. She turned to look at me, her eyes slightly out of focus, as I came through what had been the door.

"Damned if I can remember the code right now," she said.

All three kids were standing in doorways in the hall, their eyes huge. One of the twins called out the code to his mom, and soon the alarm shut down. No sooner did it stop than the phone started ringing. In the distance, a siren wailed.

Jeannie took a few steps into the living room and looked around for the portable phone. "Geez," she said as she stared at the damage to her door and wall. Her hands still gripped the shotgun tight across her body, and her fingers, wrapped around the stock, looked white and bloodless. I peeled her hands open and took the gun from her so she could answer the phone. As she lifted the phone, she winced and reached up to massage her shoulder.

The door frame scraped open, and Rusty slipped into the room, holding a handgun down low with both hands. I started to tell him that everyone was okay, but he swept past me, running in a sort of simian crouch, checking every room down the hall. Jeannie finished talking to the alarm company on the phone and hung up about the time Rusty came back into the living room, tucking his gun back into its holster on his hip.

"What happened, Jeannie?" I asked.

Rusty crossed to the front door and looked down into the yard.

"The bastard cut the screen with a machete," she said. "I grabbed the gun when I heard the alarm go off. When I got into the hallway, he was coming through the door swinging that big old blade. I guess he heard me pump the action on the gun. He must have jumped back and to the left, behind the wall. I'm pretty sure I winged him, though."

"The cops are here," Rusty said, looking through the remains of the screen. He turned around and looked at Jeannie. "You definitely grazed him. I followed the guy through the backyard, over the fence, and into the street, but he must have had a car waiting back there. He was losing blood all the way. Anyway, get the kids settled back down. The cops will be up to talk to you when I'm done." He started out through what was left of the door.

Jeannie made coffee after the kids got settled, and we sat in the living room, wired on caffeine and adrenaline but too tired to talk. A couple of uniformed cops had searched the apartment, examined the torn-up doorway, then just stood there, hands clasped behind their backs, staring at us, waiting. For what, I wasn't sure. I should have known that a call that involved Solange and me would end up getting to Collazo. I shouldn't have felt surprise when the raggedy screen door scraped open and I heard his voice saying, "Miss Sullivan . . . again."

After Collazo, more uniformed officers came through the door,

followed by several folks in plainclothes. I didn't know if they were detectives or technicians. The living room was getting damned crowded.
Rusty brought up the rear. They all huddled around the door and
mumbled, examining the damaged wall and wood.

Collazo pointed to the shotgun lying where I had left it. He looked
at Jeannie. "That weapon belongs to you."

"You asking me?"

"Jeannie, that's just his way," I said. "He doesn't ask questions.
You get used to it after a while."

She shook her head. "Yes, that shotgun is registered to me, and I
am the one who fired it tonight at some dirtbag who was trying to break
into my house, waving a machete around."

"He was entering through the front door."

Jeannie glanced at me as though to say "What is this guy's problem?" I just shrugged. I was enjoying the fact that his nonquestions
weren't aimed at me.

Jeannie told the story with the accuracy that one would expect from
a lawyer. Her description of the guy made me certain it had been Le
Capitaine.

Cops and technicians had been coming and going, and none of us
paid them much mind, but when Agent D'Ugard arrived, there was a
noticeable straightening of the spines of all the men in the room. She
nodded to Collazo and then headed straight for Rusty. When the two
of them disappeared into Jeannie's bedroom in the back of the house,
my imagination went into overdrive. I was still staring down the hall
when I heard my name.

"Miss Sullivan, your story."

I blinked. "Oh, okay. Well, I need to back up a little and tell you
about what happened earlier this evening. Then, maybe all the rest of
this will make sense." As I told Collazo what had happened in Pompano, I kept glancing down the hall, wondering what they were doing
back there. Collazo took in the dead chickens and Voodoo rituals
without so much as a blink. Unlike Rusty, this man knew his home
turf. "I thought I had really paid attention on the drive back from
Pompano, and I didn't see anybody follow us back here. I don't know
how he knew where to find us."

"That's the problem with amateurs," Collazo said.

—

"I have to agree with Detective Collazo." It was Agent D'Ugard, with Rusty close at her side. They'd just come out of the bedroom. I checked for disheveled clothes or hair, then felt silly for doing it. I cursed my own dirty mind and wondered why I would even care.

"The events of this evening," she continued, "as related to me by Agent Elliot, are proof enough that you cannot guarantee this child's safety here." She turned to Rusty. "You mentioned a group home where you house alien children."

Jeannie opened her mouth and started to protest, but Rusty jumped in and through sheer volume took control of the conversation.

"We need to move them all. Not just the child. None of them are safe here tonight. Even if we remove the girl, there's no way of being certain they won't come back here later looking for her. We need a safe house where we can keep this entire family protected."

Collazo turned to Rusty, a faint smirk dancing around his mouth. "Mr. Elliot, nobody at the department is going to authorize taking all of them to a safe house. There is no evidence Ms. Black is in that kind of danger."

"Look at my door," Jeannie shouted.

"Ma'am, there are break-ins in this neighborhood every night."

"Oh, so you think this was just some crackhead looking to make a score? With all the million-dollar waterfront homes less than two blocks away, you think some whack with a machete is going to choose this dump to rob?" Jeannie threw her hands into the air and began walking in circles, talking to herself. Collazo was right, though. There wasn't really any way to prove that this incident had been directed at Solange.

"Listen, Maria, Detective Collazo"—Rusty nodded at them each in turn—"what about this idea: I have a little condo down on Hollywood Beach. What if I take them down there? It's a three-bedroom unit. We could ask the Hollywood PD to keep an eye on the place, and I'll sleep there tonight. What do you say?"

Agent Maria D'Ugard shook her head and whipped out a tiny cell phone. She walked over to the kitchen as she dialed.

Collazo wandered over to the door frame. The crime scene team had finished with their photos and the removal of several pieces of shot from the wooden door frame. He picked at the plaster with his fingernail and looked outside through the gaping screen.

When Agent D'Ugard finished her call and snapped her phone shut, I said, "May I speak to you for a minute?"

She jerked her head in the direction of Jeannie's kitchen. Once out of earshot of the others, she crossed her arms and said, "Go ahead, Miss Sullivan."

I didn't think she looked too receptive, but I dove in anyway. "There's something I found out tonight about this alien smuggling ring. Something I thought you and the DART people ought to know about."

"Why not tell this to Collazo or Elliot? Why me?"

"I don't know. Maybe because you're a woman? I know that doesn't make much sense, but what I am going to tell you is going to sound farfetched. I'm certain the guys in there would dismiss it. You're my best bet. Anyway, here's the deal. It seems these people are importing kids and placing them as *restaveks* in homes here in the States."

"And what are *restaveks*?" Her tone of voice couldn't have been more mocking.

"In Haiti, when a family has too many kids, and they can't feed them all, they send off some kids to live with and work for other families. They are basically child slaves. Now they are importing this practice to the United States."

"So you think they've started up the slave trade again? Haiti? The first country in the Americas to outlaw slavery?"

"Yes, strange as that sounds, that's exactly what I'm telling you. There are child slaves working in the suburbs of Fort Lauderdale, right under our noses."

"Miss Sullivan, why don't you leave the investigating to the professionals? That's preposterous."

"Think about it. They double their money. The family in Haiti pays to have their children taken to the U.S., and the families in the U.S. pay the smugglers to get a domestic worker who needs no Social Security or even wages. They don't even send these kids to school. Remember the two girls who drowned off the *Miss Agnes*? Don't you think it's odd that we're seeing so many more unaccompanied minors?"

She uncrossed her arms and smoothed out the fabric across the front of her skirt. "I'll certainly keep it in mind." She turned and left the room, and I heard the sound of the screen opening.

When I stepped into the hall, I saw Collazo standing in the dark at the doorway to the kids' room. He was watching Solange sleep, and he looked up, surprised when I joined him.

"Isn't she sweet?" I asked. "She's got nobody, you know. Do you really want to send her back to the streets of Port-au-Prince?"

"You get them settled into Elliot's condo. Tomorrow"—he turned and looked straight at me—"I want to talk to the child about this captain."

We piled toys and clothes and sleepy kids into the back of Jeannie's van. It took me several minutes to convince Solange that she couldn't go with me in the Jeep, that she needed to stay in the van with the other kids. Looking like a regular caravan, we pulled out of Jeannie's driveway—the van, then me in the Jeep, and Rusty taking up the rear in the Border Patrol Suburban. When Agent D'Ugard had left earlier, Rusty walked her down to her car, and although I couldn't hear what they were saying, I did hear their raised voices.

When we exited Sailboat Bend onto Broward Boulevard, Rusty had us divide up and drive around in some convoluted routes while he backtracked behind each of us, checking for any possible tails. It was nearly two in the morning when we met up in the parking lot at the Howard Johnson's on the beach. Jeannie and Rusty were there ahead of me, and a Hollywood cop pulled into the lot at the same time I did. Rusty went over and leaned into the car to talk to the officer.

I jumped out of the Jeep and went over to the window of Jeannie's van.

"How're the kids?" I asked.

"They zonked out in the first five minutes. I'd like to do the same. What's Mr. Green Jeans doing, anyway?"

I was trying to come up with a clever remark, but my brain was too exhausted to even approach the realm of slightly amusing.

Just then Rusty stepped away from the cop car, and he motioned for us to follow him. We drove another three blocks north and parked in the lot of a condo building on the Intracoastal side of US-1. The complex wasn't huge, just a single building four stories high with a rustic wood sign out front that said "Heron Heights Condominiums." There was no ground floor; the building was built over a covered parking area. Rusty waved as the Hollywood cop cruised slowly past the building, and we each took a sleeping kid and carried them up to the fourth floor.

The door to Rusty's condo was at the end of the hall, facing north. When I stepped inside his unit, I realized it stretched to both sides of the building, overlooking the Intracoastal to the west, and when I crossed the living room to the sliding glass balcony doors, the ocean loomed as a distant dark mass beyond the rooftops of the low apartment bungalows between US-1 and North Surf Road.

Rusty flicked a switch and the soft light of a ceramic lamp lit the room. The lamp rested on a dark wood table next to a big leather reading chair.

"Wow," I said. The place was like something out of an old Key West magazine photo—hardwood floors, ceiling fans, built-in bookcases, and a few perfectly placed antiques.

"In here," Rusty said, carrying Jeannie's son Adair into one of the bedrooms. He laid the boy down on the queen-size bed and unfolded the armchair, which was then transformed into a single futon. I knelt down and placed the girl's thin body on the futon mattress, though it took me several minutes to get her to let go of my neck. Even in her sleep, she was clinging to me in a way I found both unsettling and reassuring, as though whether or not I believed in myself, this child believed in me. Jeannie and I covered all three kids with the sheets and blankets Rusty provided, while he fiddled with the air conditioner to clear out the stale air. He pointed Jeannie to the second room, promising to bring up the rest of the luggage. Jeannie just waved a limp hand in the air and closed the door behind her.

"You can have the bedroom. I'll take the couch," Rusty said.

"Nah, I'm not staying."

"But you must be exhausted." He rested his hand on my shoulder, and I felt the muscles beneath his touch tighten. "You shouldn't drive anywhere."

I shrugged. "Yeah, but I've got the dog at home and—" I couldn't finish the sentence. I looked at him, saw the way his shaggy hair fell across the tops of his ears, the way the light made his blue eyes appear iridescent. I had enjoyed that kiss earlier, and the prospect of another wasn't exactly unappealing. B.J. and I had agreed to a break. There really wouldn't be anything wrong with it, would there? My brain felt foggy.

I turned and stepped out of his reach, trying to get the weight of that hand off my shoulder before I did something really stupid. "You got a Coke or something with caffeine? I think I just need a little fresh air." With barely a touch of my hand, the balcony doors slid open with a soft *whoosh,* and the moist sea air blew into the opening. I stepped outside and sucked in what a yoga instructor years ago had called a "cleansing breath." I exhaled loudly through my mouth. Rather than revived, I felt even more dizzy. I was hyperventilating.

Rusty joined me at the balcony rail and handed me an icy soda can. I drank so much, so fast, my chest hurt. Out on the horizon a small pinpoint of light appeared and then disappeared, then came back and grew steady—a small vessel crossing the current, heading for Port Everglades. There was no other traffic in sight, which was unusual for this stretch of the coast. I wondered then, how many boats were out there running dark—running drugs or human cargo?

"This is really a nice place you've got here, Rusty. View's sure spectacular."

"Yeah, I like it, but I don't get to use it enough. I keep my boat at the dock out back on the Waterway, and most times I just go out fishing, come back, and never even make it upstairs."

"I hope you're going to be ready for three rowdy kids in the morning."

"Bringing them here solved the problem for tonight, but this is not a long-term solution, you know."

"Why'd you do it? Invite us over like this?"

He tried to laugh, but it came out a single "Ha," without humor. "Good question." He leaned his arms on the balcony railing and stared out to sea. He seemed to be struggling to find the words to say something. I was afraid of what that might be.

I drained off the last of the soda. "Well," I said, and turned to head for the door.

He reached for my shoulder and slid his big hand around the back of my neck and under my ponytail. He pulled me to him, saying, "It took inviting the entire crew over just to get you here."

"Now that's funny, because they're going to stay and I'm not." I must not have sounded very convincing at that point because he kissed me. Again. And again, I didn't protest. In fact, my body became a regular cheerleader for the idea. All kinds of little nerve endings were shaking their pom-poms.

But then I pulled away. "Rusty, it's late and we both need to get some sleep."

He tried little kisses then, down the side of my neck, around my ears, and *that* came very close to making me forget everything.

When I got to the door and had my hand on the doorknob and was almost out of there, he called my name softly. "Seychelle."

"Yeah," I said, but I didn't even turn around.

"Are you sure you won't stay?"

I couldn't answer him. My voice would have given too much away.

When I got back to the Larsens' place and saw Abaco crawl out all sleepy from under her bougainvillea bush, I sat down on the bench outside the cottage door and gave her a good body rub. She groaned in contentment. I patted the bench next to me, and she hopped up and sat there panting. I looped an arm around her and buried my face in the soft fur around her neck. I pulled back quickly.

"You need a bath." I looked down at my clothes, the dark smudges from the chicken blood still apparent on my shirt. "Me too, I guess." I scratched her silky ears. "Girl, do you think we'll ever understand men?" She just smiled her doggy smile.

I started to tiptoe past Pit snoring on the couch, but then I stopped and stood there for a while in the dark, watching his chest rise and fall with each breath. In the face of the man I could still see the features of the boy I had grown up with. The hair at his temples reflected what little light there was in the room. He was going prematurely gray. We were all growing older—Maddy was already quite gray. We had tried to gather as a family at least once a year as long as Red had still been alive, but now we were forging our own lives and seeing less and less of one another. I tried to memorize every small detail of Pit's features because I knew he was already itching to leave.

I crawled into my bed after a quick rinse in the shower. I was too tired to sleep and still tossing and turning as the sky began to go gray. Rusty's words, the sound of his voice, the feel of his touch. I kept going over and over every minute of the night, from the restaurant to Jeannie's to his gorgeous condo. And I kept trying to avoid the question that my mind couldn't let go. How does a Border Patrol officer afford a half-million-dollar condo on the Intracoastal Waterway?

xx

I'd slept about an hour when I woke to the noise of an exceptionally loud outboard motor headed downriver, and I knew I wasn't going to get back to sleep. It was not yet six o'clock, but I threw back the sheet and swung my legs to the floor.

My head felt like it was stuffed with dirty gym socks. I knew because I could taste them. After a bathroom trip, and pulling on shorts and a T-shirt, I grabbed a bottle of water out of the fridge and locked up the cottage, my brother still snoring contentedly. I noticed the dining table and floor were covered with charts, and my plotter and dividers were on the bar next to several empty beer bottles. Pit had been hard at work.

The Larsens have a shed full of water toys, and they don't mind if I use them from time to time. And alternating running, paddling, and swimming did help keep the exercise regimen from getting too boring. I pulled the red, sit-on kayak down to the dock, gritting my teeth as the plastic slid across the gravel; holding on to the bowline, I tossed it into the river. Getting onto the thing from the dock ladder without capsizing was a feat, but once settled, I paddled upriver, pulling against a river current made weak by the rising tide.

The hour of morning after the sky first starts to turn gray but before the sun's top curve peeks above the trees and homes of my neighborhood is the part of the day I cherish most. I hadn't seen much of it recently. Along the banks of the New River, the early morning is when the animals relinquish the world to the humans. The raccoons scurry across backyards and hightail it up trees to their daytime sleeping roosts. The herons stand regal and still on the seawalls, their bills pointed down at the slow-moving water, their dark, sharp eyes their only moving parts.

After I'd passed through the heart of downtown, where the cars were already moving over the drawbridges and aproned men were out sweeping between the waterfront tables, I heard a sharp exhale as I approached the fork where the river split in two directions. I slowed my paddling and watched the surface ahead. Circles again on the surface. Finally, I saw the nostrils blow off my port bow. Our late-season manatee was making her way downriver, and now that the sun was nearly up, the water around her reflected the pink clouds, making it look like she was swimming in a bubble-gum-colored river.

The morning air was still and heavy with humidity. No more than ten minutes after I'd slowed to watch the manatee, the sunlight's reflection on the river ripples seared laserlike into my eyes. Soon, the sweat was dripping off the tip of my nose, and I was starting to wake up.

I paddled up the north fork of the New River where it meandered undeveloped through some of the poorest neighborhoods of Fort Lauderdale. The riverbanks were thick with trees and grasses, but I knew that less than one hundred feet beyond those wooded banks ran some mean, tough streets. At least it was quiet up there, and only the occasional friendly fisherman waved to me from the riverbanks.

The railroad bridge was down, and I was paddling in slow circles, waiting for the freight train to pass, when I sensed a boat approaching me closer than I would like from astern. I turned around and saw Perry Greene's white blond hair as he leaned over the side of his *Little Bitt* with his arm outstretched, reaching for my ponytail.

"Don't even think about it, Perry," I said, keeping an eye on him.

"Hey, babe, what you doing in that little bathtub toy?"

"It's called exercise, Perry. Not that you'd understand the meaning of that word."

He put his boat into reverse and I stopped paddling. We both eased to a stop, side by side and still in the water, but traveling slowly with the tide. The last car of the freight train rumbled over the trestle, and it grew much quieter as we waited for the automated bridge to reopen.

I grabbed the gunwale of *Little Bitt*. While he was here, I might as well ask him a couple of questions. "Perry, I saw you in Flossie's yesterday. I'm guessing you were there talking to Gil Lynch."

He pressed his lips together like he was getting ready to spit, and I cringed. He turned his head aside and blew a mouthful of spittle into the water off the stern.

"God, gross, Perry."

"So what if I was talking to Gil. It's a free country."

"No big deal. I'm just curious what you guys were talking about, and why he ran when Mike and I tried to talk to him. Do you have any idea why he took off like that?"

"He's crazy. You do know that, don't you? But the thing is, he's still got connections. We was just shooting the shit. I told him about towing in your friend Mike and then I was asking him about the owner of that Eye-talian boat we worked. He was just starting to tell me about that dude when he split. So I went back to Flossie's last night."

"Perry, you're at Flossie's every night."

He nodded. "Nearly. Anyways, when Gil showed up, he was acting real skittish. Said he didn't want to have nothing to do with that one-legged cop. Meaning Mike Beesting, of course."

"That's kind of weird. What's he got against Mike?"

"Hell if I know what goes on in that dude's head. It's all scrambled in there."

The railroad bridge sounded the buzzer and the span began to rise. Perry said, "Much as I love chatting with you, sweetheart, I got a Hatteras down at Bahia Mar waiting for Perry to make his magic."

The rest of the trip downriver hadn't taken nearly as long since I had the current flowing with me. That was fortunate because the last half hour on the main river, with all the Saturday-morning boating crowd who were jockeying like it was rush hour on the Interstate, churning up the water and impatiently revving their engines, had come close to making me seasick.

My arms burned and my palms were blistered when, finally, I feathered my paddle to ease the kayak into the dock off *Gorda*'s stern. When I reached up to grab the cleat on the dock, I saw a pair of familiar handsome brown legs walking toward me.

"Morning, Miss Sullivan," Joe said. He was carrying two covered paper cups and a grease-stained brown bag. "Your cappuccino's getting cold."

"Where's my brother?"

"Nobody here but the dog when I arrived. I knocked on your cottage door and was about to drink your coffee when I saw you come paddling this way."

"I'm surprised Abaco let you back here."

"Onion bagels are her favorite. She wouldn't have done it for honey wheat. I tried that first."

"Ah, so, do you always bribe women to get what you want?"

He grinned. "I usually don't need to."

I was attempting to execute the rather complicated maneuver required to climb off a kayak alongside a dock, and I nearly went into the river at this comment. The tide was high, so very little of the ladder was left above water, and I made an extremely ungraceful landing by sliding onto the dock on my belly. After tying off the kayak's bowline, I dusted off my hands on my shorts and stood up. Joe's mountain bike was propped against the trunk of an old oak tree, and he was again dressed in Lycra bike shorts, this time with a baby-blue tank top. He handed me a cardboard coffee cup.

"Thanks." I inclined my head in the direction of the wood picnic table closer to the Larsens' house. "Let's get a ways back from the river. I've inhaled enough exhaust this morning."

"So how're things?"

I didn't say anything, just looked into the bag he'd brought, pulled out a cinnamon raisin bagel, and spread the cream cheese on with a plastic knife. I knew what he was doing. Joe was trying to get back on my good side by bribing me with bagels. I'd take the bribe, but as for forgiveness, he was going to have to work for it.

I bit off a big piece and chewed slowly. "Hmmm. These are really good. The coffee, too. Thanks."

"So, how's that kid?"

"Fine."

"Have you been to see her?"

"Yup."

He tried to wait me out, make me need to fill in the silence. Not this morning. Not after what he'd said yesterday.

"Seychelle, look, I want to help you. I like you. I'm a retired cop and I'm bored, so I'd like to help out any way I can. You're not experienced. You should use me. Use me and abuse me."

"It's nice of you to offer, Joe, but . . ."

"You're still pissed off at me, aren't you. First my daughter, now you. I seem to piss off all the women I try to help. This is about yesterday, isn't it. About what I said about your old man."

"Don't call him my 'old man.' "

"Okay, this is about Red, then. Hmm. I thought you were better than that, Sullivan."

I glanced quickly at him, frowned, and turned away. The bagels tasted lousy all of a sudden.

"You said you were going to find that kid's father," he said, "and you sounded like you meant it. I believed you." He balled up his napkin and crushed his empty coffee cup. "But now you're so hung up on some old news about what did or didn't happen more than twenty years ago, you're gonna turn down a chance to use thirty years of investigative experience because you're pouting over your daddy." He stood and collected the bag with the remaining bagels.

I sighed. "Sit down."

He stood there, waiting.

"Would you sit already?" I said.

"Why?"

"You're gonna make me say it, aren't you. Okay. Maybe I could use a little help. There. See, I kinda screwed up last night. Somebody followed me, and it nearly got ugly. I thought I'd made sure I didn't have a tail, but I guess I'm not a very good Nancy Drew after all. I don't want to make that mistake again. So, yeah. I'll take you up on your offer."

He sat down on the wood bench. "Okay, so you need to find this kid's father."

"Yeah. She says her father is an American, and she thinks that she was being brought to America to join him. I figured the place to start, then, was the boat that brought her to America. I've set up a meeting today with someone who knows something about the *Miss Agnes*."

"Would you mind if I tag along? I could watch your back."

I looked at his bike shorts and clean blue tank top. "I don't know that you'll still want to when you hear where we're going."

"Where's that?"

"The Swap Shop."

—

What we now know as the Swap Shop had started life back in the six-
ties as the Thunderbird Drive-in Movie Theater. When the owner
began running a flea market on the blacktop expanse on weekends, the
concept grew and grew, eventually becoming an indoor/outdoor collection of permanent booths with a food court and full-time entertainment including a circus, complete with elephants, rides, and an
outdoor carnival. The place still showed movies at night, but the main
business now took place during the day when the Swap Shop resembled
the outdoor markets of third-world countries more than an American
shopping mall.

We got lucky and found a minivan pulling out of a parking space. I
whipped Lightnin' into the spot before a hooked-up Honda Civic with
booming bass could beat me to it.

"You like to live dangerously, I see," Joe said.

Although most of the sky was blue, a small dark cloud just overhead
began to spit raindrops on us as we walked across the parking lot. We
picked up the pace and ducked under the tent that covered the long
rows of outdoor stalls.

"You ever been here before?" I asked Joe.

"No, can't say that this is my sort of spot." He seemed to draw into
himself, as if he were afraid he might catch something.

I like grit. Always have. And the Swap Shop was one of the grittiest
places you could find in South Florida. And that was saying something.

Within a few minutes, the rain had stopped, and the fierce sun was
out again, pushing the humidity into the nineties. The odors from
fried foods, sweet cotton candy, and sweat mingled with the steam that
was rising off the asphalt, making it difficult to breathe. I half expected
Joe to pass out.

Hispanic families and East Indian men manned most of the stalls.
They called out to us as we passed, offering us their assorted car parts
or their knives and sword collections or their T-shirts with off-color
slogans. The blacktop beneath our feet was throbbing with the bass
from the reggae music as we passed a huge array of subwoofers. I didn't
see many Haitians among the stall owners, though folks in the crowd

seemed to speak more Creole than anything else. I figured that most of the Caribbean islanders probably sold fruits and veggies over in the food market. Joe and I asked an elderly security guard for directions and discovered that Paris Kids was a children's-wear store inside the main building.

"What's the plan?" Joe asked as we headed toward the double glass doors.

"I don't have one," I told him. "I'm supposed to talk to a girl who works in this booth. She supposedly knows something about the *Miss Agnes,* maybe came over on board herself. I'd like you to just keep back, see if anybody shows an interest in us. The Capitaine guy is a dark-skinned man, well over six feet tall, with a goatee and a mustache. If you see anybody around fitting that description, let me know."

"Sounds like a plan to me. Consider me invisible."

From inside the building, we could hear an announcer's voice booming over a PA system. "Ladies and gentlemen, boys and girls . . . " and it was clear that we had arrived in time for the circus performance. The crowd was so thick that we had to turn sideways to fit through the doors and fight our way into the building. An old mir-rored ball flung dancing spots of light around the crowd, and neon signs advertising gyros and pizza and Tic Tac Dough lottery cards pro-vided the only other light. I saw the sign for Paris Kids on the far side of the food court and squeezed my way through the crowd in that di-rection. I'd already lost track of Joe.

When I made it to the shop's door, I felt like I had just paddled my kayak into a side eddy of the river. I paused to catch my breath, and be-fore I became aware of anything else in the shop, a woman was at my side.

"Can I help you?" She was a matronly Haitian woman in her mid-forties.

"No, thanks. I just want to look around."

"Do you have something special in mind?" Her fingernails were long and painted with some kind of intricate designs. Little jewels glued to the nails glinted in the fluorescent lights.

"No, I just want to look around, okay?"

The store was filled with hundreds of little white dresses. There were maybe ten out of the hundreds that were either a pale pink or blue. The rest were all white.

"How old is your daughter?" the saleslady asked.

"I don't have any kids."

She made a sympathetic sound. "Awww, I am so sorry," she said. "Are you shopping for something for a niece or nephew, perhaps?"

Hey, lady, I wanted to say, bug off. There's nothing wrong with not having any kids.

Then the phone rang. "*Pardon,*" she said, and hurried into the back of the store. On her way through the door she hollered, "Margot! *Viens ici!*"

The young girl who emerged wore a deep, permanent scowl on her face and a large loose gray T-shirt that hid her body almost to her knees. A blue-and-white bandanna covered her head, and her face was makeup free. She looked about seventeen years old.

"Hi, Margot. I'm Seychelle Sullivan."

She jerked her head toward the racks of dresses on the far side of the front door.

When we got there, I pretended to look through the dresses, sliding each little hanger around the metal bar. "Do you know who I am?"

She nodded.

"Juliette told me you would talk to me," I said. "You know something about the *Miss Agnes?*"

"Yes."

"Do you want to tell me about it?"

"Yes." She didn't say anything more, and I was beginning to think this was pointless when she added, "He killed my brother."

The suddenness of her revelation startled me. "Who did?"

"Le Capitaine."

"The captain of the *Miss Agnes* killed your brother?"

"*Oui.*" It sounded more like a sharp inhalation than a word. She looked out at the crowd and scanned the faces, then turned back to me. "Very bad man. In Haiti, he was Tonton Macoute. Everybody afraid of him." She looked to the back of the store, and she sniffed. "I not. My brother was come from Haiti take me home. He pay Le Capitaine eight hundred dollar to come for me. Get away from Madame. That why Le Capitaine, he opened his head."

"Your brother died of head wounds?"

"*Oui,* they told me Le Capitaine put everybody in the sea, then he cut Jean-Pierre. Push him in the sea, too. He like it when some can't swim. He laugh."

"I'm so sorry," I said, my voice shaky. Her dark eyes gazed past me, reflecting the red circus lights like a pair of smoldering coals, and I actually felt scared watching the hatred in her face. I didn't know much about Haiti, but I had heard of the Macoutes—Papa and later Baby Doc's much-feared security force. No wonder this guy was so good with a machete. "Your brother didn't want you to work as a *restavek* any longer?"

She shook her head. "I come to Florida eight month ago. No school, only work. Jean-Pierre say he take me to school. Now . . . " She shrugged.

"Margot, I am trying to help another girl. She's younger than you are, and she came on the *Miss Agnes* this week. She was coming to live with her father here in the States, and I need to find him."

She shook her head. "All the girl come on *Miss Agnes* are *restavek* here in Florida."

I turned from her and held up a dress as though for her approval. My eyes swung across the crowd, and I noticed a familiar face. Then the face was gone. He had melted back into the sea of faces, but I would know that pockmarked skin and that zigzag eyebrow anywhere. What was Gil Lynch doing at the Swap Shop? Following me?

"Margot!" The saleslady emerged from the back of the shop shouting.

"Ma'am," I called out to her, "is it okay if Margot helps me pick out a dress for my niece? She's a very sweet girl."

The shop owner looked astonished that anyone would call this scowling girl sweet, but she was afraid to lose the sale, so she left us alone.

I pulled a dress off a rack and held it up, asking Margot to tell me what she thought. The music from the circus swelled, and the audience oooed. Apparently the elephants had entered the ring. I scanned the crowd again, trying to spot Gil. For just a second, I questioned whether he had really been there. Where was Joe?

The girl pointed to the lace around the collar of the little dress, and she said quietly, "You stop Le Capitaine?"

She wanted something from me that I couldn't promise. I put the dress back, moved a little farther down the rack, and examined a pale blue dress with a deep V neckline. Why the hell would a seven-year-old kid wear a neckline like that?

"He know Madame," she said.

"You mean the woman who owns this store?" I jerked my head toward the woman with the fingernail jewels and then whipped a dress off the rack and held it up as though for her opinion. "She's a friend? Of the captain of the *Miss Agnes*?"

Again, she nodded almost imperceptibly. "No friend. Business. He name Joslin Malheur. He come see Madame two day ago. He pay her money."

"Margot! *Qu'est-ce qui ce pas?*" Madame called from across the store. I didn't know what she was saying, but I could tell from the tone of her voice that she was suspicious.

I grabbed the biggest dress off the rack. "I'll take this one," I said, handed it to the girl, and followed her back to the cash register. The older woman rang up the sale, her lips pursed, her long nails clicking on the machine's keys. Margot bagged my purchase, her eyes downcast. When I'd received my change, I said to the girl, "You were going to point out the ladies' room?"

We walked to the store's entrance and were once again enveloped in the music and roar of the circus crowd. She pointed to the stairs and explained that I should turn left at the top to find the ladies' room. I whispered to her.

"Do you know where I can find him?"

"He tell Madame he go back to Bahamas on *Bimini Express*."

"Thank you very much, Margot." I turned to go, but Margot reached out and grabbed my forearm.

"You help Juliette?" She gripped my arm even tighter and moved in, her mouth close to my ear. "Monsieur Gohin. He hurt her." She turned around and hurried to the back of the store.

I plunged into the crowd and made my way away from the store and the prying eyes of Madame. My stomach churned as I thought about Margot's last words. She had to have been referring to sexual abuse. *Child slavery.* I looked at the smiling crowds leaving the circus bleachers.

Would any of them ever believe such a thing was happening in their backyards?

I'd heard of the *Bimini Express*. It was a little interisland freighter that usually sailed in and out of either Port Laudania or the Miami River. Back when I was a kid, Red used to work some jobs down on the Miami River. I'd gone with him, and I vaguely remembered seeing that name on a little freighter.

Clutching my purchase, I wormed my way through the crowd that was now breaking up. Evidently the circus had finished. I looked everywhere for a familiar face, but there was no sign of either Joe or Gil. I decided to head over to the stairs to see if Joe was on the upper level, and he seemed to magically materialize at my side.

"How'd it go?" he said.

"I've been looking all over for you. How come I didn't see you till you were right next to me?"

He winked. "Trade secrets." He pointed at an electronics booth jammed with stereo gear. "See that store? It's owned by a buddy of mine. He let me stand behind the counter. You weren't looking at the people behind the counters."

"You're good," I said.

He shrugged. "My buddy and me, we've been catching up a little about the old days. Things were really good back then."

"Hey, Joe. You didn't happen to see Gilbert Lynch go by while you were standing behind that counter?"

"Gil? No, why?"

"I could have sworn I saw him in the crowd. But, you know, it was just a glance and he was gone."

"Even if it was him, Seychelle, I wouldn't make too much of it. Gil's pretty harmless. From what I hear, he's not exactly firing on all pistons these days, but he's never hurt anybody."

"Yeah, I guess you're right."

"So, we done here?"

"Yeah," I said. "Let's go."

"Is it okay with you if I stay? My buddy over here"—he pointed toward the booth—"offered to buy me lunch at a little Cuban place he knows about. That is, if you don't need me anymore."

"It's okay with me," I said. Actually, I felt relieved. I'd been wondering how I was going to get rid of him now that I had accepted his offer of help.

I tossed my bag in the back of the Jeep and headed out of the parking lot. I had no doubt about where to go next. After talking to both Juliette and Margot, I figured Martine Gohin had some explaining to do. Abusing children may be an acceptable practice in her own country, but not here.

XXi

The traffic on Sunrise was miserable, and it was nearly thirty minutes later that I pulled into Martine's drive. Her minivan was there, so I assumed she was home. Juliette answered the door, and she drew in a sharp breath when she saw it was me.

"I need to speak to Martine." The child backed away, opened the door wide, and lowered her eyes. I could just about smell her fear. I would have to be careful that Martine never learned that Juliette had spoken to me.

"Seychelle," Martine crooned, "what a nice surprise. Come join me out on the patio."

"Martine, this isn't really a social visit." I stopped in the foyer and refused to follow her any farther into the house.

"Ah, you want to know if we have received any information at the radio station. I am sorry, but no one has called."

"Thank you. But no, that's not why I'm here."

"Oh?"

"I want to talk to you about Juliette."

"I do not understand."

"Martine, you know I've been running around trying to figure out how to get in touch with Solange's father. Well, it's become obvious to me that the *Miss Agnes* was in the business of bringing young girls to Florida who weren't coming to see fathers or join relatives here. They were coming to be sold, to work as *restaveks*, like Juliette here."

Martine's mouth opened in a round *O* as she inhaled sharply. "That is ridiculous," she said. "What do you mean coming in here and making those accusations? Juliette is my niece."

"Oh, please. Martine, don't lie to me."

"Miss Sullivan, you don't understand a thing about Haitian culture." As she talked, Martine's hands flew through the air, making wide gestures. "We have traditions in my country that you will never be able to understand, but at least you could respect them. But no, not you Americans. You think all the world should be like you. You are so arrogant. You would like to see a McDonald's in every city, your music on the radio, and all the world just like your country."

"Martine, child slavery is not some quaint Haitian custom that needs preservation."

She made that sound again with her mouth, expelling a puff of air through her pouty lips, and she rolled her eyes. "You come into my home. You make these ridiculous lies, these accusations—"

"And what about the captain of the *Miss Agnes*, this Joslin Malheur. You know him, don't you?"

"Of course not." She turned away and busied herself going through a stack of papers on a console table in the hallway. She had not turned away soon enough, however, and her eyes had widened almost imperceptibly at the mention of his name. She knew Malheur.

A phone started to ring in the kitchen. "Excuse me," she said, still not meeting my eyes with hers. She hurried off into the other room. I could hear her muffled voice as she spoke, but mostly she seemed to be listening while the other party did all the talking. From the entry to her house, the living room opened up off the hall to the right, and I took a few steps forward to explore while I waited. The room was decorated with paintings and artifacts from Haiti. There was a carved gourd and a beaded flag on display on the bookshelf. On the top shelf of the unit lay a machete in an intricately designed leather scabbard. I was just reaching for the machete when Martine appeared in the hall, almost breathless. She had her pocketbook slung over her shoulder.

"Miss Sullivan, we are going to have to cut our visit short, I am afraid. That was the police dispatcher, and they need my translation services. I must go."

"What happened?"

"There's been a homicide," she said, and waved me in the direction of the front door. "They need me to interview some of the possible witnesses. I really must be going."

Martine opened the door, and we both walked out onto her driveway, squinting into the glaring sunlight. As she put the key in the driver's-side door of the minivan, she turned to watch me leave. "We are finished, Miss Sullivan, *non*?"

I wondered if she was referring to our friendship or just this afternoon's meeting, but I supposed she was right in either case. "I'm not giving up, Martine. I'm not going to let them send Solange back, and I'm going to report this *restavek* business to the authorities."

She looked at me thoughtfully, then opened her door. Just before she climbed in, she paused. "Miss Sullivan, I am a civilian contractor for the Fort Lauderdale Police Department. I have worked with them for almost five years. You think they are going to believe a word of this nonsense of yours?" She made that dismissive spitting sound again, then looked at her watch. "This is going to take most of the day. The Swap Shop," she said, shaking her head. "They couldn't have picked a place with more Haitians."

"It's at the Swap Shop?"

"*Oui,* probably some kind of gang activity. Kids these days, eh?" She slammed her door and the van started up.

I jumped into Lightnin' and backed out of her way. After she had turned out of sight, I followed. I hadn't been willing to ask her if it was a boy or a girl, but in my gut I knew.

When I pulled back into the Swap Shop parking lot, there were more than half a dozen police cruisers, several unmarked county vehicles, and a white van with the words *Fort Lauderdale Police Crime Scene Unit* emblazoned across the side. The sad part was how little attention the crowd of police vehicles warranted among the weekend shoppers; they passed by as though this level of police activity was something they saw every day.

Inside the building, it was different. A crowd had gathered around to peer in under the circus bleachers at the shrouded body lying on the cement floor next to a dusty carousel horse. Mothers stood on tiptoes, holding their children's hands, the children's eyes wide in their painted faces, their helium balloons bobbing overhead. An older black gentleman wearing red suspenders to hold up his sagging black trousers was mumbling a prayer, though it was barely audible over the calliope music being broadcast over the PA system.

On the far side of the building, families sat eating their McDonald's burgers, people were buying Lotto tickets at the Tic Tac Dough window, and ladies were bargaining with a turbaned shopkeeper for imitation eelskin handbags.

She was just a kid who was trying to help me, trying to get back at the man she suspected of killing her brother. What part had I played in her death?

A woman started wailing somewhere in the crowd. I pushed my way to the front where bodies pressed up against the crime scene tape. The woman stood between two uniformed officers, her face covered with both hands, her fingernails brightly detailed little jewels sparkling in the flash of a camera. She lowered her hands suddenly and turned her back to me. She began to speak to someone on the far side of the crowd, but I couldn't see who was there because the two patrolmen, who supported her on either side, blocked my view. I tried to get the attention of the female cop who was handling the crowd, to ask permission to speak to the saleswoman, as if I didn't know who was there under that black plastic sheet.

I was concentrating so hard on getting her attention that I didn't even notice who had walked up on the other side of me.

"It's happening again, Miss Sullivan," Collazo said.

Even with all the noise in that place, hearing his voice startled me. I jumped back and collided with him.

"Geez, Collazo, give me a heart attack, why don't you."

"I go to a scene, and somehow you are involved." He had removed his jacket, and when I bumped into him, his freshly ironed shirt felt damp. He mopped the back of his neck with a handkerchief.

I pointed to the covered body and said, "I didn't have anything to do with this." But even as I said it, I knew I was protesting more to convince myself than the detective. She *was* dead because she had talked to me.

"Madame Renard, the store owner," he said while flipping through the pages of his note pad. "She just identified you as a customer who was here this afternoon. You talked to the victim and bought a dress."

He didn't have to finish the thought. I'd been accusing myself the entire drive here.

I could not stop staring at the tarp. "She just wanted to go to school, Collazo."

He pulled at the neck of his shirt, and the movement drew my eyes away. He ran a hand around the back of his neck where the tufts of black body hair curled over the top of his collar. The air-conditioning in the building was practically nonexistent, and the humidity was off the chart. "You came here to the Swap Shop to see her, and you were one of the last to see her alive."

I nodded. "Someone set up the meeting. I wanted information about anyone who had been on that boat that sank up in Hillsboro, and this girl"—I pointed to the draped body—"her name was Margot. She had come over on the *Miss Agnes,* but several months ago." I looked around at the crowds and the lights. "Collazo, are you telling me that this girl was murdered here in this crowded place, and no one saw anything?"

He nodded. "Either saw nothing or will say nothing."

"What about the store owner. What does she say happened?"

He shrugged. "The girl was there. The owner went into the back room, came out, the girl was gone."

"What about that snitch, that guy, Gil Lynch. I saw him in the crowd while I was talking to the girl."

"Interesting."

"And I came with Joe D'Angelo. After I talked to the girl here, Joe took off to have lunch with some buddy of his."

"Miss Sullivan, start over. Tell me how you got here, what you talked about." He had his gold pen out, and he flipped to a new page in that little notebook of his. I found it reassuring somehow: As long as Collazo made those little notes in his neat writing, he might help me make sense of this.

After telling him the whole story, I added, "The Haitian term for them is *restaveks,* but they are really child slaves. It's not unusual for them to be molested by family members—they are seen as the property of the family. Apparently this *restavek* business has been going on for decades in Haiti, but Joslin Malheur, the captain of the *Miss Agnes,* and all his crew, they've imported the concept here to the U.S. They are in the business of bringing girls here and selling them into slavery. Margot said Malheur is a former Tonton Macoute. He likes to hurt people. Gets off on it." As I was telling him the story, it began to sound more and more far-fetched. "I think he's responsible for all these DART killings. Including this one."

"Miss Sullivan, you are telling me that these killings are about child slavery, here in Fort Lauderdale."

"Yes, Collazo, that is exactly what I'm saying. Okay, so the *restaveks* aren't the only part of their cargo—they do make money from bringing in your standard, old-style, illegal immigrants, too. In fact, this girl, Margot," I said, "told me that her brother paid eight hundred bucks to come here to the States in order to take her away from these people."

"These people. You mean the slavers."

The tone of his voice told me what he thought about my theory.

"You're telling me," he continued, "that the police translator who is here somewhere right now taking witness statements is really a child slaver."

"I know it sounds crazy, but it's true, Collazo."

"And this young Haitian girl was telling you all about this when most Haitians won't say anything to an American."

"The only reason she was helping me out was because she wanted to bring this Malheur guy down. He killed her brother. She said he was going back to the Bahamas on the *Bimini Express*—a little freighter that usually sails out of Port Laudania. Please, check that out, even if you don't believe me."

He didn't say a word for almost a minute.

"Come," Collazo said. He walked over to the body, now abandoned and covered and waiting for transport. I followed him, thinking he wanted to speak to me out of earshot of the crowd. He bent down and, with a flourish, pulled back the sheet. It was the last thing I expected him to do, and I didn't have time to avert my eyes.

"What the . . . " I turned aside and felt the bile rising in the back of my throat. A porous blackness began to creep in around the periphery of my vision. I put my hands on my knees and dropped my head, breathing deeply. I had seen her, and already I wished I could erase those few seconds from my memory. The left side of her head looked like someone had cut a deep groove from the top of her scalp all the way down to her eye, and dark blood mixed with grayish brains spilled out across the concrete and across her face. Her eyes and mouth were open, as though she were still screaming.

"They have determined that he does it with a very sharp machete. He must be an immensely strong man. The MO's the same as the other four victims."

"You could have just told me, Collazo. My God. I think I might be sick." I was having trouble breathing, and my eyes filled with tears. "You bastard. I was just talking to her a couple of hours ago."

"And that's exactly why I showed her to you. Child slavery." He cleared his throat and stepped in close, invading my space, making me feel sicker still. "I'm going to tell you a little secret about people." He paused for effect, then said, "They lie." He stopped and smiled, showing the wide gap between his front teeth. "All the time. People lie to us to try to get us to do things. Things they want us to do for them. Go home to your little tugboat, Miss Sullivan. Amateurs like you, you go out and try to play detective, and people wind up hurt or . . . " He gestured at the body. "I don't want to be scraping your brains off the pavement next time."

I thought about Collazo's words all the way home, thought about what I'd seen beneath that tarp. How could someone do that to another human being? Even that scowl of hers, the anger she'd wrapped herself in, none of that had obscured the fact that she was a beautiful child. Could Margot have been lying to me? I didn't think so. The hate for Malheur I had seen on that girl's face was real. She had taken a risk by talking to me. And I had put her in terrible danger by talking to her. If only I hadn't gone to speak to her, if only I had taken her with me, put her in the same house with Solange. If only the world weren't a place where children were abused and killed. And then there was Juliette. I had seen it in her eyes, too. Someone was hurting her. On the one hand, I was terrified that my blundering around would result in someone else getting hurt or killed. Yet, on the other hand, no one else was doing anything to stop this *restavek* business. Whether or not Collazo and D'Ugard believed me, this was real.

When I came around the hedge on the side of the Larsens' house, I saw Pit sitting at the picnic table in the backyard, charts and papers and books spread out on every surface of the table and wood benches.

He looked up. "Hey, I got something to show you. Come here."

After scratching Abaco's ears, I joined my brother in the shade of the live oak.

"What have you got?"

"I think I can see what might have happened that night. From what you told me earlier, and from looking at the charts, I'd say their base camp is probably out in the bush somewhere on Bimini."

"Yeah, that makes sense. A girl I met who came on an earlier trip on the *Miss Agnes*" —and a girl who is now dead because she talked to me, I thought but didn't say— "told me that Malheur, the captain, is heading back to Bimini on one of those interisland freighters."

"Here's the way I see it." He pointed to the chart of the Straits of Florida, and we both stared while he gathered his thoughts. The coast of South Florida and the Keys ran down the left side. The Great Bahama Bank bordered by the Biminis, Gun Cay, Cat Cay, and, to the north, Great Isaac's Light, were on the right side of the straits. Flowing north through the middle of all this was the Gulf Stream, pouring through this narrow slot at speeds of three knots or better. "So they house the people over here" —Pit pointed to Bimini— "until the weather is calm, and then they try to make a quick run across the Gulf Stream to dump their load and run back to the Bahamas. Their boats are primitive, and they don't have fancy navigation gear because it's only a forty- to fifty-mile run. They count on conditions being the same for each run. I suspect the night Solange was set loose out there the current wasn't exactly cooperating."

"What do you mean?"

"Sey, you found the kid right here" —he pointed to a penciled letter *X* on the chart— "on Wednesday morning around eleven A.M. The *Miss Agnes* had sunk going into Hillsboro about thirty hours earlier. In a two- to three-knot current that kid would have traveled sixty to ninety miles north by then."

"Right. That's why I couldn't make any sense out of it."

"I think the *Miss Agnes* was originally headed for Miami Beach. Say they left Bimini early Monday morning planning to unload their cargo late Monday night. They assumed the current was hauling ass as usual, so they cranked an extra thirty degrees into their course to compensate. Only, due to a cross current and a slowing of the stream from the previous week's norther, they ended up down off Elliot Key by mistake. I still can't explain how Solange and that woman ended up in the boat. But if they got in the boat off Elliot, and the stream was running at less than two knots, which, by the way, I have verified to be the case with a windsurfing buddy of mine who works down at the Rosenstiel School—"

"Where?"

"You know, the oceanography place down at UM? They do satellite imaging of the oceans and, by looking at temperature and all that, they can determine how fast the current is running. Very cool stuff. Anyway, it was abnormally slow that night—that whole week, as a matter of fact."

Trying to keep Pit on track sometimes took some nudging. "Okay, so they're down off Elliot Key, and they dump those two into the dinghy. Then how did the *Miss Agnes* end up at Hillsboro sixty miles north?"

"Easy." He reached under the chart and pulled out a wrinkled newspaper. He pointed to a story he had circled with a yellow highlighter. "This article is about the huge Art Deco festival they've been having on the beach. Been going on all week. There were concerts and lights and all kinds of stuff happening down on Miami Beach. Scared 'em off. They've been dredging Haulover Inlet, so the lights on the barges there probably made them pass on that entrance. They kept heading north, looking for a quieter place to land. Coming into Port Everglades was too dangerous with the Coast Guard station right there. Eight hours later they were coming into Hillsboro Inlet in the wee hours of the morning. That captain must have been desperate to get rid of his cargo by then."

"So you're saying the *Miss Agnes* motored up the coast in eight hours, but the dinghy drifted the same distance in just under two days."

"That's how it would have happened with the current running less than two knots, which my buddy says it was."

"Okay." I shrugged. "That makes sense. Lots of things are beginning to make more sense."

He cocked his head to one side and looked at me. "This kid, why are you putting yourself in danger for her? These guys have killed people, Sey."

"I know it doesn't make much sense. I don't know how to explain it." From down the yard, out on the river, the deep rumbling of a high-powered ocean speedboat's idling engines was making the brass dividers jump and vibrate on the picnic table. My world was boats, engines, salt-water. I knew nothing about kids, how to do their hair, what kind of toys or clothes to buy them, and I was so afraid I'd end up like my own mother, unable to handle it. But for some reason something was different with Solange. "Pit, if I hadn't found her, she probably would have died. Yeah, maybe someone else would have come along, but the thing is it wasn't someone else. It was me. That makes us connected somehow. And if I just let them send her back to Haiti, there's a good chance she'll die there. I can't just sit back and watch that happen. Do you know anything about what it's like for a street kid in Haiti? Okay, I know I'm not going to change the world, but if I can just save this one kid..."

Pit was shaking his head. "Okay, I get it, I get it. Why did I even need to ask? I should have known. Just tell me you're not planning on talking to this captain dude."

"Pit, I'm sure he knows where this kid's father is. I mean, if he was just bringing her over as a *restavek*, she'd be dead by now. He's had two chances to kill her, and he hasn't done it. I know a Haitian woman who thinks it comes from some sort of magic. I'm not quite ready to go that far yet. But I do think there's something special about this kid."

"So you're just going to find this Haitian captain and walk up to him and ask him where the kid's dad is?"

"Not exactly. I'm still working on that part. I think if I can find some evidence that he is importing these kids as child slaves, and locate him, the police will take him into custody and maybe I'll get the answers to my questions then. I hope to get some help from this Border Patrol guy I know."

"Sey, sometimes I wish you were as concerned about yourself as you are about all these wounded birds you adopt."

We both started collecting the charts and books and instruments that were spread out on the picnic table. When my arms were full, I headed into the cottage, dumped the stuff on my dining table, and went to the fridge for a cold beer.

"By the way, sis," Pit said as he came through the door. "B.J. came by looking for you earlier. He told me a little bit about what was going on with you two. All joking aside, what's up? B.J.'s a great guy, and last time we talked on the phone, it seemed like you thought so, too."

I carried my beer bottle across to my bedroom door, then turned to face him. "Pit, I told you, I don't want to talk about that. Besides, look how late it is. I've got to change, then get down to Hollywood and check on how things are going, say hello to Solange. Want to come along?"

"Can I bring my board?"

I rolled my eyes at him. "You haven't changed."

As soon as I parked in front of Rusty's building, Pit pulled his sailboard out of the back of the Jeep and was ready to go. I noticed the

Paris Kids bag back there and I picked it up. Might as well give it to her. She probably wouldn't like it anyway.

I undid the clasp on the dive watch on my wrist and handed it to him. "Meet me back here at seven, okay?" He disappeared across A1A in the direction of the beach. The breeze was decent, a solid twelve to fifteen knots out of the south-southeast. Storm clouds lined the eastern horizon, but that wouldn't matter to Pit. I figured I wouldn't see any more of my brother until it grew too dark to see the waves, which, in June, wasn't until after eight.

There was no sign of Rusty's vehicle in the parking lot. Back at the cottage I'd found myself standing in front of my closet trying to decide what to wear, knowing that there was a chance he would be here. Then, of course, I had felt really stupid and had just thrown on some baggy cargo shorts and a T-shirt. At the last minute, on my way out of my bedroom, I'd grabbed a Hawaiian print shirt and tied the shirttails around my waist so I could at least look a little feminine.

Jeannie opened the door with a curt nod, and when I stepped into the condo, I was hit smack in the center of my chest by an airborne miniature helicopter.

"Ouch, that hurt!" The slightly larger of Jeannie's twins had collapsed in hysterics at my dismay, and his brother pounced on him and took away the 'copter launcher.

"Mom!" the older boy screamed, and punched his brother in the back as he fled into a bedroom.

"Welcome to the madhouse," Jeannie said. She sat back down on a tiny chair in front of a computer and seemed to ignore the screaming and the sound of fists hitting flesh that was coming from the bedroom.

"Don't you think you should do something?" I pointed to the bedroom door.

She didn't even look up from the computer screen when she said, "They'll work it out."

And I felt it again, that I could never be a mother.

"Where's Solange?"

Jeannie inclined her head toward the other bedroom. "She's been asking about you all day."

Solange didn't hear me enter the room. She was sitting on the bed, playing with two stuffed animals, and while the bear was neatly tucked

in with the covers up to his chin, it appeared that the monkey was getting a hell of a chewing out in Creole. I didn't understand the words,
but I sure knew that tone of voice.

"Hey, kiddo, how are you?"

Her face lit up, and she slid off the bed, dashed over, and wrapped
her arms around my waist, her head pressed against my tummy. I patted the back of her head and hoped that was a correct response to this
kid hug.

"Everything going okay? You having fun around here?"

"I don't like boys," she said, looking up at me with a very serious
look on her face.

"Trust me, kiddo. You'll change your mind one day."

I remembered the bag I'd brought and I told her to sit on the bed.
I pulled out the white dress and held it up. "This is for you," I said.

She reached out and fingered the lace at the hem, a look of disbelief
on her face. I could see already that it would be much too big for her.

She jumped off the bed and hugged me again, rubbing her cheek
against the fabric of the dress where she had pinned it against my body.

I heard the sound of the front door opening, and then someone
else was enduring an attack from the twins. I let go of Solange to go see
who had arrived. After I'd spread the dress on the bed, she slipped her
hand into mine and followed close by my side.

On his back in the middle of the living room, Rusty Elliot, special
agent to the INS, lay pinned to the floor by two blond dervishes who
straddled his body, threatening him with Super Soaker squirt guns
nearly as big as they were. Jeannie looked up from her computer and
shrugged. "He didn't know the password," she said.

"It's his house! Doesn't that count for something?"

She indicated her sons and smiled. "Not with them."

At that point the floor erupted with flying limbs, streams of water,
and giggles. Apparently the special agent was fighting back by tickling,
and he was winning. The boys tumbled off of him and retreated to the
far side of the room. Then Rusty held up his hand.

"Hold it." The water streams stopped. "I think this battle needs to
continue in the pool. What do you say, kids?"

The boys cheered and Solange smiled. I didn't think she understood the word *pool,* but the entire scene had been extremely entertain-

ing. I wondered if she'd ever seen an adult horsing around with kids like that before.

Rusty got up and brushed the water off his clothes and hair. He was wearing a white knit sport shirt and khaki cargo shorts. There was no avoiding it. The man looked good. He nodded to me. "Good afternoon, Miss Sullivan."

"Hey." I started to say something, but he'd turned and disappeared into the bedroom. He came out a few seconds later, drying himself off with a towel. "You're good with kids."

"I got a bunch of rugrat nieces and nephews. They keep me in shape."

"You seem to like them as much as they like you," I said, thinking that if most men had any idea how attractive it made them to be comfortable around kids, they'd all be pushing strollers.

"What's not to like? They're great. Anyway, how're things around here? You been here long?"

"I just got here a few minutes before you. Jeannie? How's the day been?"

She turned from the computer as the page she was browsing shut down. "Nobody but me's been near these kids today—not that I haven't felt like killing them myself a few times this afternoon. My boys are set on getting that girl to play with them, and she doesn't want to have a thing to do with them. She's a quiet little thing." She heaved herself up out of the chair and walked to the bedroom door. She turned back to Rusty. "You sure it's safe to take these kids down to the pool? I'd love to get out of here for a while. I've got a serious case of cabin fever."

"We'll be all right. I've checked with the local PD, and they say no one has shown the least interest in this place all day. The pool is screened from the road, and we'll all be there watching them."

She turned into the bedroom. "Okay, boys, swim trunks on, now."

"What about Solange?" I asked.

A pair of red swim trunks flew out of the bedroom and hit me on the side of the head. I handed them to the girl. "Go put these on."

She started toward the bedroom, dragging my hand. "You don't need me to come with you." I looked around the room and my eyes lit on Rusty's. He was smiling.

"Don't look to me for help, Sullivan."

The kid squeezed my hand even tighter and looked up at me with those big brown eyes.

"Oh, all right," I said. "Let's go."

The pool deck at the Heron Heights condo complex was on the north side of the building, just two steps higher than the wood docks where a collection of power and sail craft were tied up to pilings and small finger piers that jutted out into the Intracoastal. A rough wood fence shielded the pool on three sides, effectively keeping out the neighbors and the noise and prying eyes of the motorists passing on A1A. The view, however, was open on the water side, and when Rusty opened the gate and the boys darted through, I thought about how nice it would be to live like this someday. Across the tops of the boats in the marina, on the other side of the Intracoastal, I could make out a flock of egrets roosting in the mangroves of West Lake Park. Except for the occasional passing boat and the balconies up above, the little pool area was surprisingly private. Solange pressed her body against my side and held my hand tight as I arranged a chair in the shade at one of the umbrella tables.

"Don't you want to go into the water?"

She shook her head.

"Tell you what. We'll go check it out together in a few minutes," I said, and pulled her onto my lap as Jeannie and Rusty installed themselves in chairs around the table. Jeannie, whose webbed pool chair was creaking in a disconcerting manner, was the only adult who had changed into a swimsuit, although she was still wearing her muu-muu over the top. Today's version had green curly-tailed lizards pictured in the tropical print.

"Seychelle, we need to talk," Rusty said. "I heard about what happened this afternoon."

"Hey, not here," I said, nodding my head to indicate the child sitting on my lap.

"Then let's go where we can talk. Collazo called me. This situation is becoming very difficult to defend. After today's events, it's time to turn her over—"

I cut him off. "Rusty, I said we'd talk later. After we let these kids burn off a little energy and we give Jeannie a break."

"Speaking of which," Jeannie said, "I think I'm ready to try out that water before this chair demonstrates what happens when you exceed its load capacity."

"I think we are, too. Right, kiddo?" Solange didn't look too happy about it. She was wearing red boys swim trunks and a bright yellow tank top. We both sat on the edge of the pool, dangling our feet in the water, and watched Jeannie as she unzipped the front of her muu-muu and stepped out in a matching lizard-covered swimsuit. The great thing about Jeannie, though, was how at ease she was in her body and how light on her feet. She walked down the steps and lowered herself into the water, bobbing right into the middle of a splash fight between her boys, dunking one and splashing the other with a playfulness and ease I envied. Some people seemed to be born knowing how to act around kids.

Little fingers tapped my upper arm. Solange was looking up at me and speaking softly. "I go home with you? I stay with you and Abaco?"

"No, look, I can't keep you at my place. I . . . you know, I'm not set up to take care of kids, with the right food and all that."

"I don't eat much."

"Ah, geez, Solange, it's not that." I put my arm around her narrow shoulders and hugged her to me. "It wouldn't be safe. We're keeping you here because the Capitaine doesn't know about this place. He could find you at my place." Bringing up the Capitaine's name reminded me that I needed to get over to Port Laudania to look for the freighter. After another half hour or so around here, I'd have to bow out and take a quick trip up to Dania.

Solange tapped my arm again to make me look at her. "You stay here, too. You be safe."

"Oh, I'm okay. And I'm hardly ever at my place these days. You know, I'm going to have to leave in a few minutes. I've got to find your father, your papa."

She didn't say anything after that. We just sat together and watched as Jeannie threw her boys into the air and the three of them laughed and hooted and splashed.

Rusty stood and called out to us, "You guys want to see my boat?"

His boat was the last one at the north end of the condo complex's docks. He'd trotted on ahead and was already standing in the boat tying a canvas strap to the side of the hull when Solange and I arrived on the dock off the stern of his boat.

"Oh my God, Rusty. Why do rational people completely lose it when it comes to naming their boats?"

"You like it?" He looked so damned cute standing there grinning up at me, his shaggy blond hair falling in his eyes, that knit shirt showing off his sculpted chest.

"Folks must figure you either work for Immigration or Allstate," I said, pointing to the lettering on the stern that read "*INS AGENT.*" "What were you thinking?"

Rusty's boat was not the prettiest thing on the dock, but the man kept it immaculate. For a boat that was over twenty-five years old, it looked great. He had repainted the fiberglass hull with one of the new polyurethane paints when the gel coat had begun to chalk, and all the stainless was polished to a mirror finish. The blue canvas bimini that provided the shade Rusty was standing in looked brand new. The tide was such that the deck of his boat was almost perfectly level with the wood dock, and even Solange had no trouble hopping aboard. The steering wheel was offset to the left, and just forward of that and down a step, double wood doors stood open, revealing the tiny sink and V-berth in the cuddy cabin.

Solange let go of my hand and moved away from me for the first time since I'd arrived. As she scampered down into the cramped forward cabin, I thought that I should feel relieved, but I was starting to enjoy the attachment.

"There you go, young lady," Rusty said, bending forward at the waist to look into the cabin. Solange was stretched out on the bunk. "You're just about the right size for that cabin." He stood up and faced me. "She's a twenty-five-foot Anacapri with double bunk V-berth in the cuddy cabin along with an enclosed head. Well, the head is mostly for people about Solange's size, too." He went on to show me his collection of rods stowed neatly in the cabin's overhead, his fresh bait well, his cast net for catching bait, life jackets, flares, the inflatable dinghy in the seat locker with CO_2 cartridges so it could double as a life raft. I understood that he was damn proud of that boat, but it wasn't like I had never seen a standard boat U.S. flare kit. I was beginning to think the term *obsessive-compulsive* might apply. Then I saw him rub my fingerprints from the gel coat after I touched the rail, and I was convinced.

"So, this is your 'classic,' eh? I gotta admit, you keep a clean boat, Agent Elliot. I assume your engines are just as clean?"

"You bet. Twin Mercs. They're not the newest engines, but if you spend the time and give them a little TLC, they'll keep running for a long time."

"I wish more people thought that way. If it weren't for all the yahoos out there breaking down every weekend, there probably wouldn't be so many people jumping into the towing business. It's getting harder and harder for a slow boat like *Gorda* to make it."

"You do all right."

"How do you know? You been checking up on me, Agent Elliot?"

"Let's just say I wouldn't have let this child go into the hands of people I knew nothing about." He pointed down toward the cuddy cabin where Solange, lying on her belly on the blue canvas mattress, watched us with her head propped up on her two fists.

Rusty looked at his watch. "Hey, it's almost five-thirty. You getting hungry?"

"I guess I could use a little something. I haven't eaten much all day."

"What do you say we take the boat down the Intracoastal a bit and hit one of those waterfront restaurants? That would also give us the chance to talk in private."

I had just been thinking about getting a look at Port Laudania, and here was the perfect way. "Sounds good to me, except, there's this place up the Dania Canal—"

"Sure, I know the place. Tugboat Annie's? Perfecto. Then I'll be able to say—"

"Just stop it right there," I said. "There is nothing original about making a Tugboat Annie joke to me."

Tugboat's was a favorite waterfront bar and restaurant with an outdoor dining area that served up barbecue and reggae, along with cans of Off on weekend afternoons for those brave enough to face the no-see-ums. Their logo and namesake was a caricature of an old crone smoking a pipe, leaning out the wheelhouse window of a tug. I'd been the object of way too many jokes that noted some physical similarities between the crone and me. I kept pointing out to folks that I'd never smoked a pipe.

"Okay, I promise. No Tugboat Annie jokes if you'll lay off the name of my boat."

"Deal." I shook his hand, then peered down into the cuddy cabin. "Come on, kiddo. Let's get you back to Auntie Jeannie."

The boys were still splashing and shouting in the pool, but Jeannie had installed herself on a wrought-iron bench that looked far sturdier than the webbed pool furniture. The bench backed up against the wood fence around the pool and Jeannie looked absolutely regal surveying the pool deck from beneath the brim of a white floppy hat. She turned to us and waved as we came around the corner and up the steps from the docks.

"I wondered where you two had disappeared to." Rusty had stayed behind to prepare the boat.

I pointed to the north end of the dock. "Rusty's boat." I sat down on the bench next to her, and Solange squeezed in next to me. "I don't get him, Jeannie. On the one hand, he does a damn good job of playing the rustic redneck type. But then there's this condo with a million-dollar view, furnished like something out of *Southern Living* magazine. And his boat down there? It's old, but it's immaculate. He wants me to think otherwise, but my guess is it's professionally maintained. Where does a Border Patrol agent get the money for all this?"

"You like him, don'tcha."

"What?"

"Seychelle, my friend, you are so transparent. Soon as you like a fellow, you start picking on him. I pity the poor man you marry."

"Marry? Why's everybody got to talk about marriage all the time?"

"Everybody? Seems like I'm the only one around here just now." She leaned forward and looked past me at Solange. "Tell me, missy, did you discuss marriage with this lady?"

Solange giggled and hid her face behind my back. Whether or not she understood Jeannie, the tone of voice and the face were enough to make anybody crack up.

"Seems to me, Seychelle, that you are the only other one around here who could have been contemplating marriage just now. Hmm . . . Was it to B.J.? Or to Rusty?"

Rusty came bounding up the steps from the docks.

"You ready?"

"Oh, uh, Jeannie and I were just talking. Jeannie, Rusty and I are going to run up to Tugboat Annie's in his boat and get some dinner. That is, if you don't mind."

"You go on. After all, this is just what I went to law school for—to be a baby-sitter."

"I'm sorry. Forget it. We'll stay."

"Girl, you are taking me way too serious today. You two go on. You've got a lot to talk over. Besides, my boys are always with me. And this little thing?" She reached over and poked Solange in the belly button. "She's so quiet you don't hardly notice she's around."

"You want us to bring you something back?"

"Barbecue? Absolutely!"

I told Rusty I would meet him at the boat after I put a note on the Jeep for Pit. He ran upstairs to grab his wallet. I peeled Solange's hand out of mine, knelt down next to her, and told her good-bye for now. The look on her face made me feel like a real creep, and I could feel her eyes on me as I crossed the pool deck on my way to the parking lot.

After I'd finished the note to Pit, I noticed the dark clouds gathering out west over the Everglades, and I decided to take the time to snap the side windows back onto the Jeep. I didn't have a rain jacket, but I did find an old zip-front hooded sweatshirt.

Rusty and I arrived back at the boat at nearly the same time. Without a word, I untied the dock lines while he started the engines. We were like a couple of kids trying to sneak off.

"So," Rusty said over the noise of the idling outboards when we were about five yards from the dock, headed north up the Intracoastal. "I hardly recognize you without your shadow."

I turned away from him and looked through the windshield, up the waterway toward the Sheridan Street Bridge. The sun had slid behind the mass of clouds and squalls out to the west, bringing on an early twilight, and the cars driving over the metal grate in the bridge already had their headlights on. The air had that thick, menacing feel of an impending storm.

"I know what it's like," I said, "to really want to have a mom. At least when I was Solange's age I still had my dad." Rusty put his hand on the back of my neck and squeezed lightly. I felt his touch course through my body like heat lightning.

"Hey, I was just kidding," he said.

"I know, but I can't get over thinking about how alone she must feel." I looked into his eyes. "Sometimes 'alone' feels really rotten." I turned away again and spoke to the mangroves on the west bank of the Intracoastal. "The thing is, I don't know how to be a mom, and I can't be *her* mom."

"Don't sell yourself short. You're doing all right with the kid. In fact, it's kind of neat watching you with her. There's some kind of special bond between you two."

"Thanks," I said, turning my face toward the mangroves, not wanting him to see how much I wanted that to be true.

XXIII

We squeezed into the last little bit of space at the restaurant's dock. Before long, boats would start rafting up, tying to the outside of other boats, and later in the evening, they would be three deep in places. The restaurant was already crowded, but we got one of the high bar tables outside with a low powerboat at the dock in front of us. There's nothing quite like waterfront dining when your view turns out to be the glossy fiberglass sides of fifteen-foot-high sportfishermen. Although we were a little downstream of the port, I sat on the side of the table that looked up the canal and had a great view across the water to Port Laudania. The lights around the port were blinking on as the last traces of daylight were swallowed by a low, dark sky.

Directly across from the restaurant, the pitted concrete dock was empty. The only things tied to it were the huge tires that served as bumpers along its entire length. A hundred feet or so back from the dock was a large white aluminum building with a green sign that read "G&G Marine, East Terminal." A crane, tractor-trailers, and containers all sat idle. It was well after quitting time, and if there was anybody over there, I sure couldn't see them. There wasn't any sign of the *Bimini Express*. But, really, I wasn't even certain this was where the little freighter was likely to dock. Here or in Miami? For all I knew, Capitaine had already left. On the other hand, would Malheur leave without tying up that last loose end that was Solange?

Once again, I flashed on the image of the girl Margot on the concrete floor at the Swap Shop when Collazo had pulled back the tarp. She would still be in the shop, scowling at Madame, if she had not spoken to me.

"What are you thinking?" Rusty asked after the waitress left with our orders. My eyes had been focused on the docks across the way, but my mind was filled with images from the past few days. The sound of Rusty's voice brought me back to the restaurant.

"Huh? Oh . . . I don't know. I guess I was thinking about the people who are so desperate to get to this country that they'll get involved with monsters like this Capitaine Malheur. Think about how bad it must be if the alternative to Malheur is even worse than he is. They climb aboard these crowded, rickety boats, leaving behind their families and all that was familiar. For freedom. And then they end up in the hands of a man like Capitaine. God, Rusty, what he did to that girl?" I pressed my hands against my eyes, trying to wipe the images away. It didn't work. I tried to focus on Rusty's face. "It probably wouldn't have happened if I hadn't talked to her."

"Hey, stop talking like that," he said.

"Think of the courage it took. She went against her culture. She spoke to me, told me Malheur killed her brother. She was trying to bring Malheur down for that."

"See, so if it hadn't been you, she would have talked to someone else. It certainly wasn't your fault."

I propped my elbows on the table and leaned my chin on my clasped hands. "Maybe. But your saying that won't make this feeling in my gut go away. He's got to be stopped. I've got to make sure the same thing doesn't happen to Solange."

"Seychelle, why do you think that hasn't happened yet? Malheur could have killed her. I mean, let's go all the way back to why she was alive in that boat. Why did he take the risk that someone would find her?"

"We don't know that he put her in the boat. Maybe she escaped?"

"I don't know," he said, and his eyes focused on something in the distance on the other side of the canal. It was almost totally dark, but across the way, in the branches of a dead tree, I could see the silhouette of an osprey against the pinkish gray sky. "I think if she was just any restavek, she would be dead by now."

He reached across the table and took my hand. I felt that titillating surge of excitement and dread that I get when I know my relationship with a man is about to change from friendship to something else.

"Seychelle, there's something I've been wanting to tell you," he said.

"Rusty, the other night—"

"Yeah, that's what I wanted to talk about. And I'm not real good at this kind of thing. Talking about it, anyway."

His "aw shucks" demeanor was incredibly disarming. "I can't figure you out, Rusty Elliot."

"What do you mean?"

"You come across as this simple down-home Georgia guy who's trying to stem the tide of illegal immigration, and then . . . I would say that little 'second home' of yours back there is worth close to half a million. Either Border Patrol agents make a lot more than I thought, or you're not who you let on to be. You tell me."

The way his white teeth glowed in contrast with his tanned cheeks, it made me want to forget all my questions and just kiss him.

"Okay. I do wonder what kind of thing you've been imagining, but here's the truth. The beach condo was my mother's. *Her* second home. We always had a beach house in South Florida, this one's just the most recent. My mother was a Depression baby and she saved everything. Over the years it mounted up. The real family homestead is up on Jekyll Island in Georgia. I keep that rented out most of the time now. I've tried to dodge around it, make my own way in the world, but the fact is, my mother was wealthy, and I was her only child."

"In other words, you don't need to work. You just chase after bad guys for the fun of it?"

His grin grew wider. "And to meet beautiful women."

"Hey, I thought you said you weren't very good at this?"

The waitress arrived, bringing our appetizer of blackened grouper bites and a couple of beers. He let go of my hand, and I dug in with relish.

After what I had been thinking about earlier, I was worried I might have lost my appetite, but not with Tugboat Annie's grouper sitting in front of me. Rusty didn't try to talk as we ate, and he jumped another notch in my esteem as a result. When we finished, he waved to the waitress for two more beers.

"I really need to check in with the station, and I left my cell in the truck back at the condo." He looked around at the interior restaurant. "There's got to be a phone around here. I'll be right back." He headed through the double doors into the bar. Once he was out of sight, I took the opportunity to get up and stroll up the dock to see Port Laudania from another angle.

At the far end of the dock I heard the noise of a large engine firing up somewhere across the canal. Through some shrubbery I saw another terminal building and could make out the outline of a small ship's bow poking out of the trees. I didn't remember that the port continued that far up the canal, but they are always building new docks at the commercial ports in Florida. I closed my eyes for several moments to get them accustomed to the darkness. When I opened them, I could easily make out the first few letters of the name on the bow: *BIM*. Just then the red navigation and masthead lights blinked on.

"Shit!" I said aloud. I began running, dodging between the tables, barely aware of white moon faces and startled eyes staring up at me. I had to find Rusty.

I pushed through the swinging glass doors that led to the inside bar and hollered at the bartender, "Phone?" He pointed at the opening in the wall next to the front door. After shoving my way through the crowded bar, I finally made it to the phone, only to find some young, heavily made-up twenty-something in a miniskirt and tube top screaming into the handset.

"I don't give a fuck what you say, you son of a bitch," she said, holding the phone away from her ear and hollering directly into the mouthpiece.

"Excuse me," I said. "Did you see where the guy went who was on the phone here?"

"Fuck you," she said, and turned her back to me.

Try as she might to be intimidating, it wasn't working. I was tempted to try one of B.J.'s fancy aikido moves on her, but I just used the strength in my swimmer's arms instead. I grabbed her by the shoulder, spun her around, and pinned her to the wall with my forearm across her throat.

"I asked you a question. Have you seen a blond guy, late thirties, wearing cargo shorts and—"

"He got pissed off waitin', cussed me out, and took off out the front door. Now let me go, bitch."

Part of me wanted to take her into the ladies' room, stick her head under the faucet, wash all that makeup off her face, and continue the soap treatment on the inside of her mouth. Instead, I said, "Thanks," and pushed my way out the heavy wood front door.

The parking lot was full of cars, but there was not a single person in sight. I called Rusty's name a couple of times but knew that if he was in a car or on a boat with the air-conditioning running, he'd never hear me. Thinking I'd missed him somehow, I pushed my way back through the bar and out to our table. Still no sign of him there, and I knew that if I searched much longer, the *Bimini Express* would be long gone. I had no desire to take on Malheur myself, but maybe I could delay the little freighter from leaving until Rusty could get there with the authorities.

I saw our waitress standing by another table, and I interrupted her recitation of the daily specials. "When my friend comes back to our table, tell him I took his boat and went across the canal to that big ship down there, okay?" I pointed at the *Bimini Express,* and she nodded, turned to the young couple at the table, and started reciting the night's specials all over again. I just had to hope she would remember.

I trotted back to Rusty's boat and breathed a sigh of relief that no one had rafted another boat alongside it. Once aboard, I threw off the dock lines and gave the piling a good shove so the boat would drift into the canal. The engines purred to life at the first turn of the key, and I silently thanked Rusty for taking such damn fine care of the old girl.

My blue sweatshirt was where I'd left it, tucked up on the dash against the windshield, so I pulled it on, zipped it up, and pulled the hood up over my head. When I was a lifeguard, this had been my uniform on cold mornings, and with my broad shoulders, I'd often been taken for a man. I hoped the same would be true tonight.

Pulling up next to the little ship might attract too much attention, so I slowly idled past her bow and into the large basin with the commercial shipping docks on one side and the yacht yard docks on the other. Just a few days earlier, B.J. and I had towed the *Miss Agnes* through this same basin. I tried not to look at the *Bimini Express* as I slowly passed, but out of the corner of my eye I could see three men standing outside the wheelhouse up on the wing deck, two island men close together in conversation, the third man standing apart, talking on a cell phone. I couldn't see well enough to tell if one of the two islanders was Malheur, but even at that distance, I recognized the third man's wide mustache and protruding belly. They belonged to Gil Lynch.

XXIV

I pulled Rusty's boat into one of the haul-out slips at the Play-boy Marine Boat Yard and grabbed hold of the rungs of the iron lad-der that was bolted to the concrete walls of the slipway. We were at about mid-tide but, even so, when I was standing up in the boat, my head was several feet below the top of the wall. I raised the hatch on the seat locker and pulled out the cast net Rusty had shown me earlier. The weight of the net surprised me. The lead weights attached to the nylon were quite small, but there were enough of them that I worked up a sweat just hefting it around. I threw a couple of hitches around the ladder with the bowline, flipped the fenders over the side, and hoped that the barnacle-covered walls wouldn't chew too badly into Rusty's flawlessly painted topsides.

Before leaving the boat, I paused for a couple of seconds, checking to see if I'd forgotten anything. How had my search for Solange's fa-ther and my search for the truth about my own father converged on this former drug smuggler on a Bahama-bound freighter on the Dania Cut-off Canal?

At the top of the ladder, I raised my head slowly over the lip of the concrete dock. I didn't see any movement, didn't hear anything. Sev-eral of the sailboats were propped up on the hard in the boatyard, and warm yellow light spilled from their port lights. Playboy Marine was often used by live-aboards. The dark hulk on the far side of the yard I recognized as the *Miss Agnes*. She would certainly be stickered all over with U.S. Customs impound stickers.

The Playboy yard butted up against the G&G West Terminal, but I could see that the fence separating the two didn't extend all the way to the end of the dock. It was simple enough to slip around. Then I ducked down behind some pallets of brick pavers to reconnoiter. To my left, out by the road, was a security guard shack. A spotlight lit the area around the little building and there were about twenty wild cats scarfing down food from dozens of plastic bowls and tins. The music from a Spanish-language radio station was playing inside.

Keeping my body low, I ran across the concrete dock to a small school bus, waiting for transport to some island. I leaned my back against the vehicle. The net I was carrying was so heavy that my thick sweatshirt was already damp with sweat. The security guard's shack was north of me, and the *Bimini Express* was south. It was hard to find a spot where I wouldn't be seen from one direction or the other.

The *Bimini Express* was stern-tied to the wharf. She was probably no more than eighty feet long, with her bridge and superstructure all jammed up forward in the bow so that everything aft could be used for cargo. There were big doors in her stern that flopped down to form a ramp onto the ship. They loaded her first with the vehicles they could drive on, and then they used a forklift to add the pallets. The cargo looked mostly like building supplies. No doubt in the Bahamas they were doing the same thing as in the Everglades. Like the lyrics to that old Joni Mitchell song my mother used to play, "They paved paradise and put up a parking lot." At least this one would be a nice parking lot with pavers.

What I needed to do was to get at her prop. Fishermen throw their cast nets so they open into a perfect circle, and then the weights sink the net down over their prey, little baitfish. *My* intended prey was the ship's prop. I hoped the net would wind around the prop and disable the ship until Rusty, who I was sure must be freaked back at the restaurant, could get here with the cavalry.

At least that was my plan.

I ran from the school bus to a forklift to a huge pile of plywood. As far as I could tell, no one had seen me. I was now only about two hundred feet from the stern of the vessel. They had already raised the transom doors, and they were pretty damn ready to depart. Only a small gangway remained on the dock. I wondered what they were waiting for.

The men I had seen earlier on the bridge had vanished. I could stay hidden among the cargo pallets and the empty shipping containers, but at some point I would have to dash across the wide-open space and run down that gangway onto the ship. That was when I would be the most vulnerable. I worked my way forward, and at one point I could have sworn I saw movement behind me, but when I looked back, directly at whatever it was, there was nothing there. I rubbed my hand over my eyes and my fingers came away dripping with sweat.

I don't remember making the decision to go for it. I was just standing there one minute and then I was hurtling across the open concrete wharf, my feet pounding across the gangway, then ducking between the stacks of shipping containers that covered the stern of the vessel. I stopped and leaned against a pallet of lumber, breathing so hard that I was sure the guys up on the bridge would hear me. I simply couldn't catch my breath. When I heard the sound of footsteps on the gangway, I stopped breathing entirely.

They were light footsteps, like someone sneaking. There was no question now that I was being followed, and whoever was there knew exactly where I was. I slid around the corner of a container and onto the stern, but it was far too exposed back there. There was the housing for some crane machinery a bit farther forward up the ship's starboard side, and it looked like something to hide inside. I eased my way forward, trying to figure out how to use the net as a weapon. I started unfolding it, readying myself to throw it the way I had seen the surf fishermen do. Half the net was over my shoulder, hanging down my back, the other half in my hands in front of me. The crane machinery didn't provide much of a hiding place, but I pressed myself back into a shadowy crevice and waited.

I heard something like a snort or a sniffle. Evidently the guy had a cold or a bad coke habit. Then I heard it again, so close this time that I tensed, ready to throw the net at the first sign of movement in front of me. I was looking for some giant Haitian captain, and when I finally realized there was someone right in front of me, it was too late to throw the net. Arms wrapped around my waist and a head pressed hard against my belly.

The name escaped my mouth before I had time to think. "Solange?"

XXV

She was crying. She didn't make any sounds other than the occasional sniffling, but I could tell by the way her shoulders were shaking that she was crying hard. It was a good thing she wasn't bawling like most kids do, because the guys up on the bridge were outside again, talking to one another and pointing toward the dock.

I let the cast net fall to the deck, and I knelt down next to her. How on earth did she get on the *Bimini Express*? Her snuffling grew louder, and I tried to comfort her so the men above couldn't hear us. I could tell from their voices that the two black men were Bahamians, and they shouted to someone as a vehicle approached on the dock. I could see all the way forward along the starboard side of the vessel, and to my surprise I saw motion up on the starboard ladder to the bridge. A deckhand had been sleeping on a pile of lines about twenty feet from us. It was a wonder he hadn't heard me when I cried out. He passed around the aft end of the deckhouse and headed for the stern. If he was headed aft to throw off the dock lines, then we had better get the hell off this ship.

The approaching vehicle sounded like a truck. It stopped on the dock, and I wanted to see who or what was being delivered. The ship's engines, which had been turning over at a very gentle idle, now revved up and smoke billowed out of the stacks above the wheelhouse. I heard voices over by the gangway and held my finger to my lips so Solange would know to be quiet. Then I loosened her arms from around me and pushed her back into the shadows of the crane's machinery. I slipped over to the end of the containers to try to see across to the other side of the boat. What I saw made my stomach threaten to eject the dinner I'd eaten at Tugboat Annie's. Climbing the stairs to the bridge deck, dressed all in black and wearing wraparound shades, was Joslin Malheur. He began slapping the Bahamians on the back like they were old friends. Gil was nowhere in sight.

It was then that the deck beneath my feet began to shudder as the screws bit into the water.

I'd waited too long. The two deckhands threw off the lines, the gangway clattered aboard, and the *Bimini Express* slowly eased her way forward. The gap between the ship and the dock was widening, already too far to jump. If I didn't do something fast, Solange and I would be on our way to the Bahamas.

Now was the time. The ship would soon be reversing her screws to pivot around, and the prop wash would suck in whatever I threw down there.

"Stay here," I whispered, my lips close to her ear, and I again motioned with my finger to my lips for her to be quiet.

Keeping my body low between the piles of cargo, I huddled down over the net, which I had balled up in front of my body. I hurried toward the transom.

The crewmen were gone, so I quickly divided the net weights and threw half of the bulk over my shoulder. Bright lights shone from the bridge onto the aft deck, and I wondered if anyone was watching me as I stood and ran to the rail. Bending down as I'd seen the surf fishermen do, I made ready to cast the net.

Even over the noise of the roaring engines and the churning water, I heard her scream. I turned back, and though I could make out only his silhouette, I knew that the man standing there, his right elbow askew as if he were holding a weapon against Solange's body, was Malheur.

I moved my head off to one side and squinted into the brilliant light. "Leave her alone. Please. Don't hurt her."

He laughed. It was a big, loud, booming laugh, and I heard Solange take two quick sharp gulps of air. She knew to be terrified of that sound.

Another man materialized out of the darkness and grabbed my upper arm, squeezing so tight that the folds of my sweatshirt cut into my skin. I let out an involuntary cry. Malheur said something to him in Creole, and both men laughed. I shaded my eyes with my free hand, and I was surprised to see that the man gripping my arm was Gilbert Lynch.

The *Bimini Express* had made her turn and the small ship was starting down the Dania Cut-off Canal. We would be passing Tugboat Annie's in a few minutes—my last chance to attract Rusty's attention. If only I could break Gil's grip, I might be able to run and jump over the side. But then I immediately dismissed that thought. I couldn't leave Solange behind. I flashed on the image of Margot on the cement floor at the Swap Shop. I could not leave Solange alone with Capitaine.

Malheur spoke again in Creole, and Gil pushed me forward, up the starboard side, just as the lights and music from Tugboat Annie's started to spill over the little ship. Although I could see people sitting at tables, they weren't looking up or paying any attention to the ship passing on the canal. For a moment, I thought I saw Rusty standing at the hostess station, talking into the phone, and I raised my free hand, tried to shout and wave. But the words strangled in my throat when Gil slapped me open-handed on the side of my head and dragged me forward, then shoved me down between two stacks of plywood. He held me down and mumbled something unintelligible. We were now amidships in the shadow of the upper deck, and I could see Malheur, his skin so dark I could barely make out his features. The white skulls on the sides of his sunglasses reflected the light from the floods on the aft deck. He was wearing a tight-fitting black T-shirt, and around his elbow and upper right arm were white bandages, evidence that Jeannie's shotgun had inflicted some damage. The weapon he held across Solange's chest was a machete with a long shiny blade, narrow at the hilt but broadening out to four inches of steel at the tip.

Malheur lowered the machete and pushed Solange over to Gil, who pulled me to my feet. I stood facing Malheur, staring at the black lenses that covered his eyes. He brought the tip of his machete up under my chin and pressed the sharp end against the soft place at the top of my throat. I stopped breathing, though the steel barely touched my skin.

Malheur smiled broadly and began to raise his other arm. I thought he was going to hit me, kill me, but I was determined not to let him see me flinch. He took hold of the zipper on my sweatshirt and began to draw it down, slowly. I could feel the vibration as the slider passed over each metal tooth. His knuckles pressed into the flesh of my breast and then my belly as he dropped his hand lower.

He wouldn't have to hit me. I was going to kill myself if I didn't breathe. I swallowed and felt a sharp stab of pain as my muscles pressed against the blade at my throat. I felt sick with shame. I was letting him humiliate me. That tiny touch of cold steel had turned me into a victim.

When I couldn't take it any longer, I looked away and found Solange's frightened eyes, her features otherwise calm.

I knew I had to make him stop. So I lied.

"You don't scare me," I said. My voice trembled and my chin quivered, but I never again took my eyes off those shades.

Malheur threw back his head and laughed, then spoke for what seemed like forever in Creole—either to me or to Gil, I couldn't be sure—all the while still holding the machete to my throat. In midsentence, he lowered the machete and turned, grabbing Solange. He headed for the door that led into the crew's quarters. I dropped my head and inhaled a deep lungful of air, and though it was scented with diesel exhaust, it tasted sweet to me.

Malheur turned and spat some words at Gil, and I thought I understood the words *gra kochon*—in French class we'd giggled over the phrase that meant "fat pig."

Gil grabbed my arm even harder, scowled at Malheur's back, and pushed me to follow them. Malheur held Solange's arm so high in the air that her feet barely skimmed the ground, and he lifted her into the air to get her over the steel threshold of the watertight bulkhead door. When I came out from behind the stack of plywood, I tried to look for Rusty on shore, but Gil grunted and pushed me through the door. I tripped and almost went down, slamming my head and shoulder into the steel bulkhead inside the dark companionway. My vision blurred while I struggled to remain standing, and tears began to fill my eyes. I was reaching up to feel if there was any blood in my hair when he shoved me again, through another door. This time I did trip—my feet got tangled up and I fell—and while it occurred to me as I was going down that I needed to protect my head this time, something hard and cold came out of the darkness all too soon.

The first thing I became aware of was the motion—that feeling that the deck beneath you is suddenly falling and you are falling, only your stomach has decided not to fall, and then you are rising, and your stomach is trying to relocate somewhere down in your bowels.

I moaned aloud when I tried to move. I was all twisted up and my neck was cramped and hurt like hell. As soon as I tried to move, however, I forgot all about my neck as my head started throbbing from the inside out. It felt like a cartoon character's thumb after he's banged it and it's ballooned to three times its normal size. I wondered if my head was three times its normal size.

I felt a lump the size of a walnut just back from my hairline above my left temple. My hair was encrusted with dried blood.

A small hand brushed across my forehead and pushed the stray hairs out of my face. Although the room was pitch dark, I didn't need to see her to feel her fear.

"Solange?"

"*Oui,*" she said, pronouncing it as an inhaled gulp of air.

"They didn't hurt you, did they?"

"No." I felt her hand on my head again. "You hurt." It wasn't a question. She knew.

"I'm okay. How long have I been sleeping?" Through the ship's deck I could feel the vibration of the engine and the sudden surge of the RPMs as a wave lifted the stern of the ship, causing the prop to spin faster. Waves would have to be at least ten feet high to do that. We were out in the Gulf Stream already.

"Long time," she said.

It was a stupid question for me to have asked her. She had no way of measuring the time. Ten minutes alone in the dark, not knowing if I was dead or alive, would seem like an eternity. She didn't even sound like she'd been crying. But I guess it wouldn't have been the first time she'd ended up on a boat with a dead woman.

I felt around my surroundings and realized that I was sitting on the floor of a crewman's cabin, my back against the bunk—probably the same bunk I had hit my head on when I fell. When I got to my feet, my legs almost gave way again from the wave of dizziness that grabbed hold of me. I reached out and placed my palms on the wall, bent my knees to the corkscrew motion of the ship, and waited to get control of my body again. When I opened my eyes and turned around to face the bunk, I wasn't expecting to see anything. I was surprised to make out a dim light from what looked like a porthole in the hull just above the bunk. In the faint glow, I felt around the cabin to familiarize myself with the space.

The door was locked; no surprise there. There were a couple of built-in drawers under the bunk, and they were filled with men's clothes, neatly folded. I felt under and around everywhere, but there were no shaving articles with razor blades, no pocketknives—nothing we could use as a weapon. I crawled onto the bunk, feeling for Solange, and put my face to the porthole.

The cabin we were in was on the starboard side of the ship, and in the distance, a bit off our aft quarter, I could make out the horizon with a bright glow above it. There were only a couple of places where actual building lights were visible; the lights of the city had just dipped below the horizon. The ceiling of clouds hung very low, and it looked like it might be raining out there. If we were headed for Bimini, that would put us on a southeast heading and that would be the North Miami skyline I was looking at. Judging from the brightness of the sky-glow, we were probably ten miles offshore, about fifteen miles out of Lauderdale.

"I guess I really was out a long time, wasn't I," I said as I reached for Solange and pulled her over onto my lap. I remembered the rough way Malheur had been treating her, and I was terrified to think of what he could have done to her while I was unconscious. "You're sure no one hurt you?"

Although I couldn't see her in the dark, I felt her nod.

"Boy, have I ever gotten us into a mess." I pushed her away for a minute, tried to see her in the dark. "How'd you get here, anyway? I suppose you hid on Rusty's boat when I went out to the Jeep?"

Again I felt her nod.

There was something else I wanted to ask her, but I wasn't sure her English would be good enough, or even if I was ready to hear the answer. "Did you understand what Capitaine and that other man were saying in Creole?"

Her head bobbed up and down.

"Can you tell me?"

She didn't answer right away. "He say Bwon Samedi going to take you over."

I'd heard the phrase before, I just couldn't remember what it meant. "What is Bwon Samedi?"

"He is a *lwa*. Capitaine say when we get to the island, Bwon Samedi, he going to take you over."

After she said this, she began to cry softly. I had no idea what it meant to her, the phrase "take you over," but it was obvious she thought it was pretty bad.

"Okay, kiddo, listen. I'm not going to let the Capitaine or this Samedi guy or anybody else hurt us. I'm going to figure out a way to get us out of this mess. Okay?" I gave her a quick tight hug, and she squeezed back so hard I thought my pounding head would explode. "I reckon this little ship does about ten knots." It didn't matter that she didn't understand ninety percent of what I was saying, I had to talk out loud to convince myself, since it was wildly improbable that I was going to come up with any sort of workable plan. "It's roughly fifty miles across to Bimini, not taking the Gulf Stream into consideration." I reached for my wrist to illuminate my watch, but it wasn't there. I'd forgotten that I'd given it to Pit. "So let's figure this out. We got to the restaurant around seven. The *Bimini Express* probably left after eight, and it's about ten now. I'd say, given this weather, we should get there in about four hours, maybe a little more. That will be two A.M. There's really nothing we can do now. The best thing for us is to try to get some sleep."

There were bedclothes on the bunk, and though the room was hot and stuffy, I pulled back the sheet and tucked Solange in, kissing her lightly on the forehead as my mother used to do to me. I lay down next to her on top of the covers, though I didn't intend to sleep. I thought I might have a concussion, and I couldn't remember whether it was good or bad to sleep. The fact that I couldn't remember didn't make me feel so great about the health of my head.

"Solange . . ." I spoke softly in the darkness, not sure she was even still awake. "What happened on the big boat with Erzulie?"

She didn't speak right away. I'd about given up when she whispered, "Le Capitaine and Erzulie fight."

"Why?"

"Erzulie *mambo*, le Capitaine *bokor*."

"Oh, she was a *mambo*. Okay, I see. She didn't like what was happening on board the boat. She challenged him."

I heard the covers rustle as she pushed herself up to a sitting position. I could barely make her out in the thick darkness. "Le Capitaine make—" I felt her hand give me a soft judo chop to the side of the head. It didn't help the pounding inside, but I knew what she was trying to say.

"The captain hit her in the head with a machete."

"*Oui.*"

"So how did you both get in that boat?"

"Le Capitaine go inside. People put Erzulie in boat."

"The other Haitians on board the *Miss Agnes* put her into the boat's tender to save her from the captain?"

"*Oui.*"

"And she was still alive?"

"*Oui.*"

"And you, how did you get into the boat?"

"Erzulie say come. People make me go."

She lay back down and rolled onto her side, and her breathing started to deepen its rhythm.

"Miss?"

I thought she had fallen asleep, and her whispered voice surprised me. "Yes?"

"Don't cross over."

"What do you mean?"

"Don't cross over," she repeated.

"Solange, it's not like we have a whole lot of choice. If you mean the Gulf Stream, this boat is crossing the current, and we've got to go where the boat goes."

"No. *Cross over.* Like Erzulie."

I understood. The crossroads. I searched for the words to comfort her, but in the end, I said nothing. I didn't want to lie to her anymore.

By the time I could tell Solange was truly asleep, when her breathing had evened out and the tension in her body had fled, I was thinking about what Rusty had said back at Tugboat Annie's. He agreed with me that there was something special about Solange, that she was not just another *restavek*. What took place on the *Miss Agnes* seemed to bear that out. Why had the other passengers felt it was important to get her off the boat? What was the reason Malheur wouldn't or couldn't just kill her? Why hadn't we been deep-sixed as soon as the boat got offshore? Unless, of course, they were just waiting until we got a little farther out into the Gulf Stream.

I woke when the RPMs on the engine dropped down, and I noticed immediately that the rocking and rolling motion had steadied out. We had to be in the lee of the islands. The inside of my mouth tasted like stale beer and rancid grease, and when I tried to sit up I got another monster case of the dizzies. I felt like I was going to puke. I forced myself to swallow the acid taste; whatever it was, it seemed to get stuck halfway. Finally, the nausea began to subside.

Through the porthole I could see the dark outline of a low island off our starboard beam. The dense cloud cover hid the stars, but I knew that on this night, clouds or no, there would be no moon. Just as city people always know when it's legal to park on the street, knowing the phase of the moon comes with my job. Had Malheur planned this trip for a night with no moon?

The little ship was starting to make her turn in the inner harbor when I heard voices outside in the companionway. Solange was sleeping, so I shook her shoulder and sat her up. I'd taken off my sweatshirt so she could use it as a pillow, and it was too hot in the cabin to bother putting it back on. Solange was still rubbing at her eyes when the door to our cabin swung open and someone shined a flashlight into our faces. I threw up my hand to try to shield my eyes, but the light seared my eyeballs and intensified the pulsing pain in my head. The light clicked off just as abruptly, and all I could see were bright red and white dots swimming in the darkness. The footsteps I heard enter our cabin sounded like they came from leather-soled shoes, and while I flinched just a little, expecting brutality, the arm that grabbed hold of mine did so almost gently.

"Come. Please, make no noise or I will have to hurt the little one." As my eyes began to readjust to the darkness, I saw that the voice belonged to a slender Haitian man. His voice reminded me of Racine's husband, Max, when he said "leetle wun." They both had that same touch of Maurice Chevalier.

My eyes had cleared by the time we passed through the companion-way door and out onto the cargo deck, and though I looked, I saw no sign of Gil or Joslin Malheur. The Haitian man who was leading us had me on one side and Solange on his other. He paused in the shadow of the ship's superstructure, waiting for the deckhands to secure the ship to the dock.

I had never been to Bimini before, but I had been to Nassau and Eleuthera on a former boyfriend's sailboat. Most Bahamian towns had a government dock for cargo ships and a place for yachts to get their customs clearance. I figured that Alice Town, the only real town here on Bimini, would be the same. The floodlights that lit up the ship's cargo deck illuminated the dock as well. It was a concrete dock now slick with rain; though it was not raining at the moment, the humidity had to be in the upper nineties.

The captain of the *Bimini Express* had dropped a bow anchor out in the middle of the harbor, and he was backing into the dock so he would be able to roll off his cargo. Other than a sleepy-looking dockworker who was securing the ship's lines and a pack of five or six wet and bedraggled stray dogs who stood scratching themselves, Alice Town looked to be fast asleep. My estimate of a 2:00 A.M. arrival time might have been a little on the short side. Judging from Bimini's reputation, I would have thought there would still be some music and bar traffic if it was only 2:00. Instead the town seemed eerily quiet.

As soon as the cargo ramp had clanged down onto the cement dock, our escort hurried us back through the pallets of building materials and shipping containers and led us off the ship's stern. We turned to our left on the government dock, and there, tied alongside, at the south end, was a twenty-foot open fishing boat, outboard idling, the single man aboard holding on to the concrete dock with his hands: It was Gil.

I thought about screaming for help, trying to escape, running into town, throwing myself on the mercy of some of the local Bahamians, but then I remembered how strong Gil's grip was. I remembered, too, the Haitian man's comment that he would hurt Solange if I did anything foolish.

As I slid into the boat, Gil turned around and directed me to the stern.

"I've got to help her," I said, pointing to Solange. I reached up to the girl, got my hands under her arms, and started to lift her into the boat. Gil came up alongside me and took the child out of my arms. He startled me, and when I turned to look at him, I saw that his eyes were clear. Once you got past the scars, big mustache, and misaligned features, there was an intelligence there. Was the craziness an act he could turn on and off at will?

He settled Solange gently on the stern.

"What are you doing with these guys, Gil?"

He whirled around, his arm upraised as if to strike me. "Shut up."

I turned my head aside, waiting for the blow, but none came. When I opened my eyes, he had his back turned to us, and he was watching the bridge on the *Bimini Express.*

"You knew my father, didn't you?" I said.

He remained standing facing the ship, but I could see his profile. "Your father?"

"I saw pictures of you," I said, "with Red in Cartagena almost twenty-five years ago. You and Joe D'Angelo were—"

Once more Gil surprised me with how fast he could move. In an instant, he was at my side, sqeezing my arm in that grip. "I said, shut up," he hissed, and shoved me hard toward the back of the boat with Solange.

Then I heard another voice behind us, speaking Creole. Malheur had arrived, and he was castigating the slim Haitian man for not doing something to his liking.

Gil had done his best to hide any reaction, but I had seen his eyes widen slightly at the mention of Red and Cartagena. He had been surprised.

Once we were all in the boat, Gil shoved off and headed the boat back toward the harbor entrance. Our leather-shoed friend pushed Solange and me down in the back of the boat, making us sit on the wet deck so that our heads were not visible above the boat's gunwales. The boat would look like it carried three men going fishing. When they were all deep in conversation, I raised myself up on my knees and took a look over the rail. We were idling along, passing a marina, and I nearly did a double take when I saw a familiar boat tied up to the sea-plane dock. It was an Anacapri with two big outboards, just like Rusty's.

I sat down quickly when Gil turned around to check on us. He glanced over at the seaplane dock, and even in the darkness, I could see the recognition on his face. That boat meant something to him, too, and he turned around and shoved the throttles forward. We surged up into a plane and sped across the channel toward South Bimini. Like the Anacapri, this boat could do maybe twenty knots—more than twice the speed of the *Bimini Express.* Now, with our bow raised and the stern lowered, I didn't need to get up on my knees to see over the top of the outboards. Under the bright dock lights, I could just make out the name of the boat tied to the seaplane dock: *INS AGENT.*

We had not yet left the harbor basin when we abruptly slowed and turned into a canal on our left. What we call Bimini is really two islands—North and South Bimini—and the harbor entrance is through a slot where the two islands overlap. The canal entrance on South Bimini was next to a dock. I'd heard there was a ferry between the two islands, and I presumed we were passing the ferry dock as we idled into the canal. Although the night was very dark, I could see that there were a few homes lining the canal as we motored back in. The farther we traveled, the more numerous the homes, though all looked dark, per-haps deserted. At one point we took a hard left turn, then passed what looked like an abandoned hotel. Soon after, there were no more con-crete seawalls, and then, finally, we were traveling through something that looked like a scene out of the old Bogart movie *The African Queen*—a narrow creek with low-hanging branches forming a canopy over the waterway.

Swamps have never been on my list of favorite nightspots. There was no breeze whatsoever, and as the outboard slowed, and we inched our way up the creek, I felt the mosquitoes on my back and arms and legs. I couldn't swat them off one patch of bare skin before another bug landed somewhere else. These weren't really the kind of mosquitoes you swat, either; these were the kind that smeared into your sweat, leaving a black sooty smudge mixed with blood across your skin. The odors of ammonia and rotting vegetation combined with the gas fumes from the outboard engine that was right next to Solange and me, and it made me start to feel sick. I was grateful when I heard Gil shift the engine into neutral and we glided up to a rickety wood dock, where the waterway dead-ended.

Something about Gil's docking was not to Malheur's liking. As the other Haitian man tied up the boat, Malheur yelled at Gil, his nose almost touching Gil's, and then Malheur spat in his face. The two men stood with their faces inches apart as a large wad of spittle slid down Gil's cheek. When the Haitian captain turned his back, Gil's lip under that huge mustache curled back in a soundless snarl.

Malheur then jumped onto the dock and disappeared into the brush without a glance back. I helped Solange out of the boat and held her hand as they led us into a dark passage someone had cut through the mangroves. Gil was in the lead with the flashlight that, this time, thankfully, was not pointed into our eyes. Someone had attempted to build a dirt path above the tide line, but the earth underfoot gave with each step, and when I walked through a puddle, the water that seeped into my boat shoe felt more like mud. My feet were soon slipping around in the grit inside my shoe. The Haitian crewman brought up the rear, apparently guarding us, and I wondered how he was doing in his leather shoes.

The smell was the first thing I noticed. The stink of the rotting vegetation in that mangrove swamp was nothing compared to the stench coming from somewhere up ahead. I pulled my shirt up over my nose. The deeper into the mangroves we walked, the more putrid the air grew.

Then I noticed the quiet. It seemed as though even the insects and the slithery mangrove critters had decided to take a night off. The stillness was giving me goose bumps in spite of the sweat that had now completely soaked my shirt.

We came to a piece of high ground in a clearing; there the cause of the stench became clear. A cinder-block house stood in the center of the clearing. It had been built on big concrete columns so the tidal surge of a hurricane could pass beneath. But tonight, it wasn't water moving under the house and spilling out across the cleared land. Gil swung his light across the silent ground, and I saw eyes. As the flashlight beam played across their faces—black, white, Asian, Hispanic, Indian—they all turned their heads away, as though ashamed to be found living in such conditions. Hundreds were trying to sleep on the ground, on top of one another, with no shelter from rain or bugs or whatever might come crawling up out of those dark mangroves.

Above us, I heard a door slam, and from the middle of the sea of people came a cough—a chest-rattling, wet, phlegmy cough. Then another. From the other side of the clearing, I heard a young child start to cry and then a mother's voice speaking softly to him in Creole, trying to calm him. The moaning began from several directions at once and in a variety of pitches, all of them resonating with a hopelessness that was painful to hear. From beyond the tree line, somewhere out in the mangroves, came sputtering noises from somebody suffering from a case of explosive diarrhea.

They'd somehow kept quiet as Malheur had passed.

"My God, who are all these people?"

"None o' yer business," Gil said as he stopped at the bottom of the stairs, clicked off the flashlight, and drew a pack of cigarettes out of his pants pocket.

As my eyes grew more accustomed to the dark, I saw next to the house several rusted drums attached to a water catchment system on the roof and a two-burner propane stove resting on a plywood sheet on sawhorses. I wondered if this was the place Solange had worked with Erzulie. No wonder she'd been so thin.

"But they're human beings. The smell, these conditions—so many kids, too—and they're sick, Gil."

He sucked on the end of his cigarette, making the ember glow bright, then nodded his head toward the top of the stairs. "You think he gives a fuck?" His voice sounded different from that of the man who had been yelling at me to shut up in the boat.

I thought about the immigrants who had been killed in Florida and about Margot at the Swap Shop. "But if he is going to sell the *restaveks*, he must want to keep them healthy."

"They don't normally stay here this long," he said, then he took another long drag on his cigarette. He blew smoke toward the upstairs. "He hasn't been making runs across since he's been trying to track down the kid there. He don't usually stay in Florida."

"What is it about her? What do they want with her?"

Gil ignored my questions. He dropped the half-smoked butt and ground it out. "You really Red Sullivan's kid?"

"Yeah, I run *Gorda* now. So, you *did* know Red."

From upstairs came the sound of a door opening, and streams of angry-sounding Creole poured out. Gil mumbled something unintelligible and pointed to the concrete stairs. "Git moving," he said, and nodded toward the upper landing. "He wants you upstairs."

I helped Solange up the stairs and through a wood door at the top. Gil was breathing hard just from the climb up the stairs. The room we entered reminded me of Racine Toussaint's place in Florida. The main light came from two pressurized kerosene lanterns, but at one end of the room was an elaborate altar with dozens of flickering candles, as well as dolls and shells and what looked like a real human skull resting on a crossed pair of thigh bones. Off to one side was a wooden cross that looked like it had been removed from a grave—the downward stake was caked with dirt on the lower third of its length. A rusty shovel leaned against the wall.

Gil and the slim Haitian left us and began talking to some men in an adjoining room. I had no idea what they were saying, but I recognized Malheur's voice. As the conversation continued, Solange squeezed my hand tighter and she pressed her body against mine.

Seconds later, Malheur made his entrance. He had changed clothes and was now wearing what he had worn that night at Racine's— black suit, white shirt, narrow black tie, and top hat with a skull and crossbones made of metal studs. His machete was in an elaborate beaded and fringed scabbard on his belt. The slim Haitian entered the room, pushing two other fellows dressed in rags. The three of them crossed to the altar and pulled out drums from beneath the cloth. Malheur produced a bottle of rum and began passing it around. The men drank from the bottle, tipping their heads back, their Adam's apples pumping as they gulped the liquor. The volume of their voices increased in direct proportion to the amount of rum they consumed, but all the talk was in Creole. Malheur and the other men exchanged comments, looked at me, then burst out laughing.

You don't have to know the language to know when men are talking about sex. It's in their eyes, in the way they laugh. I remembered the Capitaine's little game with my zipper on the ship. I began to understand why Solange was acting as though she feared she would never see me again, and I imagined that anyone looking at the side of my neck would see my pulse pounding in the veins there.

Malheur seated himself with a flourish on a big wooden spool next to the altar. The spool's wood was weathered to a silvery gray. Probably, it had once been used to run wire around the island, but now it served as a throne for the leader of what seemed to be shaping up to be a Voodoo party.

Solange and I were still standing against the wall about ten feet from the door. I squeezed her hand, and she looked up at me. Inclining my head in the direction of the door, I raised my eyebrows slightly to ask her if she understood. She nodded. Very slowly, we began inching our way toward the exit.

Malheur lined up several bottles and clay pots and produced a mortar and pestle from beneath the table. He began adding ingredients from the pots—dried leaves and dark, foul-smelling liquids—and grinding them together. After pouring some of the rum into the stone bowl, he lit the mixture with a wooden match. He waved his arms in the air over the blue flames and spoke aloud, but his voice was blotted out by the drums that had just started. I had thought the drums at *Mambo* Racine's were loud, but these were brutal. It felt as though the drummers were beating directly on my body.

I pressed my hand against my chest and felt for the pouch that Racine had given me. The drums, candles, lanterns, potions, real human bones—these produced some kind of irrational fear. Potions couldn't hurt me. To be afraid of a six-foot-four-inch murderer was perfectly logical, but it was the blank stare of that skull that made me want to clutch the pouch and start talking to La Sirene.

Malheur had his back to us, but because he was sitting at an angle, I could see part of his face. We had halved the distance to the door when he called out my name.

"Seychelle Sullivan," he said, his voice loud enough to be heard over the drums.

Gil appeared at my side. He grasped my arm and put an end to the progress we had made toward the exit. He shoved me in front of Malheur. I never let go of Solange's hand.

Malheur's eyes looked really out of it—drunk or high. The look was not the same I'd seen on the faces of the people at Racine's who claimed to have been possessed by the *lwa.*

"The *bokor* is gone. I am Bwon Samedi."

He grabbed at the front of my shirt and pulled me down to him. I tried to twist out of his grip, to turn my head aside, but he just held me there, my face not two inches from his. I could feel and smell his breath on my cheek. He didn't try to kiss me or bite my nose off—he didn't do anything. The longer we stayed like that, the more frightened I grew. What was he doing? Then he leaned in until his nose almost touched my cheek and his nostrils flared. He was sniffing me. I squirmed when his nose actually ground into my ear, and he made grunting noises like a foraging pig. Then he leaned back, though he still held the front of my shirt. I felt a second of relief before he smacked me open-handed across the face.

I was dazed, couldn't see a thing out of my left eye, and probably couldn't have told you my own name. I stumbled back, the room spinning out of control, but I was determined to stay upright. Too late, I realized I had let go of that little hand.

I heard her call out over the noise of the pounding drums and saw the blur of her yellow tank top and bright red shorts as the Haitian crewman disappeared with her into the other room.

"Solange!" I cried as I started toward the spot where the blur of color had disappeared.

The second slap rocked me even harder, and I tasted the blood where my teeth had pierced the inside of my cheek. The pain must have shown on my face because Malheur threw back his head and laughed again. He was standing now, and he motioned to Gil, who stepped in and grabbed my arm again in his viselike grip. I shook my head to try to clear my blurry vision. There seemed to be only one other room in the house, and though I called out her name, I could barely hear my own voice inside my head. Malheur lifted the bowl that contained the mixture he had cooked up earlier, then shouted something to the drummers, and the rhythm grew even faster. Gil dragged me out the front door and onto the landing. Malheur followed, bringing one of the kerosene lanterns to light up the clearing. Whatever he intended to do to me, he wanted an audience to appreciate it.

The drumming stopped and the silence was nearly as painful as the noise had been. My head had taken too many blows; it felt as though my brain had been jarred loose. The hiss of the pressure lantern was the only sound in the night air when Gil pressed me against the railing at the edge of the landing. Though my vision was blurred, I could still make out the countless white eyes looking up from the dark ground. Malheur held the stone bowl over his head, and he began talking to them in Creole. In the flickering lantern light, it grew clear to me that this man, this *bokor,* thought himself some kind of charismatic leader. Power. And fear. These were what he fed on. The machete on his belt, the potion in his hands, the death images on his hat and glasses—these were the instruments of fear he used to gain power over these people, just as he had done years ago in Haiti under the Duvalier regime.

As my eyes grew more accustomed to the dark, I realized that, from the balcony, we were able to see across the tops of the mangroves to the ocean beyond. We'd entered on the west side of the island, and now I could see open water ahead through the mangroves. I knew South Bimini wasn't very big, but I didn't realize that we had nearly traversed the width of the island on our canal passage. As Malheur continued his speech in Creole, I scanned the water off to our right and understood that I was looking at the Great Bahama Bank that stretched out eastward toward Andros. And there, traveling not more than a quarter mile offshore, I spotted the dim light of a small boat. I wondered if it was Rusty.

"Don't look this way," a voice whispered right next to my ear.

I gave a barely perceptible nod of my head.

"Don't swallow," Gil whispered, so quietly that I could barely hear him over Malheur's rantings.

"What?"

Malheur abruptly stopped speaking and motioned to Gil to bring me closer to him. Gil grabbed my ponytail and yanked my head back, while Malheur's huge ring-covered hand pulled on my chin to open my mouth. The move took only seconds and surprised me. I couldn't clamp my jaw shut in time. Malheur splashed his mixture on my face, getting equal parts down my throat and all over my shirt and hair. The taste was foul, and as I gagged and choked, some of it went down my windpipe. When Gil finally let go of my hair, I bent forward from the waist, coughing and trying to spit it all out on the ground. But I knew, as I gagged and tried to make myself vomit, that I had swallowed some as well.

Malheur spun around and went into the house, calling out instructions to Gil.

Gil let go of my arm for a few seconds, walked to the door, and checked to make certain it was closed. Malheur had taken the lantern with him. It was now pitch black outside. My coughing had just started to subside when Gil emerged from the dark, grabbed me, pried my jaws apart, and stuck his fingers down my throat. I heaved what tasted like pure stomach acid, and Gil jumped back while I puked over the railing.

"Geez, Gil," I said. My throat burned. Then I had another, milder coughing fit.

"He uses drugs. He wants the people to think he's a hot shit Voodoo priest, that he's making people into zombies. He makes it look like a potion, then he just mixes in some drugs—roofies. Makes people kinda paralyzed. He does shit to 'em then. Plays with 'em."

"Why are you telling me this?"

"Go. Get out of here."

"What? Why?"

"You're right, I knew Red. He was all right. Malheur's a psycho prick and I'm sick of his shit. Thinks he's my boss. That's the last time that asshole's gonna spit on me." Gil spat onto the deck. "Now get outta here." He pointed down the stairs. "He expects you inside."

I looked out across the mangroves. The white light was still out there. It wasn't moving now. Maybe it was just some fisherman anchored out there. Maybe it was someone coming to help. "I can't leave Solange."

He shook his head. "Shit." He walked away and then returned. "Act like you're totally drugged out."

He grasped my arm and dragged me to the door. Inside the Voodoo room, the drummers were gone, and the bright lantern was out. The only light in the room came from a couple of candles on the altar. There was no sign of Malheur or the other Haitian man. Gil took me to a chair at the far end of the room, and I sat, slumped over, eyes closed.

Gil and Malheur were speaking in Creole in the other room for quite a while before things grew quiet. Then I heard footsteps crossing the room. They stopped in front of me. I had ingested enough of the drug that I was feeling woozy and disoriented. It was growing more and more difficult to remain still. It felt as though the room were tilting, and I was in danger of slipping off the chair.

A hand enclosed mine where it rested, loose at my side. I could feel the cold metal of the silver rings, so I knew it was Malheur. He lifted my hand level with my shoulder and then let it drop, evidently testing my drugged state. I let the hand flop free and swing.

His breath smelled of rum and cigarettes, and the odor mixed with the earthy smell of the potion he had spilled all over me, making me feel like I was going to vomit again. His face was so close to mine that I could hear the noise his breath made in his nose.

Then a new sound. An odd sort of *swish*. The sound of two surfaces sliding against each other. Then something cool touched my cheek, and I knew that the sound I had heard had been the noise of his machete being drawn out of the sheath on his belt. The steel lay flat against my face. He pulled it away, and the smell of his breath disappeared. Then the thin sharp edge came to rest on my upper arm. I'd seen how much damage that blade could inflict. It took every ounce of willpower I possessed not to flinch as he drew the steel across my arm and began to cut into my flesh.

I heard running footsteps, then the scream. At first I thought it was me screaming, until I opened my eyes and saw Solange on his back, her tiny fists pounding around his shoulders and knocking the sunglasses off his face. When he stood, she rose with him, still clinging to his back, shrieking at him with words I could not understand. I looked down at the blood dripping to the floor from the cut in my arm, and I felt that it was all happening to someone else. I didn't feel any pain. Then Malheur reached around and threw the child to the ground. She landed in a still heap, and he was looking at her, laughing, his face turned away from me, his shoulders shaking.

I laced my fingers together, shot up out of the chair, and slammed my hands down across his injured arm just above his grip on the machete. The weapon flew from his hand, and I kicked it across the floor. He roared like an enraged animal and backhanded me across the face with his ring-encrusted hand. I fell against the altar table and heard the sound of breaking glass, saw the flames where the candles ignited the rum, and then I fell to the floor when the table collapsed beneath me. At once, Malheur was standing over me, the whites of his eyes made red by the flames and the rum, his goatee and mustache making him looking like Lucifer incarnate. I reached through the rubble, trying to get my hands on a piece of a broken bottle or splintered wood. The flames caught at the nylon tablecloth that had covered the altar and raced toward me. Malheur bared his teeth in a sickening grin, then his eyes grew unfocused and he fell forward on top of me.

The cloth of his black suit was suffocating me as the weight of his body pressed down on my abdomen, nose, and mouth. I couldn't move his massive chest off my face because my arms were pinned down where his arms crossed mine. I squirmed and struggled, unaware at first that he was not trying to rape me, that he was not, in fact, even moving.

Then the weight was lifted off my face, and I gasped for air and crabbed my way across the floor, away from the *bokor* and the flames, into a corner of the room. Gil was holding one of Malheur's arms, and when he released it, the Capitaine flopped back to his facedown position. I saw the machete driven deep into the back of the big man's skull.

I retched up more stomach acid as I crawled toward Solange's still form. I hovered over her protectively, eyeing Gil, who stood frozen, staring at the body. I knew the drug was affecting me, and I wasn't even sure if any of what I was watching was real. The whole table was in flames now, and the smoke was making it difficult to breathe.

Solange began to cough. "Are you okay?" I asked when she opened her eyes. She sat up, rubbing the back of her head, and coughed some more. "We've got to get out of here." I stood up, took Solange's hand, and gave Gil's shoulder a shove. "Come on."

We crossed to the door, and before I opened it, Gil put his hand on my arm, touched the blood. "You're cut," he said.

I nodded. "It's not deep. Come on."

"I've got to stay. He's coming."

"Who's coming?"

"You go. Take the kid. Stay away from the dock—go the other way. You don't want him to find you."

"Come with us, Gil."

"I can't." He shrugged. "Get her out of here before he gets here."
He pushed open the door, then grabbed a blanket and started beating
at the flames that were now licking around the body on the floor. He
looked up. "Get the fuck out of here," he shouted.

I grabbed Solange's hand, and we raced down the steps, then bore
right, away from the direction of the dock where we'd arrived. There
was a pathway of sorts through the bodies stretched out on the ground,
but as we passed, the path widened as the people drew back. They were
clearly accustomed to violence, and they did everything they could to
stay out of reach. At the edge of the clearing, we stepped onto a crudely
built wooden walkway that led out through the mangrove swamp toward the island's eastern shore.

The wooden walkway led out to a short pier over open water, at the
end of which was a small shed. I'd seen this type of thing before in the
islands. No plumbing required for this head; it was a straight shot
down to a tidal flush.

We stopped at the base of the pier, and I looked at the dim white
light bobbing about half a mile offshore. It was all shallow out there.
The banks stretched for miles. Probably just some fisherman. But it
might be Rusty. The light looked like it was dancing, and every time I
tried to look right at it, it swerved out of my line of vision.

I looked down at Solange.

"Can you swim?" I asked.

xxvii

She cocked her head at me, not understanding. I pantomimed an Australian crawl, and she shook her head.

"Okay, get on my back and put your arms around my neck." I adjusted her around behind me piggyback style. I could feel her body trembling, and I knew it was not from the night air. "See that white light?" I pointed the light out to her, attempting to focus my own eyes. I figured she would be less frightened if she could see our destination. "I think that's Rusty's boat." I felt the cut on my upper arm. While not deep, it was still oozing blood. "I'm going to swim us out there, okay?" I tried to sound more confident than I was.

For the first hundred yards or so, I was able to walk across the uneven bottom, my sneakers crunching on the shell and coral, the soles of my shoes getting sliced up in the process. I began to worry about someone seeing us, so I lowered my upper body into the water and started a slow but strong breaststroke. I was glad no one was there to watch my technique—I'd never felt so uncoordinated in the water. It was as though part of my consciousness were standing aside, looking at the rest of me, which was impaired—mentally and physically. The night was so dark, I couldn't even make out the line of the horizon, where the clouds ended and the waters of the Bahama Banks began. The white light we were headed for looked like it was suspended in a black sky. I began to feel that vertigo again, like I was swimming uphill.

We were not far enough away from the little pier when I heard voices from the island. I didn't dare waste the energy to turn around and look. My strength has always been in my arms, but my deltoids were burning already. Back when I was working the beach, I had pulled in guys who weighed four times as much as Solange. Tonight, I began to worry I wasn't going to make it.

The voices on shore multiplied, and I judged I was only about halfway to the boat. I hoped Rusty didn't hear the ruckus and decide to lift anchor and split. I hoped the boat really was Rusty's. The cool water was helping my wooziness, but I found the best thing was just to concentrate on that light and block out all other thoughts.

My arms were starting to go numb. It should have been an easy swim, would have been had I been clearheaded and on my own, even wearing all the clothes that weighed me down. I didn't want to think about the blood I might be losing from the wound on my arm. Or what it might attract. Not only was I fighting off some kind of poison in my system, but I was also trying to keep a low profile and hauling a kid on my back. Not that she weighed much of anything, but she kept trying to climb higher up my shoulders, almost onto my head, and that pushed me down, under the water. I'd gulped seawater a couple of times when I came up for air, and in her panicked state, she'd pushed me back down.

I could make out the outline of the boat finally, but I couldn't see any sign of a person in it. It sure looked like Rusty's. From the sounds of the voices behind me, they seemed to be searching among the mangroves along the shore. I didn't want to confirm my position for them, but I did want Rusty to get that anchor up and get ready to haul ass out of here.

"Hey," I tried calling out, not too loud, between panting breaths. "Rusty, hey, over here." There was still no sign of anyone on board. I wondered if he was below in the bunk. Surely he couldn't sleep out here, knowing that Solange and I were ashore with Malheur.

When I reached the fiberglass hull, I banged on it to awaken him, then swam around to the stern to climb aboard. Where the hell was he? I pushed Solange onto the swim platform first, and then I crawled up. When I stood up and started to lift her over the transom onto the apparently deserted boat, I heard the first gunshot.

"Shit. Stay down," I said as I dragged her the rest of the way into the boat. "Get in the cabin."

The next bullet entered the water with a *pfft* noise just off our stern, a fraction of a second before the boom of the shot rang out. I spaced out for a few seconds, staring at it. Solange reached through the cabin doors and put her hand on my leg. I blinked, then slid into the helmsman's seat and reached for the keys. I gave silent thanks when I found them in the ignition. I turned the key and the engines fired right up, still warm from having made the trip over here.

"Stay here," I told her as I leaned into the cabin and turned off the anchor light at the panel. Then I stepped up onto the foredeck cabin to retrieve the anchor. I heard two more gunshots from the shore, but thanks to the dark night, none came close.

Maybe I should have waited around for Rusty to return, but with bullets hitting the water all around us, I pitched the little CQR into the foredeck anchor well, ran back to the helm, and shoved the outboards into gear. I tried to picture a chart of South Bimini. The island was roughly rectangular, running about two and a half miles long, east to west. We'd entered a canal on the northwest corner, and I was now on the north coast. The quickest way back to deep water and the straightest shot to Florida was to head west, back to the town and the harbor entrance. I'd also have to pass the canal entrance, and they might be heading out that canal right now in their boat. If I headed away from Alice Town, I would have to go a couple of miles in the opposite direction, and I knew there was very thin water over the coral.

Knowing there was a good chance I'd kill us both if I ripped the bottom of this boat out doing twenty knots, I turned the wheel to head for the faint glow of Alice Town.

We still had roughly half a mile of very shallow water to cover before we would reach the main channel and pass in front of the canal that led to Malheur's camp. I'd sweat gallons along the way, hoping we had enough depth under the outboards, because on this dark night I couldn't see a thing.

I motioned for Solange to come closer. She wrapped her arms tightly around my waist and pressed the side of her face against my ribs, staring up at me. She opened her mouth as though to say something, but with the noise of the outboards and the constant jarring of the boat as it pounded across the flats, she closed her mouth again, gritting her teeth in a terrified grimace. Clearly, she did not like small boats, nor did she like the speed we were traveling. "Life jackets?" I said. "Do you know what they are?"

She answered me with a puzzled look.

I lifted up the driver's seat and found a big foam life jacket in there. "Like this. Find a small one for you, okay?" She nodded and turned slowly, making her way back down into the cuddy cabin.

After what seemed like an eternity, we reached the end of the island and the deeper channel. As we made our turn and passed in front of the entrance to Malheur's canal, I saw the red and green of a pair of running lights far back in the canal. A boat was coming out.

A little nudge to the throttles didn't do much to change our speed. Rusty's boat was giving it everything she had, and I just had to hope that it would be enough. I wondered if he was somewhere on the dark island, watching his boat speed off. I was confident he could take care of himself and find his way to the ferry and back to Alice Town, but I was also pretty sure he'd be pissed at my stealing his boat a second time.

Bimini is not a harbor to go in or out of at night without local knowledge or a chart. The channel runs parallel to the island for about half a mile with a sandbar and reef between the channel and the open sea. In places, there was four feet of water over the reef, and I'd have no problem crossing over; in other spots, though, there was only inches over coral heads that on this dark night would be absolutely invisible. Though heat lightning now flashed intermittently on the horizon, and the pregnant-looking clouds overhead appeared about to burst, there was little wind and the surface of the sea in the lee of the island was oily smooth. There were no breakers to show me the end of the reef. I would have to guess.

For some reason, the boat had not followed us out into the channel. I could see their lights behind us, and they were headed across to Alice Town.

Solange came up from the cuddy cabin holding two life jackets. I quickly showed her how to step through the crotch straps, then snapped the front of her jacket.

I slung the larger one onto the deck as I saw a house on the beach off to our left. I knew there were range markers somewhere around that house, but I'd never find them in the dark. I decided it was time to go for it.

"Hold on tight," I shouted over the roar of the engines, and I swung the wheel.

I braced myself, waiting for the crunch, for the jarring stop that would send me through the windshield, but it didn't come. We sailed on out into the dark sea.

We had been on a course heading roughly due east for about ten minutes, making a good speed of about twenty knots, when we began to clear the lee of the island. The increase in the wind chop and swell wasn't all that gradual. I was down in the cabin, digging out Rusty's binoculars, when the boat became airborne and slammed nose first into a big swell. So much for a quick trip back. I tossed the binoculars out onto the deck and jumped to the helm. After I'd disengaged the autopilot, I lowered our speed and checked the gauges.

"Shit."

Solange poked her head out the cabin door and looked up at me with alarm.

"Hey, sorry. Just go back and lie down, okay?" There wasn't any need to make her even more scared. I had no idea what the boat's fuel tank capacity was, but I was pretty certain that a gauge reading less than a quarter of a tank meant we did not have enough fuel to get back across the Gulf Stream to Florida. That was probably why we had no pursuers—they were at the fuel dock.

Maybe we'd get within VHF range of the coast, and I could call for a tow. There would be a lot of charter and towboat captains who would find *that* highly amusing. I'd probably never live it down, but given that just an hour ago I was wondering if we were going to live at all, I guess it wasn't so bad.

I made a quick 360-degree check around the horizon. To the north, a nasty squall loomed like a black hole and seemed to suck what little light there was into its dark curtain of rain. I was running without lights, trying to make sure I saw any other boat traffic out here, because they sure as hell weren't going to see me.

I went below to dig around and see if I could find a chart. The mainland wasn't all that hard a target to hit, but I was certain we didn't have enough fuel to get there. I wanted to make sure we were in the most populated shipping lane when the tanks ran dry. Thinking about how this boat with no power would wallow in the swells, I knew we would need to get found pretty damn quick.

When I came out of the cuddy cabin, the air temperature had dropped a good fifteen degrees and the wind was starting to pick up. Ahead, the rain was visible, even on this dark night, and it looked like we were about to drive into a black wall. I checked the autopilot and the fuel gauge. We'd already used half of the fuel we'd had when we left Bimini. I didn't know how much longer the boat would run, but hopefully, it would run long enough to get through this squall.

The wind hit us about thirty seconds ahead of the rain. It was as though someone had turned on a hurricane-force wind machine. Some of the gusts must have been clocking at over forty-five knots, and when the rain hit, it felt like we were being attacked with an air stapler. The stinging raindrops made it nearly impossible to open my eyes, so I huddled behind the windscreen for cover. Within minutes, I was drenched down to my underwear, and the rain was so cold, I trembled uncontrollably. Solange opened the doors to the cuddy cabin and stuck her head out. I could see she was crying.

"So much water," she said.

"Yeah, I know. It's the rain," I shouted over the noise of the storm. "It will be over soon."

The wind and rain had not yet let up when the outboards started to sputter. I throttled back, thinking I could keep the engines running a little longer at the lower speed, stretch out our fuel, but both engines immediately quit. The boat didn't glide to a stop, she just lurched down, dead in the water, and immediately began to roll in a wild corkscrew motion driven by the waves kicked up from the squall. Solange opened the doors to the cuddy cabin, and when I saw the water sloshing over the cabin floor, I realized what she had been trying to tell me earlier.

"Watch out," I said as I pushed her aside and dove below. I located the electrical panel and tried the manual override on the electric bilge pump. Nothing happened. "Okay, Rusty, where's your hand pump?" I started going through lockers and finally found a cheap little plastic pump under the bunk. Of all the things for him to cheap out on, I thought. I handed Solange the end of the hose and told her to hold it out the doors as I pumped the water out of the cabin, onto the deck, where I hoped it would drain through the aft drain holes—if they weren't already underwater.

I started strong, pumping like our lives depended on it, which of course they did. After about five minutes, I still couldn't tell if I'd made any progress, and I had to switch arms. I stood for a second to shake out my shoulders, and I watched as a large green wave dumped across the boat and gallons of seawater sloshed through the companionway into the cabin. I shook my head. This was futile. She was going down.

I went back to pumping, but I started directing Solange to put together a survival bag of things that we would need in Rusty's life raft. She found bottles of water and a box of protein bars. I took a couple of the candy bars and stuffed them in the pockets of my jeans. I'd need to keep my strength up to keep going with this pumping.

When she came across a diver's buoyancy compensator, I had her hand it to me, and I put it on, checking to make sure the CO_2 cartridge was in the pocket. I hated life jackets, but with this less bulky vest, I could inflate it only if I needed it. I took the whistle and small strobe light off an adult life jacket and attached them to my buoyancy compensator.

Sound travels better through water than through air. When you're inside a boat, and another boat approaches, you will always hear the engine through the water first. I knew exactly what that rumbling noise meant the minute I heard it.

From down below, it was impossible to tell what direction the boat was coming from. I told Solange to stay in the cabin, and I went out on deck. The squall had let up, and the gray light of morning had increased visibility tremendously, but the sky still hung very dark and low. When we rose to the top of a swell, I looked all around the horizon, but I didn't spot the boat before we immediately plunged back into a trough. I tried the VHF radio at the helm but discovered that all the electronics on the boat were dead. I could see now how low Rusty's boat was riding in the water, and I understood why the waves were breaking over the gunwales, swamping us. I remembered Rusty's flare kit in the seat locker and dug it out, fitted a flare to the gun, and shot it into the air.

I waited until we had crested an entire series of waves, and I still didn't see anything. The noise was growing louder, though. I had just decided to try another flare when the approaching boat went from being a distant possibility to being right there, coming over the top of a wave, headed straight for us. Although I couldn't see anyone on board, the high white fiberglass bow of what looked to me like an ocean racing boat seemed to appear out of nowhere. For an instant, I feared the captain didn't see us, wasn't slowing down, and he was going to run us over, slice our boat in two. At the last minute, the racing boat veered off, the stern swung around, and I saw the trademark name Donzi painted along the waterline. The boat looked to be about forty-five feet overall, and as it slowed and the engines went into neutral, a man stepped away from the helm and leaned over the side. I realized that I knew him.

"Seychelle?"

"Joe?"

"Are you okay, honey? What the devil are you doing out here? Take this." He tossed me a line, and I tied it off to a midships cleat on our sinking boat.

"Man, am I ever glad to see you," I said. "This boat's taking on water, and we were getting ready to abandon ship."

Then I felt a small hand on my thigh. I reached down and pulled Solange up so that Joe could see her, too.

I started to speak again when Solange called out at the top of her voice.

"Papa!"

I looked at him and then at her. "No, Solange, this is Joe," I said. When I turned back to look at him, he wasn't alone anymore. Gil Lynch stood to one side and the slender Haitian man who worked with Malheur stood to the other.

Solange cried out, a plaintive wail so full of pain that I wrapped my arms around her and turned my back to the men on the big ocean racer. I stroked her head as she gulped for air.

Joe D'Angelo was Gil's boss? I wanted to cry out, too. There was nowhere left to go.

Joe called out to her. "It's okay, kid. Don't worry. These are my guys. I won't let them hurt you." I watched over my shoulder as the Haitian man, lying on his belly on the stern of the ocean racer, reached for the side of our boat.

Joe reached his arms out for Solange, and she buried her sobbing face in my neck. He handed the line to Gil, who shoved his handgun under his belt at the small of his back, then pulled our boat in tight alongside theirs. I saw the Haitian man tying us together at the stern as well.

"Go to hell, D'Angelo," I said. Gil stood back behind Joe, and his eyes flashed at me. He was trying to tell me not to push him, but I wasn't going to give Joe the satisfaction of watching us just climb into his big ocean racer.

Joe laughed even louder that time. "Hell? Isn't that where all us smugglers go? Like Red?"

I turned and opened my mouth, started to speak, when over Joe's shoulder I saw Gil, frantically shaking his head.

Then Joe was right there, holding his arms out in my face.

"Hand her to me, Seychelle."

"I don't get it. She's your daughter? And you left her in Port-au-Prince all these years as a *restavek*?"

Joe turned to the Haitian and pointed at the sinking boat. The man fired several rounds into the hull, only hurrying along the obvious.

"I said give her to me," Joe said. He had his hands on her shoulders, yet she held tight to me, screaming as he pulled at her. "Seychelle, now."

He was hurting her. "What do you want with her?" I yelled at him. "You left her once. Leave her again." I struggled to hold on to the child, the water sloshing around my knees. I was sinking down, farther from his grasp, but he wasn't letting go.

"No," he shouted, and then he enunciated very clearly: "She belongs to *me.*"

In the end, he was stronger, and she was gone, yanked out of my arms, crying like a lost child, only she was in the arms of her father. I scrambled over the gunwale and across the upholstered white vinyl on the racer's transom.

"I go wherever she goes, Joe."

Gil and the Haitian untied the lines, and Rusty's boat disappeared in a vortex of bubbles.

Joe turned away from the sight and looked at me with a half smile, then looked at Gil. "Shoot her," he said.

Solange began kicking and screaming even louder as Joe tried to haul her toward the companionway leading to the cabin below decks.

Joe shook her tiny body hard. "Shut up," he yelled. Solange sobbed, even as her head flopped on her shoulders as he bounced her body back and forth. Then he turned to Gil, who was standing next to me in the stern, head lowered, eyes fixed on the gun in his hand. Joe yelled, "I said shoot her."

Gil looked up, and his handlebar mustache was twitching. "Boss, let's just leave her out here."

"Son of a bitch," Joe said, and nodded at the Haitian man, who had been watching the scene with a perplexed look. "Take this kid below and shut her up." He handed the bawling child to the slender man, and the two disappeared below. Joe turned back to Gil. "When I tell you to do something, Gilbert Lynch, you damn well better do it."

I watched Solange disappear into the cabin, and all I could think of was that I hadn't said good-bye.

Gil said, "Just let her get in a raft. She probably won't make it. Boss, she's Red's kid."

"I don't give a fuck whose kid she is."

"Cartagena, Joe. Remember? I owe him."

"You crazy son of a bitch. The only person you owe a damn bit of loyalty to is me. I own you. You'd be rotting in some federal cell right now if it weren't for me. And now when I tell you to do something, you're talking back to me about some piddly-ass tugboat captain?"

Gil was still holding the gun, but it was lowered, hanging at his side now. He turned to me. "Look, I'd been drinking and whoring down there. On my way back to the boat, a bunch of locals tried to rob me. They knifed me in the gut, left me for dead. Your daddy found me, woke up some local doc, saved my life."

"Shut up, Gil," Joe said, "nobody cares about that old story. It's all a fabrication from that burnt-out brain of yours."

Gil continued as though he hadn't heard Joe. "I wanted to send your daddy back to the States—didn't want him involved, but it turned out I'd cut one of them Colombians, too, and the Federales come looking for me. Joe told the Federales a pack of lies, and we sailed out of there that night, straight shot back to Florida. We never told Red what was under the floorboards. Red was such a straight shooter, he woulda turned hisself in if he knew—and us in the process."

"Gil, shut your mouth and take care of business."

Gil turned from me and raised the gun, his hand shaking, pointing it at Joe. "I ain't gonna shoot her, Joe," he said.

"Shit. First I lose Malheur, and you try to tell me he fell off the balcony, busted his head." Joe's voice remained steady, even calming, as though he were talking about taking out the trash.

Gil's mustache started to twitch again, and his lips were bulging over his teeth, the hand holding the gun shaking wildly.

"And now you're turning on me. Telling drug-induced lies about something that never even took place. I think you've finally gone off the deep end, Gil."

When Joe made his move, it happened so fast, I didn't realize what had gone down until I heard the shot. Joe had spun around, come up alongside Gil, and taken the gun from his hand. Then he'd stepped back in front of Gil, raised it to the man's forehead, and fired. A spray of red spewed across the stern cushions seconds before Gil's body fell backward onto the vinyl.

Joe squatted, lifted the man's legs, and said, "The very deep end." He slid the body into the water, then rubbed his hands on his pants. "Shoulda done that years ago," he said, standing and surveying the blood-spattered stern. "Shit, what a mess. Sullivan, get a bucket out of that deck box and clean up my boat."

A part of me wanted to scream and give in to the horror of what I'd just witnessed, but at the same time I felt numb to it. This whole thing couldn't really be happening. I wasn't really about to die.

I found the bucket and a scrub brush and dipped the bucket full of seawater. As I poured the water over the racing boat's padded stern, I watched the red turn pink when the blood mixed with the sea. My arm was moving across the plastic, but I wasn't aware of being in charge of that arm. It was as though I were watching someone else scrub away the streaks of Gil's blood.

They had chased us out here, and now both Malheur *and* Gil were dead—and all for this little girl, Joe's daughter. I remembered him shaking Solange, her head bouncing around on her shoulders. I had to know. "Joe, what do you really want with her?"

He waved the gun, motioning me to keep working while he sat down on the helmsman's seat. "You're as much of a pain in the ass as your old man was," he said. "Maybe more. At least Red knew when to look the other way. Didn't go butting into other people's business, trying to save the fucking world."

With the barrel of the gun, he pointed at a spot I'd missed.

"The world's a fucked-up place, Sullivan," he continued, "and there's not a damn thing you can do about it. This was all supposed to be so simple. All I asked Malheur to do was to bring this kid into the States on one of our boats. I mean, shit, this is what we do for a living. No big deal, right? Ninety percent of our runs slip straight through, no problems. It's not like I was gonna go to the embassy and claim the little shit and do the paperwork to try to get her in legally. Right, and wait years? Then some bitch on the boat gets Malheur pissed, he whacks her in the head, and when he's not looking, the fuckin' Haitians stick the two of them, my kid and the bitch, in their tender. Malheur doesn't even realize the kid's gone until the boat is off Hillsboro, ready to go in. He looks around for the dinghy and the kid— both are gone." Joe spread his hands wide, still holding Gil's gun. "I got nothing but fuck-ups working for me."

I dropped the bucket into the ocean and pulled up another load of clean seawater, then sloshed it across the vinyl. I wanted to keep him talking, but I also really wanted to understand the how and the why of all this business. "Joe, she's your daughter."

He waved his arms in the air. "Don't talk to me about daughters. When a daughter won't let her old man see his own grandson because of some half-breed kid down on a shithole of an island, you know the world is fucked up. I never should have told her about the kid in the first place. But there it is. I don't get to see my grandson, my one and only *male* heir, until I can prove that the kid is in America, living with a family. Ha!" he said. "I'll place her with a family all right."

"A *restavek*? You plan to make your own daughter a child slave, in the States?"

"Beautiful, right? Get paid coming and going. Plus, I get my grandson. Best gig I ever come up with. Used to be my guys took a boat south and bought the product—coke—now the product pays them! Best part is the kids take up less room on the boats. And the market in the

States . . . you would not believe it. No wages, no Social Security, and they work twice as hard as any Yank kids would. We've had a waiting list from the very start."

I was scrubbing the last of the blood off the vinyl, and I sat up on my heels when Joe said, "You about done there? Good." One minute I was sitting on top of the engine housing on the back of this ocean racer, getting ready to climb down into the cockpit, and then I saw Joe slide the throttles forward as he shouted, "So long, Sullivan."

The boat leaped into motion like a panther after her prey, and I tumbled in a backward somersault off the transom, back into the sea.

I came up sputtering, having swallowed a mouthful of seawater in my surprise. I heard the engine roar through both the water and the air. As the distance between the boat and me grew, a wave lifted me, and I saw Joe at the helm. He didn't even bother looking back. When I crested the next swell, I could no longer find him. The boat must be in a trough, I thought. He couldn't have disappeared that quickly.

Or could he? I stopped dog paddling for a few seconds to listen, and the weight of my shoes and clothes pulled me down so that a wind wave broke over my head, and I went under. I pushed back up to the surface and sucked in a breath of air so violently that it hurt. It seemed to scrape the back of my throat and stretch the limits of my chest. I clawed at the surface of the water, thrashing, trying desperately to keep my head from going under again. Finally, I recognized what I was feeling: panic. I'd seen it in a hundred near drowning victims but had never expected to experience it myself. I kicked off my shoes while I blew some air into my buoyancy compensator, then I rolled onto my back and floated, slowing my breathing and my heart rate.

Too bad I couldn't slow my mind as well. Thoughts kept tumbling in this chaotic montage. When people talked about that cliché of your life flashing before your eyes, I always thought it would be like a feature film played on super-fast-forward, and you would watch yourself grow up and then old, like in time-lapse photography. But that wasn't what I was seeing at all. One minute I was trying to calculate how long we had been traveling in Rusty's boat, and at what speed, in order to figure out how far we'd made it across the current, and then, *bam!* My mind jumped to an image of my mother laughing and tickling Pit, and then, *bam!* An image of her cold and wet and blue on the beach, and then, *bam!* I'd see a seventeen-year-old girl I once pulled from the sea, her hair dry, still wearing her life jacket, no water in her lungs, dead from hypothermia three days after her family's fishing boat sank out in the Gulf Stream.

Images flitted in and out of my brain as though I had lost control of my own mind. I saw Gil's face again when the gun was pressed to his forehead, his eyes showing something that looked almost like relief. His body was here in the water with me, floating somewhere, possibly not far off, leaking blood and attracting . . . what? I lifted my arm out of the water and looked at the puckered white skin around the wound in my own arm. At least there was no more blood there. Straight beneath me, thousands of feet down, was an unexplored world. Humans had never walked down there, and no one really knew much about those depths or what lived down there. Sharks? I saw myself then from beneath, floating at the surface, as though I had stepped outside my body, swum underneath, and looked up, and then I realized I was just replaying a scene from the movie *Jaws*. My mind pictured whales and sea monsters, even Nemo's giant squid. None of that frightened me.

Hypothermia. That was how I would die.

xxviii

Swimming seemed pointless. The buoyancy compensator was inflated just enough so that I could float on my back. Which direction would I go? As far out into the Stream as I was, the current would be pushing me along no matter what I did.

My thoughts bumped around my brain so haphazardly that it occurred to me that "train of thought" was grossly inaccurate. It wasn't a straight rail in my head, but more like a traffic jam, a major snarled-up mess in a place with no roads. The ocean is like that. A place to get lost.

I'd been dozing, floating on my back, when the vibrations started up. I didn't know what it was at first. I'd only heard the sound of outboards through the water before. When I realized it was an engine of some kind, I stopped floating on my back and searched the horizon. As I crested the top of the next swell, I saw a long white cruise ship three to four miles off and coming my way.

The damn thing passed me less than a mile off. I flailed my arms and screamed, but a lot of good *that* did me on that rainy, overcast day. I wished like hell that I had some of the flares that went down with Rusty's boat. Why hadn't I tucked one or two of those in my pockets? I was laughing out loud at that thought when the ship passed at its closest point. I could even see people leaning over the rail on the upper decks. Not many, just a few loners in rain slickers, out enjoying the dark, brooding afternoon. I thought about the dry beds and hot meals and long lives that awaited them. The ship disappeared over the horizon in a matter of minutes. That was when I cried for the first time that day.

At some point, a band of blue appeared at the horizon—I did not know whether it was east or west or whatever. The sky that had been this big gray dome slowly metamorphosed into individual clouds with depth and design and beauty. B.J. would have loved those clouds, and he would have started seeing shapes and pointing things out to me—animals, mountains, and faces, shapes that I never would have been able to see on my own. I tried to look at the clouds as B.J. would, tried to see the world and my predicament as he would see it, and thinking about him, trying to get at the essence of him like that, made me feel angry. I'm not ready to let go of him yet, I thought, not ready to say good-bye to that . . . what? What did I call what I felt for him?

How poor our language was with this one word: love. The Polynesians had dozens of words for coconut, the Eskimos had their variations to describe snow, but we had only this one word to communicate the most important aspect of life, the multitude of ways we can connect with other beings. What I felt for my parents, my brothers, Jeannie, my dog, B.J., and now Solange—all were variations of this emotion, yet all were so different. How could that one little four-letter word encompass all that range of pain and joy and sorrow?

I tried to focus, to slow my mind down. I felt that I was on the verge of some moment of enlightenment. Then a larger than normal wind wave slapped me on the side of my face, and I snorted seawater up my nose and swallowed a mouthful. Coughing and gagging, fighting against the burning sensation in my sinuses, I thought, I'm not ready to drown yet. I need more time, dammit.

Time. It appeared to lose all meaning out there. The day seemed to not want to end, yet I was not looking forward to the dark. When I became aware that I was cold, I realized that I had been cold for a very long time. I began kicking and rubbing my skin, trying to warm myself up. The wind had dropped down to almost nothing, and while there was still some swell, there were no longer the little wind waves that splashed me in the face.

Three times during the day I saw helicopters or planes pass overhead, and I waved and shouted as I had at the cruise ship, but I'd flown in an airplane over these same waters before. I knew how unlikely it was that anybody up there would be able to spot a person in the water. I wondered if all the air traffic had anything to do with me. Had Rusty reported his boat missing?

Two large clouds parted and a column of sunlight lit up a small circle of ocean not far from me. It reminded me of those paintings of angels or Jesus, where they stood in a shaft of celestial light. Maybe this was a sign, maybe a miracle was about to take place, another boat would appear, and I would be plucked from the sea. I waited, allowing myself a tiny bit of hope. The lovely shaft of light broadened as the clouds drifted apart, and soon the whole sky was flecked with spots of blue. No boat appeared, and I beat my hands against the surface of the sea, splashing my own face, angry at myself for wanting to believe.

When the sunlight finally reached my part of the ocean, I could feel the temperature change. I closed my eyes, pointed my face to the sun, and let the heat soak into my skin. I leaned the top of my head back, and my feet floated right to the surface. I began to feel some warmth, even in my legs.

For a time, I actually dozed off into real sleep. That bit of late afternoon sunny warmth reenergized me, and when I woke, I remembered that I had those candy bars in my pocket. The saltwater had not penetrated the vacuum foil wrapper, so when I tore it open with my teeth, the chocolate bar inside was squished but dry. I usually complained about the chalky taste of those health food store protein bars when B.J. offered me one, but this one tasted so good, I nearly gobbled down the second as well. I pulled it out of my pocket but then stuck it back, thinking that night was coming, and it would take every bit of energy I had to survive through those long dark hours.

Night came on as quickly as the cruise ship had passed. It seemed as though one minute there was sun, then a flamboyant red sky had melted into a million stars. The sky was not as dark as it had been the night before. Out of reach of all the mainland lights, there were so many stars there was little black sky left. I couldn't ever remember having seen so many stars. No, that's not true, I thought. There was that time, down in the Dry Tortugas with Neal, my former boyfriend. Neal, who had shown me the stars, named the constellations, and made love to me on the sand of an island that disappeared at high tide.

Was Neal waiting for me at the Crossroads, along with my mother and Red and my dear friend Elysia and Margot and all the others I had not saved?

The skin on my fingers had lost all sensation. When I touched my fingers to my dry cheeks, it felt like I was pressing slimy sea creatures to my skin. I put a finger in my mouth, and it was more like a cold thin pickle than a part of me.

Sleep was the enemy, and I battled against it by singing songs I'd learned as a child, songs like "This Land Is Your Land" and "America, the Beautiful," by gliding my hands through the water and watching the blue green contrails of bioluminescence sparking off my fingertips, by naming the stars and constellations I could remember: Orion, Betelgeuse, Altair, Sirius.

Just in case there really was some kind of search-and-rescue effort happening out there, I turned on my little strobe light. It had a big pin on one side, and I had attached it to one of the straps on my buoyancy compensator. As I adjusted the straps on the BC, I felt Racine's pouch float up under my chin. I grasped it tight in my fist and stared upward, but the bright flashes of my strobe blinded my night vision, ruining my view of the stars. I was way beyond caring what seemed rational and what did not. I called her name out loud, La Sirene, and I told her that I didn't believe, but if she wanted to help me anyway, I wouldn't turn down the offer. That made me smile, and I wondered if it would be the last time.

It didn't take long once it was dark for the cold to set in. I tried curling my body into a ball, swimming, rubbing my limbs, but nothing worked. A part of me welcomed the numbness because it stopped the aches in my body and the pain in my head. At one moment, I was sure I heard my mother's voice, and we had quite a long conversation. She told me drowning really wasn't so bad. "Sey, dear, when you've really had enough, just breathe the water. Simply put your head under and breathe."

"Mother," I said as I kicked my legs, spinning my body around looking over the waves. "Mother, where are you?"

She wouldn't answer me, and I was so cold. And so sleepy. I would never do as she said, never breathe in water, but it would be nice to stop struggling and sleep for a little while. Maybe, just maybe, the darkness and cold would be gone if I could only sleep through the night. Yes, sleep.

I was down in a deep, dark cave where the cold and damp got
into your bones. Waiting, but for what, I wasn't sure. Then I saw a shaft
of light shining in the cave, just like the light I had seen at the surface.
And she was there, crying, asking me to hurry, please. I pushed back
the strands of my long black hair that were floating in the water, waving about my head as she reached out to me. Help me, I heard her say
inside my head, just like that first day I'd found her. Help me. You
promised. I called out to her, Where are you? I could see her, but I
could not reach her. When she answered, she asked, Who are you? and
I told her, La Sirene.

A hand grabbed hold of my clothing and started pulling me up toward the surface. I struggled, and I wasn't sure I wanted to go. Then I
heard the voice of a man speaking Creole, and I knew I was not going
to let them take me away from Solange again.

"No," I cried out, and swung my fists at the arms that grasped my
clothes. I was dragged into the bottom of a boat, and a plastic tarp was
thrown over me. I felt the weight of several people lying on top of me.
I stopped struggling because if they didn't get off me, I would soon suffocate.

The corner of the tarp lifted. My strobe light was still flashing in
my eyes, and I couldn't see anything. A hand reached in and turned off
the light. Red lights continued to dance in my vision.

"Lady?" someone said. It was a young man's voice, and the accent
was distinctly Haitian. Maybe this was another of Malheur's hench-
men. "You okay, lady?"

I tried to blink away the red spots. My eyes began to focus on the
person nearest me, a woman. Her skin was very dark, and she was wearing a headscarf. She was the one sitting on my midriff. The young man

was behind her, and there were other faces behind them, more and more as my eyes started to see better.

"What—" I tried to speak, but with the woman sitting on my diaphragm, it was difficult to get enough air. Then I looked up, above all their faces, and I saw the sail. It was made of flour sacks and other odd bits of fabric. It puffed out, round-bellied and pulling hard in the strong night winds. I looked back at the woman sitting on me. "Can I get up?" My voice sounded strange even to me.

A puzzled look crossed her face, and she looked over her shoulder at the young man. He smiled and nodded, saying something to her in Creole. She laughed and wiggled her way to a stance.

When I tried to stand, I discovered my legs could not support me, and I collapsed back to the deck of their boat. In the moment I had tried to rise, however, I had seen that the boat I was on was only about thirty-five feet long. People were packed into every square inch of space. They had squeezed even closer together to make space to pull me aboard. There, where I collapsed on the deck, exhausted and suffering from hypothermia, the lady who had been sitting on me took over and began to undress me.

I didn't have the strength to object. She removed all my wet clothes and paused as she fingered the pouch at my throat.

"No," I told her, not yet wanting to remove the pouch.

She smiled and muttered to herself as she wrapped me, naked, in a blanket. She was telling a story to the others in Creole as she began to rub my arms and legs, and I heard the same words repeated, passed from person to person across the crowded vessel. In the starlight, I saw face after face smiling in my direction. The woman handed me a plastic water jug and I drank the water in great gulps.

When the young man came close to the woman rubbing my legs, I asked him, "Do you have any idea how far we are from Florida?"

He shook his head. "We leave Haiti five days ago. Weather very bad." He pointed toward the bow of the boat. "Florida, soon."

He looked to be no more than eighteen years old. "What is your name?" I asked him.

"Henri Goinave."

"Will you please tell the captain, thank you, thank him for saving me."

The young man smiled shyly. *"Oui,"* he said. "He is my papa."

The woman who had been rubbing my back then handed me a plastic glass. Thinking it contained more water, I took a big gulp, then grimaced at the taste of the raw burning liquor. Many of the people near enough to see me laughed and talked around me. Their voices reminded me of Solange. I returned the glass, and she handed me a comb and a fragment of a mirror.

"Thank you," I said to the woman, and I began to comb some of the knots out of my hair. The voices around me grew louder, and it seemed everyone on the boat was watching me. Then, to the young man, I added, "Can you tell everyone thank you?"

"You make them very happy."

"Why?"

"La Sirene will guide us to Florida."

"What's that got to do with me?"

"When we saw you in the sea, we spoke, and you say your name is La Sirene."

"No, I was dreaming."

He shook his head. "Eyes open," he said. "And we asked you in Creole."

Henri was shaking my shoulder. "Miss," he said. He pointed to the bow. "Florida."

I sat up and stretched my legs out. I'd been dreaming again about Solange. She kept crying out, Help me. It took me a few seconds to get her voice out of my head. I tried to stand and realized I hurt in every part of my body. The woman who had undressed me earlier arrived with my shorts and T-shirt. They were stiff with salt, but nearly dry. Once I had dressed, Henri motioned for me to follow him. When I stood, I saw the bright lights of the Florida coastline no more than a mile off our beam. Henri led me through all the people sitting, sleeping, but mostly standing and staring at the lights. At the bow of the vessel, he introduced me to a distinguished-looking gray-bearded man who stood staring at the lights.

"Papa, ici c'est La Sirene."

The older man was wearing a dark shirt buttoned to the neck. He nodded and shook my hand, then turned to his son and acted as though I were not there. While they spoke to each other in Creole, I searched the coastline for a familiar landmark, trying to figure out where we were. Finally, I spotted the Hillsboro Light to the south of us. We would be off the coast of Deerfield Beach, then. I was amazed that the Coast Guard had not yet intercepted us. It looked to me like the boat was making a good four to five knots through the water, and we were headed straight for the beach.

"Henri, can you tell your father that there is a harbor entrance back to the south of us. It isn't very far." The young man translated what I said, and then the older man spoke to him at length, frowning and ignoring me.

"My father says if we go into the harbor, they will only send us back to Haiti. He says we will land on the beach."

I could see even from as far out as we were that there was surf breaking on the beach, swell left over from the weather system that had passed over us. The hotel lights lit the mist from the breaking waves. I'd seen boats go on the beach in weather like this, and it wasn't a pretty picture. "Henri, tell your father that people will get hurt and drown if he beaches a boat this size." Again, he translated, and again the father was very emotional in his reply, but he would not look at me.

"My father says everyone on the boat agrees. We didn't come this far to look at the sand and trees of Florida and then get sent back to Haiti. We come to stay, even if some die getting there. Some will live, and they will be free."

I looked around me, and I saw weak, sick, tired adults, some teens, and a few younger children. "Do any of these people know how to swim?" I asked.

"Few," Henri said. "I do. I lived in Miami for two years, and I learned to swim in school."

"Good. Henri, will you tell your father that I am a trained life-guard, and I am the captain of my own boat, a tugboat. If he will listen to me, maybe nobody will get hurt."

The old man looked at me for the first time, and I saw questions in his eyes. He was trying to decide whether or not to believe me. I held his gaze, willing him to trust me. Finally, he nodded.

"Okay, Henri, this is what we'll do." I explained to him that we would have to get just outside the surf line and then sail parallel to the coast, luffing the sails until we felt a big set of breakers pass. We'd then make our turn and try to sail in on the smaller set. The point was we didn't want the boat to broach, or turn sideways and roll over while surfing in on a wave. The shore was so close. This section of the beach was where the private homes north of Hillsboro ended and condos began. The swim ashore would be nothing for me, even as exhausted as I was. That beach was life and liberty and happiness for the folks on this boat, and it was very possible some of them would not make it.

The sky was just starting to lighten along the eastern horizon when we tightened the sheets and felt the wind begin to push us onto the beach. Some early-morning beach walker whipped the T-shirt from around his shoulders and waved it at us, swinging it round his head. I wasn't sure what he was signaling, if he was saying come on or go back. The first couple of waves passed under us as mere ripples, barely lifting the heavy island boat. It was the third wave that came and lifted our stern, and when I looked at the old man, I could see that though he gripped the wheel, he had lost all steerage as we started to surf toward the shore. I clutched the pouch at my neck and figured it couldn't do any harm to ask La Sirene once more to watch out for us, to help us make it ashore.

The old boat must have had a nice long keel on her, as we held a steady course and made it through the surf without broaching. It was only when the bow grounded that the stern swung around, and the whole boat rolled onto its side. We had grounded on a sandbar about forty feet from the beach.

People were scrambling everywhere. Many had been thrown off the boat when she rolled. Children were crying, and I heard splashing and saw folks running up the beach in every direction. I jumped off the boat and was surprised to find the water nearly over my head. Many of the smaller people on board would need help getting to shallow water. I ferried children and women to where they could reach shore. The waves continued to roll in, battering the sick and the weary even when they'd found bottom under their feet. Many jumped off the boat and went straight down and had to be plucked, sputtering, from underwater. My body ached in every fiber, and each time I turned back toward that listing wreck, I thought my arms would not be able to grasp another person. On my fourth trip, I carried in a little boy, no more than five years old, and looked around for an adult to take charge of him. I was startled to look up and see Racine Toussaint standing there at the water's edge, holding up the hem of a long black dress.

"I'll take him," she said, reaching with one arm.

Someone a few feet away shouted something in Creole, and I felt the temperament of everyone change. Racine took the child, turned, and without another word disappeared into the darkness. Beyond the sand, I saw blue and red flashing lights, and I knew that some would get caught, but others still might make it away. I stayed in the water until the last person was off the boat and clear of the breakers, then I swam away from the wreck down the beach to where a small unit of condos had a back door onto the beach. To the east, the sky had turned a whitish blue and the clouds on the horizon looked like ash-covered charcoal with the glow of the occasional burning ember shining through. I exited the water, not sure I had the strength to stand, and staggered right into the building. No one paid any attention to me. There were far more Haitians than there were cops on the scene.

I walked through the condo lobby, down the driveway, and out to A1A. I could still see blue flashing lights to the south, so I turned north and began walking along the highway toward the city of Deerfield Beach. I was gauging the distance to a small minimart where I might locate a telephone when an older-model station wagon pulled up alongside me and stopped. I bent down to look inside the dark car, but before I could make out the identity of the driver, I heard Racine Toussaint's gravelly voice say, "Get in."

Racine drove north until she found a driveway large enough for her to be able to make a U-turn in her big station wagon. She paused before pulling back out onto A1A and sat looking at me in the dark car.

"I lost her," I said, my voice breaking with emotion.

Racine reached over and placed her hand on my arm. "Yes, I know."

"She's in terrible trouble."

"Tell me what happened."

I swallowed hard to try to get the tears under control. The place where Racine's hand rested on my arm grew warm, and when I placed my hand on top of hers, I felt a sense of relief flow through me, knowledge that I was not alone in this. "We had moved her to this condo on Hollywood Beach, thought she would be safe there, but when Rusty and I went out to dinner, she must have hidden in the cabin of his boat. She followed me." I went on to explain all of it—the boat trip on the *Bimini Express*, the camp on South Bimini, Malheur, the encounter with Joe, and getting rescued by the Haitians.

Though we were still in the shadow of the tall building, I noticed the tops of the coconut palms were lit with the first bright rays of the sun. I said, "I didn't think I was going to see this morning. I really believed I was going to die out there, Racine."

She squeezed my arm. "La Sirene would not allow it."

Staring out the car window at the silver blue sky, I touched the still-damp pouch hanging around my neck. "I'm not sure who to thank, but I am thankful." I twisted around on the car seat and faced her. "But now, I'd be so much more thankful if I could find Solange. Her father is going to make her a *restavek* again, here, as soon as he's used her to get what he wants. But there's something even worse. I don't know what, but she needs our help, now." I could not explain how I knew, not even to Racine.

She stretched her hands out toward me, palms up. I placed my hands in hers, and she said, "We will find the child, and the *lwa* will take care of this man. You are not the only one who has suffered a loss to him. Many have died on his boats. I told you I came that night looking for the *Miss Agnes,* hoping to find my sister?"

"I remember."

"Her name was Erzulie."

If my pounding on his hull didn't wake Mike up, I had decided I was going to climb aboard his boat and roll him out of his bunk. The companionway hatch slid back just then and Mike's tousled hair was the first thing out.

"Jesus H. Christ, what the blazes is going on out here?"

"Mike, get dressed. I need your help."

During the drive south on the coastal highway, Racine and I had discussed how best to get Solange back. My first thought had been to go to the police, but Racine pointed out to me that I had absolutely no evidence to prove any of my story. And to make matters worse, she said, Joe was a retired law enforcement officer. Yes, I had witnessed him kill a man, but where was the body? It was my word against his, and whom were they more likely to believe? And, as for Solange, what could I accuse him of? Kidnapping his own daughter? I wondered if this was Racine's natural Haitian fear of the police, or if she was right. She kept telling me not to worry, we would get her back and that the *lwa* would protect us.

I finally explained that I'd feel a lot more protected by a guy with a gun.

Mike rubbed his eyes. "Seychelle? I heard you were missing."

"You heard wrong. Now come on. Put your pants on and let's go."

Mike emerged a few minutes later wearing a wrinkled T-shirt that read "Arms Are for Hugging" and had a circle and slash over a rifle. He sat on the cabin top and began strapping on his leg.

Racine looked at me with raised eyebrows, as though asking "This is the fellow who is going to protect us?" I knelt down and began to untie the dinghy painter and pointed for Racine to get into the boat.

"Geez, it's hot out here already," Mike whined. "What time of the god-awful morning is it, anyway?"

"It's six forty-five, Joe. We're taking your dinghy. Like your shirt. You've got your gun?"

He finished with his leg and smoothed his pant leg down over the prosthesis, but he made no move to get up. He said, "Sey, you asking about my gun makes me think I need to know just a bit more about where we're going."

This was the moment I had been dreading. Just because Mike was now retired didn't mean that he no longer thought like a cop.

"Okay, Mike, here it is. Your buddy Joe D'Angelo is the brains behind this whole immigrant smuggling outfit. I've been to their place in the Bahamas. Mike, he shot and killed Gil Lynch right in front of me, then left me to die, dog-paddling in the middle of the Gulf Stream. Yeah, Malheur was the instrument that Joe usually used, but Joe's a killer, too. And now he has Solange, and I've got to get her back." I paused, knowing that what I was saying to him would sound so outrageous, he was probably thinking about hauling me off to a psych ward. "I know this is a lot to take on faith, and I've got nothing to prove any of it is true, but please, Mike, I need you to trust me here."

Mike shook his head, then he looked up at me, squinting his eyes. "Joe D'Angelo?"

I nodded.

Mike sat there without moving for so long that I thought for certain he was going to say no. I had about given up and was beginning to formulate Plan B when he finally said, "Okay. I'm going to agree to go along on this one, Sey, against my better judgment. If this was *anybody* but you, I'd be saying you're full of shit—and so would any cop. But the guys on the force don't know you like I do. If it was a toss-up as to who to believe, they'd go with Joe. But I'll go along with you—to a point. Let me talk to the man, alone. I don't like what I see or hear, and" —he lifted the pant leg on his good leg and showed a small stainless revolver in a holster strapped to his ankle— "I'll keep Mr. D'Angelo tied up while you ladies call the police. You realize, we'd better figure out a way to do this so he doesn't know what's up. Joe was a hell of a good cop."

"From what I've seen, Joe was never a good cop. But he's mighty good with a gun."

On the ride up the river, we ignored all the speed limits, the manatee zones, and the no-wake areas. Even with the three of us in his dinghy, that twenty-five-horsepower Honda four-stroke of Mike's pushed his dink up onto a plane, and we rounded the curves in the river sliding sideways, barely missing the yachts tied along the seawalls. Racine sat on the seat in front of the center console, her body rigid, her back straight, black dress flapping around her legs, eyes squinting into the wind. The closer we got, the higher the sun crawled up into the sky, the stronger I felt it. Solange needed help now.

After I told Mike the details of what had happened on Bimini, he brought me up-to-date on what had happened in Florida since I'd left. "You disappeared Saturday night along with the kid. Jeannie told me nobody realized Solange was gone until you all were off at Tugboat Annie's. Then, when Elliot called in, and when they told him the kid was missing, it really hit the fan. Seems there was some girl on the pay phone at the restaurant, so he had gone to use the phone on the boat of a friend of his. He got back to the table at the restaurant, and you were missing, and so was his boat. He was pretty damn pissed, I reckon. By the time they figured out you musta been on that island freighter, the ship had been gone over an hour. Rusty found his boat and took off straight away. Your brother Pit was on the first morning seaplane over there. Far as I know, they're both still over in Bimini looking for you."

We were passing the Larsens' estate, my cottage, and *Gorda*. All looked deserted. I turned to Mike, but he had guessed my question. "Jeannie's been taking care of your dog. She might have taken her over to her place last night."

After a few more minutes, he said, "So what makes you so sure the kid's in terrible trouble?"

"I can't explain it exactly. What I do know for sure is that Joe told me he needed her to prove something to his other daughter. He evidently told her that he had a child in Haiti, and she wigged out. She wants him to take care of this half-sister of hers. She's refused to let him see his grandson until he can prove that Solange is safely in the U.S. and being cared for. Joe doesn't seem to give a damn about either one of his daughters, but this grandson is the male heir he's always wanted. In fact, he intends to sell Solange as a *restavek*, but as far as the daughter knows, she'll be living with this American family. I'm just hoping he's still got the kid with him and that he hasn't already sold her off to some family we'll never find."

When we were still around the bend from Joe's house, Mike pulled over to a dock, and he had Racine and me lie down on the floorboards. He covered us with a couple of dirty, musty-smelling beach towels that he pulled out of the bow locker.

As he put the outboard back in gear and began the approach to Joe's, he filled us in on what he saw. "There's no sign of anyone on the pool deck. With the sun shining on the windows, I can't see too much inside. It's just going on eight o'clock. They might not even be up yet. I'm going to tie the dinghy up here, out of the sight line of those pool-deck windows. You two stay down till I get back."

We never heard voices or knocking, but Mike didn't return, so we assumed he was in.

Now, I will be one of the first to admit that patience is not one of my stronger character traits. That wasn't the only thing that made me want to get up out of that dinghy and do something, though. We hadn't been there five minutes before the heat began to suck all the energy out of us. It was already in the upper eighties outside, but under those towels, with the sun beating down, it must have been over a hundred. I couldn't even remember how many days ago it had been since I had either bathed or changed clothes, and my shorts and shirt, which had been stiff with salt, were now drenched with sweat. Breathing was becoming impossible. I don't know how Racine stood it as long as she did. Droplets of sweat rolled across my forehead and into my eyes, across my belly, and out of the creases behind my knees. I had to move.

"Racine?" I said, looking at the back of her head in the filtered sunlight. "How long do you think Mike's been gone?"

"Fifteen minutes?"

"What if something's happened to him?"

She didn't say a word.

"Racine, we could suffocate under here, or die of heat stroke. What do you say we go look around? Think we can do that without anybody seeing us?"

"Whatever you choose. The *lwa* will protect us," she said.

When we peeked out from under our cover, we saw that our dinghy was tied up at the far end of Joe's dock where the fence divided his property from his neighbor's. The bow of the Donzi ocean racer was just off the dinghy's stern, and it helped to screen us from the side windows on the house. The stainless-steel bow rail was still coated in salt from the trip across from Bimini, and judging from the condensation on the port light windows in the hull, whenever Joe had returned, he'd just tied up the boat, locked it, and left. He seemed to have a penchant for asking others to clean up after him.

I climbed out of the dinghy and turned around to give Racine a hand. I needn't have. She hopped onto the dock without help, and we both slipped into the bushes that ran along the fence line.

The blinds were drawn in the guest bedroom window. From inside the house came the sound of unintelligible shouting. Someone, it sounded like a man, was barking orders. I inched my way back toward the river side of the house to see into the den. Holding my breath, I took a quick peek past the edge of the sliding glass door. In that one second, the tableau inside told me the story. Mike was sitting on a dining room chair in the middle of the room. Joe had his back to the window, but I could see the small silver gun he was waving around—probably Mike's—and Joe was hollering at Celeste to get something for him.

I jerked my head toward the street. "Come on, Mike's in trouble. We need to get some help."

The dinghy was too exposed, but I figured we could run to a neighbor's house and ask to use the phone. A narrow concrete walkway led around the side of the house to the front circular driveway. I could see, before I reached the end of the house, that a black iron electric gate blocked our exit out the driveway. The fence closest to our side of the house was shielded by a tangled thicket of bougainvillea, but ahead, on the far side of the drive, was a stretch that was free of the prickly shrub.

I turned back to Racine. "Think you can climb over that iron fence?"

The look she gave me told me not to underestimate her. "Okay, then, let's go," I said, but when I reached the corner of the house and made my turn, I ran straight into Celeste.

"*Bon dieu!*" she exclaimed, her hand rubbing the spot on her chin where our heads had collided. She was wearing a tiny, strapless, tropical-print minidress, a matching headwrap, and high wedge sandals. She looked like she should be posing for *Vogue*.

I held my finger to my lips. "Shhh, please," I whispered.

"You must go. Get away from here."

"Yeah, I know. But we need your help. Please."

"He won't be happy if he finds you here."

Racine stepped forward and placed her hand on the young woman's neck, just under the curve of her elegant jaw. She whispered something in Creole. Celeste closed her eyes for a moment and bowed her head.

"Celeste," I said, "I know that Joe doesn't want to see *me* here. But listen, we're looking for a little girl. Did he bring her here? She's Joe's daughter. Her name's Solange." Celeste just stood there, frozen. She cocked her head as though she had just heard something from the house. Obviously, she didn't want him to find her out there talking to us. "Celeste, when did he get back from Bimini?"

Celeste looked at me with vacant eyes, as if she were looking through me instead of at me. "Yesterday afternoon, four o'clock."

"Shit," I said, jerking my head down and turning aside in frustration. "It wouldn't have taken him more than a couple of hours if he'd come straight back here. Means he went somewhere else. Probably to dump her off with someone."

Abruptly, Celeste turned and walked toward the front door.

From inside the house, Joe hollered, "What's going on out there, Celeste?"

She glanced back at us with a raised eyebrow. I shook my head at her and mouthed the word *Please*. Her gaze jumped from me to Racine, and suddenly Celeste stood up straighter and nodded her head curtly in the older woman's direction.

"It is nothing, Joseph," she called back into the house. "Just some kids." She reached inside the door and touched something on the wall. The gate began to slide open.

She held out her hand, indicating the gate, and mouthed the word *Go*.

Racine took my hand in hers, and we started running across the drive toward the gate.

We'd taken no more than a half dozen steps when Joe called from the doorway, "Well, if it isn't Sullivan. Back from the dead. Keep going, ladies, and you can say good-bye to Mike here."

"Sey, go, keep running," Mike yelled.

I slowed and glanced over my shoulder, just in time to see Mike's head bounce in recoil from the blow Joe had delivered with the fist that gripped the small stainless gun. Blood trickled from a cut under Mike's eye. Racine and I both stopped and turned. Celeste had twisted her face away from the violence.

"Smart decision, Sullivan. Come on inside and join us."

Joe stood by the door, dressed in white shorts and polo as if he were ready for a morning tennis match. He was holding Mike's arm with one hand, pointing the gun at his ribs with the other. Racine and I approached them, and Joe said, "What's with the old woman, Sullivan? You haven't got enough people killed?"

"You're the killer, Joe."

"I don't think so. Gil and that kid at the Swap Shop—they'd both be fine if you hadn't stuck your nose where it didn't belong."

"You killed Margot?"

He shrugged. "Couldn't let her talk and get away with it. There were plenty of places there to buy blades, and I figured I'd make it look like another of Malheur's temper tantrums. See, that was the beauty of his whole *bokor* bit. I was pissed the first time he killed one of the cargo, but then I realized it worked for us. Kept the Haitians too scared to talk." He jerked his head toward the front door. "Inside now. Head left," Joe said, "into the den."

We entered the same room Joe and I had been in a couple of days earlier, with a bar along one side and windows that overlooked his pool deck. Joe pushed Mike into the room after us, and then he turned to Celeste and spoke in a voice I had not heard from the man, all soft and almost like baby talk. "You go stay in your room, sugar. This is business."

Racine then said something softly in Creole, and Joe swung around and yelled at her, "Shut up, old woman. Think I don't understand Creole?" He pointed the gun at her head. "You say another word of that Voodoo shit to my woman, and you're dead."

I put my hand on Racine's arm, trying to tell her not to upset him any more. When Joe crossed to the bar, she turned to me, her eyes sparkling with humor, and whispered, "He doesn't know it, but he is dead already. Here." With her fist tight she pounded her chest just over her heart.

Joe slid behind the bar and took a bottle of water out of the fridge back there. "So how'd you do it, Sullivan? Back from the dead, eh?"

My mind was spinning, looking for any excuse, any way out of this. Mike had a defeated look about him that made me think he wasn't going to be much help. Whatever had transpired between him and Joe had taken away something more than his gun. "I guess I just got lucky, Joe. Who'da thought I'd get picked up out there? By a Haitian boat, no less."

Joe laughed at that and pointed his finger at me. "That's a good one." Then he looked at his watch. "Well, I'd say you've about used up all your luck. No Haitians to rescue you this time. I do have an appointment later this morning, but it can wait. Mike tells me you all came in his dinghy, so we'll just tow her along behind my Donzi and take a little trip up the river, over into Pond Apple Slough. Won't be the first time folks went missing in that swamp. Let's go." He pointed Mike's little gun toward the sliding glass doors.

We were walking ahead of Joe across the den, and I had almost made it to the glass doors when a voice called out in a commanding tone, "Monsieur Blan, where is my child?"

Mike and I turned around to see Celeste standing in the hallway, both hands holding the wood-handled gray gun Joe had taken from Gil. She had it aimed at Joe's midsection.

"Listen, sugar, put that gun down. That's a Sig. That's got quite a kick. You know how you hate loud noises." There was something sickening about the babyish voice he was using.

"Where is she, Joseph?"

"You don't know what you're doing, sweetie. This is your Big Poppy here. Now I told you, your baby girl is gone. She's been dead, honey, a long time." Joe was moving toward her slowly, his right hand reaching out to her.

Mike stepped between me and Racine and put his arms around the two of us. He began to steer us toward the side of the room. He'd faced a gun once before and knew enough to keep us clear of her line of fire.

"Don't you lie to me, Joseph. That woman told me you just brought her here. She did not die in Haiti like you told me. Where is my child?"

"Celeste, baby, who you gonna believe? After all I've done for you?" He continued to take small steps, closing the gap between them. He was measuring her determination, judging whether or not she really could fire the gun. "Honey, I love you. I wouldn't lie to you."

"You stay back, Joseph. You think I won't shoot? You taught me to use a gun to protect myself, and I will use it. Where is Solange?"

"Babydoll, you don't need to protect yourself from me. I'm not going to hurt you."

Only five feet separated them when Joe made his move. Unlike Gil, Celeste didn't hesitate. She fired the instant he began to lunge, three quick shots, and his legs buckled under him. Instinctively, I dropped to the floor in a squat and put my arms on top of my head. In the aftermath of the shots, the only noise was the high-pitched buzz inside my head. I didn't want to stand up and look, but I couldn't play ostrich forever.

I rose slowly from where I had crouched behind a white leather chair. Joe's body lay sprawled on the floor, one leg bent awkwardly under him, his eyes open but dull as unpolished pebbles. His arms were flung wide on the floor, his right still loosely wrapped around Mike's gun. A growing red stain colored his white shirt just above his left breast.

Racine, still standing, had not flinched at the piercing noise or from the horror of what now lay on the floor. When our eyes met, she nodded, and with her clenched fist she hit her chest again, just over her heart.

Celeste knelt and laid the gun on the floor next to the body. Without so much as a slight quaver in her voice, she said, "Let's go find my child."

XXXI

Mike made us sit in the living room, away from the body, to wait for the police, and from the moment the first patrol car arrived, things seemed to shift into slow motion. The head count on law enforcement personnel multiplied exponentially within the first hour, as photographers and crime scene techs wandered throughout the house, but no one appeared to be accomplishing anything, other than gawking at Celeste's legs as she offered them Styrofoam cups of coffee from the kitchen.

I wanted to yell at them, *Get on with it.* We have to get out and start looking for Solange. She needs help.

When Collazo arrived, he, too, seemed to be moving as though he were underwater. He questioned us in the living room while several patrol officers searched the house, the pool cabana, the garden shed, and he had each of us slow down and repeat our stories over and over. Agent D'Ugard arrived and she dove right in, asking us to start again, from the beginning. Judging from the angle of the sun, I figured it was nearly eleven o'clock, and I was exhausted, but every time I closed my eyes, I saw that image from my dream. Long black hair floated around the periphery of my vision, and Solange called to me, *Help me.*

Collazo believed me this time when I told him about his police interpreter, and they sent a car over to Martine's house. Later, an officer reported to Collazo that Martine Gohin had given the police permission to search her house, not thinking that they would search her whole property as well. In her backyard gardening shed, sleeping on the floor on pallets, the officers found thirteen Haitian girls, aged eight to eighteen. Martine claimed they all were nieces before she asked for a lawyer and stopped answering any more questions. Solange was not among the girls.

On hearing the word *lawyer*, I excused myself and went to a phone to call Jeannie. After the expected tirade about how I better not scare her like that again, she informed me that B.J. had taken off the day before in Jimmie St. Claire's partially remodeled Chris Craft, headed for Bimini to join the search.

When I returned to the living room, Celeste was telling Collazo and Agent D'Ugard for the third time that Joe had not returned to the house until four o'clock the day before. He had not said anything to her about a child, and they spent the afternoon and the evening together at home. He had been in a very bad mood, throwing things around and cursing at her for nothing. He became furious when he asked her to pour him a drink and she told him they were out of rum. She offered to go out to the boat and get a bottle out there, but he exploded, screaming at her about her incompetence, and he hit her. She pulled back her headscarf to show the bruise at her hairline.

One minute it seemed as though I could not breathe, as though I were underwater and drowning, and the next thing I knew I was in my element. I saw her, and I saw where she was. The condensation on the windows, the appointment this morning, Joe not wanting Celeste to go for the rum. I jumped to my feet and said, "Come on," and ran to the sliding glass doors.

The Donzi's cabin door was secured with a stainless hasp and a padlock. Rather than look for the key, Mike kicked at the doors with his good leg. On the third kick, the wood splintered, and I had to turn my head aside as the blast of superheated air poured out the companionway.

Every year, I see the stories in the newspapers about some child who got left or locked in a vehicle in the Florida sun, and the result is usually death or permanent brain damage. We found Solange bound and gagged, locked in the forward cabin, behind another door that Mike kicked in. I could not detect any respiration when I tore off the gag. I sat down on the bunk next to her and felt her neck for a pulse. Faint, but it was there. "Solange," I said as I picked her up and carried her limp body off the boat, "I'm here. Like I promised."

When we entered the living room, Celeste was sitting alone on the couch, her head bowed, her hands covering her face. It had not occurred to me until then that the men had not told her what we had been doing outside. Solange and I were both dripping wet—I'd taken her into the pool to bring down her body temperature. She was now weak but conscious.

"Solange . . ." I stopped in the middle of the living room, set her on her feet, and knelt next to her. She looked at me with questioning eyes. She did not recognize this woman, but she sensed I wanted her to try.

Celeste's head had snapped up at the sound of my voice, and she watched the child, hungry for some reaction.

"Solange," I said, and raised my hand to indicate Celeste. "This is your mother."

At first the kid didn't move. I watched her face, the lines of concentration etched in her little forehead as she tried so hard to remember something from a life she had once known but had long forgotten.

Then, in a soft voice, Celeste began to sing:

Dodo ti pitit manman'l
Do-o-do-o-do ti pitit manman'l
Si li pas dodo
Krab la va manje'l

"Maman," Solange cried out, and ran to her mother's arms.

When we still hadn't heard anything from Pit or B.J. by that afternoon, I called my brother Maddy, and he offered to run me over to Bimini on his charter sportfishing boat, the *Lady Jane*. I met him at the fuel dock, and I was surprised to see his hair had gone completely gray in the few months since I had seen him last. The size of his beer gut hadn't changed, and I wondered if I would believe he was only thirty-two if he weren't my brother.

I spent most of the four hours of that crossing slumped in a chair up on the fly bridge, my feet on the dash, looking out to sea, trying to figure out why the world was such a shitty place. Yeah, I *know* the world is full of ugliness. I didn't need Joe D'Angelo to tell me that. But I still couldn't fathom a father who didn't love a kid as great as Solange. We're not talking about a crime against strangers here, *she was his own kid.* I thought of the way the little kiddo had looked up at me all the time, the way her serious face would be transformed when her lips parted and those small, perfect teeth showed in her shy, tentative smile. I thought of her hand, how it slipped into mine and squeezed with a slight pressure that asked me to love her. And oh, damn, how I did.

The June storm had passed several days before, and any traces of that wind and swell were long gone now. As we charged across the stream at over twenty knots, we created our own wind up there on the bridge. I was wearing a baseball cap to tame my hair and as protection from the sun, and I kidded myself as I tugged the brim lower that the tears on my cheeks were caused by the wind burning my eyes. The still water out in the Stream was back to the familiar luminescent inky blue strafed with golden shafts of sunlight. The current looked both beautiful and benign, though it had been neither when I'd watched the sun set the night before, assuming that sunset would be my last.

On the drive down to Maddy's dock in Surfside, I had learned from Jeannie that Rusty was still over on Bimini, working as a liaison with the Bahamian government to deal with the illegal immigrants who had been at Joe's camp on South Bimini. They had reportedly found over four hundred people living there in squalor.

Rusty told Jeannie he had been hiding in the mangroves that night, trying to spy on Malheur, when Solange and I had surprised him by taking his boat. There he was in the mangroves, his binoculars trained inland, trying to figure out how to rescue us from the clutches of Malheur, when we tore past him on our way out of the cut. He saw the smugglers go out the canal shortly thereafter, and he wound up swimming across the harbor back to Alice Town.

"He called me this morning," Jeannie said, "before I heard from you. I told him not to worry, you were a survivor, and he asked me to call him if I heard anything. He said he was staying at the hotel that has all the Hemingway stuff, what's it called?" Then she snapped her fingers. "Oh yeah, the Compleat Angler," she said. "He sounded pretty damned upset, girl. Both that nobody'd heard from you, and that there was no report of his boat showing up at any ports along the Florida coast."

I was watching the road outside my window flying past in a dizzying blur of asphalt, cars, and strip shopping malls. "I hope he cares enough not to kill me when I tell him what happened to his boat."

We got into Bimini just before dark, and Maddy tied up the *Lady Jane* in a slip at Freddie Weech's Bimini Dock, moving easily around the boat in spite of his size. The little fifteen-slip marina was where he usually brought his long-term charter guests. Freddy rented the guests rooms, so he offered captains, like my brother, a discount on the dock rental. Maddy took care of Immigration while I hosed the boat down.

When he got back with our papers, Maddy said he wanted to eat dinner on the boat first, but there was no way I could sit still knowing that Pit and B.J. were out there somewhere, worrying that I might be dead. I convinced him that we should go out and have a look around, see if somebody couldn't tell us where we might find a crazy American windsurfer and his big Samoan friend, maybe spot the Chris Craft B.J. had brought over.

The sun had set behind the island, but the sky above the collection of concrete- and plywood-buildings was filled with salmon-colored furrows of cloud, the sky behind a washed-out, waxen blue. The precision of the formation reminded me of the ridges in the sand bottom back at Hillsboro Inlet, and I remembered B.J. standing on *Gorda's* deck, the water dripping off his bare chest where he had unzipped his wet suit. Was it really possible that was less than a week ago?

We stopped in at the Compleat Angler, and while Maddy was playing at big game fisherman, asking the other American yachties in the bar if they had seen anything, I spotted two Biminite ladies working the barbecue in the courtyard, turning the blackening chicken quarters with large tongs. I admired their cooking and asked after the health of their families, and soon I was on a first-name basis with Charlotte and Liz. When we got around to what I was doing there in Bimini, they told me that they had heard that there was an American camped out on the beach at the north end of the island, off Paradise Point.

"There is an old house out there, we call Rockwell House," Liz told me. "Nobody live there now. They say he sleep in a tent," she said, and she chuckled softly, shaking her head as though this were something only an American would do. She said that her son worked on a fishing boat, and he'd told her that the American had been inquiring on the docks about the whereabouts of a young woman who fit my description. Her son told her that this American traveled everywhere on his sailboard, she said, sneaking a nod to Charlotte, confirming this wild report. Whether coming to town or visiting South Bimini, he treated the sailboard like it was his dinghy.

I headed back into the bar to find Maddy and in the entry of the old inn, I literally ran into Rusty.

"Sey!" he shouted, and scooped me up in those football player arms of his, squeezing me in a breath-stealing hug. After holding me just long enough that I was beginning to think I might suffocate, he kissed my ear through my hair and dropped me back to the ground. He was wearing a long-sleeved white T-shirt and worn blue jeans, and he smelled of shampoo and shaving cream. From his days over on Bimini, his tan was even darker, making his deep blue eyes look electric. When he cupped his hands around my face and kissed me gently on the mouth, he fired up all the same tingles as on our first kiss, and I gave in to it, tasting his minty mouth and reaching up and over those strong shoulders of his.

"I was so worried," he said when I pulled my mouth away and placed both hands on the center of his chest. Brushing his hand against the hair on the side of my head, he said, "I thought I'd lost you."

I looked around the room at the hundreds of black-and-white photos hanging on the walls from years of Bimini fishing, gray, blurry images of men standing next to their hanging catch. There was a lot of history in that room.

I shook my head. "Rusty, I'm really sorry. Your boat . . . I shouldn't have taken it . . . that was yours, and it really is lost. Gone, sank." I thought about how to say the rest, and there didn't seem to be an easy way.

"Hell, Sey, I can replace the boat, but if I were to lose you—" He wrapped his arms around me again and squeezed. I couldn't breathe, but it wasn't because of his embrace.

"Rusty?" He let go and held me at arm's length, staring at my face. "I spent a long time treading water out in the Gulf Stream, yesterday. Had lots of time to think about my life and, you know, think about the big questions, like why are we here and all." I paused and took a deep breath.

He hugged me again before I could go any further. His lips were next to my ear, his breath hot on the side of my head, when he said, "You're trying to tell me I never had you."

I squeezed him tight, thankful to him for saying it for me. I broke the embrace so I could see his face as I said, "Rusty, I'm so sorry."

He smiled. "I'm gonna miss you, Sullivan. And what might have been."

"No doubt about it, Elliot. We would have been great."

The walk to the north end of the island was only just over a mile, but Maddy complained all the way out there. It was past nine o'clock, and he had neither eaten nor had his evening quota of beer. I tried to tune him out. The slender new moon had already set, and the walk through the Australian pines was dark. Little animals scurried in the underbrush, lizards probably.

We smelled the campfire first. The abandoned house loomed dark at the end of a driveway that once had been paved but now was a mass of weeds and broken concrete. Liz had told me this place had been built in the forties and fifties as a private home for an American from Detroit who invented car bumpers. Three stories high with a small tower up top, it looked like a ferryboat perched out there on the limestone bluff. The east side was lit by the firelight from Pit's camp, and as Maddy and I approached, he looked up from the flames.

"Sis!" He jumped up and trotted over to me and threw his arms around me, lifting me off the ground and twirling me around. When he put me back down, he looked up and nodded at Maddy, who stood off to one side of us. "Cool," Pitt said. "A regular Sullivan family reunion." Then he collared Maddy in a hammerlock, bringing him into our little circle. We stood there in the firelight together, arms over one another's shoulders, the tops of our heads touching, each of us lost in thought about those who weren't there.

Maddy pushed away first. "Okay, enough of this mushy stuff. You got any beer, bro?"

Sitting around the fire, I told my brothers about the camp on South Bimini and Solange and my hours out crossing the Gulf Stream. I told them about the picture in the trunk and what Gil had said about our dad and what he had done, and *not* done, down in Colombia. I was able to tell the whole story without breaking down, but telling the end about the kid and her mother, and how Agent D'Ugard had said they would probably both be able to stay since Celeste had her green card—that part made me miss Solange even more. Pit said B.J. had left that morning, taken the Chris Craft down to South Bimini and Gun Cay to continue searching for me. Maddy promised to take the *Lady Jane* down there to find him in the morning.

I'd left my brothers chattering around the fire then, told them I was going off to explore the big vacant house, but really I just needed to get away.

The Bahama Islands are made of old coral reefs that once were beneath the sea, but when the sea level changed, these reefs dried out.

They are limestone islands, made of the skeletons of long dead animals, and now with a thin layer of soil, a few struggling plants eked out an existence in the salt spray. Out along the edge of the bluff they'd named Paradise Point, the bumper man had built an iron-and-concrete walkway around three sides of his elaborate island home. Salt and rust, and perhaps even hurricanes, had eaten much of it away over the last fifty years, but I wandered out onto one of the remaining sections of concrete and looked down the fifteen feet or so at the ocean that was rising and falling around the rocky bluff. There must have been a small cavern below me, because when the swells came in, the air was expelled with a loud rush.

I didn't even hear him walk up behind me, but in an instant the scent of coconut soap mingled with the iodine smell of the sea, and I sensed the size of him standing next to me. There was a comfort in his presence. I didn't need to look to know he was there, leaning on the rail, looking out at the ocean as I was. We stayed like that for the longest time, not saying anything, not knowing what to say, but comfortable in the silence.

In the end, I was the first to speak.

"I found her mother," I said, breaking through the weight of the humid night air that seemed to be pressing down on me. "They say she can stay in the States now." The rocks below exhaled with another powerful *whoosh*. "That should make me feel good, shouldn't it?"

"Sure," he said. "That was a great thing you did."

We both watched as a local fishing boat motored by, her running lights lit, her outriggers heavy with nets.

"So tell me, why does it hurt so much?"

"Because you love her."

"And I'm going to miss her."

Neither of us said anything more for several minutes. We stood there watching the stars and their reflections on the blackened swells, listening to the rocks' rhythmic breathing.

"You'll still get to see her," he said. "You know, families come in lots of different shapes and sizes these days. You decide what feels right for you." He slid his hands into the pockets of his cargo shorts and took a deep breath. "You could be Auntie Seychelle. Make Solange and her mother part of the family."

I leaned back and looked up at the broad bright band of the Milky Way. "I like that: Auntie Seychelle," I said, trying out the sound of it. "Come on, we'd better get back," I said, slipping my arm into his and starting to walk down the concrete toward the campfire. "And what about you?" I asked, turning my face up toward his.

White teeth glowed against his dark skin. "Uncle B.J. works just fine for me."

CHRISTINE KLING is the author of *Surface Tension*.
She spent more than twenty years on and around boats
and has cruised the waters of the North and South
Pacific, the Atlantic, and the Caribbean. She received
her MFA in creative writing from Florida International
University in Miami. She lives in South Florida
with her teenage son.